HERS TO DEFEND
THE CHAINED HEARTS DUOLOGY
BOOK 2

ASHLEY DAVIS

Copyright © 2026 by Ashley Davis

Cover design by Ashley Davis

Formatted by Ashley Davis

All rights reserved.

No part of this book may be reproduced in any form or by any electronic or mechanical means, including information storage and retrieval systems, without written permission from the author, except for the use of brief quotations in a book review.

This is a work of fiction. Names, characters, places, and incidents are either the product of the author's imagination or used fictitiously. Any resemblance to actual events, or persons, living or deceased, is purely coincidental.

No generative artificial intelligence took were used in the writing, editing, or creation of this book. All content is original and authored solely by the human writer.

 Formatted with Vellum

For the broken, the brave, and the men in masks.

CONTENT WARNINGS

This story contains themes and situations that may be difficult for some readers. Please take care of yourself while reading, your mental health is the most important thing.

Potential triggers include:

- Violence and terrorism
- Kidnapping and captivity
- Guns, knives, and combat scenarios
- References to torture and past trauma
- PTSD, anxiety, and panic attacks
- Strong language
- Explicit sexual content
- Attempted sexual assault

This story explores systemic corruption, abuse of power, and violence that may echo real-world events. While this novel was written well before recent developments unfolded, some similarities may feel striking and hit close to home.

While these elements are part of he characters' journeys, your well-being as a reader matters most. If at any point you need to step away or put this book down forever, please do.

PROLOGUE

Riley screams as the rusty hook tears through the muscles of his back, matching the wound on his other side. Every thrash of movement opens the medley of fresh cuts covering his chest and abdomen. Metal rings out across the courtyard as he tries to pull his arms from the handcuffs holding him against the table beneath him.

Cheers sound, hiding his screams of agony. Dmitri's forces gather around the man who spent years ruthlessly hunting them, eagerly watching their leader ready him to be strung up for their entertainment. Every day has been spent fighting off ruthless beatings from his captors. Riley can only fight back so much before the little strength he has is gone. A dangerous mix of starvation, dehydration, and delirium quickly threatens to ruin any plans of escape he has.

Today is not that day. Riley was so hopeful when they moved him from the makeshift cell to the courtyard. Those hopes died the moment he saw the gathering crowd. There is no doubt he can free himself of his restraints, but with so many of Dmitri's men surrounding him, he won't make it far. Riley does the only thing possible: he waits. He endures everything they throw at him, knowing every cut, every stab of the knife, every fist slamming into his already desecrated body, is one that Liz will never have to experience again. Riley swore he would never allow himself to be thrown back into this situation.

Now, his capture is a sacrifice he would happily make one thousand times over if it means she stays safe.

He blocks out the searing pain coating every inch of his body, pushes everything out of his mind, but her. The way her silky hair feels twisting around his fingers or the way her eyes light up when he surprises her with her favorite snacks. The feel of her small, reserved hug when he carried her down the mountain, telling her about his past.

Weeks have gone by since he gave himself up to make sure Dmitri couldn't get his hands on her. Every day has been an endless cycle of attacks. Dmitri visits every few days, trying to beat information out of him. But he doesn't break, he can't. Breaking means everyone he cares for is in danger, and if getting his ass beat from sun up to sun down is what it takes to keep his loved ones safe, then he will take it.

His team knows to reconvene at the bunker and decide if they should rescue him, or admit it is just too risky and leave him to die. Riley wishes they would pick the latter. Every time he thinks of the love he left behind, he knows she'll make every man on the team find him and drag him home, for no reason other than to tear him a new one for getting captured.

Another scream tears from him as the hook in his back lifts him off the table until he is upright, held by hooks meant for nothing more than cattle carcasses. He sucks in a sharp breath, running through every training technique that taught him to fight past the pain and keep from passing out. Rocks crunch beside him, footsteps drawing closer. Face to face with Dmitri, Riley greets him with a smile, his normally brilliant white teeth now a deep shade of red.

"Are you ready to tell me where you are hiding my pet?" he asks coldly. A sinister smile creeps up his face as his icy blue eyes dart from the various wounds peppering Riley's exposed body. "How about what your leader has planned? I–" A spray of warm, red liquid over his face stops his rant.

"Why don't you go fuck yourself," Riley chokes out before a hard fist slams into his head, sending him spinning in the air. Cheers erupt around him. His head spins faster than his dangling body, the near constant abuse taking more of a toll on him than he would ever admit.

Dmitri reaches out a hand, stopping Riley's slow rotation. His eyes simmer with contempt, glaring at the man hanging before him.

"I will make you an offer, Reaper," he spits. "Tell me what I want to know, and I will end this. I will grant you a fast death." Dmitri brings his hand up and pats Riley's bruised cheek. "I have many men who want to watch you bleed. You can make it stop; all I ask in return is information. A small price to pay, I think."

An eerie silence blankets the courtyard. Every man huddled together waits to hear if the man they have spent years fearing will finally break and accept the sweet release of death.

A hiss escapes Riley's lips while his eyes sweep the small crowd. The adrenaline that has kept him conscious is starting to wear down, leaving his vision fuzzy. He rallies every ounce of strength left in him to drag his point across one last time before he succumbs to the loss of blood pooling from his wounds. With his head high, speaking loud enough for everyone to hear, he seethes, "You should kill me while you still have the chance. When I get out of here, and yes, asshole, I will get out of here, I'll be waiting for you, right up there..." He cranes his neck to look at the building towering beside them. The blood drains from Dmitris's face as Riley turns back to face him, "Waiting to flay the skin from your fucking bones."

Dmitri's eyes widen with fear as each word sinks in.

Pride swells in Riley's chest as he watches the man reach up and gingerly touch the scar across his eye. A reminder of what Riley will do to be free.

Dmitri knows all too well Riley feeds on the fear of others. He will become the nightmare who watches his victim squirm before he takes their life. With a small shake of his head, Dmitri tries to ignore the pit growing in his stomach. Plucking a rusted piece of rebar off the ground, he connects it with Riley's abdomen. Deep, guttural screams fill the air like thunder. His ribs crack from the blow, the force of the impact sending him swinging, the metal hooks threatening to rip clean out of his back.

"You are never getting out of here. As I told my pet, I have my own men in your ranks. I made sure your general will not send help, and your partners do not care enough to risk their lives for you. No, one way or another, you will die here." He sneers before turning on his heels. "Someone stop his bleeding, we wouldn't want him to die before we've had our fun," he adds without looking back.

This is exactly what Riley needed. Dmitri may have power amongst his organization, but he has never been a smart man. His anger and need to be seen as someone worth fearing has always been his downfall. He is too busy preening, thinking he has outsmarted his enemies, to realize he is feeding them information. He will take every beating with a smile on his face because when he does, Dmitri will do anything to wipe it off. Including telling him his next plan of attack, and just who he has working for him on the inside. Riley can only hope his team makes it to him before Dmitri makes good on his promise.

Once his cuts are sutured and glued, the bleeding slows. He is left alone in the dark of night, hanging from the flesh of his back, fading in and out of consciousness. It's then he realizes he may have pushed too far this time. Mentally, he can take whatever is thrown at him, but even he has physical limits that can't be ignored.

A wave of regret settles over him. He pushed too much. All the information he squeezed from his captor will never be heard, all his work will be for nothing. He thought Dmitri would keep him alive long enough for his team to find and extract him, but it's too late. His heartbeat thrums in his ears, a sad, irregular sound mixed with a wheeze from every breath he draws. Riley quickly comes to the conclusion that his lung must have been punctured by the broken rib. He allows his eyes to drift closed, his pain growing lighter as his thoughts flood with the memories he made with Liz. If he is to die tonight, her face is the last thing he wants to see. Shimmering green eyes flash before him, but they are not right. He was supposed to see her, glowing with happiness, living her life once more. Instead, he sees her how she was when they first met: blood running down her face, eyes laced with fear as she screams at him.

Riley refuses to let that be it. He compels his mind to go utterly blank before his world falls dark.

CHAPTER 1
FORTY-EIGHT DAYS AGO

Footsteps echo through the empty room as the team steps out of the elevator. No one dares talk, still too raw from the battle they just lost.

Liz peels her eyes from the fluffy pink slippers Mikey brought her—a gift for finally leaving the hospital. She knows it was a sad attempt at distracting her from the fact it was him walking her out instead of Riley. The heavy weight of returning to the empty bunker without Riley crushes her. She shouldn't be here, not without him. It feels wrong. Everywhere her eyes land she pictures him and their times together. She replays his words over and over again from the first time Riley brought her to his home, their home. It was built to be a sanctuary, but without him it feels more like just another prison.

She takes one painful step after another, floating toward her room like a ghost. After all, that's what she is now. A ghost, a shell of the person she grew to become with Riley. A slow exhale escapes her lips as she makes her way down the hall, knowing she cannot let herself fall into the pit of despair she is balancing on the edge of.

Seventeen days have passed since her entire world changed.

Seventeen long, agonizing days stuck in a hospital bed when she should have been doing everything she could to find him. Playing nice with her doctors and nurses got her out earlier than they would have liked, with the condition that Mikey makes her take it easy. An agreement she made that she has no intention of sticking to. There is only one thought in her head, bring Riley home. She knows what is happening to him at this very moment and it makes her stomach churn. He has been through so much already. One capture is one too many, two is unthinkable. She will not let him suffer. He came for her when she needed him most, now it's her turn to do the same.

Liz changes into her gear, leaving the guns on her bed along with her vest, ready to throw it on at a moment's notice. She storms back to the men gathered around the table. The sight of the empty chair Riley preferred threatens to send her breakfast back up. Somehow, she finds the strength to push through.

"Alright boys, when do we leave?" she asks, sliding into an empty chair at the far end of the table. "I assume you've been making arrangements since he was taken? Has anyone been able to get information out of the general? Is he locked in that stupid little prison cell he loves so much, or did he get brought somewhere with more guards?" The questions pour out of her, unable to stop herself. Glancing around, each of the men in front of her avoids making eye contact. They look toward each other, brows knit together as they shift nervously.

They may be highly trained soldiers, but they suck at hiding things from her. "You do realize it's obvious you're keeping something from me, right? You all look like you're scared to tell your mom you broke a window. Someone needs to tell me what the hell is going on and fast."

"Look, Liz," Tyler starts before a hand covers his. She watches the two men sitting hand in hand, a pang of jealousy in her heart.

Alex shakes his head at his partner and picks up the conversation. "You already hate me, so please, don't take anything out on them. Riley trusts you, he made you a part of the team, so I am going to tell you everything we know, but you need to be prepared to hear things that are going to upset you." His stern tone sends a chill down her spine. Whatever he is going to tell her very well could be the thing that breaks her for good.

Her thoughts go to that dark place she tries so hard to ignore. Heart thumping in her ears, she knows what Alex is going to say, but she can't lose Riley. She will never be able to come back from the death of another love.

"Scott isn't in jail. I know you think he has something to do with Riley going MIA, but he is the leader of our unit. He may be an asshole, but he wouldn't risk his top commander. We still need to follow his orders."

A silent tear rolls down her cheek as she lets her eyes close. She knew they would never believe her. They all know their general's true nature, but they still don't know her. The only thing they know is that she is a victim and she hates Scott with every fiber of her being. "Is he dead?" she asks, her voice quivering. "Is Riley dead? Is that what you're too scared to tell me?"

"No darlin, he's alive, we know that much, it's just... we just don't know where he is. We have an idea, but nothing solid," Mikey reassures her. His hand envelopes hers, rubbing back and forth just as he saw Riley do so many times before.

Tyler then speaks up, wanting to share the awful task of explaining everything to her, knowing only months ago she was the one being held captive. "The three of us talked while you were in the hospital, and we all agree you should hang back while we find him." Before they know what is happening, Liz is out of her chair, knocking it over with a loud crack.

"What? No! You can't... no... just no," she shrieks. Three sets of concerned eyes track her every move as she walks circles around the kitchen island, the gears turning in her head. Liz opens her mouth to say something, snapping it shut before she can. There are no words. Nothing she can say to them to make them understand. Deepseated guilt grips her. He fought to protect her, and when it was her turn to defend him, she failed. She was willing to die to keep him from turning himself over, instead, her actions guaranteed his capture. How can they expect her to give up on him like this?

"You just got out of the hospital—" Mikey starts.

"I don't care," Liz retorts

"You were blown up," Tyler says, trying to help his friend.

"I don't care."

"You're still training," Alex says, only adding fuel to the fire growing in her.

"Oh my fucking god! I do not care," she says, slamming her open hands against the smooth marble island. Riley is alive and they are going to find him; they will have to throw her back in chains to keep her from helping. "If you are going after him, I am too. I don't give a fuck if I was in the hospital, and I certainly don't give a fuck if I'm not fully trained. Wounds heal, and you can train me while we search for him. Look me in the eyes and tell me you wouldn't do the same if it was Tyler who was missing." Alex's eyebrows shoot to his forehead. Sheer will and determination shines in her eyes, and he knows she will go toe to toe with each of them to be included in Riley's rescue. "Will you follow orders? No matter who they come from, even if you disagree?" he asks carefully, gauging her reaction.

She gives him the smallest nod of her head, not wanting to make him change his mind by being a hot head.

"You can't be serious," Mikey shouts, looking between the two. "Do you have any idea what Ry will do to us if he finds out we took her on a mission? No, scratch that, do you have any idea what he will do if she gets *hurt* because we took her on a mission?"

"Okay, so I just won't get hurt, problem solved," Liz interjects, "When do we leave?"

"We don't! We—" he shouts, gesturing to himself, Tyler, and Alex, "leave after speaking to the general and working out a plan of action. You stay put." He grows more frustrated with every word. He was the one tasked with keeping her safe. If anything were to happen to Liz because he allowed her to tag along, Riley would kill him. Not in the way friends joke about killing each other, no, Reaper would come out in full force and rip the soul from his body.

Twiddling her thumbs, watching Mikey with her cheeks puffed out, Liz waits for him to calm down. She already got their interim leader on her side, there is no going back now. She only talks when the storm churning in his deep blue eyes slows.

"So, here's the thing, sweetie. I know Riley is like, the big, bad, scary guy whose morals are a teensy bit grey, and I get where you are coming from, I promise, I do. However, I am not afraid of him. The man knows damn well that if he's getting rescued, I will fight alongside you to get to him, and if he has a problem with it once he is safe, then he can take it up with me," she says, leaving no room for argument.

The men exchange knowing glances. There is no denying she is right. If Riley were there, he may fight her on it, but in the end, he would acknowledge she is a grown woman who makes her own choices, and they need to do the same.

"God damn it. Fine, but you need to promise me you will follow every order we give. Every step you take out of line puts all our lives, and more importantly, Riley's life, at risk." Mikey's voice is firm, dripping with an authority she has never heard from him.

She extends her pinky to him, a promise she will do anything she is told. The smile spreads across his face before he can stop it as he links his own pinky with hers.

"Okay, now that it's settled, I should go get the general so we can brief him on everything we know," Tyler announces. Chair legs scrape across the floor like nails on a chalkboard as he stands, heading to his borrowed room down the hall. Mikey follows suit, strutting to his own room to gear up for the fight ahead. Alone with Alex, a mix of fear and anger claws its way up at the thought of the general coming to Riley's home while he isn't there. If she fights them on it, effectively breaking her promise, they will never trust her, and there is a good chance they will use that as an excuse to force her to stay behind.

"Hey, Alex?" her timid voice says, drawing his attention from the map laid out in front of him. He looks up at her, his deep brown, almost black, eyes are kind, even with the dark bags sitting below them. "Don't bring him here," she says. Her voice matches the slight tremble in her hands. "Please."

He can see it then. The fear she tries so hard to hide from everyone. The one person who has brought her strength in the months since she was rescued is now gone, and she doesn't know how to cope without his steadying presence. He gives her a small nod, knowing how hard that bit of vulnerability must have been for her.

"Go gear up. We will take the information to him." Turning on her heels, she starts back to her room when Alex calls out to her. "And Liz, bring some of that fight to this meeting. I have a feeling we are going to need it."

CHAPTER 2

Setting foot in another military base is something Liz had hoped she would not have to do for a long while. Unease grows with every step she takes, regardless of how safe she feels with the trio of men surrounding her. The base looks the same, yet so different from the one she was held prisoner in. The same brick buildings are adorned with the same perfectly manicured lawns scattered inside the walls. Helicopter pads and aircraft hangars line one side of a brilliant green yard with a flagpole stretching into the clouds. Administrative buildings line the other. Rows upon rows of soldiers march by in unison, their boots nearly shake the ground as they pass.

Liz tries and fails to ignore the many pairs of eyes glaring at their small group. She never did good with large crowds, and it seems like military bases have a near constant flow of people running around. Her shoulder bumps into Mikey, not realizing she has been stepping closer to him on their trek across the lot. He wraps his pinky around hers once more, keeping them locked as they walk, a silent promise that she is safe with him.

The team stops just outside what looks to be the main administrative building, forming a huddle away from prying eyes. Standing tall, Alex carefully watches a squad of soldiers stroll by, eyeing them carefully as they do. Once clear, he takes a step forward, closing their small circle.

"I need everyone focused in there. We don't have much to go on right now, but we do have an approximate location where we believe Riley is being held. Whatever you do, do not let Scott know that. You tell him we have a game plan and a location. I will present him with a list of equipment and units to approve. Once we get his seal, we get the hell out. Understood?"

Liz will never have the strength to tell Alex how much she appreciates him stepping into Riley's role, allowing Mikey to stay by her side as the friend she desperately needs. Liz's heart swells as the men step back into position, forming a protective triangle around her. Despite only knowing her for a short time, they understand how hard things have been for her and have been sure to make her feel safe. She assumes this is what having brothers would be like, or rather, brothers who don't abuse you and murder your family.

She takes a steadying breath and follows Tyler into the dimly lit corridor. Cool air washes over her as soon as her boots hit the polished tile. A wave of nausea hits her, the walk feeling too much like when she was brought to the interrogation room. It's Alex who notices the change first, seeing her begin to pick at her nails while they walk, her pace slowing ever so slightly. Heartbeat pounding like a war drum in her ears, she stops, whirling around the moment a hand lands on her shoulder. He yanks it back to his side when she looks at him with wild, panicked eyes.

"I'm sorry. I didn't mean to scare you," he says, stepping back into formation. "You look like you're not doing well, and I've seen how Ry and Mikey help you when you start to freak out. I didn't stop to consider that I would make it worse."

Words evade her. She and Alex have not exactly gotten along well, but she has seen a shift in the way he treats her. She has proven her innocence, and he accepts that. In his own way, he is trying to treat her as a member of the team, and that means looking out for both her physical and mental wellbeing. Putting the moment behind them, their pace picks back up as they make their way down the maze of hallways to where the general is waiting.

Faces blur past as Liz forces one foot in front of the other, swallowing the fear threatening to rise again. She made a promise to be on her best behavior and follow all orders. Following orders is not the problem, however, following orders that will directly harm Riley, is. The last thing she wants to do is something stupid that will get the unit punished, but if they can't convince the general to let them find Riley, she may finally snap and do what she has wanted to do since the moment she met him.

Growing increasingly angry at all the faces watching the team while they hurry up the stairs to the third floor, Liz looks anywhere but the men and women they pass. The pale brown walls are adorned with an unbalanced mix of cheap modern art and paintings depicting different events in history. The decor fades into walls holding portraits of top leaders. Smaller frames holding various badges, medals, and awards are nestled between sets of double doors that line the hall. Liz sucks in a deep breath, knowing the man they are here for is waiting on the other side of one of those doors. Wondering what room he is in, Liz almost doesn't notice the soldier standing at attention outside the only single door in the hall. Her heart sinks at the sight. She knows exactly where he is hiding, but she is not ready to face him.

As they approach, the man seemingly guarding the door turns to them and smiles, his eyes landing on Liz. Her eyes roam over him, trying to remember if she has seen him before. He is tall by her standards, but shorter than the rest of the men with her, still easily six feet. His rich bronze skin and chiseled jaw make him look like he just came from a day at the beach rather than a military base in Montana. Liz can't help but be suspicious. He is clearly here by orders of the general, but does he know just how evil the man is? Or is he just doing his job? None of that matters when they finally reach the door. Riley's fate lies just on the other side. The man standing guard silently pushes the door open when the team approaches.

The moment Liz steps into the cramped office her gaze lands on the general. He is perched in a plush leather chair, a pompous look staining his face. Flexing her hands, Liz looks around the office, trying to focus on anything but launching herself over the desk, standing between them, and physically removing the look he has. Tyler steps around them, plopping into one of the chairs in front of the desk. He gets right into digging through his bag, pulling out all their hard work, and tossing it on the desk. The chair next to her squeaks before Mikey's hands find their way onto her shoulders, urging her to take a seat. Although she reluctantly agrees, his hands never leave, staying firm as her emotional anchor.

"I don't have much time. What's all this about, gentlemen?" the general asks, eying the growing pile of maps and charts atop his desk. Liz glances up to Mikey, his jaw clenched tight like he is trying to stop himself from saying something.

"Sir, we have located Riley," Alex begins, taking a small, folded paper from his pocket and handing it to the general. "We just need you to sign off on our equipment and we can bring him home."

The energy in the room shifts.

"Now, you know I can't approve that," he says, matter of factly, a scornful smile playing on his lips. "Even if you did know where Reaper is, I won't risk my best men going after him. He made a stupid, impulsive decision that got him caught, now he has to live with that choice. If he is even still alive, that is." He looks directly at Liz with those last words, smiling as his verbal attack lands. The room goes quiet. They all knew he would be difficult, but no one thought he would refuse their request, no one but Liz.

"But sir—" Mikey says, stepping around the chair.

"You got my answer, soldier, or did you forget who you really answer to?"

"No sir. I understand you call the shots, but Riley is one of ours. We can't just leave him to die," Mikey argues, trying not to let his anger get the better of him.

"We know exactly where he is. I believe with minimal equipment and a small tactical unit, we can get in, get him, and get out," Tyler adds, sliding another stack of papers to the general, who now sits with his arms crossed and leaned back in his chair.

"They're right. This is a low risk, high reward, mission. Riley would fight like hell to get any one of us back, and I'll be damned if I don't do the same for him," Alex shouts, shaking the desk when he slams his hands against its metal surface.

The general's face twists with anger. This is not how the meeting was supposed to go. Liz stays silent, racking her brain for anything she can use while the rest of her team argues with their boss. Then it hits her. She takes a moment to calm her nerves, sitting straighter in her chair, crossing her arms and legs.

"Enough guys. He made his choice—"

"What the fuck, Liz? Now is when you're going to listen? What about Riley? He almost died trying to save you from the same cocksucker that has him now," Mikey shouts at her, instantly regretting it when he sees her flinch.

"We knew he would leave him to die, and this way he won't have any blood on his hands," Liz says, staring down at the man in front of her. She can't help but smirk as she watches his face grow red. "I guess we resort to plan B and release the footage." She stands and starts for the door when a voice calls out behind her—

"What footage would that be, Elizabeth?"

She would give anything to be able to slap him, just once. She pushes the feeling out of her mind, replacing it with the burn in her chest when she sees Riley. Solely focused on getting him home, she turns, smiling wide, "Oh, the footage from the bar. You did know there were cameras everywhere, right?" Her smile turns genuine when the color drains from the general's face.

Mikey, Tyler, and Alex exchange confused glances, looking between the general and each other, hoping someone has answers.

"They might not have seen you that day, but I did. While I was screaming for help, willing to sacrifice myself to keep Riley safe, you were aiming a fucking RPG at him, weren't you?" she shrieks. "No one believed me, but Riley's truck has a dash cam, and Mitch has cameras all over the bar. Your own fucking soldiers had cameras on their helmets. It was simple enough to go back and get the footage." His eyes dart between Liz and the men surrounding her. He tries to form words, but Liz cuts him off. "Now, you can either sign those fucking papers and give us permission to go find him, or we will release those videos and turn you into a pariah. I will make sure your career and credibility die with Riley."

The general stammers, quickly realizing he is losing control over the situation. Liz has run out of fucks to give. The guys may not know it, but she knows without a doubt that the general wants Riley dead. His actions directly led to Riley being captured, and there is nothing in this world that is going to stop her from getting him back.

"No such video exists—" the general is cut off by Liz, growing more inpatient by the second.

"Then why do you look like you've been caught? If you have nothing to hide, you would have told me to release it, called my bluff, but you didn't. Approve what Alex asked for, and we will be on our way. You can look like a hero when Riley returns home safe, or don't, and the world will know you're a traitor and a coward."

"I will be keeping you all on a short leash." he chokes out, reaching for the crumpled list of demands. "We will meet at the bunker before and after each mission. I will expect a full report the moment you return, and, since you are down a man, I have someone joining the unit." he states, looking directly at Alex, clearly expecting him to nod dutifully and go along with whatever he says.

"With all due respect, sir, their home is off limits," he says quickly, glancing over to Liz. Only able to put out one fire at a time, he continues, "We will come here for our meetings. That bunker belongs to Riley, and it is not my place to bring you there without him."

"Fine," the general says through gritted teeth. "If you insist on doing things here, I am going to insist on seeing you work here, too. You do not get to hide away, working from that hole, only setting foot on this base when you need something. You are soldiers for god's sake. You may be a special operations unit with your own set of rules, but this is still your job!"

Alex gives him a slight nod and steps back into formation, placing his hands behind his back, waiting to be dismissed. The four of them exchange glances, unsure of what else is to be said. They did it, they got what they needed, and they are free to gather their resources and pile into the next plane to Russia.

"Now, who exactly is joining us? How much training do they have? I need to know everything about them before I can re-work the plans, and we can't leave until I get that done." The questions pour out of Tyler.

Liz steps away from the desk, striding back to Mikey's side.

Her anxiety spikes. There is no telling what she will do if she is not near someone who will stop her from ruining everything.

"I'm glad you asked," he says with a sneer. "Matt, come in and meet your new team," he shouts toward the door. Nausea rises as the handsome man standing outside strides in. This answers all the questions she had when she first saw him. If he is hand picked to join the team, there is no doubt in her mind he knows exactly what kind of man the general is. Now, this mystery man is on their team, and she is expected to just trust that he won't kill her the first chance he gets.

"Meet Matthew Solano. He just returned from a mission along the border of Kazakhstan and Russia. He has outgrown his current unit, and I believe he will make a good addition to this one. Matt will be an asset to you, and you will show him the same respect you have shown Riley's little stray," he says, sneering at Liz, smiling to himself as his insult lands.

Anticipating her next move, two strong arms wrap around her waist, pulling her back and pinning her against a hard body. Mikey leans down and whispers, "Think of Ry, darlin. If you do anything right now, he will back out."

She relaxes slightly, furious how he's right.

"That was uncalled for, sir," Matt says, winking at Liz as he steps further into the room. "I think it's honorable that she is so willing to fight to find her commanding officer. Especially after he publicly rejected her in front of all the men and women she now has to work with. That takes a strength not many have."

Liz seethes at the backhanded compliment, ready to turn her anger on him. The loosened grip retightens. Mikey knew the moment her body went rigid things were about to turn explosive.

"Well, thanks for this. I'm going to take this one and start gathering supplies. Alex, text as soon as plans are set and we will meet you on the runway." With that, he pulls her out the door, steering her back down the hall before dropping his hands.

CHAPTER 3

While Alex and Tyler hang back to go over plans with the general, along with their newest addition to the team, Liz reluctantly agrees to stay with Mikey and gear up. Their first stop is the central issue facility to finally get her some gear that fits. Men and women cleanly march from one building to the next while jeeps whiz by. Everyone has a purpose they execute with a scary precision.

Her head drops, feeling out of place, so she resorts to watching her feet and the dust kicking up around them rather than all the people moving too close for comfort. A deep sadness settles on the long walk across the base. They both know Mikey should not be the one beside her, getting her ready for her first real mission.

When they reach the small brick building, Mikey pulls the door open, ushering Liz inside. The noise from the rest of the base fades away as they make their way deeper into the facility, nothing but squeaking shoes and the dull hum of an air conditioner to fill the silence. Rows of shelving are spaced along one section, holding all the clothing anyone could need, all a mix of blacks and camouflage. On the far side is a wall of shoes with shelves upon shelves of various accessories.

"C'mon, we don't have much to get. You need some real boots and a vest that fits. The rest of what you wear should be fine," he says, guiding them toward the shoes waiting in the back. He begins looking through the boxes, trying to find her size.

"So, I don't have to wear the army uniform?" she asks, picking through boxes to help speed up the process. The boxes thunk onto the discolored tiles as they start to pile up. Liz isn't even sure what she is actually looking for, she just knows she needs shoes in her size.

"Nope. That's one of the many perks in being in a super secret spec ops unit. It's definitely unfair, but we can dress in whatever works for us, although that usually means black to stay hidden. Sometimes we need to be in full tactical gear, but not very often," he says, picking a box and holding it above his head like a trophy.

Finally having what they were after, they make their way to the racks holding hundreds of kevlar vests. Finding a vest in her size goes much faster than the shoes. The third one Mikey forces her to try on fits like a glove. He tosses it over his arm, tucks the shoe box into the crook of his elbow, and weaves through displays until they make it to the large desk in the middle of the room where a man waits.

"Hey, Ted. I'm snagging these for her," Mikey says, nodding his head in Liz's direction. "Just throw them on my account. Alex should have sent over his list of demands if you don't mind getting everything together for us."

Liz watches the man with caution even though he is fully engaged with Mikey. The man seems to only be in his late forties to early fifties with neatly cut grey hair and deep wrinkles around his eyes. He turns to walk away when she sees the prosthetic leg. Liz pulls her eyes away, hoping she wasn't rude for noticing.

"He said we are in hangar two. If you could get someone to deliver everything there, I would really appreciate it."

Ted stays silent, giving Mikey nothing more than a nod before walking off, list in hand. A sharp chirp rings out from Mikey's pocket. He slides out his phone and checks the message, not bothering to reply before stuffing it back into his pants. They leave Liz's new gear on the desk and step back out into the controlled chaos outside.

"The guys are done, and apparently Scott had some info he was holding onto that helped pinpoint where Ry is being held. We have just over an hour until we can gear up," he says, guiding her once again through the endless stream of people and vehicles roving around. "We don't have time to go back home. Are you good at eating in the mess hall? Ty and Alex will meet us."

Her shoulders drop at the thought of being around so many strangers. Despite everything, she still gets nervous around crowds, especially when she does not know anyone or their intentions.

"Yeah, that's fine. Honestly, though, I don't think I'll be able to eat anything."

Mikey can't help but feel for her, knowing all too well the nervous jitters before the first mission. Unfortunately for Liz, she has so much more to worry about than it just being her first. She has been through more than anyone ever should in such a short amount of time. Mikey glances at her, seeing the strength and determination she carries has him beaming with pride. They may not have known each other long, but she has quickly become one of his closest friends.

"Did you hear about the man who installed a window in his butt?" he asks, holding back his laughter. "It was a pane in the ass."

Liz lets out a melodic giggle, letting it take some of her anxiety with it. She loops her arm through his and lets him guide her across the courtyard, not speaking again until they reach their destination.

Mikey holds the heavy glass door open for Liz. Only a few small steps into the mess hall and she freezes. A cacophony of voices ring out, making it sound too much like a high school lunchroom. She should be happy with the normalcy of it all, the men and women finding joy in their everyday lives, but she isn't. She is bitter and jealous that while they get to sit here, laughing with friends, and enjoying their food while so many of their fellow soldiers don't get to. She hates herself for doing the same thing only moments before when Mikey started joking with her again. How can she let herself feel any type of joy with what is happening to Riley?

A hand finds its way to the middle of her back, pulling her from her thoughts. "They got a table over there in the corner. Pick what you want and load up a plate," he says, grabbing a tray and plate.

Liz follows his lead, picking up her own tray and following close behind to the salad bar. She watches, slowly putting greens and some veggies onto her plate, as Mikey piles salad onto a second plate. Her eyes go wide as the mountain of lettuce, cucumbers, and tomatoes grows. He finally tops it with two heaping scoops of chicken, cheese, and a rich orange dressing. Liz, on the other hand, adds a small spoonful of chicken and ranch dressing. They make their way over to the hot line. Once more he starts filling his plate with more food than any one person should eat. Chicken cordon bleu, mashed potatoes, roasted carrots, and broccoli. Despite the amazing smells wafting all around, she can't bring herself to take more than the measly salad and a bottle of water.

When Mikey's tray is practically overflowing, they make their way over to the table where the rest of their team waits. A wave of relief washes over her when she sees its only Tyler and Alex sitting at the table. Hopeful that they were able to convince the general to get rid of Matt, she slides into a chair between Mikey and Alex. They have a pleasant enough time eating together. Alex takes time to go over the new plans, breaking everything down for Liz. She knows she will be partnered with Mikey, and he will keep her from making any huge mistakes, but her nerves won't stop until the adrenaline takes over.

The mood of the entire table shifts when a chair is pulled over and the newest member of their rag tag squad sits down. Liz seethes the moment her eyes land on Matt. She wants to get up and drag him from their table. She wants him to know she will never welcome him into their unit.

Her fork clangs against the plate as she aggressively stabs at her salad. "I thought you guys were getting rid of him," she snarls before shoving the fork into her mouth, eyeing him with disgust. She can't help herself; the promise she made was to play nice with the general, not this new man who lobs insults then winks like he did her a favor.

"Woah, what the hell did I do to deserve that?" he asks, clearly taken aback by her anger.

"Oh, you mean other than how you insulted me back in general fuck faces office? We don't need someone trying to come in and fill the hole Riley left. We are getting him back and our little team will be just fine until then," she says, staring him down. She doesn't miss the rest of her team exchanging worried glances.

"First off, that wasn't an insult. I am genuinely impressed with your dedication to a man who embarrassed you the way he did. Personally, I would let him rot and move on to someone who reciprocates my feelings, but if you want to hold out hope for a man who treats you like that, then that's your choice to make." Liz is so angry she cannot even form words, and her jaw drops open as he begins again. "And second, the only hole that man left behind I wouldn't mind filling, is yours."

The chair under her flies back, and she's on her feet across the table. Before anyone can register what is happening, Liz has brandished her fork like a knife, seconds from plunging it into Matt's smug face.

Mikey snatches her hand, roughly pinching the area between her thumb and pointer finger. The fork drops to the table with a loud clang, and he shoves her back into her chair.

"Enough. Both of you," Alex shouts, trying to get control of the situation before more eyes see what is happening.

"Shit, you were really going to stab me, weren't you?" Matt asks with a smile plastered on his face. "Look, it's a ten out of ten for the dedication, but we both know this face is too pretty to stab." Leaning back in his chair with his arms crossed, his hazel eyes scan hers for any hint of amusement. "Has anyone told you you're like a little honey badger? Small and cute but mean as all hell."

"I said that's enough, Solano," Alex snaps. One look at the mountain of a man now standing over them would get anyone to rethink their choices. "You're not needed here. Go to hangar two and make sure all our supplies are in order, and if I hear another word out of you, I will throw your ass off the team so fast your head will spin." Alex slams himself back down into his chair, not bothering to see if his new recruit is doing as instructed. It's not long before the whispers of what happened start to make their way around the mess hall.

"I'm sorry," Liz whispers to Alex, knowing her outburst is going to once again make more work for him to deal with. The last thing she wants is to cause problems.

"It's not your fault. The guy is an asshole, but we need to work on your temper. You can't go around attacking fellow soldiers," he says, finishing up the last of his food.

"I know. I promise it's something I will work on. I tried so hard not to let it get to me. I know Riley didn't mean what he said, at least I don't think he did, but the other thing…" She trails off, pushing her still half full tray to the middle of the table so she can lay her head down. "The last thing he said was just too far. I can handle a lot, but I won't tolerate anyone speaking to me that way." A soothing hand rubs gently up and down her back, a light, comforting touch of a trusted friend.

"I take things like this very seriously. Right now, we need him to find Riley, but I will talk to him and make it clear I won't tolerate that shit. He does anything like that again, and he's gone, no questions. You have my word."

"Thank you. That means a lot to me, but we both know if you get rid of him, general stupid face will go back on his word. My comfort will never be more important than Riley's life. I just need to focus on getting him back and not fucking up my first mission."

CHAPTER 4

The hangar housing the rest of the crew and the C-146A Wolfhound waiting to start the long journey overseas is far more intimidating the closer they get to it. Logically, it doesn't make sense, but Liz had just assumed they would be taking a helicopter or something similar. No time is wasted as they approach.

Alex barks orders, getting everyone onto the plane and seated so they can take off. Liz did not expect the plane to look so commercial. It's small, with a bathroom at the front, two rows of seats lining the walls, and a wide walkway down the middle leading to a large door. They hurry down the aisle, taking seats near the back, as the pilot guides them onto the runway before shooting into the air.

The moment the plane is at its cruising altitude, Alex removes his seat belt and stands at the end of the row, facing his soldiers. "Alright, listen up," he barks with authority. All the voices and chatter cease. "We are in for a long trip. We have six days, most of that will be spent in the air. We will be flying in six-hour intervals, only stopping long enough to refuel. Make sure you are eating and getting rest while you can. You have all been assigned your duties. Read your briefing packet, and when you finish, read it again. When we reach the drop zone, you will rendezvous with your assigned team. Once your team is together on the ground, you will go on foot to your assigned coordinates and wait for confirmation. When all teams are in position, I will clear you to push into Dmitri's compound. Our goal is to find commander Corson and bring him home. Understood?"

"Yes sir." The plane responds in unison, sending chills skirting over Liz's skin.

She read through the small packet of papers Tyler gave her, twice, trying not to get confused by the language she has yet to fully understand. Mikey is doing his best to explain and answer all of her questions on the long flight to the White Sea. She is immensely grateful to Alex and Tyler for making sure she is able to stay with Mikey, being the last pair to go into the drop zone. Her job would seem simple to the more experienced members of the team: stick with her battle buddy, watch his back at all times, keep your gun up, and sweep the cleared areas to find where they are holding Riley. When he is found, radio the rest of the team and call for an extraction.

No one is sure of what awaits them when they finally make it to their destination. The intel they received showed a small group of houses in a clearing just west of the White Sea, but they have been unable to find satellite photos to confirm. After two stops to refuel, and a total of thirteen hours into their flight, Mikey and Alex excuse themselves to help prepare a small dinner for the team.

Mission brief in hand, Liz is ready to focus and read through the plans for the umpteenth time when the seat next to her is filled. Her eyes flutter closed, and she takes a deep, steadying breath before she does something she can't undo.

"Don't attack," a smooth voice says from beside her.

Her eyes snap open, glaring at Matt, silently praying the plane crashes and takes him out for her. "What the fuck could you possibly want right now?" she snarls, kicking herself for lining him up to make another obscene comment.

"Calm down, honey badger. Your guard dogs will be back soon to drag me away. I just wanted to apologize." The shock on her face must be obvious because Matt shakes his head and a small laugh escapes. "Don't look so surprised. I'm not a total asshole. Scott told me the only way to get on your good side is to get you mad. Says that's how Reaper won you over—"

"He doesn't know shit about me, or Riley, let alone anything that went on between us. Riley was kind and protective. He made sure I felt safe, even in my worst moments. He may have pushed me, but he never took things too far. He didn't just waltz in, make some backhanded comment about being rejected, which I wasn't by the way, and finish it off with saying he wanted to fuck me like some delusional fucking pig," she snaps, trying to keep her voice low and tone as calm as she can given the situation.

"You're right. I swear, I was not trying to be disrespectful when I said you were dedicated to him. I read your file when Scott first asked me to join, I really do admire your strength and determination. Reaper is kind of a legend, like a ghost story that gets told around the bases. That day and what he said about you spread like fucking wildfire. I'm sorry, but you won't convince me he didn't mean it. No one has ever seen or heard about a woman in his life; he's known for being completely dedicated to the job." He glances over, seeing the anger brewing behind her eyes, he quickly finishes, "The moment I saw you walking down the hall, all I could think was how bad he fucked up that day. Still, it was not my place to make assumptions or sexualize you, and for that, I am deeply sorry. I shouldn't have blindly listened to the boss man and just gotten to know you for myself."

Matt was there one minute and gone the next. Now tossed into the aisle like a pile of dirty laundry, an angry Alex stands over him, looking like he is ready to open the cargo door and toss him out. Matt scrambles to his feet, attempting to stutter out a poor explanation of what he was doing. "I thought my orders were pretty clear, soldier," Alex barks, gaining the attention of almost everyone currently awake.

Mikey comes running up behind them, his arms full of sandwiches. His wild eyes scan everywhere, trying to figure out what is going on.

"I was just apologizing and heading back to my seat, sir," Matt stammers.

Alex turns to face Liz, looking to her for confirmation, though it may not matter at this point.

"He was, it's fine." Liz gives Alex a soft smile. He steps aside and lets Matt slink back to his seat. Wordlessly, he walks away, grabbing a handful of the food Mikey is passing out to their unit and starts handing it to everyone waiting on the other side. When the crew has their food, the two men find their way back to their seats. A tightly wrapped sandwich lands in Liz's lap as Mikey plops down next to her. One look at the food sends her stomach into knots. Wondering how anyone can stomach eating this close to a mission, she tries to hand it back to him.

"Oh no, you're eating, darlin. Remember what Ry said when he first agreed to train you? Gotta take care of yourself; no food means no energy. No energy means you get sloppy," he says through a mouthful of his own sandwich.

Liz watches him with a mix of awe and disgust, tearing into his food like he hadn't eaten four plates before leaving. The wrapper crinkles as she opens it, and she quickly wipes away the tears welling in her eyes. The sound reminded her so much of the first meal she had with Riley, when her brain shoved her fear and mistrust aside and let her enjoy the smallest moment with him.

"You want to tell me what happened or should I go beat it out of Matt when I'm done?" There is not a hint of sarcasm in his voice. While grateful he pulled her from the spiral she was about to embark on, Liz has no clue how to explain what happened. She digs into her food before she starts.

"Nothing really. I think he apologized, in a fucked-up kind of way." Mikey doesn't bother asking her to elaborate, just raises his eyebrows and continues to eat. "He did apologize, but he said he's never going to believe Riley didn't mean what he said to Dmitri. He also said general dick bag told him to be mean if he wants to get on my good side."

"Damn, I guess it's good he apologized but try to keep your distance. Alex will get rid of him, you know, just say the word and he's gone. Once he likes you, the guy is almost as protective as Ry," Mikey says through another mouthful of food.

Liz wonders if he even has the ability to talk if he's not chewing at the same time. She nibbles her food enough to make him happy, trying not to run to the bathroom and throw it all up. One more stop and they will be on the last leg of the long journey to Russia. By this time tomorrow, they should be on a plane back with Riley in tow.

"Has Riley ever brought women around? Like, had a girlfriend or anything?" she asks quietly, leaning over, hoping everyone is asleep. She tries to forget what Matt told her, but the little anxiety gremlin in her brain keeps forcing her to replay every word Riley said, remembering how he could not look her in the eyes. Her heart so desperately wants to believe it isn't true, but her brain keeps doubting.

"What? Why would you ask that?" His brows knit together. He turns to find Matt sitting a few rows back, paying them no mind. "Did he say something? Ry only has eyes for you. You know that, right?"

"I want to believe that, but ever since that day, I can't stop thinking about it. Matt told me he is like some mythical person everyone tells stories about. Word got around about him 'rejecting' me, and he may have mentioned no one has ever heard about Riley being with anyone. Apparently, he is married to his mission." She pulls her feet under her on the small seat, loops her arms around her friend's, and rests her head on his shoulder, the day finally catching up to her.

"I didn't know him very well before all his shit went down, but yeah, he has had flings, never a full-blown girlfriend or anything, but that was before he was taken. You've been the only woman he's shown any interest in since then. Try not to worry about what idiots like Matt say. Focus on tomorrow, and I promise when we get home, I'll tell you what happened after that rocket got fired." Mikey holds out his free arm, allowing her to loop her finger through his.

He is right, she shouldn't be worried if a boy likes her or not, she needs to focus on the fact that in nine hours, she is going to be strapped to her friend, thrown out of a plane, and into a battlefield. She forces her eyes closed, taking slow, controlled breaths until sleep creeps in and takes hold.

CHAPTER 5

Jumping from a plane and plummeting twenty-seven thousand feet to the ground wasn't nearly as terrifying as Liz thought it would be. The moment their boots touch soil, Mikey releases the clip holding Liz securely against his chest. She brushes off the embarrassment of having to tandem jump while all the others have been trained and jump alone.

Mikey expertly unhooks his harness, dropping it behind him, and picks up his rifle in one swift movement. Meanwhile, Liz embarrasses herself further while she struggles to get everything unhooked as fast as possible. She sucks in a sharp breath, trying to steady herself. This is not the time to break down and she knows it. She forced them to let her join the mission, and she needs to prove to not only them, but to herself, it wasn't a mistake.

After three miles of walking through the dense forest, Mikey signals for the team to slow. Gunshots begin to ring out ahead of them, echoing through the trees, signaling the other squads have made it to the hideout. Sticking close to her battle buddy, Liz walks through the trees with her gun up, keeping her head on a swivel, just as Riley had shown her. The gunfire lasts only a few minutes before ceasing. Something has either gone right for once, or really wrong once again.

As they approach, Mikey radios the rest of their squad to break off. Two head in one direction, two more in the opposite, while Liz and Mikey continue straight.

The trees thin, opening to a wide expanse of tall grass and wildflowers. Giant rocks and flower-filled bushes dot the field, perfect for cover as they trudge forward. Another half mile from them sits the small, seemingly abandoned town Dmitri has taken over. They keep pushing forward. The closer they come to the town full of shacks, the more everything feels off. There are no alarms blaring, no voices shouting. Gun fire no longer rings, the only noise is the sound of two sets of feet moving through the foliage. The pair exchange silent glances, keeping pace with the rest of the team. They make it to the edge of the town where half their unit is waiting. Mikey spots Alex standing in the front, talking to a small group of soldiers. A handful of bodies litter the ground, but it's clear they have not used this location to hide for a while.

"Where the hell is everyone?" Mikey asks, approaching the group huddled together.

"I don't know. The intel we got from the general said he was here. There should have been more than twelve men on guard. I don't like this," Alex says, intently watching his portable radar system.

When it doesn't detect movement from anywhere in the town, he turns to the group to reorganize. "Alright, listen up. Our intel is bad. We need to find anything we can and get to the evac point. We are clear, but keep your radars on. Radio if you find anything or anyone."

The moment he is done speaking, the soldiers scatter. Liz still isn't sure what she is supposed to be doing, but she promised to follow orders, so that's what she does. Grateful for all the long days of forced training, Liz runs through everything in her mind as she goes from shack to shack in the abandoned town. She moves slowly, keeping her rifle in a low, ready position, making it easier to navigate. Meticulously, she clears every room in two buildings, on her way to the third, something behind it catches her eye.

A bulkhead door, nearly covered in grass and debris, is tucked against the back of the house. It's too perfect, like someone was trying to hide it without making it look hidden. She creeps over, checking the coordinates on her MGRS. Moving closer, she radios to the team and informs them she is going in to check it out. Nothing but static comes back over. The heavy metal door groans, dirt sprinkling onto the crumbling stairs as Liz pulls it open. She flicks on the light attached to her gun and slowly descends the stairs, ignoring the crackling voices coming over the radio.

Doubt and anxiety flood her body—she is not ready for this. Refusing to admit to being a failure, she pushes on until she reaches an open door leading to a room at the bottom of the steps.

The overwhelming smell of must hits her before the scene. Maps and charts cover the crude cinder block walls, photos of Riley and other familiar faces dotted amongst them. An old computer sits atop a small desk on the far side of the room, while a makeshift table filled with papers sits in the middle. Metal clinks gently with each step she takes, bullets scattered all over the dirt floor. She tries to radio the team just like she practiced in her head to no avail, her radio still not working. The hairs on the back of her neck stand up seconds before she hears the slow, careful footsteps. Alex had said the area was clear, but she won't take chances.

Liz positions herself in a darker area, clicks her light off and raises her gun, waiting for the owner of the footsteps to show themself. She takes a deep breath, finger resting next to the trigger, when Matt steps into view, shining his own light in her face.

"I found the honey badger. I'm with her now," he announces

into the radio on his shoulder, adding, "You may want to come see this, commander."

Trying her best to ignore the awful name, she prays the rest of the squad didn't hear. They silently look around, Matt taking pictures of the mounted maps while Liz grabs whatever folders she can, shoving them into her pack. Footsteps approach from the door, Alex strides in, followed by a very angry looking Mikey.

"Why the hell did you take off?" he seethes. "You were supposed to stay with me."

"You guys told everyone to look for anything we can use. Literally, everyone else took off. I assumed I was supposed to do the same," she shoots back, unsure of if she actually did something wrong or not. "If I wasn't, maybe you should have said something." Papers crinkle behind her as Alex loads up the rest of what is spread across the table into his bag.

"Has anyone else found anything?" she asks, terrified to hear the answer. She watches as Alex claps Matt on the shoulder, nodding his head toward the stairs. Her heart sinks. Neither one speaks until the sounds of the receding footsteps go silent.

Then, and only then, does Mikey dare speak. "I'm so sorry, darlin. I don't think he was ever here."

She blinks away the tears threatening to form, breathing deeply through her nose, and letting it out slowly through her mouth. She can't react, can't break no matter how much that tiny bit of information is crushing her soul. The moment Alex announced their intel was wrong, she should have known they would not find him, but she so desperately wanted to believe she would. Not only did they not find Riley, but they dedicated a week to this mission for nothing, a week that could have been spent traveling anywhere else he may be.

Liz knows it's stupid to think like that. She knows he could have been here, and there is no guarantee they would have found him if they had gone somewhere else, but she cannot stop herself from thinking it was all a waste.

"We should probably get back." There is no emotion in her voice, completely numb to her world falling to pieces around her. She turns on her heels and climbs the crumbling dirt stairs, marching right back to the group gathered together and waiting to start the long trek to their evac point.

The hours blur together, aimlessly following her leaders across miles of terrain to an old airstrip where the plane waits to bring them home empty handed. Liz holds it together, blocking out anyone who tries to speak to her. She runs through the motions until she is back home, and she can throw herself into bed and let out everything she is holding in.

CHAPTER 6

It has been eight days since returning without Riley in tow. Thirty-one days and a countless amount of tears since he was taken. Still, Liz attends every meeting the general will allow, absorbing as much information as possible. The only thing keeping her from a full-blown mental breakdown is all the hours of extra training she has convinced them to give her.

Mornings are spent in the gym, sparring ring, and gun range, training with Mikey. Alex takes over with more advanced training. Small unit tactics, combat-casualty care, and every other day Liz goes to the base and trains on airborne operations so she can eventually jump alone. When she is not with either of them, she is with Tyler, trying to understand land navigation and how all their special equipment works.

Her hand cramps with the amount of notes she has taken, scribbling down every detail she is allowed so she can go back and study it in the minuscule amount of down time she is left with. Mission plans are still left for Alex to coordinate, working with all the new information the general is somehow getting. She keeps trying to make the team understand how suspicious it is. Scott may be their leader, but something about the information seems wrong. It is far more detailed than anything she has seen Riley receive. Granted, she has not been around anything like this before. Her concerns always fall on deaf ears. Liz knows she would have better luck talking to her guys if Matt would leave them alone, her concerns falling on deaf ears.

Since the moment the general introduced Matt to the team, he is always popping up wherever they go.

Despite his apology, Liz still can't stand the man. Constantly sliding himself into their training regimen, trying to give tips on how to improve. Matt has perfected the art of simultaneously overstepping professional and personal boundaries, offering to take over certain training aspects and take her to dinner after.

Liz begs Alex to drive her to base today, hoping the switch will throw Matt off, allowing her and Mikey to train in peace. She sits at the island, head resting on the cool marble, arms sprawled out in front of her, waiting for Mikey to finish whatever it is he is doing when Alex comes down the hall.

"Alright, let's go. I wanted to talk to you anyway," he says, tossing a large backpack over his shoulder, walking to the elevator without looking back.

Nervous energy fills her as she hops from her chair and follows him into the elevator and outside to his waiting truck. "So, this is weird, right?" she playfully asks buckling into the passenger seat. "I don't think we have ever been alone outside of you going all drill sergeant mode when you train me." The tension eases when he lets out a deep chuckle.

"Yeah, it is. That is why I wanted to talk to you." The truck roars to life and speeds off down the wooded area leading to the road.

"Alright, so that was ominous," she says, peeking at him from the corner of her eye.

"Sorry. Not great at this. I owe you an apology," he says. Liz doesn't miss the genuine sympathy in his tone. Of all the things he could have said, offering an apology was not what she expected to hear.

"I haven't treated you the best, and for that I'm sorry. Riley and I have a... complicated relationship," he starts, taking a big breath before continuing.

"We're both so stubborn and pig headed that it causes problems. I didn't want him going after you the day you got taken, and we had a big falling out over it. Even after he proved you weren't involved, I tried to get him to get rid of you. He got too attached, and I didn't want him to end up getting hurt or being thrown out of the military for some woman who could never feel the same way. Clearly, I was wrong. His demons don't scare you, and now you are fighting just as hard as any of us." The way his knuckles turn white from his death grip on the steering wheel says everything she needs to know. This is hard for him.

"Thank you. I appreciate it, and I appreciate how you have stepped into the leader role and kept pushing everyone to find him. You are doing so much, and it hasn't gone unnoticed." She lets out a breath of relief, happy to have the animosity being put behind them. "I do need to ask, though, when you say 'complicated relationship', do you mean you guys were like, a thing? Not that it would bother me, but it would explain a lot."

He barks out a rich, throaty laugh, one she has never heard before. The openness brings a smile to her face.

"No, nothing like that, although he did help me realize I was attracted to men as well as women."

"So, he was your sexual awakening? I get that, dudes a fucking smoke show," she practically purrs, picturing Riley at their lake, glistening in the moonlight.

"God, no. I met Riley at basic and he became like a brother to me,"

We got stuck in the same unit and just hit it off. We've gone through the ringer together. He is my brother and nothing else. I was supposed to be with them on that mission, but he got promoted before me. We got in some stupid fight that ended with me thrown off the roster, that was the mission he got shot down and taken. I took a step back in my career to help him through all his shit. I hated the idea of him getting his own unit to destroy the Komarov Empire Imperial Movement, but I didn't hesitate to join when he asked. We fought a lot, but I was there through it all. It's hard to watch him risk his life over and over again. It sounds stupid saying all this out loud. He is a grown man who can handle himself." Alex sighs, shaking his head at his own realization.

"I get it. You worry about him; there is no shame in that. I'm glad he has you in his corner. He is going to need everyone supporting him when we finally get him home."

The conversation fizzles out, uncomfortableness finally fading between the duo. Trees touching the clouds shoot past as they navigate the winding roads. Eventually, the clearing thins, opening to a small town outside of the base. Dread oozes the moment they pull past the gate.

"Well, we're early. Tank should be here soon. I have to meet with Scott and get the okay for us to leave in a few days. You should be clear to hide in the gym and get a head start. Text me if you need anything," Alex says, pulling his truck into a parking spot and hopping out, not bothering to wait for Liz.

She follows his lead, climbing down and power walking in the direction of the gym.

"Honey B, wait up!" an agitating voice yells from across the lot.

Unsure of what irritates her more: the obnoxious nickname or the fact he found her within minutes. Liz keeps her head down and pretends she didn't hear. She can't ignore it for long before footsteps quickly approach, slowing their pace when they catch up to her.

"Mikey not coming today? Do I finally get to train you?" he asks, a little too hopeful for her liking.

"He's on his way. You can go bother literally anyone else," she snaps, keeping her head down, continuing on her way.

"I'm just trying to help. Part of the team now, remember?" he utters.

"Then go follow Alex around and not me," she argues.

"I would if he had an ass like yours," Matt blurts.

He stops in his tracks, hanging his head at his mistake. Liz ignores it, still marching her way to the gym. Once Mikey gets there she will be in the clear and left alone, she just has to hold out until then.

"I'm sorry!" Matt calls after her, jogging to catch back up. "That one slipped out. I'm sorry—"

"Oh my god, will you just leave me alone!" she shouts, stops, and turns on her heels, not caring about the attention she is drawing "We have known each other for what? A couple of weeks? And yet you track me down and follow me like a lost fucking puppy. I don't know you, and you sure as hell don't know me, definitely not enough to speak to me the way you do. So, for the love of god, back the fuck off."

"I said I was sorry. I'm trying to get to know you, but you won't let me. Excuse me for wanting to be friendly with the people in my unit. I'm cool with every single person, but you, and do you want to know why I think that is? I think you're just as attracted to me as I am to you. You know, if you let yourself accept that you're not in a relationship with your commanding officer like you want to believe, you would realize that we would get along really well. You act like a bitch to distance yourself—"

"Did I just hear that right," a booming voice rings out across the lot. Soldiers of various ranks scatter across the blacktop, trying their best to look like they weren't watching the fight between Liz and Matt. They both snap to attention as Mikey strides over, looking like the sergeant he truly is. "I will ask again. Did I just hear you call your fellow soldier a bitch?"

"Yes sir, but—" Matt stammers, only to be cut off by Mikey's domineering voice once more.

"Miller! Front and center." A scrawny kid, no older than nineteen with buzzed blond hair and thick glasses, rushes to his side, quickly standing at attention. Mikey ignores him, still aiming all his anger at the man in front of him. "Since you have no respect for the women at this base, you get to apologize to each and everyone for being disrespectful. Private Miller here will help you get a list of names and make sure you do a thorough job. I expect every name on his list to be checked off by morning, and start with the highest rank, I'm sure they will be thrilled to know how you treat their sisters in arms."

The two men sulk away, heading in the opposite direction. They watch as Private Miller leads Matt to the admin building, taking his babysitting task very seriously. When they are far enough away, Mikey spins, smiles ear to ear, and pulls Liz into a tight hug, lifting her effortlessly off the ground.

"My hero." Liz fake swoons, giggling into his neck before he places her back down. She loops her arm through his and nearly drags him the rest of the short walk to the gym, ready to focus on anything but their failed mission.

The room is nearly empty when they arrive, nothing more than a handful of soldiers trying to fit a workout into their busy schedule. An hour into their cardio, Liz is dripping sweat. She's jogging fast on the treadmill when Mikey finally speaks up.

"So, the last week has sucked." Beeps sound from the machine and the belt slows. Mikey drops from a run to a fast walk. Liz follows suit and slows to match his pace.

"I think sucked is an understatement. I don't even know how to describe how scared and miserable I have been. I thought the missions were going to be the worst part, but they aren't. Coming home without him and having to live with that is..." she chokes, wiping a tear from her cheek before anyone notices.

"I would say, now you know how he felt, but what you are going through is so much worse. How about we try to have some fun tonight? Just me and you?" It is clear he is trying to make up for something, but Liz cannot think of anything he has done to warrant it.

"Why? What did you do? I mean, yes, obviously I would love some best friend time and have a couple of hours where I don't want to bash my head into a wall, but the way you're saying it, something is off." She eyes him carefully, and he won't meet her gaze.

"Sometimes I forget how scary good you are at reading people. I have some not so great news. I promise I will tell you more tonight after Alex is done with his meetings, but right now, the general is forcing you to sit this one out." The words come in a rush that he can't stop.

"He can't fucking do that," Liz shouts, forgetting where they are.

"He can. He is our commanding officer, and if that is what he orders, then that is what will happen." Mikey leaves no room for argument. She can see in his eyes how much he wishes things were different. "It gets worse, darlin. He says you still need to be supervised by someone who can get you to and from base and keep up with your training. I'll give you one guess as to who that is." His tone is much lower this time, knowing how much it's going to upset her.

"You have got to be fucking kidding me," she angrily whispers. "You know why he is doing this, right? He is not coming to our house; I won't let him."

"It's not safe to talk about this here. I will tell you everything at home, but I think we need to consider moving back to base for a while. Alex and Tyler already have a room, and they pulled some strings to get us one, too."

Liz is fuming by the time they finish their cardio. Mikey decides to cut the workout short, knowing there is too much for them to talk about once they leave. He needs to get everything out on the table before they can have their fun.

CHAPTER 7

The moment the elevator door groans open, Liz sees what has been laid out before her. She can't stop the shriek that rips from her chest. Mikey stumbles back as she launches herself into his arms, landing in a laughing pile on the floor. Scrambling to her feet, Liz stands in awe of the sheer amount of planning and effort her friend put into his surprise. The already plush couch is covered in thick, luxurious looking throw blankets. The coffee table is littered with all her favorite snacks and candies, a bottle of her favorite white wine sitting in the middle. Before she can throw herself over the back of the couch and get lost in the expanse of blankets, two hands land on her shoulders, guiding her to the table.

"I told you, talk first, slumber party later."

Liz slinks into her chair, pretending to pout even though she knows whatever he needs to say is far more important than any plans they have for fun. "Okay, quick like a band-aid. Tell me everything you need to tell me. I won't say a word until you're done," she says, wanting to get the conversation over with.

"Cool, that works. Things are weird, and I mean unsafe weird.

We have our own guy on the inside, and he won't talk to the general, says he doesn't trust him. Well, turns out, he knew the camp we raided was empty. Dmitri pulled his men a week before we showed up. Scott told us he got satellite images of the town crawling with KEIM followers the day before we left. His info may have been wrong, but something feels off about it. I guess when Alex brought it up, Scott argued that you must have sent word back to your 'Russian lover' and made him pull his men. He wants you sitting this mission out, and he wants one of his guys to keep an eye on you. I already assumed that was why Matt got added to the team, but now it's obvious." He pauses for only a moment, watching her to make sure she isn't too overloaded with information. He can almost see the gears turning in her head when he starts again.

"I know you are really against it, but I think moving back onto base is for the best. It's only temporary. You and I will bunk together. Tyler made sure to get rooms across the hall from each other, so we can all stick close.

When Ry comes home, they are going to force him to stay for a medical evaluation, then he will have a psychological decompression. It's better to be prepared and have a secure space waiting for him so he isn't kept in the medical building. Luckily, this has happened before, and he has had extensive psychological and resistance to interrogation training, so he should bounce back faster."

"Is that all?" Liz sarcastically asks, so quiet he almost missed it.

"Almost. This needs to stay between us, and I mean you and I us, not the team us." Mikey waits for Liz to nod in agreement before continuing. "Do you remember what you did before you tried to murder me in cold blood?" he asks, smiling as the color drains from her face.

"I told you I was sorry, and I remember everything perfectly. I just don't know what you're getting at here,'" she says with a small shrug. Being reminded of how awful she was to him isn't making this any easier. She is amazed at how far they have come in just under six months.

"You know how you pushed past wanting to stab us in the eyes every time we talked to you and pretended to play nice?"

"How the hell do you know that?" she shrieks.

"Shh, you said no talking until the end. We're highly trained military operatives, of course we knew that the woman who was just rescued from captivity wasn't going to be okay with us after only a few days. We never expected you to try and use us, but we knew what you were doing the whole time. Lucky for us, you are good at reading people, and realized we were never going to hurt you. So, you opened up, and ended up getting close to us really fast. I need you to do that with Matt, maybe ease in a little slower, but I need you to play nice. Apologize to him, lie to him, whatever, but I need to know why he was so interested in joining our unit. I know Scott loves the kid and that's how he got on the team, but he is a low rank, yet the general trusts him more than anyone. Something is off about the whole situation."

"Um, okay, I have some thoughts, but I don't even know where to start." She inhales deeply, running all the information through her head again, trying to figure out what she can even say at this point. "I guess, first, if you think moving to the base is a good idea and will be what's best for Riley, then we can, but I'm not going to lie and say I'm fine with it. It terrifies me to be back there with so many people. In Nevada, Riley's room was safe, it was *his*, this one won't be. Also, I have been telling you guys there is something up with that asshole. You said it yourself, I'm really fucking good at reading people, and Scott is not a good person. I want as many updates while you're gone as possible. If you're going where general fuck face is sending you, I can almost guarantee Ry won't be there." She tries to mask the pain in her voice, but it's no use. Mikey is her best friend, and he always seems to know when she is hurting.

Horrible conversation finally out of the way, Liz rushes to her room to find a new set of silky pajamas resting on her bed. She takes a quick shower to wash the sweat off before she slips on the black and white cow print shorts and matching tank, rushing back into the living room.

Finally, throwing herself over the back of the couch, she gleefully giggles when she lands smack dab on top of Mikey who's wearing a matching pair of pajama pants. Scrambling off his bare chest, Liz grabs the fluffiest blanket she can get her hands on and curls up in the corner, flicking on Netflix. When she finally finds the perfect girls night movie, her feet get propped on Mikey's lap. A bright pink bag lands in her lap and she happily digs into it.

"Really, darlin? Twilight?" Mikey asks, pretending to not be thrilled with her choice.

"It's the best worst movie. Perfect for a slumber party when you don't actually want to watch the movie. Now you're free to paint my nails and tell me stories, starting with what happened when I exploded." She pops a rainbow candy into her mouth, wiggling her bare toes at him. He plucks the bottle of bright red polish off the table and gets to work.

"Once upon a time, there was a small pain in the ass who fell in love with a big pain in the ass. Both of them loved to get captured–" He is interrupted by a foot kicking him in the stomach, the woman attached to the foot giggling beside him. "Fine, but I thought that was a great start. I'll be honest, not a lot happened, and some of it you need to hear from him, but the general fired an RPG at you. We think. It was somewhere between you and Ry. The fear in his eyes still haunts me. I ran for you, because I'm the best at field dressing wounds, so you became top priority, but I could still see him. He picked up that gun with superhuman speed, and killed anyone in his path to you." He finishes painting her last toe, placing her foot to the side, and picking up the next, ready to get to work. "He picked you up like a rag doll and ran you through the damn firefight, begging you to stay with him. I thought he was going to leave with you, but he told me he needed to make sure Dmitri is never able to hurt you again. Holding your lifeless body, kissing your head, begging you not to die, that was the first time I have ever seen that man shed a tear." He looks up to find tears streaming down her face. Maybe this wasn't the best idea for their night off.

"Do you think things will be different when we find him? It's ironic that after he saved me, he gets taken, and I help to save him, but is he going to see that we did the same thing and stop feeling so guilty? What happens to us if he does? I know it's stupid, but every single day I think about those things he told Dmitri. I want so badly to believe it wasn't true, but there is a stupid, nagging voice telling me it is," Liz finally confesses.

It has been weeks of Liz pretending they are in a relationship. Even if Riley hadn't been taken, they never talked about what they were. There has always been a seed of doubt growing roots in her mind, and no matter how hard she tries to smother it, it remains.

"I told you, some things need to come from him, but if you could have seen what I did that day, you would see that you two are soulmates. Now, this is supposed to be a night off. No more sad stories," he says, capping the bottle and tossing it aside.

Enthralled in the movie playing in front of him, Mikey absentmindedly pours two glasses of wine, grabs an armful of snacks, dumps them on the couch between them, and gets himself settled in.

"Tell me another story. How did you guys meet?" Mikey adjusts himself, sprawling across the oversized couch. Her freezing fingers pick up his feet, placing them into her lap so she can begin painting the hottest pink he has ever seen onto his toes.

"Did you know I didn't know Riley before all his shit went down? We were on the same base, so I knew of him, but that was it. I heard about him the same way Matt did. He really is a legend. I heard he was building a team, and being the mature fangirl I was, thought working under him would be the coolest thing ever. I followed him to the tank field with no idea what he was actually looking for. Somehow, my dumbass, who had never even been in a tank before, convinced him I was not only an amazing driver, but a sharpshooter with the tanks weapon system—wow that is blinding," Mikey lifts his leg into the air, eyeing the almost neon color now meticulously painted on five of his toe nails.

"Where was I? Oh yeah. I don't know if he saw through it or not, but he told me he wanted to see what I could do and sent me to bring it out. Please remember, I am a dumbass who was just trying to impress a total stranger. I knew a few of the guys working in the garage and got them to give me the gist of how to run it. I didn't understand the best and somehow turned just enough to plow through the wall between two huge bay doors."

"Oh my god! When he said you drove a tank into a building, I thought he meant, like, outside. I can't believe you crashed just pulling it out," she says through the laughter bubbling out of her.

"Hey, I own my mistakes. I apologized to everyone and admitted what I did to Riley right away. He found me the next day sweeping the sun off the sidewalk so a crew could rebuild without it getting in their way, called me Tank, and told me he was taking me for his spec ops team." He beams, kicking his feet back and forth at the sight of them.

"How the hell did you manage to be the luckiest person ever?" she teases, pushing his feet away from her.

They spend the rest of the night telling stories and eating too much junk food. With every laugh the stress fades, feeling lighter as the night goes on. Mikey tells her about all the times he got Riley to leave his cave and enjoy life. Hearing how they progressed from co-workers to best friends warms her heart. Meanwhile, Liz tells stories about all the trouble she got into as a teenager, trying to run from her problems and tells him only the best stories of her past life. Eventually, they both start to fade, curling up on opposite sides of the couch while the third twilight movie plays in the background. Her eyes drift close, letting the sounds of vampires fighting werewolves lull her to sleep.

Morning comes too fast. The moment the alarm blares from Mikey's phone at 6 a.m., the throbbing in her head makes her regret drinking the entire bottle of wine. Rolling off the couch, Liz pads down the hallway to find Mikey already in his room, packing a bag, still shirtless with his cow print pajamas on. Flopping onto his plush mattress, she watches him pack, knowing she only has a few minutes before he will send her to do the same.

"What do you call an Italian hooker?" she asks, sliding off the bed. "A pasta-tute"

Not a single laugh from him, just a shake of his head and a smile that reaches his eyes. His whole face looks brighter, more relaxed after their night together. They both needed it. The endless hours of stories and talking about what is bothering them took a huge weight from their shoulders. Before she can stop, Liz presses against him, arms wrapped tightly around his waist.

"Thank you. Last night was perfect." She gives him one quick squeeze before dashing to her room and tossing a small luggage bag onto her bed. She takes her time, carefully picking out everything she will need, hoping they won't be stuck staying at the base long.

After filling the bag with enough clothes to last her two weeks, she takes out a second one, stuffing sneakers, boots, and her favorite sandals into it before grabbing all her soaps from the bathroom and dumping them on top. A few personal items manage to find their way into the bags. Her pillow, a throw blanket, her kindle, and one of Riley's t-shirts that still faintly smells like him. She picks up her last empty bag and darts across the hall. Hoping he doesn't get mad she is invading his personal space, Liz grabs a few things from Riley's dresser, placing everything into the bag neatly. As she is about to leave, the small frame with their photo catches her eye. She snatches it from its place next to the bed and places it on top of his clothes before leaving their home behind.

The new room at the base is not nearly as cozy as the one Riley had claimed at the Nevada base. Even as plain as he had it, there was still a touch of life, still someone's home. The layout is nearly identical. The door opens to a living room, a kitchenette tucked to the side, the only difference is the large closet right off the living room. Two bedrooms line the other wall: one holding bunk beds, the other a full-size bed with a bathroom in between the rooms.

"You take the single room," Mikey says, heading right for the smaller room and tossing his bags inside. "I'm good with a bunk. Ry is going to need the big bed when he gets home."

"Are you sure? You do realize I'm just going to be moving in with you when he gets here right? We don't know what they are doing to him or what kind of head space he will be in. The last thing we need to be worrying about is what our relationship is... or isn't,'" Liz says.

A deep sadness fills her. That is exactly what she wants, to figure out their relationship, to know what is going on between them, even if it's the least of her worries. She can't help it, she needs to focus on the trivial things like that, if not, the endless barrage of thoughts of what he is enduring will devour her. So, she focuses on anything else. How is she going to sleep at night knowing he is lying in the next room? What if all her anxiety was for a good reason and he comes back loathing her very existence? Will she be able to handle that level of rejection? What if he doesn't hate her, but if what he is going through changes everything between them?

"Hey! Get out of there!" a booming voice shouts, making her jump. "I know where you're going, and you need to knock it off," Mikey adds.

"What the hell are you talking about? I'm not going anywhere," Liz says, genuine confusion dancing across her face.

"You were making that face: the one where your eyebrows look sad, and you kind of push your lips out like a fish. Whenever you make that face, you get lost in your shitty thoughts. You retreat into your mind. We leave in a few hours, and I need you in tip top shape while you're here. This is the first time you're going to be without one of us. You should try to find something to do in your downtime. Maybe spruce the place up so Ry doesn't come back to a shit hole." He stops in his tracks, turning to his smaller bag and mumbling something under his breath. He pulls out a small, black card and hands it to her. It is almost identical to the one Riley gave her for her shopping spree, the only difference being her name is etched onto the front rather than his. "I meant to give that to you sooner, but so much happened. Riley told me something about getting you all squared away. I don't know, I wasn't listening, but I think he got your paperwork submitted and got an account set up so you can start getting your pay."

His words hit her like a train. She has money, a job, a life. For the first time in years, she has something of her own, something she can be proud of. She slips the card into her pocket and tries not to cry. It has been so long since she has had this much freedom. She has spent years being controlled by others, whether it was her grief, her capture, or being held hostage by the general, something else was always in control. Liz knows if she dares to speak the tears will come flooding out. She brings her bags into the other room, setting them on the large bed. It looks too much like Riley's room in Nevada, the one now most likely destroyed, thanks to her. Shoving the building guilt down as far as she can, Liz carefully unpacks Riley's clothes, placing them in the dresser next to the door. Her own bedding gets sloppily put on the bed, and her own clothes stay in her bags which get tossed into the closet. The only items that hold any significance to her get handled with the utmost care. She slides Riley's shirt onto a pillow, hoping and praying he doesn't find it creepy. The small, framed picture gets placed on the nightstand next to the bed.

With only a few hours left until almost the entire team leaves without her, Liz gets to work. Mikey has left to go make sure all their gear is ready and the rest of the preparations are made. The whole trip is pointless. Whenever she thinks of them going, she gets a sinking feeling in the pit of her stomach. They won't find him. Something is preventing his rescue, and Liz is going to figure out what, or better yet, who. She has approximately ten days from when they leave to when they get back, giving her nine to figure out who is screwing them over and how to convince them to let her go on the next mission.

CHAPTER 8

By her fifth day alone, Liz has found her groove. She sneaks out early to workout, takes her meals back to her room to avoid the soldiers trying to talk to her in the mess hall. She became friendly enough with one of the other sergeants, Lauren, to join her unit on their air tactic training, allowing her to still learn and work toward her thirty solo jumps. Although that may have just been the work of Mikey, not wanting to float down to Earth with her strapped to his chest again. While trying to do what he asked and be friendly with Matt, she can't help but avoid him And when she *is* around him, she snaps. Today is the day that needs to change. Mikey kept his word, texting her as much as he is able, just to let her know they are alive. When she sees Matt in line at the mess hall, she knows it's time for her to keep hers.

"Hi," she squeaks out, picking up a to-go box from where they sit next to the trays. He looks up at her, eyes going wide in shock.

"Holy shit, did you just talk to me?" he asks, smiling so wide the dimples on his cheeks show. "Don't make me change my mind," she says. Her eyes bounce from one steaming tray to the next, waves of spices filling the air, making it hard to decide on what to eat. Her stomach growls loudly as she peers to the salad bar.

"I already figured that was all I was getting out of you," he says with a casual shrug.

"Actually, I was going to ask if we could talk. I'm not eating here, but I guess you could come back and have lunch in my room if you want," she says.

Her heart pounds in her ears, not wanting to see his reaction to her words, she moves down the line, placing a piece of baked chicken into her box. Mouth already watering at the smell of the herbs wafting around, she quickly adds a scoop of brown rice, sliding further away. Matt is next to her a moment later, filling his own container with two heaping scoops of chicken pot pie. They stay silent while Liz finishes up, adding roasted carrots and broccoli to her meal before closing it and walking off.

The scrape of Matt's boots tell her he isn't far behind. Her hands tremble as he approaches, darting ahead to hold the door open. She rushes through the lot, trying to make it back to her room before her mind changes. The sounds of boots stomping in perfect unison and jeeps speeding by keeps her focus, anything but having to have lunch with someone she can't stand.

The door to her room creaks open. The light flickers on, and she steps into the depressing, standard issue living space. The sharp whistle behind her has her rethinking every decision she has ever made. Unable to help what happens next, a sharp sigh escapes, and she turns on him.

"Problem?" she snaps

"Always so defensive, honey. I'm surprised. I thought you lived off base?" he says, only half asking.

Her eyes never leave him as he takes the food from her hands and makes his way over to the dining table. "For one, I was trying to be nice, but if you think it's okay to have some little pet name for me, I will drag your ass out of here and let the guys deal with you when they get back. And second, I was staying off base with Riley, but Mikey thought it would be better to stay here."

He simply watches her, amused as she storms over to the table. "I won't say what I'm thinking," he says.

He no doubt sees the fury churning in her eyes, and that is not a battle anyone would want to face. "Do you ever relax? Honey is short for honey badger, that's what everyone calls you after they decided the full name was too long. Congrats, you got a call sign, honey. It usually takes years for that honor, but, if you prefer, I can make everyone stop calling you that and it can be a special thing between us," he says, winking at her.

Her phone buzzes in her pocket, saving his face from being slapped. When she looks at the screen, some of her tension dissipates, and she sends a quick reply before shoving it back into her pocket and sitting down at the table. Her eyes drift close, silently counting to five. She lets out all the air in her lungs before beginning.

"I think I owe you an apology." The attitude never leaves her voice, even if her tone is much lighter, mentally questioning if she will ever be able to speak to Matt without wanting to throttle him. "Other than your incessant flirting, and weird attempts to convince me there is nothing between Riley and I, you have been trying to be part of the team and I keep pushing you out. I'm sorry for that." She opens her box of food and starts eating, ignoring the blatant shock plastered on his face.

"Thank you. I understand why you don't like me, though. You and Scott have some crazy anger toward each other. I didn't know he hadn't told you guys I was joining, and I definitely should not have inserted myself into your relationship. It doesn't matter if I think it's real or not, what's between you two isn't any of my business. If someone did that to me, I would be pissed," he says, digging into his own plate of food.

"True, but it's more complicated than that. I think you're right, to an extent. I know what is between us. I know with every fiber of my being that we have feelings for each other, but ever since that day, there has been some doubt. Then you told me everyone thinks he was just being honest, and now I question everything. Maybe he was just trying to get laid and maybe the only reason he was nice to me was guilt. I keep reminding myself we only knew each other for a few months. Not only that, but I stabbed him, and threatened to do it again. I was a disgusting mess when he found me. No one could fall for someone who went through what I did, especially someone like him." Her fork clatters onto the table, her mind spiraling into her worst fears.

"They might if you let them," he says between bites.

"You're right, but that's not something I can do until Ry comes home, and I know if what's between us is real or not. Until then, I'm going to live in my delusions. If you can respect that, and me, then I can try to be nicer. I'll stop avoiding you and let you do your job, at least until my guys get back."

"Deal," he says, finishing his food. He picks up after himself, and re-joins Liz at the table. "So, if you don't live with Reaper—""

"Riley," Liz interjects.

"Sorry. If you don't live with Riley anymore, why haven't you spruced this place up? If he's not coming back, you're going to be here for a while. That was the first thing I did when I move onto a new base. If you want, I can help you move your things out while everyone is away. Honestly, I'm kind of curious about his secret cave."

Her stomach churns at the admission. Making a mental note of it, she shrugs it off, trying to remain nonchalant.

"Thanks, but no thanks. I was kind of a prisoner for a while, and I don't exactly have a lot of stuff. Eventually, I will make this hell hole a little nicer, but I have to wait for Mikey to get back and take me shopping."

"Why do you need him to take you? I thought you were a strong, independent little badger." He leans back in his chair, smirking as he watches Liz compose herself before answering.

"Well, being kidnapped by terrorists, having your entire existence wiped out, and having to start your life over makes it just a teeny bit difficult to get a car, or license, or I.D., or literally anything an adult needs to function."

"Go grab what you need. I can take you. There's a huge mall not too far from here, and I'm free for the rest of the night." He gets up, ready to rush out the door with Liz in tow, but she is not so sure.

"I can't let you do that. We don't even know each other. I'm not going to drag you around a mall buying home decor, that's weird."

"Is it weird? Or is it a good way to get to know me?" A smug smile plays on his lips, knowing she can't argue with his logic.

Mikey's words echo in her mind, she needs to get closer to him. She sighs and goes to her room, changing into the pants with the gun holster built into the waistband that Riley had gifted her, tucking her small pistol into it. Trying to multitask, she stuffs her minimal things into a small bag while trying to send Mikey a text, letting him know what is happening, just in case.

"Lead the way," Liz says, motioning to the door.

They walk out to the parking lot, and he takes her straight to the brand new, sharkskin metallic Camaro. She can't help but giggle, not surprised at all he drives the most stereotypical douchebag car a man could own. The only thing worse would be a modified Subaru. Matt opens the door for her, and she climbs into the passenger seat, heart racing while he jogs to the other side. The engine roars to life before they speed off and away from base.

They return to the base hours later. Both the back seat of the car and small trunk are stuffed full of bags. After being dragged around the mall for hours by Matt, who was clearly enjoying himself far more than Liz, she spotted a tattoo shop and bolted in. After hours in the chair, she was done, finally ready to go home. When they pull into the parking lot, Liz lets out a breath of relief, happy to finally be back. Pretending to be friendly with someone she cannot stand has her mentally drained. Matt insists on helping her carry everything back to her room, even though she is sick of making small talk, she agrees and thanks him with a smile, hoping and praying he doesn't try to stay.

Fumbling with the bags hanging from her arm and the keys in her hand, Liz finally gets the knob to turn and kicks her door open, dropping the bags the moment she is inside. Matt chuckles, bringing in the rest of her things and tossing them onto the couch. This is her best opportunity to get rid of him.

"Thank you," she says, a little too sweetly, adding, "And thank you for today. I guess you're not as bad as I thought."

"I knew you would like me once you opened up a bit." He smiles, making his dimples pop. "Do you want some help putting away this stuff?" he asks, peering into one of her bags. "Like I said, I have nothing going on for the rest of the night."

"I think I can handle it," Liz says from her spot in the kitchen, pulling all her groceries out and placing them on the table. "I'm pretty tired, probably just going to put the food away and get some sleep." Liz watches his reaction carefully, his shoulders slum and he stops walking toward her. "I'm not great at things like this...the whole friend thing. I never have been, so I'm sorry if this isn't what you were hoping for," she admits.

"You don't seem to have a problem being friends with Mikey, you two are inseparable," he remarks.

"Mikey is different. He has been there through it all, and he has never once sexualized me or made me feel uncomfortable. He never wanted anything more than a genuine friendship, and you can't even begin to imagine what had to happen for us to be at this point," she snaps, slamming her bread onto the counter.

"Seems more like a guy waiting around for you to get over your infatuation with his uninterested friend so he can fuck you."

Her head whips around so fast it makes her dizzy, just in time to see him throw his hands over his face and look up to the ceiling, clearly regretting his choices. "That was stupid. I'm sorry. After spending the day with you, I'm a little jealous of the relationship you two have." He drops his hands, turning to her with big, sad eyes.

"I think you should go. I will see you at the gym tomorrow." She snips, turning back to her task at hand. She holds it together for a count of ten after the door clicks closed before she rips a pillow from the couch, stuffs her face into it, and screams until her throat burns. When the anger subsides, Liz gets to work on unpacking the rest of her bags, placing each item as she goes. A plush, charcoal grey rug gets unrolled and pulled to sit under the front legs of the small couch, carefully placing the coffee table back in the center. A white throw blanket covered in small black bows is placed on the back of the couch, with matching throw pillows on each side. The coffee table gets topped with a black porcelain tray which winds up holding a set of two candles and a small vase of white flowers.

Taking more bags from where they are haphazardly strewn across the floor, Liz marches into Mikey's room, dumping the bags on the floor, and getting to work. His bedding is stripped and replaced with pink and white checkered sheets, and topped with a white comforter covered in hand drawn style pink daisies and small pastel strawberries mixed in.

After swapping out the pillow cases and putting them back, Liz places a plush, furry pink pillow on top with a teddy bear sitting front and center. While she lucked out on finding a princess canopy for the bunk, she did find pink cherry blossom string lights that she hangs around the perimeter of the bed. Satisfied, she balls up the old bedding and shoves it in the closet, making a mental note to deal with it in the morning. By the time she is done, the clock reads 2:24 a.m. Unable and unwilling to do any further decorating, Liz crawls into bed, staring at the photo of her clinging to Riley, until she can't hold her eyes open any longer.

That night, Liz dreams of being back in her cell. She knows she is not there––huddling in the corner, arm chained to the ground, gently rocking herself back and forth. Liz tells herself over and over again it isn't real. But if it's not real, why does it feel like it is?

The same sharp bite of pain as the metal cuffs cut into her raw wrists. The crumbling concrete floor freezing beneath her nearly naked body as blood slowly trickles from her freshly cut leg. Reaching for the cut, she remembers doing it once before, but it's not a cut. It's a small lump. The tracker, that was when they put it in her, the blood coming from the sheer size of the needle.

She takes a deep breath, trying to get her bearings, but the smell of urine mixed with blood has her gagging. She wonders what the point of knowing she's in a dream is when she can't change anything.

Footsteps echo in the distance, moving closer to her cell. Every hair on her body stands on end. Her heart rate picks up and she breaks out in a cold sweat.

She hoped to never hear those footsteps again in her life.

He was coming for her. She screams in frustration, wondering how she remembers this day but does not remember him coming to her cell.

Gunshots ring out in the distance, and the men in the halls start screaming at each other, yelling that he is there. It's not right. She got sedated and stabbed in the leg, she never knew what happened in the time between that and when she came to. Everything begins blending together. One moment Dmitri was screaming at his men about getting chirinda ready, and the next, Riley is in front of her.

She springs to her feet, yanking as hard as she can on the chain holding her in place. She cannot 'stop the tears from flowing, telling him how happy she is to see him. He steps over and crouches down, like he can't even see she is standing in front of him. She begs him to look up, to talk to her, and cries that she needs to see him. Her cries only grow louder as he starts to fade away, the walls around them morphing to a deep, endless black. She screams until her voice breaks, begging him not to leave her, crying pleas that never make it to his ears.

Her eyes snap open, face wet with tears shed while asleep.

Peering around the dark room, she wishes she could go back in, just to see him for a moment longer. She lies there, unmoving, wondering why her subconscious would force her to relive that day, more importantly, why it would make her remember that day wrong.

It hits her then, what if her mind wasn't remembering wrong, but showing her what she heard while drugged?

She leaps from the bed, sprinting into the kitchen to grab the notebook she's been using to write down all the strange things about Matt. Scribbling down every detail, circling chirinda until a hole nearly forms in the paper. The word was so out of place in her dream, she needs to ask Alex about it when they get back. She just has to endure four more days until then.

CHAPTER 9

The days leading up to the team's return dragged by at a snail's pace. Liz stands on the tarmac, bouncing on her toes with nervous energy. The plane should be emptying any minute, and when it does, she will finally know if they found him. One of the worst parts of being spec ops she has learned, is the fact that they cannot share any information while in the field. Any message can be intercepted at any time, so no details can be shared. Mikey sent sporadic messages letting Liz know he was alive, but other than that, nothing.

The hangar door groans open. Men and women in uniform slowly start filing out of the plane. Liz's heart drops.

Riley isn't with them.

If he were, he would be the first one taken off. She tries to hold out hope, thinking maybe they held him back so there isn't a crowd. The look on Mikey's face when he walks down the ramp says it all.

He finds her in the small group gathered to greet the team, dropping his eyes and giving his head a small shake. Her heart shatters in her chest. Panic claws at her core, wanting to go to her friends and welcome them home, but she just can't. She bites her cheek until she tastes blood. Turning on her heels, she jogs back to the housing complex, weaving through the people filling the halls until she is tucked safely back into her room. She doesn't cry, doesn't scream or throw things. None of the things she wants so badly to do. Instead, she goes into her room, sliding down the closed door, and stares into nothingness.

Liz has no idea how long she sits like that when the door to the apartment opens. The moment she hears that the familiar creak of the unoiled hinges, the wall she put up comes crumbling down. Violent sobs wrack her body, wishing so badly that Riley was the one walking through that door.

Mikey's heavy footsteps rush through the apartment, going through their shared bathroom and into hers. He drops to his knees, pulling her into his arms, and rocks gently back and forth. The scream that escapes between sobs comes from her soul. The kind of scream only someone who lost a piece of their very being can make.

"Why?" she screams through broken sobs. "Why can't we find him?"

It's a question he will never be able to answer.

"I don't know, darlin. I don't know. He was supposed to be there." His arms squeeze tighter, heart breaking for her.

Two more sets of boots run through the apartment, throwing open the connecting door to find them huddled on the floor, crying together. Liz looks up at them through wet lashes, unable to stop herself from the anger churning inside, and she screams.

"IT'S YOUR FUCKING FAULT!" Shoving Mikey off, Liz stands, storming to where Alex and Tyler stand wide eyed. "You all fucking did this. I told you. I told you so many fucking times that man is trying to make sure Riley is never found! You keep pretending he wants to find Riley but he wants him fucking dead!"

she shrieks, stepping up to Alex until they're practically touching, chest heaving with each shuddering breath. "Get out. I want everyone out right fucking now," she orders as calmly as she can muster. She sees the hurt in their eyes as they file out the door, but she can't be bothered to care, instead slamming the door behind them.

Dragging her feet over to the bed, she sits on the edge, picking up their picture as she does. She lets the tears fall, dripping onto the glass in the silence. Trying to steady her breathing, she takes two sharp breaths in, anything to trick her body into calming down.

"It's all my fault," she whispers, looking down at the picture. Even through his mask, she can see his smile. "I'm the reason you got taken, and now I don't know how to get you back."

She stays like that for a long while, letting the grief and anguish wash over her until it's almost too much to take. She knows it is her fault, and she lashes out at the only people fighting for the same cause.

Wiping her eyes, she gets up and goes into the living room where she finds Mikey, sitting on the couch, eyes red and puffy from his own tears . Without a word she goes to him, pulls him into her own arms, and holds him the same way he had her. His head drops to rest on her shoulder. Her arms stretch so far around him they don't even touch.

"Fuck, we must look ridiculous right now," he laughs. "I'm too big to be held like this." He tries to wiggle out of her arms, but she just holds tighter.

"Big strong men need to be held sometimes, too," she coos, rubbing his arm. "I'm sorry I snapped earlier. That was the last thing you needed after everything you just went through. None of this is your fault."

"I'm fine. It sucks, but it's a risk of the job that I'm used to.

You're hurting right now. We may have known him longer, but you have a connection with Ry none of us could ever have. You're not just worried about your friend, you're terrified for the man you love. Anyone with half a brain could hear the pain in your screams," he says, successfully escaping her arms and pulling her into his instead.

"I'll be right back," she mumbles against him, sliding from his arms. She walks away, disappearing out the door. Knocking on the door across the hall, she secretly hopes they don't answer, unsure of how to apologize to them for everything. They heard cries and came running, and in return, she blamed them. She feels like such a bitch, cursing herself under her breath, and she gently knocks again. The speed in which Alex whips the door open is astounding. Liz stumbles back, peering up at him with wide eyes.

"I need to apologize... to both of you," Liz says just loud enough for him to hear. Tyler perks up, walking to the doorway to stand next to his partner. "What I said was wrong and uncalled for. I was projecting my own insecurities onto you. None of what happened is anyone's fault but my own. I never should have taken my anger out on you, and I am truly sorry."

"Thank you, honey. That couldn't have been easy. I don't think either of us blame you. If Tyler had got taken, I would do the same," Alex says.

"Oh, good. Mikey got my message," she says, hearing the nickname. "I'm sure you guys have a lot going on, so I'll leave you to it, but I am sorry for the way I treated you."

She doesn't wait to see if they say anything more before turning and going back to her own room where she finds Mikey digging through the cabinets.

"Looks good in here," he says, going back and throwing himself down on the couch. "How did you manage to get it delivered so fast?"

"I took notes!" she proudly states, opening the book to begin telling him everything. "The guy really loves bragging about himself and how great he is. Apparently, Scott wants him to take over the unit. I told you he isn't trying to help Riley. Also, I don't think he realizes he did it, but when we talked about the mission, he said Scott knew the town was empty."

"What?" Mikey interrupts, eyes simmering with anger.

"Yeah, I got him talking about himself and..." she trails off, flipping through the pages, before jumping up and running out the door. She throws herself against the door opposite her own, pounding both her palms on it until Tyler yanks it open, looking angry.

"I need you guys... now," she shrieks, darting back into her own room once more.

Mikey looks at her, brows pinched in confusion, watching her rub her hands together, pacing back and forth. When the rest of the team walks in seconds later, she flicks the locks and ushers them to the table.

"Now that everyone is here, I can finish. The day Matt took me shopping, he started talking about himself. He wants to be commander, I guess that's his end game. While he was ranting, he told me general shit for brains knew the town would be empty. Said he thought it was weird, but questioning his commanding officer wouldn't help him rise in rank, so he ignored it. And he let it slip that Scott wanted someone who could handle you guys. Why would he need someone who can handle you if Riley is coming home and leading you again?" A heavy silence fills the room as they all start to put the pieces together.

"Did he say anything else?" Alex asks, jaw clenched so tight it looks like he could crack a tooth.

"Not really, the rest of the time he was just bragging about how amazing he is and how it's almost guaranteed he is going to lead the unit. It's weird though, he didn't out right say it, but he kept telling me I need to get over Riley. The way he says it sometimes is really creepy, like he knows Ry will never make it home. He said *if he doesn't come back* and said he is curious to see Riley's cave." Her pacing slows, and she joins them at the table, flipping through her notebook, anxious to tell them about her dream.

"One more thing. Does chirinda mean anything to you guys?" she asks innocently. Her heart drops when she sees the same pained look on each of their faces.

"Where did you hear that?" Alex asks sternly.

"So it does mean something?" Liz fires back.

"That depends," Tyler replies.

"Well, now that I know it means something, I can tell you, but please don't make fun of me... I had a dream a few days ago, a nightmare. I was back with Dmitri. It was the day he had the tracker put in my leg, but everything was wrong," she starts to explain.

"What do you mean wrong?" Mikey asks, concerned.

"I knew it was a dream. It was almost like lucid dreaming, but I couldn't change anything. I was scared, covered in blood, and everything felt so fucking real, but I knew it wasn't. When I checked on my leg, there was a bump, not a cut. Here's the weird part, I remember that day. I was drugged, stabbed by a giant needle, then out of it for a while before Riley came in, but it was all wrong. I heard Dmitri walking to my cell, then guns. He started yelling in the hall about someone being there, and making sure chirinda was ready, but the gun shots didn't happen until I woke up, and I never heard him come anywhere near me that day. Then Riley came in. I tried so hard to get to him. I was screaming his name, but he walked in and crouched next to my bed, like he didn't even see me fighting to get to him." She scans the table, looking at each man wearing the same pale expression, as if what she said holds some deep-rooted trauma.

"Chirinda is where they were holding Riley when he was first taken. It's where it all started. That was our first thought, but the general said he's been keeping an eye on it," Alex says, too quiet for her liking.

"It sounds like your subconscious was showing you what happened when your mind wasn't fully there. You likely did hear all that, but you were too far gone to really understand what was happening," Tyler says.

"Holy shit. That has to be where they are keeping him! We have to go now." she yells, jumping from her chair.

"We can't just leave. There is a process. We need to te--"

"Don't you dare say it, Alex," Liz snarls, turning back and storming over to them. "How can you want to tell him after everything? We can't tell him! The moment you do, Riley will be moved. I understand I have my issues with Scott, but he knew Riley wasn't going to be at any of the places he sent you. He does not want him found. If he were here, Riley would trust me. I wish you would do the same."

Footsteps echo around the room as she begins pacing again, no one daring to talk. Her words weigh heavily on all of them.

"Look, if I'm wrong, I'm wrong. I will accept any and all consequences, but you know I would never risk Riley if I didn't know in my soul this is the right move. And if I'm right, and he is there, then we have a lot more to worry about than you guys realize."

"Fuck!" Alex shouts, standing from the table. "This could ruin us. If this goes wrong, we could all be thrown out, dishonorably discharged."

"I would rather go back to living on the streets than leaving him to die," Liz says solemnly "I lost everything: my home, my job, even my identity, and now that I have some of that back, I would throw it all away if it meant saving Riley."

"He would do the same for any of us," Mikey says. "I mean, he already did to get Liz out."

"Alright. I need some time to pull this together. I don't know when we can leave, so stay ready." Alex says no more. Tyler stands and joins him as he walks out the door, pulling it closed behind them.

Mikey and Liz simultaneously go into their rooms, ready to load their packs so they can leave at a moment's notice. She only makes it a few steps before she hears thunderous laughter from the other room. Her feet carry her to him before she even registers she is moving, giggling the whole way.

"What did you do to my fucking bunk?" he chokes out through laughs.

"Surprise! I made it pretty," she says, beaming with pride. He pulls her into his arms, lifting her right off the ground.

"I love it, now go pack a bag. Alex says he isn't sure, but he is and he is going to get shit done quick, and we need to be ready."

Feet firmly back on the ground, Liz prances to her room, tossing her go bag on the bed as she does. Running through the mental checklist Riley coached her on, she places each item on her bed in neat rows, making sure she has everything she may need. A thermal blanket and change of clothes are the first thing she puts in, followed by a bottle of water, and two MREs. Next is the multi tool, flashlight with extra batteries, scissors, and the biggest first aid kit they own, placing it right on top in case she needs to use it fast. The bag gets placed next to the door, much like Liz, ready to go the moment she gets the call.

CHAPTER 10

"Time to go," Mikey says, barging into Liz's room and ripping her blankets off. She is on her feet in an instant, pulling on the clothes she left laid out next to her bed for days. She stuffs her feet into her boots, which she leaves untied until they make it onto the plane, just as Alex instructed. Her bag gets slung onto her back and they are out the door where Alex and Tyler are waiting. Wasting no time, they take off in a silent sprint, heading to the tarmac where their plane awaits. After forty-eight days, Riley is finally coming home.

A small group of soldiers stand ready and waiting for them to arrive. When the four of them get close enough for Liz to start making out familiar faces, everyone jumps into action. Before they reach them, the rest of the team is loaded onto the plane, leaving the door open, allowing them to run on as fast as possible. Her heart pounds in her ears, terrified for what could happen to Riley if someone is able to stop them before they take off. She picks the first empty seat she sees, throwing herself into it and buckling in right away. A sharp whistle rings out from down the aisle as the plane thrums to life.

"Seats, now!" Alex yells over the hum of voices, the plane lurching forward and picking up speed faster than Liz is used to. "This is an unauthorized mission. You all know what you are risking by coming. We have no time to lose. Once we are in the air, prepare yourselves, prepare your gear, prepare your weapons. I don't know what we will find when we arrive. We have very little information. What we do know is Dmitri has been seen arriving every few days. He is not there now, and his forces that stayed behind are small. If you do what you are told, this should go easy. Until then, no one is to leave this plane or speak to anyone when we stop to refuel. Turn all phones and tracking off."

She does exactly what he says. Once they are in the air, her boots get tied nice and snug, she straps her holster onto her legs and waist, with the addition of a second belt holding Riley's knife sheathed on her lower back. She braids her hair into two, neat French braids, making sure they can't come undone during a fight. After the third time checking her bag, Mikey pulls her back into her seat, urging her to sleep as much as she can before they reach their destination.

"How am I supposed to sleep at a time like this?" she whines, tossing her head back in frustration. "He is there, I know it. I need to stay alert. Anything could happen between now and then."

"Darlin, you can't save the world if you don't take care of yourself first. I told you, exhaustion will make you sloppy. You will make mistakes and someone will get hurt. This flight is not as long, so I don't have time to fight you on this. It's the middle of the night. We are all going to sleep. If anything, and I mean anything at all happens, we will know the moment it does."

She won't admit it even though she knows he is right, but right or not, she can't imagine sleeping at a time like this. Maybe it's just something that will come in time, the ability to pass out anywhere at any given moment, something only the ones who have been through this too many times have perfected. A large hand lands on the side of her face, roughly pulling against a hard shoulder. Mikey slides his hand into hers, stroking his thumb back and forth until he can feel her begin to relax, not stopping until the full weight of her head is pressed against him. Hours of fitful sleep drag by. It gets harder to stay asleep the closer they get to their destination.

Sometime after the first stop to refuel, the symphony of snoring comes to a stop. As they wake up, Liz spots the unit checking their gear once more. While Mikey is still fast asleep next to her, she turns his hand over to check the time on his watch: 10 a.m. They have been flying for nine hours, with only two to go until they refuel next. People have already begun pacing the aisle and doing any type of workout they can in the small open area around the cargo door, desperate to get out some pent-up energy.

The hours tick by. Liz feels as if the entire flight is going in slow motion. Their final stop for fuel took longer than expected. When she tried to talk to Alex about what took so long, all he could tell her was it's taken care of. She tried to ignore how ominous it sounded, instead focusing on their strategy, running it through her mind on repeat. This is going to be her first time seeing action.

Tyler confirmed the camp is full. Although not as many enemy soldiers as they expected, it won't be a quiet mission. Slowly but surely, things start to settle. An eerie quiet takes over the team as everyone moves to find seats closer to the door that will be opening soon. Liz and Mikey claim two seats right in the front, determined to be the first boots on the ground. From the corner of her eye, she sees Alex stand.

It's time.

She sits by the cargo door, double checking the chute strapped to her back, anxiously bouncing her knees, watching Alex pace the narrow hall. Two rows of men and women line either side of the plane, carrying them to their next mission. Her heart sinks, thinking about the last two. Their teams raided two of Dmitri's camps with no sign of Riley. Every day they returned without him, Liz lost a piece of herself.

Mikey reaches over and takes her hand, giving her a sad smile. "We are approaching the drop zone. When you touch down, find your team, and go, do not wait for orders, do not wait to make sure the other teams are assembled, just get into your position."

"Mikey, Tyler, Neil; head to the main building, take the tunnels on the far side. There will be less resistance, but stay alert. John and Lauren, lead your team around the other side. Make sure their path is clear when they get there."

He turns and makes his way next to where Liz sits, eyes falling to the large scar across her neck. He goes silent, reflecting on everything that brought them to this moment. No amount of intel or planning could have prepared them for what happened that day. She has more than proven herself and just how far she would go to keep them safe.

"If you are not designated to a team, you are just men on the ground, you will be clearing a path to the cells ahead of Liz and I. If you see someone being held anywhere other than the cells, get them out. Leave no prisoner behind. Understood?"

"Yes, Sir," the team says in unison.

He glances over to Liz who is watching him prepare their team. She may be proud and appreciate how he stepped up, but she hates herself for knowing someone else should be standing where he is, giving those orders. Alex walks to the back of the plane, pushing a big red button on the wall. The door behind them slowly falls open, filling the room with deafening winds. Everyone stands, forming two lines, ready to hurl themselves into the air.

"Riley is down there. He has saved every one of our asses more times than we can count. Right now, finding him is our top priority. The general doesn't know we are here, so let's keep it that way.

We get in, get what we're here for, and get the hell out," Alex shouts over the wind whipping through the cabin of the plane. "You know your roles, don't fuck it up. Let's bring our boy home," he says, giving Liz a sad smile.

The wind is near deafening when Liz approaches the edge of the ramp. Nine people have jumped safely, but now that it is her turn, fear grips her and refuses to let go. This should not have been her first solo jump in action, the stakes are too high to not be strapped to someone more experienced. Any longer and she will be holding up the line, throwing off the flow of the whole mission.

Her eyes close and she takes a deep breath. Her toes balance on the edge, and with one powerful push, she is flying away from the plane and falling to the ground. The static line breaks free, opening her chute. She opens her eyes, seeing nothing but black and the red smoke signaling where to try and land.

With the few minutes she has before reaching the ground, Liz goes over the battle plan one last time. The moment she lands, she needs to get her chute harness off. Her gun comes out and stays up, even while she finds Alex and the handful of soldiers going ahead of them. It is a four-mile march to reach the perimeter of the camp. Luckily, it's the middle of the night and no one knows they are coming.

Somehow, Mikey managed to secure the entire unit night vision goggles, making everything go smoother than they had originally planned. After an estimated four minutes, Liz pulls the goggles over her eyes, pushing the button to turn them on as she does.

The world below her illuminates into different shades of grey. Men and women on the ground scramble to find their teams and head off to their destination. Too busy spotting her team from the air, she miscalculates the landing. The air is thrown from her lungs as her body slams into the ground. She takes a few gasping breaths, trying to force oxygen back into her body while she fumbles with the straps. Embarrassed, she climbs to her feet and makes her way over to the huddle, pushing past her own feelings to focus on finding Riley. She sticks as close to Alex as she can, picking her path carefully, stepping as quietly as possible

It's not long before they reach the river, where just across it lies Dmitri's first camp, and somewhere inside is Riley. Gun over her head, she wades into the waist deep water, crossing just as Alex had demonstrated on the plane. The moment they are free of the trees, Liz sees the compound lit up in the distance.

"Hold positions. Everyone down." Alex's voice comes over the small com built into her helmet.

The team drops onto the ground in unison, waiting for their leader to give his next order. Liz peers at him as much as she is able through her goggles, watching intently as he looks through some type of binoculars. He reaches for his helmet, fumbling with a dial on the side before speaking again.

"Everyone hold. They have four men patrolling the front. Lauren, can you see them from your side?"

"Yep," a confident voice replies.

"On three, we drop the ones on the right, then left," Alex says, pulling the sniper rifle from where it has been perched on his back.

Liz watches in amazement as he pops out the attached bipod, holding the gun steady while he aims. He counts to three and releases two, simultaneous muffled shots. She can't see if they hit their mark, but the following shots tell her they must have. They remain, holding their positions, inching their way forward, waiting to see if any reinforcements come after their downed men. Every step they take sends her heart racing. She knows she should not be doing this. It has barely been six months since she was rescued, and even she knows that's not enough time to be doing what she is. It does not matter if she has been training ten hours a day nearly every day for six months. It has taken the rest of them years to be doing what they are.

Finally, they make it to the scattered buildings surrounding the towering abandoned structure at the center of it all. She flips her goggles up and follows her team into the light, trying her best to follow orders and hang back, allowing them to do what they do best. That works for a while, staying behind and sweeping each building they pass as gunshots fill the air around them. Screams ring out from all directions and Liz ducks into the next door. A towering figure jumps out of the dark, running toward her, wielding a knife the length of her arm. A deafening crack explodes from her weapon, followed by a sickening gurgle from the man as he falls to the ground, blood pooling. Bile rises in her throat. She hunches over and vomits onto the floor, heaving to catch her breath.

Alex pulls her back, spinning her around so she is no longer looking at the man she just murdered. Liz didn't think she would have such a horrible reaction. She has killed men before, although each time was out of desperation.

"You're okay, but we need to move. Now," he says, guiding her out of the building. Her gun is back at attention, checking the rest of the buildings, shoving the image of the man and the way his eyes glazed over out of her mind, trying to replace it with one of Riley.

It feels like hours have passed when they reach the looming structure in the distance. An abandoned hospital, Alex had told her. Dmitri had the entire construction crew killed when the massive stone frame was complete. Bodies litter the ground around her as she walks next to Alex.

"All teams should be here by now. They are clearing the floors of hostiles. If they find him, they will tell us, but we need to keep looking until they do. You take the left, I'll go right. This floor should be safe, but keep your gun up no matter what," he says into her helmet.

She gives a small nod, lifts her gun, and starts down the long hall, checking each room as she goes. Whatever team went through before her did one hell of a job.

"Floors two and three are clear," a voice Liz doesn't recognize says over the radio. "Headed to four. Seems like less and less the higher we get. I think we are almost completely clear."

"Tunnels are also clear. We're coming to you, Alex," Mikey's voice rings in her ears. Relief floods her until he speaks again. "Saw some guys come through the back on our way, so keep your eyes up."

The soft crunch of footsteps sound from down the hall. Liz ducks into the next room, making sure it is empty before she presses her back to the wall, listening to a mix of people walking toward her.

It may be Mikey, but she is not willing to take any risks. They are running out of time, and hiding isn't going to find Riley any faster. Liz takes a deep breath and steps into the hall, gun up and ready to fire. Her anxiety eases when she comes face to face with Mikey being trailed by two others she has yet to meet.

He gives a small nod, and they continue down the corridor, breaking off and searching each room on their own in an attempt to speed things up. She hears whispers when she steps into the next room. Unable to speak or signal for help, she proceeds on her own, cautiously stepping around fallen debris. The room is empty. Unable to shake the uneasy feeling, she goes to the open space where a window should be, ducking to stay hidden.

Tall bushes twisted in growing vines have had all the windows blocked from whatever is on the other side. Her blood runs cold. Whoever is out there isn't speaking English, and they are most definitely not with her.

Not thinking, she leaves the room, looking for a doorway that leads to where the men are. Three rooms down, she finds what she is searching for.

"I found a backdoor. There are a few men outside, but I can't tell how many. I am going to check it out," Liz announces.

A mix of voices take over, whispering as loud as they can to wait for someone, and not to go alone.

"We don't have time. I'll stay hidden." Her eyes dart from the floor in front of her back to the open spaces she walks through. Every step is slow and deliberate. The door leading out is shattered, leaving just a metal frame that clearly has not moved in a while. *Perfect.* The men out there must have gotten in another way, leaving this way open for her to sneak through. The overgrown brush gives her enough cover to commando crawl her way over.

"Six people, and they all have guns. I don't know what they are doing, but it seems like they are looking for something. I'm going to try and get closer." She drags her body through the dirt, crawling along the outer wall, moving impossibly slow to minimize noise until she can hear them more clearly.

They're speaking Russian, so she can't understand a word of it, but she can understand the tone. They are scared, panicked even.

She worms her way behind the impossibly tall bushes, stuffing her gun through the leaves, and peers through the scope. What she sees has her sick all over again.

All the blood drains from her only to be replaced by an anger she has not felt since the day her brother took her family from her.

There, in the center of the small expanse of mud and shrubbery, is Riley, strung up by the skin of his back, hanging like a mutilated puppet.

CHAPTER 11

Trying her best to remain calm, she pushes herself back, not stopping until she is on concrete. The moment she is, she takes off into the building, trying to move as quietly as she can into the hall where she empties the contents of her stomach.

Silent tears stream down her face. Hands grip onto her, turning her around before she has the chance to vomit again. Mikey scans her face with wild eyes, and he can see the pain she is trying to push past. There is only one person who can cause that.

"Alex, call the fucking chopper in, now! he's here," Mikey says into his microphone, calm and collected as he fidgets with his radio. "Everyone get here, now. Courtyard on the first floor. Alex is on the right, we're on the left. Lauren, get your team to the front. If you're not with one of us, get to the back and find a way in."

"You have two minutes to get into position. Helicopter is fifteen minutes out. Take these assholes down and keep Corson safe until it gets here; that is your only priority," Alex adds through the comms.

Liz is pulled into a tight hug before she has the chance to

register everything unfolding around her. The only thoughts bouncing around in her head are finding out if he is alive, and killing the ones who put him there.

"He's safe, darlin. You need to breathe. He is here, and we are getting him out. Everything is going to be okay," Mikey coos while rubbing her back. His hands drop abruptly, replacing her body with his gun. Their two minutes are up. She picks her own weapon back up, staying ready, following Mikey to the door.

The moment the first shot is fired, he kicks the frame open, rushing through with Liz close behind. She fires at the first man she sees, downing him instantly. The courtyard quickly delves into chaos. The rest of Dmitri's men try to hide while their team floods the area. Her eyes go to Riley, and everything else fades away.

Liz takes off across the space, getting to Riley only moments before Mikey and Alex. He is breathing. She doesn't try to stop the tears cascading down her face. Scanning everything holding him in the air, she tries to figure out a way to get him down without causing him more harm. The guns firing all around her make it hard to think. Each one has her flinching, knowing she won't be able to defend him from a bullet while he's strung up in the air. So focused on her own thoughts, she missed Tyler crawling into the machine

The blood curdling scream that tears from Riley brings her back to the present. Inch by inch he descends toward them, until his limp body is placed on the ground, blood oozing from his wounds. Liz throws herself next to him, rolling him into her lap to allow them to remove whatever is attached to his back

"He... did... it," Riley says through strained breaths. His eyes flutter open, his empty stare crashing into hers. "He... killed me." A smile spreads across his cracked lips. "Now--" His hand moves to her cheek, cupping it the same way he had done so many times before. Her own hand cradles his, holding it against her so he doesn't have to. "Now I get to see you again."

Their reunion is cut short by another scream from Riley. His arm goes lax, head flopping into her lap.

"I'm here, baby. You're safe. We are taking you home." Liz peppers his head with a mix of tears and delicate kisses, not willing to risk causing him any further pain.

She holds him while the guys work on getting whatever is in his back, out then bandaged enough to move. The gunfire finally ceases. Silent tears turn into chest wracking sobs the moment she hears the whirring of helicopter blades in the distance.

They stay there, Liz holding Riley in her lap until the helicopter is hovering above, lowering a gurney to the ground. Only then does she let him go, watching every movement Mikey and Alex make to get him strapped onto it. A harness lands at her feet. Without question, she climbs into it. Tyler makes his way over and explains how she is going to get strapped to go with him and Mikey. She has no time to question it before she is pulled into the air.

Safely in the aircraft, Liz and Mikey are forced to sit on a bench, watching while a trained team evaluates Riley. Her head falls on Mikey's shoulder, unable to look away. The sight of him lying with an oxygen mask covering his face while I.Vs are shoved into his veins, or the needles crudely stitching up his back, tears her heart into shreds. It's like watching a car crash. Tragic, but you just can't seem to look away. He is here, he is safe, and none of that stops Liz from the crushing fear that if she looks away for even a moment, he will disappear again.

"Hate to pull you from your dutiful watch, honey, but you need to prepare for what comes next," Mikey says, letting his cheek drop onto the top of her head.

"Another helicopter should be picking up the rest of the team any minute now. They will meet us at the airstrip to go home. You can stay with him while they get the seats taken out and litter installed, but when we move him and take off, you need to be out of the way," he says softly, knowing how much it is going to kill her to leave his side.

"When we get back, I don't know what is going to go down. Alex will call in and tell them we need medical, and they will meet us when we land to take Ry to the infirmary. The general is going to tear us all a new one, so I don't want you leaving the infirmary. The three of us are the superiors, and we will take full responsibility for what happened. I love you, but you aren't the best at controlling your smartass comments."

"I'm not that bad," she argues. "Lucky for you, even if I did have to stay with you, I wouldn't. I can't leave him, not now that I just got him back. I need to know that he is going to be okay first."

When the unit reaches the airstrip, everything seems to move impossibly fast. Liz sticks close to Riley, going wherever they take him until he is loaded onto the plane. A special stretcher was brought in for him and secures him comfortably, replacing a small chunk of seats. Seeing how distraught she is, and how much she is trying to hide the pain of leaving him, Alex has the crew leave a few seats across from where Riley is positioned, letting her stay by his side for as long as she is able, only moving her while their combat medic checks his vitals.

Liz holds out until the second stop for fuel. With exhaustion, and the adrenaline now gone, she finally drifts off to sleep, her hand firmly entwined in Riley's, neither one able to let go.

CHAPTER 12

The entire base is abuzz the moment the plane touches back down in Montana. Crowds gather around, waiting to see if the infamous Reaper was actually found, or if it was another failed mission that will be the end of so many careers.

Liz remains attached to Riley's side, watching all the other soldiers collect their belongings and line up, ready to file off the aircraft and accept whatever punishment awaits. Sneaking a peek out the window, she sees too many people, too many gathered to see if they can catch a glimpse at Riley.

"Hey Alex," she shouts over the voices. The unit commander finds her, standing over Riley, gently raking her fingers through his blood-soaked hair. "He can't go out there like this," she says, pleading.

"There is no other choice, he needs medical attention. He is stable now, but there is no telling how long he will stay that way. We have to get him to the infirmary as quickly as possible," he counters.

"What I mean is, he can't go out there like *this*." She motions to his face, completely bare except for the oxygen mask covering his mouth and nose. "He needs something to cover his face--everyone on board has already seen too much. We can't let everyone outside see, too," she argues, tears welling in her eyes.

She knows what it feels like to be violated, to be stripped bare and watched against your will. He does not deserve to be paraded in front of all the prying eyes, especially his fellow soldiers.

With a nod, Alex leaves her side, rummaging around in his bag until he finds something she considers suitable. She picks his head up, the same care and gentleness of holding a newborn baby, and tucks the scrap of cloth under it. She makes sure it covers from his neck to his cheek bones, only letting his eyes show, just as he would want.

The short walk to the infirmary is daunting. Liz is forced to walk a few steps behind the men pushing Riley across the lot, nothing more than a dutiful soldier escorting her commanding officer. The wide-eyed stares from the crowd as they pass by quickly turn into gossipy whispers. Her one and only goal right now is to keep it together long enough to get him safely into a hospital bed and start receiving real care, she will figure out the rest later.

One step after another, her eyes focus on the man in front of her until they finally reach the double doors she has been waiting for.

Inside is quiet, away from the murmurs of those wondering if Riley is dead or not, and Liz can finally breathe easier. She follows them to a room, standing just outside of the door while they get Riley moved from the stretcher onto a proper bed. Looking around, she is amazed at how quickly everyone moves to take care of him. The only experience she has had was with civilian hospitals, where even in the most dire of emergencies, you are forced to sit in an overcrowded waiting room and pray to whatever, or whoever, you believe in that you don't die before the doctor sees you. When the two men leave, she takes the opportunity to slip into the room, pulling a chair next to his bed.

Just as she is about to reach for him, she remembers what it was like for her just a few months ago. No one has any idea what he has been subjected to, and even Liz can only make assumptions based on her own experiences.

She snatches her hand back, cracking every knuckle she can, focusing on the pop each one makes to keep from touching him. Guilt courses through her. The moment he was down, she held him, she kissed him. What if he doesn't want to be touched, let alone kissed?

All the doubts about how he truly feels about her come rushing back. If he didn't hate her already, there is no doubt he will now. She tells herself she can apologize when he is awake, but for now, a silent vow to keep her distance will have to do.

They aren't waiting long before a woman in teal scrubs marches into the room like she owns it. Liz stands, placing her arms straight at her sides with her legs together, trying to remember everything her team had told her about military customs. The woman ignores her, going right to Riley's bedside where she begins checking him over.

"What can you tell me about what happened?" she asks, her voice shrill and grating.

Liz looks away when she pulls bandage scissors out and cuts her way up his pants.

"He was held for forty-eight days. There is no information on what was done to him while he was captive. How--"

"Lift his leg for me," the doctor cuts in.

Liz quickly does as she is instructed, slightly holding up his leg while she rolls him, pulling the fabric from under his body.

"He was strung up with hooks through his back, and his arms were also chained above him, although we have no way of knowing how long he was left like that. He was in and out of consciousness when the hooks were removed. Since then he has had a morphine drip that has kept him sedated. They also gave him two bags of different IVs on the flight over," Liz states, lifting his other leg so the doctor can finish removing his pants.

When she is done, she slides the chair to the other side of the room and sits, watching the woman check every inch of Riley.

After his heart rate and blood pressure are checked, and rechecked for good measure, the doctor peels his eyes open, shining her light into his pupils before moving on to the rest of his body. Liz can't help herself from looking as the doctor pulls back the sheet, revealing his torso, still strong and defined, even with the loss of some muscle mass. New injuries cover his body, everything from small scratches and cigarette burns, to deep slices that look as if they had been crudely stitched back together. She looks away, her stomach threatening to expel its contents thinking of all he has been through. Instead, she sits quietly, watching the steady thump of his heartbeat on the monitor off to the side.

"Well, all things considered, he seems to be doing remarkably well. When will your commanding officer be here? I need to speak with someone who can understand his injuries and limitations."

"Oh, um, I'm not sure. He has a lot he needs to take care of. I am more than capable of telling him everything if you would like to just tell me," Liz says, taken aback by the woman's hostility.

"He should wake up soon, so hopefully your C.O. will be here when he does. I'll speak to them then," she sneers, walking out the door.

Liz slumps in her chair, throwing her head back in frustration, and wondering what she could have done to piss off someone she has never met before.

She sits in that chair until her legs fall asleep, switching between playing childish games on her phone and getting lost in a musical, waiting for anything to change. Meanwhile, the rest of her friends are most likely being screamed at and punished for something she begged them to do. The guilt threatens to overtake her, realizing that everyone in every shitty situation they are in was caused by her.

"Princess?" A raspy, beautiful voice says from across the room. Tears spring to her eyes, rolling down her cheeks as she looks over to find Riley, barely awake, looking at her with those impossibly stunning amber eyes she thought she would never see again.

"Hi," she chokes out, not knowing what else to say, wiping the tears from her face.

"Am I dead?" he asks. His voice is too rough. He sounds as if he hasn't had a drink in weeks.

Liz looks around, hoping the doctor will come back in so she can ask if he can have water.

"No sweetie, you're alive. Safe at home," she tells him, wanting so badly to reach out and take his hand. "I'll go get the doctor and let her know you're awake." The chair scrapes across the cheap tile floor as she pushes herself up.

"No," he says with a groan. Liz is not proud of the flips her stomach does at the noise. "Stay."

She lowers herself back into her seat, doing what he commands. Their eyes meet, sending her heart racing at the intensity in his gaze. Like when they first met, neither is willing to break that contact first, so they stay just like that, looking into each other's eyes until Riley's starts to drift closed. She doesn't look away, she won't, until she knows he is back asleep.

Back in the silence, she makes a group chat between herself, Mikey, Tyler, and Alex, shooting them a quick message to let them know the doctor won't talk to her, but Riley woke up again. No more than thirty seconds after she hits send a response pops up. A warning from Mikey. Dread consumes her. Matt is on his way, and he will be there any second.

Wishing she could pretend to be asleep, she slides her phone back into a pocket and listens for the right set of footsteps to echo through the empty hall. There is nothing she can do but brace herself as the heavy door is pushed open and Matt steps in, looking more smug than usual.

"He just couldn't wait to send you to spy on us, could he?" Liz asks, making sure he can tell how annoyed she is by his presence.

"Aww. Don't act like that. Maybe I was just excited to see you."

"Well, be excited somewhere else. Riley doesn't need strangers in his room," Liz snaps, still watching his breathing, praying he doesn't wake up again until Matt is long gone.

"No can do. While your besties are fighting with the boss man, I have the pleasure of keeping you company. Someone has to make sure you don't plan on running again."

"I didn't run, dumbass. They got new information and didn't have time to make a whole thing about it. If we didn't go when we did, we wouldn't have found Riley. And if he really wants to throw a fit, what I signed said I was to remain under Riley's supervision at all times, so I was just trying to obey my orders."

"You're good. I didn't know that little detail. You still should have let someone know."

"It was either save him or stroke the general's ego. Look me in the eyes and tell me I should have let him die just to follow protocol," she snaps, glaring at him

"God, I hope you're this committed to me when I take over."

"What makes you think you will be taking over? Riley is back, and when he is cleared, he will step back into his position, until then, Alex is in charge," she remarks.

"He wasn't supposed to come back, and his position was meant to be mine," he snaps, brows furrowed and jaw tense, glaring at Riley unconscious in the hospital bed. Before she is able to ask just what he meant by that, he changes the subject, "Now that he is back, are you going to let me take you to dinner? I know a great little place in town."

"I told you, I'm seeing someone, and it's insanely fucking rude to ask me on a date in front of him." Her eyes snap to his, watching as his own hazel eyes dart between her and Riley.

"Alright, honey, it sounds like your three stooges are finally on their way so I'll step out. I promise we will get dinner again soon," he says, looking straight at Riley smirking in a way that makes her skin crawl before shuffling out the door. The tiny room is quickly replaced with three grown men in sour moods, bickering amongst themselves like their friend isn't lying unconscious in a bed next to them.

They quickly remember the reason they are there and settle down. Emotions, high or not, a hospital is not the place to handle their problems. Mikey makes his way to Liz's chair, dropping to his knees in front of her. She throws herself into his hug, needing it more than he could ever know.

"We're here now. Why don't you go shower and get some fresh clothes on before he wakes up for good." His voice rumbles against her neck.

"I can't leave him--" she protests.

"Do you want the first time he sees you to be when you smell like a wet sewer rat?" Mikey teases.

"You have my word, if he wakes before you get back I will personally put him back to sleep," Alex intervenes.

He is right. Her hair is a tangled mess, grimy from the sweat her helmet caused. Her clothes are covered in dirt and blood, soaked with now dried river water. She pushes herself up, dragging her feet to the door, not ready or willing to leave his side yet.

"And take Mikey with you. When Ry wakes up, I give it three

hours before he is fighting to go home, so you may want to have a room ready for him to go back to," Alex adds as they walk out together.

After her steaming shower, Liz digs out her favorite, buttery soft black leggings and matching long sleeve top, slipping into them faster than she thought possible. Next she tackles the absolute mess of hair she has, getting it brushed and pulled up into a messy bun, letting some of her curls spring free.

While Mikey is in the shower, Liz packs all of her belongings, leaving the bags next to the door while she strips the bed sheets and puts a fresh set on. Hopefully, Riley won't mind the white and black floral bedding she bought. The dresser is still filled with his neatly folded clothes, but she pulls a mask out and places it on the pillow, just in case.

Liz runs into the kitchen and takes an armful of bottled water and some of his favorite snacks, and displays them on the bedside table, trying to make sure he has whatever he could need. Her eyes linger on the photo, wondering if it's too much, or if he will think she is weird for taking it, so she decides to hide it in the drawer. If things go well, and they pick up where they left off, she will take it out, but if not, she can return it to its rightful place in his room at the bunker.

"You are *not* moving in here," Mikey shouts, catching her unpacking a bag into the second dresser in his room, parading in with just a towel wrapped around his waist.

"Yes I am, roomie." She pays him no mind as she shoves handfuls of clothes into the overcrowded drawers.

"He's going to be pissed. I know you keep having doubts about his feelings, but you can't just break up with him like that."

"Kind of hard to break up when you were never in a defined relationship. And besides, I know, *and* don't know, what he is going through. We don't know his headspace. He may want to be alone and untouched and until he says otherwise he deserves to have that." Her eyes plead with him to understand that it's not about her and her feelings.

"He will kill me if I share a room with you," he argues

"He will not. Now, can you please get dressed so we can get back over there? The mean doctor lady told me he should wake up soon."

CHAPTER 13

A mix of voices float down the hall as they approach Riley's room. When they make it to the doorway, the doctor is there, checking Riley over once more. Not wanting to overcrowd the already full room, Liz and Mikey stay back in the hallway, hanging on every word the doctor says.

"He is doing exceptional given his circumstances. We will need to do a psych evaluation once he is awake, but from what I can see, most of his chest and abdominal wounds are superficial. His blood pressure and heart rate are low, but not enough to cause concern," she states matter of factly.

"What do you mean *most*, Janine?" Alex asks, glaring at the chart in her hand.

Liz makes a mental note to ask about her when they are alone. Maybe one of them can tell her why she was so hostile.

"He has lost a lot of blood. His injuries look as if someone attempted to close them, but they did so too late. However, the medic you brought did an exceptional job closing them properly. He is also suffering from both dehydration and starvation, bad on their own, deadly when together."

"So, what do we do?" Tyler asks.

"I will start a blood transfusion right away as well as start an IV to administer fluids, one in each arm. The transfusion will take approximately thirty minutes to an hour, and as soon as that is done, I will start TPN. That will get him the nutrients he needs. Think of it as a liquid multivitamin. I will re-evaluate when he is awake to determine if he is able to eat and drink on his own, and we will go from there. I will be right back to get those started," Janine says, excusing herself from the room, and allowing Liz and Mikey to sneak back in, closing the door tightly behind them.

"If you two are good, we're going to take off. We have a lot to deal with now that we are back," Alex half asks.

"I'm so sorry. I hope you're not in too much trouble because of me," Liz says quietly, unable to meet his eyes.

"We all made our own decisions to go. I planned the whole thing and made it happen, don't punish yourself for my actions," he says, pulling the door back open. "Make sure someone is with him at all times. Janine said he should wake up pretty quick after she starts the IVs. Let me know when he's up."

Janine squeezes past as Alex and Tyler make their way out the door, pushing a squeaky cart topped with various bags of liquid. Overwhelmed by the revolving door of people coming in and out, Liz pushes the chair against the wall and plops herself in it, trying to stay out of the way as much as she can, given the size of the room.

Everyone stays quiet, no sounds but the beeping of machines and faint muffles from people walking by outside. Janine replaces Riley's morphine with a blood bag, flushing it out beforehand. When the fresh blood starts pumping into his veins, she moves to his other arm, placing an IV and starting him on a bag of saline to get him rehydrated.

"Press the call button when the pump goes off, it means one of his bags is empty, and I will be back in to start the next one," she says, walking out the door, leaving no room for discussion.

"I'm fucking starving, so as long as pretty boy is still napping, I'm going to go grab some food. What do you want?" Mikey asks.

"I'm too nervous to eat anything, thanks though," she says, watching him shrug his shoulders and walk out the door.

Liz loses track of how long she sits there, watching the bags attached to Riley's arms slowly drain into his body. She looks around the room, not a single clock in sight, and her phone died hours ago. It couldn't have been too long if Mikey still isn't back, unless he decided to eat somewhere else.

With nothing else to do, Liz paces the room, looking at all the crudely printed signs hanging around. So caught up with reading the random posters and loose papers taped to the wall, she doesn't notice Riley opening his eyes, watching her as she moves around the room, before flopping herself back into the chair.

"You're still here." Hearing his raspy voice has Liz practically jumping from her chair, sitting up straighter to look at him, a sad smile on her face.

"I am, is that okay?" she asks, her anxiety running wild. He blinks a few times, the same way she did when she was coming out of it, trying to get the world to focus. Fighting past the urge to go to him, she fidgets with her hands to distract herself.

Riley doesn't respond, does not speak, just looks at the various tubes in his arms, then around the room, stopping before he gets to where Liz sits. Her heart drops, every crushing thought about what would happen to them coming true. There is no denying the uncomfortable, awkward energy in the room.

"I can go as soon as Mikey gets back, but one of us is supposed to stay with you," she says just loud enough for him to hear, trying to hide her heartbreak.

"It's fine, you don't have to leave," he groans out. Of all the ways Liz saw this moment in her head, awkward was not one of them. They both look away, nothing more to say to each other. The tension in the air is palpable. Unable to stay in the excruciating silence any longer, she asks--

"Are you in pain? I can call the doctor for you."

"Everything about this is painful," he snaps harshly.

Liz recoils as if he had just slapped her. She bites her cheek so hard she tastes blood, a stupid attempt at not snapping back. If she was still wondering about his feelings, he just made them perfectly clear. She wonders how things could change so fast when just hours ago he called her by pet name and asked her to stay. A silent tear streams down her face, more following while she tries to pull herself together.

"That's no--" Riley begins, his eyes softening when he looks at her, only to be cut off by the door flying open.

"Honey, I'm home!" Mikey says, striding into the room, carrying two cardboard containers of food. "I brought your favor-- Are you crying?" His voice switches from playful to anger, laced with concern. He follows her eyes to where Riley is lying, awake and watching the two of them. When he looks back to her, she shakes her head just enough for him to understand not to push it.

"Happy tears, sweetie," she says, smiling sweetly at him.

He looks down at her. He knows she is lying, she can see in his face that he doesn't believe her. The cough that comes out of Riley has Mikey whirling on his bed, turning into a child excited to see his best friend again.

"Hey buddy! Welcome back to the land of the living!" he barks, unable to stop the smile on his face. Mikey shoves Riley's legs over, sitting on the bed next to him, not caring if he hurts him or not. He snatches the bed control from its pocket on the side, raising the bed so Riley can sit up.

"How ya feelin'?"

"Ohh, I know this one," Liz shouts, raising her hand like she's back in school, hurt getting the better of her. "Everything about this," she spits, waving her hand in a circle around the room, "is painful."

She glares at Riley. Cursing herself under her breath, Liz slumps back in her chair. So close. She was so damn close to keeping it together. Deep down she knows she has no reason to be angry with him. He has been through hell the last few weeks, of course he is going to be distant and angry.

"Okay, did I miss something? I thought the second you woke up you two would be ripping each other's clothes off, not ripping each other's throats out," he asks, confused, looking back and forth between the two of them.

Her face grows hot. She drags her gaze over to Riley to catch him watching her with a heated stare that makes her toes curl, only adding to her confusion. The steady beeping in the room picks up, growing steadily faster as they lock eyes.

Hearing that makes Mikey start to worry, pressing the call button over and over again until the doctor comes rushing into the room, frantically looking over at Riley, propped up, doing just fine.

"Why did you call me?" she remarks, spotting the control in Mikey's hand, thumb still on the button, ready to press it again if he needed to.

"He was beeping. Isn't that bad?" he sheepishly asks.

"Not necessarily," she says, checking each device he is hooked up to. "His O2 is good, you got him sitting up, alert, all good signs. His heart rate seems to be steady, all the excitement from waking up must have come as a shock, that's all. I thought he was going to need at least two more treatments to get him to this point," she says while disconnecting the now empty blood bag from his arm.

"Well, the field medics did a good job of taking care of him. They stitched him up and he got a couple bags of something from them in the air," Mikey states.

"Oh, well, that explains the miraculous recovery. That would have been the type of thing to tell his doctor," she sneers, turning to Liz. Her jaw falls open, watching the woman with sheer disgust.

"I did tell you. Maybe if you weren't so busy treating me like shit, you would have remembered," she grumbles.

Riley's eyes snap to hers and she swears he is smiling under his makeshift mask. He needs to go home with them for no other reason than Liz wanting to confront him about the mixed signals.

"So, what does that mean? Does he need another round of the IVs?" Mikey interjects before the women come to blows.

Janine stops herself from saying what she was about to say and turns back to the men. "Not yet. If you are feeling up for it, you can start small with some crackers and water. We can see how you handle food and drink and go from there." She steps closer to Riley.

"When can I leave?" he asks her, already trying to prop himself up further.

"Well, you will need a psych evaluation. You have been through so much, and I will need to continue monitoring you to make sure your body is recovering, but, as long as your vitals stay good and you can feed yourself, I would say you can leave in a few days."

"Not good enough, doc. I'm alive. I'm awake. I'm going home," His deep, raspy voice practically shouts.

Janine takes a step back, her hands tremble as she slings her stethoscope back around her neck. "I understand you don't like hospitals, but--" she begins.

"But nothing. I'm leaving," Riley argues, his voice getting deeper with each word. A loud, overly dramatic sigh fills the room, and Mikey hops down from the bed. His hand hovers next to the doctor's shoulder as he guides her out the room, shutting the door behind them.

The moment they are gone, Riley reaches with his free arm and pulls the fabric covering his face away, then rips the oxygen mask off, tossing it behind him.

Liz peels her eyes away, unsure if she should see him like this or not.

Lips pursed, kicking her feet, Liz looks around the room, anywhere but at Riley. If she does, she may just confront him right then and there, and that is the last thing he needs to deal with. She has been working too hard to keep her anger in check to throw all her progress away now. Stupidly, she lets her eyes wander back to the bed, dragging them up his body, to find him watching her every move.

"What?" she exclaims. Anger courses through her the moment he lets a strained laugh escape, flashing her his soul-crushing smile. If she didn't know any better, she would think he is toying with her on purpose.

That's all it takes. She climbs from the chair, boots stomping across the polished floor until she is standing in front of him. "What the fuck--" A slow creak cuts her off, the door being pushed open again. Sick of the near constant coming and going, she groans and goes back to her seat, facing away from Riley. A soft crackling smack sounds from the other side of the room.

"Eat that, and drink this," Mikey says entering the room with a cup of water. "Barely nine hours back on base and you're already causing problems."

Riley says nothing, simply shrugs his shoulders and downs the cup of water, handing it back when he is done.

Mikey refills it in the sink and places it on the table next to him. Taking the chance to speak while Riley's mouth is full, he starts scolding. "I know you were gone and stuff, but you should be a little nicer to people." The scoff Liz releases has both of the men turning their attention to her. "You better tell me what the fuck happened with you two tonight," Mikey snaps at Liz before turning his attention back to Riley and scolding him once more.

"I can't believe I have to be the mature one right now. They know your history, and I gently reminded Janine you will rip the tubes from your arms and get home before they even realize you are gone. She is getting me some supplies now. You can't go off base and you're on bed rest, you need to come back in the morning to get checked and another IV. Psyche will come to you in a couple of days, and you are under no circumstances to be left alone. Someone will need to be in the apartment with you at all times, so, hooray for babysitting duty, but you're free to come home. And let me be clear, you should be staying, the one and only reason you're not is because of what happened last time."

CHAPTER 14

Stepping back into their apartment, Riley finally with them, should have been a special moment, instead, Liz dreads what is to come. He will need constant supervision and assistance: someone to change his bandages, cook his meals, administer his medications, make sure he is taken care of in every sense of the word, allowing his body and mind the time it needs to heal. All of which will be easier said than done.

Mikey, Alex and Tyler refuse to tell her what happened with Scott, but they won't be able to help with Riley as much as any of them would like, leaving Liz to be his caretaker. For now, at least, she has Mikey. He was the one who pushed Riley across the base in a wheelchair, leading the small amount of conversation while she walked silently behind, carrying a large bag stuffed with medical supplies.

"Alright, I need to get out of this fucking thing," Riley groans the moment the door to the apartment is closed behind them.

Liz watches him carefully, not wanting to intervene and upset him anymore than she already has.

On shaky arms, he pushes himself up out of the chair, Mikey sticking close just in case he goes down.

"I'm just going to get the supplies set up in his room," Liz says before darting from the living room, happy to have an excuse to leave. Wasting no time, she pulls out rolls of gauze, tape, and various medicines, laying them out in order of when they need to be taken or changed. She takes her good, sweet time making sure everything is set up perfectly––expertly organized to limit the amount of time she will need to spend taking care of him, allowing him the space he seems to need.

A pair of sweatpants and one of his looser fitting t-shirts is placed on the end of the bed along with the mask she already pulled out. Liz double checks that the snacks are lined up within easy reach of the bed. Before going back out to face the men, she slides the table drawer open. Liz thinks better of it and slams it closed. Seeing them happy will only make his anger toward her that much harder to accept.

"All set," she says, striding back into the living room. She walks right past where Riley is standing. Being out of the wheelchair forces her to look up at him as she does. He seemed so much smaller lying on that hospital bed that she almost forgot just how intimidating his size is. "It's getting kind of late. I set some clothes out if you want to help him change, but I've done all I can do, so I guess I will see you in bed?" Liz asks, looking at Mikey.

His face flushes a deep shade of red, eyes full of fear looking at Riley.

The air in the room stills, like the universe is holding its breath, waiting to see what he will do. Even with her back to him, Liz feels his eyes linger on her body. Goosebumps pepper her skin when she hears the strained footsteps. Trying her best to calm her wild nerves, she turns to face him. Arms crossed and hip cocked to the side, she waits for him to find another reason to be mad at her.

"You two share a bed now?" he asks. His deep, gravely tone threatens to make her knees buckle. Riley takes another shaky step in her direction, wobbling slightly, not used to using his legs.

"Is there somewhere else I should be sleeping?" she asks, feigning innocence. She forces herself to peel her eyes away, part of her wishing they could have left him in the hospital where he would be forced to lay down and focus on getting better. That part only grows when he takes another step, more sure and confident, like her little attitude is making him ignore the pain.

"Jesus Christ, Liz! Are you trying to get me killed?" Mikey shouts from the other side of the room, keeping his distance from the storm brewing in front of him. "We share a room with a bunk bed. She's on top of me, completely separate."

Riley cocks an eyebrow at her, challenging Liz to come up with another smart ass comment. He winks so fast she isn't sure if that is what he actually did or not before he turns to face his friend. "You have her on top of you?" Riley asks, not a hint of amusement in his voice.

"She was right. You do need to get into your damn bed. I am too tired to deal with your bullshit tonight," he whines, leading Riley to the doorway. "Liz moved out and got it all set up for you, snacks, clothes and enough pillows to prop yourself in any position you could want."

"She moved out?" he asks, slowly following Mikey to the room.

"Yeah. I told her not to, but you know how stubborn she is. Said we don't know what they did to you and you should have your own space."

Riley's chest tightens when he catches Liz sneaking off to her room out of the corner of his eye. When he steps into his own room, he has to restrain himself from going to her. It's clear the only thing on her mind when setting up the space was his comfort. Mikey wasn't lying, there are too many pillows carefully placed onto the bed, and although he hates to admit it, those will come as a huge help at night.

His favorite snacks are laid out next to the bed, placed within an arm's reach. Tears spring to his eyes when he sees the mask sitting on top of the neatly folded clothes. She had put so much care and effort into making sure all his needs were met while he was a cranky asshole.

"Alright, I'm helping you change, don't be weird about it," Mikey says playfully, picking up the pile from the bed.

"I don't need to," he says, wincing while he shrugs the hospital gown off of his shoulders. He's left in just the teal pair of scrub pants he was allowed to wear in the infirmary and the hospital mask he wore to hide his face while being carted across the base. With one shaky step after another, Riley makes his way to the bed. Only when he reaches it does he let his friend help him in, groaning at the pain ripping through his shoulders when he lies back.

"It's nice to have you back, man," Mikey says, heading to his own room for the night. "I assume Liz will be by in the morning to check on things and fawn over you for the rest of the day," he says, walking to the door. "Just do me a favor and actually rest. We all know you are a big tough guy and nothing can shake you, but that really fucking shook us. We need you back, man. Things have been happening and we need you in tip top shape to help handle it," he adds. Mikey steps out the door, closing it tightly behind him without another word.

The days after Riley's return are the hardest yet. Liz spends her mornings making him breakfast and getting his medicines organized before the doctor comes to check on him. After her short gym session with Mikey, she is forced to be alone with Riley for the remainder of the day.

She cooks his meals and checks on his pain periodically throughout the day, never talking to him more than she has to. Because he can't be left alone, the rest of her time is spent dawdling around the apartment, trying to find anything she can to keep her mind busy. The only time Riley speaks to her is to ask questions: How long was he gone, how many days has it been since they found him, why won't she let him out of bed if he feels fine? She goes to his room, ready to check his bandages and prepare his next round of meds, mentally prepared for their next awkward encounter. It feels different this time. She can feel his eyes on her, tracking her every move.

"Are you ever going to fucking talk to me, princess?"

She flinches at his booming voice. The pills rattle in their bottles as her shaky hands continue their work.

"What do you want to talk about?" she asks, not caring about the tremble in her voice. Trying her best to keep the situation under control, she continues getting the supplies ready.

"I'm sorry," he breathes.

"It's alright. You are going through a lot right now," she starts.

"No, it's not alright, but that's not what I mean. I am so fucking sorry I left you. I should have stayed by your side and went to the hospital. I was reckless and impulsive trying to make sure Dmitri was dead. I wanted to make sure he couldn't hurt you again, but I only made sure he did. I fucked up, I know that. But I can't stand you being this pissed at me. Even when we found you and you fucking hated me, at least you would talk, make little smartass comments, yell at me if I did something you didn't like, now you won't even give me that much," he shouts.

Liz turns to face him, finding his legs swung off the bed, trying to stand, and she rushes over. Placing her hands on his shoulders, she applies enough pressure to hold him down without hurting him. Tears roll down her face, falling into the space between them.

"I'm not mad at you."

"Then why? Why are you treating me like you wish I never came back? Is it that guy you've been seeing?"

His words cut her to the very core. She had no idea he didn't want the space she had been giving him. "What? There is no guy," she says, shaking her head, confused as to why he would ever think there was anyone but him. "I don't know what you went through while you were gone, but from how you acted when you woke up... well, it seemed like you needed space from me."

"I didn't mean it like that. You sitting across the room, refusing to even look in my direction, that hurt more than any wound he inflicted on me."

"I never meant to hurt you, Ry."

Hearing her whisper his name is all he can take. His hands grip her waist, pulling her against his chest. Strong hands slowly move across her back until a set of arms are holding her like they never want to let go.

"I was so scared. When we first got to you, I refused to let you go. My hand was wrapped around yours the entire twenty-six hours we flew home. The only reason I stopped was because they made me, but as soon as I let you go, the doubts started creeping in. I remembered every word you said that day, and how I felt once you guys got me out. I didn't want to push anything with you. I knew we would talk eventually, but that was never more important than your healing." Her hands move from his shoulders, gliding up his neck, under his mask until her fingers find his shaggy hair, scratching his scalp the way he loves. The deep growl he lets out radiates through her chest.

"Baby, look at me," Riley orders, loosening his grip, allowing Liz a small step back. Tears rim her eyes as she does what he orders. "Every word from my mouth was a lie to get him to let you go. I thought Mikey's big mouth would have told you everything that happened after." His shimmering amber eyes drop to the long pink scar stretching across her neck.

"He said there were some things I needed to hear from you." Her hands still, wondering if he will tell her everything their friend refused.

The warmth disappears from half of her body. Riley reaches up and pulls the mask from his face, gently tossing it aside. His hand finds its way to her face, cupping her cheek, his thumb gingerly rubbing back and forth.

"Did he tell you I cried when I thought I lost you?" he asks. "Or that I begged you not to die, begged you to stay with me?"

She nods against his hand.

"Did he tell you that I love you?"

Tears pour from her, unable to control it as she shakes her head.

"Good. I should have been in the hospital with you, I should have been there to tell you the moment you woke up. I love you, Liz."

Sobs wrack her body hearing what she needed to hear for so long. Her arms wrap around his neck, pulling him into a tight hug as she cries into his shoulder. They stay like that, holding each other, crying tears of joy, refusing to let go until the sobs slow.

When they do, Riley pulls her face to his, placing gentle, loving kisses on her lips she is quick to return. A blaring alarm from across the room snaps them out of the moment. Placing a final deep kiss on his lips, Liz releases him so she can finish what she came to do.

As quickly as she can, she gathers his medication into a cup and rushes back to him, shoving it into his waiting hand, not looking away until he takes the pills. Back on schedule for the day, she helps him get nestled into bed, still insisting on rest so his body can heal.

Riley snatches her hand, not wanting her to leave now that he finally has her by his side once more. "Stay with me," he pleads.

"If I do, will you behave? I know you're in pain, even if you're too macho to admit it," she teases, poking him in the massive bruise covering half of his bicep.

"I will be good if you tell me everything that has been going on. Mikey won't tell me shit and I'm really curious who you're going to dinner with," he says, anger simmering in his eyes. "Again apparently," he adds, patting the bed next to him.

It sinks under her weight as she crawls in. Reaching down, she interlocks their fingers, holding his hand as tight as she did on the plane.

"First of all," she starts, cupping his cheek and turning his head to face her. Her lips brush his in a single kiss. When she pulls away she meets his eyes. They are lighter, the happiest she has seen since he returned to her. "I love you." A smile tugs at her lips, Riley beaming next to her, lowering his head to kiss her again. "Second, what the hell are you talking about?"

"I was in and out for a while, so I may not remember much, but some guy said he was taking you to dinner *again.* Fucker looked me in the eyes when he said it," he grumbles, anger simmering in his eyes, only made worse by Liz giggling into his neck.

"Okay, I will tell you everything that's happened, but it's a very long story, so here's what is going to happen. I am going to go get us dinner, we are going to eat together just like we used to, and when we are done, I will explain," she says, leaning in to kiss him, something she will never tire of. "Got it?"

"Yes ma'am," he says with a wink, watching her scramble off the bed and disappear out the door.

CHAPTER 15

Liz moves as fast as she can, forced to sneak across the base to avoid any undesirable attention from the still curious soldiers. The unavoidable ones look at her with nothing but pity in their eyes.

Their apartment is still quiet when she returns, heavy bag of food in hand. Snatching the small bed tray from the kitchen, Liz heads to where Riley is still in bed, waiting for her. The air is stolen from her lungs when she lays eyes on him. Even with the bags under his eyes and covered in new bandages, he is the most beautiful man she has ever had the pleasure of looking at.

After skipping breakfast, the smell of the food making its way to her nose has her salivating. Riley helps her get his table set up while insisting he has no need for it until she begins to load it up with food: roasted sweet and spicy chicken, quinoa salad mixed with grilled zucchini and eggplant, and a side of roasted asparagus is overflowing from one container. A second box with a caesar salad gets placed on the tray next to the main course.

Riley chuckles when Liz pulls out a third box stuffed to the brim with mixed fruits. The meal they share is the lightest either of them has felt in months. Laughing and joking just as they had all those weeks spent by their lake, making up for lost time. When they finish eating their eyes lock, both of them wishing they didn't have to go back to the real world.

"This is the only thing that kept me sane," Riley says, pulling Liz into his waiting arms the moment his bed is clear of the food. She curls up next to him, one arm tossed over his chest to match the leg carefully crossing his waist. Peppering her head with light kisses, he continues, "I knew I was either going to see you when I died, or you were going to make it to me before he could kill me. Either way ended with us back together."

"That explains why you said he did it," she says, kissing his chest. "You looked at me for a second, insisted you died, and said now you get to see me again. It was horrible, but pretty fucking cute."

"Speaking of cute, tell me about this guy I'm going to murder."

"No murder, sweetie. If Mikey says I have to play nice, then so do you," she coos sweetly. "Long story short, he got added to the team because you were gone, even though I said it's pointless because we were getting you back, but general stupid face didn't even want to get you back and no one believed me when I told them that. And Matt even said he was supposed to take over your job as the leader. Apparently, I'm the only one who finds that fucking weird," she rambles, words jumbling together as it all pours out.

"Slow down, princess. I know you have a lot to tell me, but you're not making a lot of sense here. I need you to take a deep breath," he says.

Liz does as he tells her and sucks in a sharp breath, holding it for a few seconds before slowly letting it out.

"Good girl. Now, tell me why you think Scott didn't want to look for me, and why do you hate this Matt guy so much?"

"The day we all went to him, Alex and Tyler worked so hard on their plans. They said we knew exactly where we were going and what we needed, but when they told him, he said no. He said you made a bad choice and needed to live with it. Who says shit like that? He only changed his mind because I remembered the dash cam in your truck. I told him it caught him aiming the rocket launcher at you. Not a single person thinks its fucked up that he changed his mind when I told him I would release the footage," she huffs, snuggling deeper into his chest, trying her best to give him actual information and not just one long rant.

"So, he agrees, but says he is adding someone to the team and brings this guy in. First fucking thing this dude says is how great he thinks it is that I'm so dedicated to a man who publicly rejected and embarrassed me." Liz scoots away from Riley, sliding herself off the bed. Pacing the room to keep herself in check, she continues, "Then says it again later, and basically says he wants to fuck me. If he's not hitting on me, he is making comments about how you don't want me or saying he hopes I am that committed to him when he takes over. But that's not all. The first time we went looking for you, we didn't go where Alex wanted. Dickbag magoo said he got 'new information' and we had to go there, but the town was deserted."

Riley peels himself from the bed, ignoring the pain screaming at him to stay put. He marches right into the path Liz is walking, wrapping his arms around her. Forced to still, she takes another breath. Her own arms wrap around his waist, letting his warmth settle deep into her bones, grounding her. Her eyes drift close, resting her head on his chest, she breathes in the rich, earthy scent of him that she missed so much. They stay there, wrapped up in each other, battling their racing thoughts.

"Oh fuck," she blurts, taking a step back. "The day you saw him, in the hospital room, he told me, like said it out loud, that you were never supposed to come back and your position was promised to him." She peers up at him, his jaw is clenched, looking like he is trying not to go find Matt right that very second.

"What's his name? And why the fuck is Mikey telling you to be nice if he is trying to take my girlfriend and my job?" Riley barks, starting his own slow pacing, causing Liz to worry.

"Matt Solano. Mikey doesn't trust him, he told me to play nice, like I did to get you guys to trust me."

"Solano? You're sure?" he asks.

"Yeah, why? Have you heard of him?" Liz asks, guiding Riley back over to the bed and helping him in. Safely tucked back in, Liz perches herself on the edge of the bed next to him.

"Unfortunately. He was stationed overseas, pretty much doing clean-up for our missions and working on smaller areas of Dmitri's operation. General always wanted him to join us. It was obvious he wanted someone to keep tabs on me, so I kept refusing. I never thought he would find a way to worm him in. Solano would suck the general's dick if it meant he got even the smallest chance to move up a rank."

"Mikey thinks he is up to something, that's why he told me to be nice." Liz admits.

"God, I hate to say it, but he's right. I want nothing more than to wrap my hands around his neck, squeezing until his eyes glaze over and he is erased from this world, but, I believe you. If he is trying to get to you, we can use that to figure out what the hell is going on," Riley seethes.

The way his deep voice rumbles the threat so easily has her clenching her legs together, trying not to throw herself at him in the middle of a serious conversation.

"Well, I may have already ruined that plan. I kind of keep

telling him I'm seeing someone and it's never going to happen..," she says, barely more than a whisper, cheeks flushed a deep shade of red. "But he doesn't think it's real, right? You said he has brought up you being rejected more than once."

"He says I have a delusional fantasy of my C.O. being in love with me. Told me the sooner I realize you want nothing to do with me, the sooner he can show me someone who does," she explains. She purses her lips, fidgeting with a loose thread on her pants, replaying the awful things he has said about their relationship.

"As long as you know how madly in love with you I am, he can think whatever he wants. Tell him he was right, flirt, act single, just remember you're not and come home to me at night."

"You're serious aren't you? You really want me to pretend to be interested in this guy?"

"I don't want you anywhere near him, but after everything you told me it's clear the general is hiding something, and if I had to guess, Matt knows what that is. So, yes, I will suffer through watching you with another man if it means we figure out whatever shady shit has been going on since I left," he states with no room for argument.

"And you're not going to get mad at me?" she asks innocently, crawling her way back over to his side.

"For doing your job? No, love, I won't get mad at you," Riley says, gritting his teeth as he lifts his arm in the air, giving Liz an opening to snuggle into. "We should probably round up the guys and let them know what's been going on."

"Will things ever calm down?" Liz asks with a sigh. The non-stop action was great at first, keeping her mind off her awful past, but after almost losing Riley, she wishes things could be normal for them. A normal life, doing normal, mundane activities instead of fighting literal terrorists.

"I'm sorry. I don't mean to complain, especially after everything you have been through. I just thought, when we finally admitted we were in love, we would get time to be a real couple without all the world ending drama. I was so fucking scared I lost you. You were being tortured just nine days ago. Tortured, Ry, and now you are jumping right back into the fight."

"No matter what, we are a real couple. We are going to go on dates, watch movies together, go grocery shopping, anything any other couple would do, and you are going to move your shit back in here so we can live together." His arms wrap tighter around her body, holding her as close as his sore muscles will allow. "If it will make you feel better, we can keep everything between us for a few days." He pulls her closer, placing a sensual trail of kisses up her neck. His fingers dig in harder when a breathy moan escapes her. "We can stay in bed," he moans into her skin, placing more kisses along her jaw. "I can do everything I imagined doing to you while I was gone."

"As incredible as that would be, you are not even close to healed and–"

His mouth captures hers before she can finish the thought.

She melts for him, opening her mouth to let his tongue sweep in. His stubble scratches against her chin as he deepens the kiss, pulling her tighter. Callused hands roam her body, goosebumps forming wherever he touches. Their breathing turns heavy, no longer able to hold back.

Riley ignores the searing pain in his shoulders. He pushes himself up enough to pull the shirt over Liz's head, tossing it to the ground before his mouth finds hers once more. He deepens their kiss, tongues swirling like they would never get the chance again.

Liz wiggles out of her pants, her mouth never leaving his. A large hand grips her thigh, the mix of pain and anticipation sends a wave of pleasure coursing through her body as he forces her to straddle him. She lets out a deep moan into his mouth, feeling how much he wants this. He lifts her just enough to shove his pants down, setting her back on top of him, chest rumbling with groans of pleasure the moment he feels how wet she is.

Liz pulls herself back from him. Sitting up, she rocks her hips against his firm body. Trembling hands dig into the soft skin of her legs. After so long apart, they both know this won't last much longer. She lowers herself onto him, grinding her hips until he is lined up with her.

"I can't take it anymore, baby. I need you more than I need air to breathe," he moans against her neck. His arms wrap around her waist, holding her close as she sinks back onto him. A breathy gasp escapes her as she takes him in, not stopping until she is fully seated against him. The bite of pain paired with the intense pleasure of him filling her threatens to send her over the edge.

"Fuck," she moans into his ear. "It's too good, Ry. I can't take any more." Liz breathes, squeezing her legs together in an attempt to stop even the slightest of movements.

Ignoring her pleas, Riley's hands circle her hips, lifting just enough to pull back before slamming himself into her over and over again. Every deep thrust has her moaning in his ear, sending him careening toward release. He can feel it, her body tensing, growing tighter around him with every stroke. He doesn't let up, relentlessly fucking her until her entire body shakes with her orgasm.

Waves of pleasure wash over him as he gets his, too, not stopping until Liz collapses against him in a sweaty pile, fighting to catch her breath.

He picks up her head, kissing her again, gentle this time, savoring her soft lips brushing against his before she slides off of him, settling against his side.

Liz knows they don't have long to simply exist together before Mikey comes home or the doctor arrives to check on Riley. Liz pulls the blanket over them, snuggling back into his side. She is content to stay wrapped in his arms until someone shoos them apart. Until then, she is staying put.

CHAPTER 16

True to his word, they spend the following days together, ignoring all the problems festering around them. Every day Riley's doctor comes in to check on his progress, and every day Liz feels lighter hearing how much better he is doing.

Twelve days ago he was held in a terrorist camp, being sliced open and strung up by the skin of his back like a sick show, and now, he is able to move around the apartment with minimal pain, so long as he does not strain his upper body. A task he claims is easier said than done every morning when he wakes up next to Liz.

She had broken her promise to move her things back in, the fresh blood seeping through his crisp white bandages after they lost control was too much for her. Liz may spend every night in his bed, but she refuses to move back in until the doctor cleared him for strenuous activity.

He pestered the nurse who came today, begging to be cleared, trying to convince him that his injuries are nothing more than paper cuts, not deep gashes and tears in his muscles that need time to piece themselves back together. Whatever he said when Liz stepped out must have worked, because the moment the nurse left

Riley pulls her through the adjoining bathroom, into the other bedroom, and begins grabbing at anything he thinks is hers.

"That's not mine," Liz says, giggling as she watches Riley, hunched over trying to pull the fairy lights off the bottom bunk. Crawling back out, he looks at the bed, eyes darting from the bottom bunk to the top then back to the bottom, brows knit in confusion.

"Mikey gave me a card and told me to go nuts, and I could decorate how I wanted. So, I wanted him to feel like a pretty princess," she says, a smug smile plastered on her face.

"That's it? I thought you would have fought about the card more," he says, marching to the dresser and digging through drawers. One thing he can't mess up is knowing what clothes belong to who.

"Why would I fight about it?" she asks, puzzled. When he doesn't respond, she pulls the card from her wallet, turning it over in her hand, unable to figure out what is wrong with accepting it.

"You're right, you wouldn't. These yours?" he asks, holding up a silky pair of cow print pants long enough to reach her chin.

It isn't until the third time the card gets turned over, just before she gives up and places it back in its designated slot, that she sees it. There, in silver embossed letters is a name that is not entirely hers. *Liz Corson*.

Her fingers brush the raised name while she wonders to herself how she could have missed that when Mikey first gave it to her.

"Those are his, and what the hell is this?" she asks, holding up the card.

"See, this is the fight I thought you already had. Did he not explain everything to you?" Riley asks, tossing the pants onto the bed.

"He told me you got everything taken care of for me, but that doesn't explain why you gave me your last name," She snaps, growing increasingly annoyed with the conversation.

"Damn, you're going to be mad. It takes a while for special paper work to go through the proper channels, so, I just added you to my account. I know we never talked about our future, but I want you to have my last name someday, and it was the easiest way to add you, so, I just did it. I'm sorry. I shouldn't have done anything like that without talking to you first," Riley explains, stuffing clothes into whatever bag will fit them, trying his damndest to avoid seeing how mad she is.

"The name thing is beside the point, that is a whole other fight that we will be having. But you're telling me the entire time I thought I was spending money I had *earned*, when I was actually draining your bank account?" she shrieks, angrily throwing her things into her duffle bag.

"Not draining. I told you before, I have more money that I know what to do with. I promise, it was the fastest way to make sure you were taken care of. Now that I'm out of that hell hole, I figured we would share a name and finances someday, so I didn't think to even bring it up, but I guess I should have," he says

Warmth envelops her from behind as Riley's strong arms find their way around her chest, forcing her body against his. Settled against the hard ridges of his abdomen, Liz closes her eyes and lets her head tip back to relax on his chest, breathing in the rich scent of his cologne she missed so much.

Guilt hits her like a truck being held the way she is. Guilt for moving on after her family suffered such horrendous deaths, and guilt for the man who saved her, and who clearly wants to give her the future she never thought she would want.

She has not had a moment's peace since being freed from captivity to think about things like this. Sure, the thought has crossed her mind in fleeting moments, but the second those thoughts creep in, she shoves them back out.

"Talk to me, princess. What's going on in that pretty little head of yours?" he murmurs into her ear. The deep, sultry sound of his voice sends a shiver down her spine, causing her to arch into him. His grip tightens, only making the warmth in her lower belly grow.

"It's nothing," she says, twisting around in his arms to face him, bringing her arms around his waist. "I just didn't know you wanted a future like that with me. All those times together at our lake, all the conversations we had, we never really talked about our feelings or where we saw things going, so it's kind of a shock you feel that way," she says, trying not to cry, thinking about how he will feel when she admits to not having the same thoughts.

"I'm sorry. It's too soon to be talking about shit like that. It's been what? Six months since you got out? Even less since things changed between us? I just had a lot of time to realize what I wanted while you were still wrapping your head around being free. We can slow down. You can stay in here with Mikey if that's what you want, or I can move in here. You should have the bigger room," he says, dropping his arms and taking a step back.

She watches in horror as he picks the bag of her clothes up from where he dropped it and works on putting them away. The wind is almost knocked out of him with the force in which she throws herself back into his arms, forcing him to drop the bag once more.

"That's not what I want. I love you, and I love how things are. Everything has just been so frustratingly hectic that I haven't thought about anything past getting you back, and it doesn't help that we've never had the super fun relationship talk." She places kisses on his chest, right on top of some of the still healing cuts.

"How about this, after we meet with the team, we kick them

out, order food, and have that talk? I want to know I am not pushing for things you don't want," he says.

Liz can't respond, the way he is so understanding of everything she tells him has her fighting back tears, she does what she can and nods her head against him. They get back to work, packing and moving things into the other room, staying busy while they wait for the rest of the team to arrive.

A calmness takes over the room as they work together to put her belongings away, tucked neatly next to Riley's. Watching him re-fold her clothes and place them in the dresser has her mind wandering to what their life could look like. He said himself they are already in a real relationship, but does she want to take it further?

Liz can see herself growing old next to him, but she would be lying to herself if that fantasy didn't involve leaving the military behind. It would break his heart for her to ask that of him. He has spent nearly half his life dedicated to his career, she could never ask him to quit. And what if he wants to be a dad someday? She never asked if he wanted children, and something tells her he would never willingly bring it up because of her past.

Kids are something she will never be able to give him. Still, she knows they could live a magical life together. Somewhere away from all the crazy, where they could spend their days not worrying if it's the day one of them will be killed.

Shaking off the thoughts, she watches him. So careful and attentive, slowly making his way around the room, making sure her things are not just shoved in drawers, but placing her small trinkets out for her to enjoy. He would make an incredible husband. Hell, they are practically married already.

What would she even say if he asks? The answer is there in the back of her mind. It's not something she would even need to think about and it terrifies her to her core. If she said yes, she would be betraying everyone she has loved before. She would be abandoning James and Maria, leaving their family behind to create a new one. But if she said no, she would be betraying her heart, and breaking Riley's.

Liz pushes the thoughts from her mind. She strides to their bed and takes the photo out of the drawer, placing it back in its rightful place on the table.

"That's been here the whole time, and you've had it stuffed in a drawer." His arms come around her like a warm blanket.

"I thought you hated me when you woke up, so I put it away. I planned on bringing it back home but I haven't been back since we left," she says, eyes fixating on the photo, on how happy they look together.

Their moment is cut short when the sounds of bickering fills the apartment. They had their time to relax and enjoy being reunited, now it's time for Riley to tell the rest of the team everything he believes is going on and step back into the chaos that is the real world.

He grabs her face, placing three quick kisses on her lips before they stride out, hand in hand, ready to get this meeting started. Liz forces Riley to settle into the couch, clearly in pain from over exerting himself while trying to help her move her things, subtly checking each bandage for fresh blood as she does. Tyler and Alex pull chairs from the kitchen and place them around the coffee table while Liz and Mikey squish together to fit on the small sofa next to Riley.

"How ya feeling?" Alex asks, pulling files from his bag and plopping them onto the table in the middle of the group.

"Eh, I'm pretty fucking sore, but I could be a lot worse," Riley tells him.

"You wouldn't be sore if you would stop overdoing it every day," Liz scolds playfully.

"Yeah, overdoing you," Mikey teases. The four collective stares he gets has him apologizing and trying to get back on track.

"We're all glad you're recovering man, and I hate to ruin that by having to tell you about the shit storm that's been brewing," Alex says.

"I told him some things, mostly about Matt and how the gremlin of a general didn't want to go looking for him, but that's pretty much it," Liz states to the group.

"There is not much more to tell. Scott not wanting to go after you threw us off, but I try to understand his stance from a technical standpoint," Alex begins only to be cut off by Liz.

"Okay, but again, what about how he got pale and switched up as soon as I mentioned the fake footage? He believes it's real, and having video of what happened shouldn't scare him if he did nothing wrong. And don't get me started on Matt saying Riley was never supposed to come back." The three men staring at her with wide eyes make her snap her mouth shut, wondering if she said something wrong.

"When did he say that?" Alex asks. His icy tone and hard stare make her wish she could slide off the couch and disappear.

"The day we got Ry home. You guys were meeting with the evil one and he was sent to keep an eye on me. I told him to leave and he told me he hopes I am that committed to him when he takes over. I asked why he thinks that, or something, and he said Riley was never supposed to make it back."

"And I know it doesn't mean much since I wasn't here when all this went down, but I believe her. She has great instincts when it comes to reading people, you know that is one of the main reasons I wanted to bring her on," Riley adds.

"Fuck!" Alex shouts, standing from his seat, startling everyone.

"What's going on?" Riley asks, concerned.

"I don't know yet, but something is not right. I didn't just brush her off when she told us, but you know there is only so much I can do. We started to get suspicious after the second mission. Scott refused to let Liz go and insisted Matt keep an eye on her, but when we got there, it was empty like the first one. He keeps telling us his intel is fresh, like hours old. Ry, there is no way Dmitri would be able to clear his forces that fast. He was sending us to another abandoned camp," Alex seethes, pacing back and forth, the betrayal clearly taking its toll.

"Did you guys see Scott that day? Right after Liz accused him of using Dmitri to do his dirty work and get rid of Riley?" Tyler asks. When no one responds, he continues, "It was just for a second, but I saw him look at his computer. It made no sound, didn't light up, but he looked at it, only when she said that."

"Dmitri bragged to me. When he had me on that table, he told me he has men in our ranks, someone high enough to send him weapons and they were making sure I would never be found," he says quietly.

"What are you saying?" Alex asks, slamming himself back into his seat.

Tyler reaches over and takes his hand, holding it firmly in his lap. One of the only signs of affection the two are willing to share around others.

"I'm saying, we don't know who we can trust outside of this room. Someone is helping the enemy, and I intend to find out who that is. I was cleared by psyche, and the doctor said I can start doing more physically, so I'm taking my position back--"

"No," Alex interrupts. "*Doing more* means nothing. You are not cleared by medical to be back in the gym let alone the field. We can handle looking into this while you handle getting your body fused back together. We need to figure out what is going on, but not at the expense of your health. I am staying in charge until you are fully cleared."

"Like hell you are!" Riley shouts, launching himself up from the couch. He tries to hide it, but Liz can see him wince with the sudden movement. "My position is not yours to take. I am your commanding officer, injured or not," he barks.

Before anyone has time to stop it, Alex is out of his seat, stepping up to where Riley is clearly seething. She can only imagine how bad this could get, and when neither Mikey nor Tyler get up to stop it, Liz takes it upon herself to get in the middle.

Wrong choice.

"Maybe we should get back to talking about what is really important——" Liz starts, trying to get Riley to sit back down.

"Stay out of this," Alex snaps, startling her enough to take a step into Riley. Cursing herself in her head, she knows what is about to happen, and knows it is not going to end well. She should have known better than to get between them.

"What the fuck did you just say to her?" Everything stills the moment Riley pushes past Liz to get to Alex, sending her tumbling to the floor.

Before he makes it a step further, the realization of what he just did hits him, stopping him in his tracks. In that moment, Tyler jumps up, pulling Alex away and forcing him into the seat furthest from the couch, standing guard to make sure he stays down.

"Baby, I–" he tries, turning to crouch next to her, only to be cut off. Rarely, in their short time together has he seen her this angry.

"Are you fucking kidding me?" she shouts, shoving his hand away and scrambling back onto her feet. "How the fuck did this go from realizing the general may be working with a terrorist who has tormented all of us, to this testosterone-fueled bullshit? I know you're protective, but really, pushing me because he was a little mean? And you," she turns to where Alex is sitting, "who fucking cares if he is not cleared yet? He is doing great and it's not like he is going to be out there brawling with every person he sees. He can lead from this room while he heals. Did you ever think that he may need to take his roll back *to* heal? No, you didn't."

"You're right. I'm sorry, honey," he says, hanging his head with a sigh that tells her he means it.

"Really, you have a fucking pet name for her now? Maybe Matt isn't the only one trying to take everything from me."

"So, it's okay for Mikey to call her names, but the minute I do, I'm trying to take her?" Alex retorts.

She can see Riley readying to lunge at his friend, fighting over nothing but neither one is willing to back down.

"Oh my god! What are you, six?" she seethes. "Mikey and I have matching jammies we wear at slumber parties. You want to get over protective and fight about that too?"

Three sets of eyes turn to him, face practically glowing with how red he turns.

"I asked them to call me that so Matt wasn't the only one. He called me honey badger but deemed it too long and switched to honey. Now, I swear to fucking god, if you don't sit your ass on that couch and drop it, every one of you will be getting thrown out, and I won't give a single fuck if you kill each other or not," she shrieks. Her cheeks are hot with anger, watching to see what the men will do.

Mikey is the only one stupid enough to say anything further.

"Now that it's out there, I will make myself very clear, matching jammies is our thing, and no, you can't get in on it," he says in his strong, sergeant tone. "Also, I didn't do anything, so it's not fair if I get in trouble, too."

Liz drops her head. With shoulders slumped, she practically drags her feet back to the couch, roughly throwing herself into it. This is not going to end well, no matter what she says, so she might as well give up and let them beat the hell out of each other instead of working to find out who is sending supplies overseas.

Closing her eyes, she rests her head on the back of the sofa, waiting to hear the sickening thuds of punches landing and furniture being thrown around. Liz is pleasantly surprised when none of that happens. Footsteps are the only sound in the room before the couch dips next to her.

"Well, this went south fast. I think I'm going to take a nap before shit hits the fan again. Do what you have to do, just leave me out of it," Liz says.

Exasperated, she goes right to her room and pulls the door shut behind her, not wanting or willing to know what is going to happen next.

CHAPTER 17

Liz sits up in the bed, rubbing the sleep from her eyes, awoken by the soft knock at the door. She already knows who is on the other side, but she is unsure if she wants to let him in so easily. After she stormed out, the men stayed relatively quiet until they left. The second the apartment emptied, she curled into a ball and fell asleep. Knowing she can't stay mad forever, Liz slides over to the door and opens it. She fights the smile as long as she can before breaking. How could she not when Riley is in the doorway, bouquet of peonies in hand, smiling down at her.

Her stomach is in knots when she looks into his amber eyes, seeing how nervous he is already. Liz should have known he would hold her to that conversation. Instead of trying to sleep her troubles away, she should have been thinking about how she feels, and what she truly wants from her second chance at life.

"I got dinner," he says sweetly, stepping aside to show off the dark living room that is now lit by all the candles she splurged on, not having the heart to tell him the mix of all the scents smells awful.

Reluctantly, she steps out, following him to the table he clearly worked so hard to set up. She sits, ready to get this uncomfortable conversation over with.

"I want to start by saying I am sorry for earlier. I never should have put my hands on you, and I swear that will never happen again. I know that's what every abusive douchebag says, but I truly never meant for any of that to happen and it will be the first thing I bring up when I start seeing the therapist in a few days," he says.

She can hear the pain in his voice, see it etched into every line of his face. His bright eyes seem dimmer, holding the weight of what happened within them. Without thinking, she reaches over and plucks his hand off the table, holding it tight.

"I know, sweetie. Trust me, I was pissed, but I get it. You have been through so much, and it's understandable that certain things would set you off. It's something I need to work on too, so we can do it together."

They eat in silence, neither one quite knowing how to move on from Riley's apology and steer the conversation to where it needs to be. It gives Liz the time she needs to think about everything she wants to say, if she can muster up the courage to say it.

"I didn't think a relationship talk would be this awkward," Riley finally blurts after too many failed attempts at small talk.

Liz can't help but giggle at the truth of it. They move over to the couch, and Liz snuggles in, resting her head in his lap so he can play with her hair like he always does when he's nervous. The silence ticks by before Riley starts chuckling.

"This is so stupid. I love you, yet I can't figure out how to even begin bringing up where we see this going," Riley says.

"I mean, you sort of just did. I think you just go for it, say whatever is on your mind, or we can play your favorite game and ask questions," she says, giggling. She glances at her nearly empty wine glass, regretting getting tipsy before having this talk.

"Okay... Fuck this is hard," he says sipping his own wine. "I just wish I knew where your head was at with us. I don't want to scare you away by moving too fast, but I have been in love with you for longer than I was willing to admit, and being taken only solidified those feelings. I can see us getting married, and spending our lives together, but I never bothered to ask if that's something you want." He picks up a loose strand of hair, twisting it around in his fingers before asking, "Is it?"

"I have been so scared of you asking that." The words come out too sad. She quickly speaks again when she feels Riley's hand still. "That's not an easy answer. If I am being honest, yes, I would love to marry you someday, but that thought gives me butterflies and nausea."

"I'm sorry?" he asks, more a statement than a question.

"*You* don't make me nauseous, the thought of getting married does," she groans, shooting back up, racking her brain to find the right way to explain. "Not that either. If we were to stay together, and make it to marriage, I would be leaving them behind," she says, holding back tears. The realization washes over him the moment she says that.

"James and Maria?" he asks sadly.

"You remember their names," she whispers.

"Of course I do, that's your family. I couldn't forget them," he says, positioning himself so he is seated facing her, opening his arms so she can crawl between his legs and be held.

"How could I get married and take your name when it means I won't share theirs anymore? It's the last piece of them I have," she sniffles.

"You don't have to take my name. Hell, we don't even have to get married if that's not something you are comfortable with. As long as I have you, I am happy."

"But that's not fair to you. I want to, but I also want to have my husband's last name, and that's where I am torn. That's obviously something you want, too, and if I give that to you, I lose them, and if I don't, I would be taking that from you."

"Hey," Riley says, tipping her head back, her vibrant green eyes swimming with tears. "You never have to worry about me. Of course, I want you to take my name, but not if it means you feel like you lose them. They were your family long before I came along, and if you really wanted to take my name, you could hyphenate."

"You wouldn't be mad that I had another man's name?"

"He's not another man, he is your husband. . I will never try to take that from you or be upset that you keep it." The kisses he peppers her head with threaten to send her over the edge. Already knowing she does not deserve him, she decides to lay it all out, even if that means they need to shake hands and walk away so he can find his happiness.

"Okay, I'm just going to throw everything out there. I will understand if you want to end things." Liz takes a deep, steadying breath, "If we were to get married and build a life together, I can't see it having kids, or being in the military." Getting it out takes a monumental weight from her shoulders, but the silence that follows is loud.

"Will you believe me if I tell you I feel the same way? Not only am I too old for diapers, but after what happened to Sara and Nick, it made me not want kids of my own. As for leaving the military, I get it. I did a shit job of explaining exactly what you were signing up for, so if you want out, I can and will get you out. It's not that easy for me, but I would do it with no regrets."

"You would really leave it all behind?" she asks, returning his kisses with her own on his hand.

"In a second. I told you, I had a lot of time to think about what I want, and I don't want to waste the life we could have wondering if each day is our last. I want to savor the time we have together, traveling the world doing everything your heart desires."

"C'mon," she says, sliding from his lap.

"Where are we going?"

"Our room. I'm going to show you just how much I fucking love you."

She pulls the shirt over her head and prances into the bedroom, giggling when she hears the speed in which he gets up to chase after her, slamming the door closed behind them.

CHAPTER 18

Things have finally started to settle down since Riley has been back, so much so that Liz isn't worried about leaving him to pick her gym sessions with Mikey back up.

Mikey woke her up, bright and early that morning, to practically drag her across the base to workout with only a promise of getting breakfast when they finish. He didn't tell her until they were gone that Alex and Tyler were stopping by to talk with Riley in an attempt to patch things up and, if all goes well, throw together some sort of a plan.

Liz stumbles through her exercises, still drained from the workout Riley gave her the night before, silently cheering when they finish, ready to get back and make sure the guys didn't kill each other in her absence.

No more than three steps out the door, Liz complains of being too tired to move, coaxing Mikey into letting her climb onto his back so he can carry her to the mess hall. Ignoring the stares from all the other soldiers moving around the base, they continue chatting and joking around, trying to enjoy the little friend time they get while they still have it.

Containers get filled to the brim with breakfast foods, more than enough to feed the four giant men that make up their team.

They were so close to being in the clear.

Walking back across the courtyard, heading to where their friends are waiting, a voice rings out from behind, the kind of voice that is worse than nails on a chalkboard. Liz feels the energy shift the closer he gets: going from a fun, cheery morning, gossiping with her best friend, to having all that joy sucked out of the air.

"Hey honey. Haven't seen you in a while," Matt greets her.

"Yeah, because I have been a little busy nursing someone back to health," she says, rolling her eyes so hard it hurts.

"I'm shocked you are still trying so hard. Janine said you two looked like you hated each other," Matt says keeping pace with them.

"We're fine," she snaps, trying to walk faster, growing more frustrated with the sound of his footsteps quickening.

"That's good. How is our benevolent leader doing, anyway? I'm sure he's been saying some pretty crazy things about what he saw when he was held captive," Matt blurts, obviously baiting them both.

Mikey and Liz share a confused glance before Mikey pulls out his phone and fires off a quick text, warning the team about their incoming intruder.

"Why would he be saying any crazy shit?" Mikey asks, trying to coax more out of the man. "No reason. I just assume being taken like that must have messed with his mind. Not all there anymore, ya know?" he says with a casual shrug of his shoulders.

"No, I don't know. We are trained for situations like his. Both for being tortured and coming back from it. Riley has more training in that than the rest of us combined. You should have learned that before Scott ever added you to the team," Mikey snaps.

"So since Reaper is doing *so amazing*, why has he not been in the gym? Or leading his team?" Matt pushes.

"Why do you keep asking questions about things you have no right to ask?" Liz finally snaps.

"Fine, sweet cheeks. How about this one? Did you and your lover finally have that talk?" he asks, trying to sound playful, but coming off too harsh for her liking.

"We did," she says, trying to figure out how she can hide what is between them without blatantly lying.

"And..." he urges.

Mikey must sense her unease growing because his hand silently slips into hers, giving her the strength to keep moving forward.

"And, he made it abundantly clear how he feels about me and what our relationship will be moving forward," she says, intentionally being vague.

Mikey drops her hand, instead bringing his arm around her shoulder and gently rubbing it, ever the comforting friend.

"Well, it's his loss, but I'll be honest, I've been waiting for this so you will finally give me a shot," Matt says, grinning ear to ear like she had already agreed to go out with him.

"I'm still seeing someone. Besides, I don't know if we will have time. Now that he is back, I'm sure we will be pretty busy hunting Dmitri down again," Liz stammers.

"Is there a reason I have been left out of all this planning the team seems to be doing?" he snaps in Mikey's direction.

"Yeah, because low level soldiers get briefed when we decide they do. You have no reason to be a part of the mission planning," Mikey clips back, the sergeant in him once again breaking through his fun exterior.

They sit with that, silently walking to the apartment. Even

with Mikey making it clear he is not welcome, Matt sticks with them, walking right to their apartment door with the pathetic excuse of needing to walk her home.

She peers over to her friend, picking up his hand when she sees the anger churning behind his eyes. She knows that with how close Matt is to the general, it won't matter what Mikey says. If he wants to join them, he is going to, whether they like it or not. Luckily, the rest of the team realized that before she did.

Mikey pulls the door across the hall open and steers her in. Stepping into the room, Liz nearly freezes in shock.

Not only did they move across the hall, but the team managed to get the entire room set up to look as if they had been going over mission details in there for hours.

Alex and Tyler are gathered around a map that spans the entire table, papers and folders scattered around it. The moment her eyes land on Riley, her breath catches. Everything else fades away. All she can focus on is the man in front of her.

Now in sweatpants and a loose muscle shirt, Riley leans back in his chair, arms crossed, seeming indifferent to the small crowd of people in the room. It's not the way his biceps bulge just right, or the expanse of tattoos and fresh scars fully on display, or even the way he twists his hips just right when he adjusts in his seat that has her heart rate quickening. No, it's the deep black skull mask with the small, spiraling horns that threatens to turn her feral. Something about the way it hides just enough to obscure his face while keeping his strong, chiseled jaw and very bottom of his lips showing in the most sensual way sends a wave of heat coursing through her.

When they lock eyes, she thinks it's all over. He looks at her with the passion and intensity that has her ready to drag him back across the hall and do everything she knows they are both thinking. That feeling is sucked away when Matt steps between them, trying to play the part of loyal soldier, ready to introduce himself to his new leader.

She could kill him, right there in the room. The guys would help her to dispose of his body, and she wouldn't have to watch the man she loves play nice with a man who is hiding his true intentions. Alex and Tyler can't be bothered to so much as glance up while Mikey gets to work handing out food to everyone but Matt.

"Nice to meet you, sir," Matt says, standing at attention.

"Why are you here?" Riley snaps.

"I was just walking Liz back, to make sure she got here safely, sir." he says smoothly, glancing over his shoulder to wink at Liz.

"Is she incapable of doing that on her own?" Riley retorts.

"She is, sir," he responds, the slight shake in his voice has her holding back laughter, knowing Riley is really a big softy.

"Then I will ask again. Why are you here?"

"General Scott has made it clear he wants me included in any and all planning because of what I have learned in my time overseas. They made it seem like there was talk of an upcoming mission, so I took it upon myself to join." He sounds like a child trying to sound confident with each word he says.

"Sit," Riley orders.

Liz glances at the open seat next to him, taking a step in his direction before remembering what he had said. They need to make it seem like they aren't together.

Heat works its way low into her abdomen when he winks at her, his devilish smile barely hidden behind his mask. The man knows exactly what he is doing. Mikey takes the empty seat next to him. Matt jumps at the chance to separate them, sliding into the old wooden chair before she gets the chance to move.

With an exasperated groan, Liz fills in the seat between Matt and Alex, the last one left. If she can't sit next to Riley, directly across is the next best thing, even if their stolen glances aren't as oblivious as they would like to believe. Lucky for them, Matt is far more interested in catching Liz looking at Riley than he is catching Riley looking at her.

"I knew you liked me. Out of all the seats you pick the one by my side," he whispers, leaning in too close for her liking, Riley's too if she had to guess by the way he is now tensed up.

"Sure, or I took the only one left because you decided to sit next to my best friend," she retorts, pushing her food away, too irritated to eat.

"Mikey would have moved for you, but you still sat with me. Does this mean you are finally going to let me take you to dinner?" he teases.

"Something on your mind?" Riley barks, watching the way Matt is speaking to Liz with a scary intensity.

"No, sir, just a private moment," he mumbles, unable to look him in the eyes.

"This is a tactical meeting, not a date. You do not get private moments. What is so important you need to whisper in her ear instead of focusing on mission planning that you insisted on being present for?" Riley challenges, sitting forward to place his crossed arms on the table.

Matt's eyes snap to Liz. She can see the fear in them, but says nothing, simply shrugs ever so slightly, just enough that he knows he fucked up and needs to repeat what was said.

"Just friendly banter, sir," he says. Every set of eyes at the table is now glued to him, watching to see if he will do what he was told or try to play it off. Sensing they expect more he adds, "I was asking Liz if she was finally going to allow me to take her out to dinner, since she keeps turning me down because of your relationship."

"Our relationship?" Riley questions, watching Liz with hungry eyes. "I thought we talked about this, soldier, clearly you need another reminder," he shouts, causing half the men seated at the table to jump. His booming voice may scare them, but it only fuels the arousal that has been building since she stepped into the room. He shoves his chair out, storming to the door.

"Thanks," she mutters to Matt as she stands and strides out, Riley only a step behind her, slamming the door loudly behind him.

A hard mask and soft lips crash into her as Riley pulls her through the door and into their room, kicking it closed so his hands can grip her waist without having to let go. Liz grabs at his mask, pushing it up just enough to kiss him fully, opening her mouth to allow his tongue to sweep in. She reaches down, stroking him through his pants. He spins her to face the couch, ripping her leggings down in one smooth movement.

"Bend over," he growls in her ear. She steps on her pants, freeing them from her legs and does as he orders. A strong hand grips her leg, lifting it to rest on the arm of the sofa, exposing her to him. "God, you're so fucking wet," he moans before, slamming into her.

She cries out, pushing back against him. One hand grips her hip, his fingers digging into her soft skin hard enough to leave marks, while the other finds its way to her throat, squeezing just enough to restrict her airflow without causing damage. He drives into her with a relentless force. Every thrust sets her nerves ablaze, feeling too much and not enough at the same time.

"Come for me baby," he orders, feeling every muscle slowly clench around him.

Her vision goes fuzzy, tears welling in her eyes at the immense pleasure that builds. It's too much. The position, the orders, the death grip on her throat all mixed with his perfect, rhythmic thrusting sends her crashing over the edge.

Her screams are muffled by the hand clamped over her mouth as tears stream down her face. Her legs shake, threatening to give out while he keeps fucking her, harder and faster until he is moaning into her with his own release.

Riley eases out of her, dropping his hands. Liz sinks to the floor, unable to hold herself up on unsteady legs, trying to regulate her breathing. He extends a hand, helping her back up, waiting until she is steady on her feet to pick her pants up and give them back.

"Don't get mad, but they may know what we did if you go back looking like that," he says, trying to hide his chuckle as he watches Liz struggle to get her pants back on. "Your makeup is running down your face."

"I'll go wash it off as soon as I can walk again" she says, starting for the bathroom when a hand grabs her arm.

"Leave it, he will either think you were crying, or he will know that you belong to me, either one is a win in my book." He pulls her close. "Unless the guys seeing you like this, knowing why we came in here, makes you uncomfortable."

"I'm fine with it," she says.

Riley gives her a quick kiss before storming out the door, slamming it behind him to keep the story going. Liz gives it a minute before she follows, knowing it will look like she needs a moment to compose herself after her boss berated her instead of what really happened.

When she walks back into the room across the hall, Riley is already in his seat, hunched over the table, and going over the map with Alex and Tyler. Mikey and Matt are the only ones who look up, each with wildly different reactions.

Mikey stifles a laugh, lips pressed tightly shut to stop from smiling. He picks up her hand and gives it a gentle squeeze as she walks back to her chair. Matt looks at her with wide, terrified eyes. He scans over every inch of her body, from her puffy red eyes and the makeup forming black lines down her cheeks, to the red marks forming around her neck.

"What the fuck did you do to her?" he yells. The three of them don't look up from their work.

"My job. I made sure she remembers who is in charge and what happens when you step out of line, although I feel like she is still going to need another refresher," he says calmly, or as calm as he can when someone is brave enough to raise his voice at him.

"You all just let him treat her like this? What the fuck is wrong with you?"

"I suggest you sit down and keep your thoughts to yourself, kid," Riley says in the icy tone Liz has come to learn means violence is coming.

"How can I? You're doing well enough to beat a woman under your protection before bringing her back crying, to be humiliated by your buddies, but not well enough to brief your boss and actually do your job?" he shouts, pushing his chair out and standing.

Liz opens her mouth to defend Riley, even if it ruins everything. She will not let someone accuse him of being a monster when he has the kindest heart of anyone she has ever known, but Tyler is faster.

"What he does is none of your concern. That man has been running this team for years. Scott will get his notes when Riley is ready for him to have them and not a minute sooner. You need to learn your place."

"I will handle it, but right now I am focused on healing and getting back into things," he starts, winking at Liz when he says it.

Her cheeks warm, knowing exactly what he wants to be getting back into. Matt doesn't miss it, looking between them as if he is going to be sick in his rush for the door.

"Oh, and kid, Scott may be our leader, but I am the fucking boss. If you ever disrespect me like that again, you will find out exactly why everyone is so afraid of me."

CHAPTER 19

"Are you sure I can't stay with you?" Liz asks for the hundredth time on their short walk to the admin building. She stays tucked between Riley and Mikey, with Alex and Tyler trailing close behind.

Most of the soldiers on base ignore them, or at least do a good job of pretending they do, but there is no doubt word got around about what Matt thinks happened the week prior. One of the few good things to come from that situation was his fear of Riley got him to stay away awhile longer.

"I'm sure, princess. This is long overdue, and I'm sure Scott is going to try and chew my ass out for that. Besides, I will have to tell a room full of people, who will one hundred percent piss you off, every gruesome detail of what happened to me in there. That's not something I want you hearing while everything is still so fresh," he explains, reaching for her hand before thinking better of it and dropping his arm back to his side.

Liz knows there is nothing she can say that will change his mind. The meeting is just the next step in getting cleared to officially lead their unit again. He is right. As much as she wishes to be in the room, Liz knows she has been too protective of Riley lately. If anyone says one wrong thing or questions his integrity, she will snap.

Her stomach churns when the towering building comes into view. Remembering how bad things went the last time she was in there, her pace slows. She retreats into her head, reminding herself everything will be okay. Riley will recount every detail of his capture, telling the men everything like a horrible bedtime story. The psychologist will explain he was cleared but has been receiving steady sessions, and Janine can confirm he has been healing incredibly--all wounds closed and faded into sensitive scars. He will still need more time for his muscle tissue to heal where the worst of the damage was,and continue physical therapy, but the worst is behind him.

"Everything will be fine. Go workout. I should be back before you are," he says, nudging her with an elbow, trying to get her out of her head without grabbing her the way he normally would.

"Good luck," she says with a smile that doesn't meet her eyes. As soon as the rest of her team goes inside, she and Mikey break into a jog back across base, looking back every now and then until the building is just a blip in the distance. She slows her pace the closer they get and she swears she spots a familiar frame leaning against the wall. Liz tries to run the other way but hands grab her, steering her back toward their destination.

"Oh, no you don't," Mikey says, pushing her to the building. "You need to deal with it, today. I called him to make sure he leaves Riley and Scott alone. You want him telling everyone Ry hits you? Because that is exactly what will happen if he shows up to that meeting."

"Dumbass. You think he hasn't already told anyone who will listen?" Liz snaps. Storming away, she walks right into the gym, ignoring both men who now follow .

She begins her cardio, refusing to speak until she is done. Her anger simmers far longer than anyone expected it to, putting in a solid two hours power walking before finally calming enough to move to weights with Mikey. She watches as he gets everything set up for them, keeping careful tabs on Matt. She needs to know where he is at all times if she is going to properly avoid him. What she wasn't planning on is Mikey calling him over to join them. Rage surges through her as they go through their routine, listening to the men chatting like old friends makes her skin crawl. Mikey excuses himself, leaving them alone and Matt wastes no time fawning over her.

"How are you feeling?" he asks with fake sympathy. She can see him in the mirror, watching her ass every time she dips into her split squats. "I wanted to come check on you. I would have if I didn't think he would put his hands on you again because of it."

"Can you ever just mind your fucking business?" she snaps. The anxiety of what is happening in Riley's meeting mixed with the burn in her muscles makes her more irritable than normal.

"I think a superior, not only berating someone under their command but getting physical, is my business. I have been worried about you."

"There is nothing for you to worry about. I'm fine," Liz grumbles, finishing her set, watching every step Mikey takes back to them, silently urging him to move faster.

"You're not fine, Liz! He made you cry, and don't think I didn't see the marks he left on your neck," he shouts, drawing the attention of the few people scattered around the gym.

"Give it a rest, Solano," Mikey's voice booms at his approach. "Go claim a ring and get it set up to spar. I could use a good fight today," he orders. Matt does as he's commanded, reluctantly pulling himself away.

"For what it's worth, I thought you looked fuckin hot, but I also know what he really did to you in there." Mikey teases, humping the air like a dog.

Her jaw drops and she stares at him, unable to form thoughts, let alone the words she would need to scold him. The weights clack against the rack as he puts them back, chuckling to himself when he catches sight of her.

"What the fuck, Mikey?" she finally chokes out. "He will actually kill you for talking like that. You know that, right?"

"Nah. He's my best friend. He makes a lot of empty threats, but he could never hurt me. In fact, I bet he would let me join if you asked," he says, shooting her a wink.

"Oh yeah, you think he would go for it? I would be lying if I said I haven't thought about it before. Two big, strong, sexy men worshiping every inch of my body," she says as sensually as she can muster, running her hands up his bare abdomen, stepping into him. "Maybe tonight I can bring you into our bed and we can see what he says." Liz can't control her laughter at the sight of the grown man before her scrambling back a few steps.

"You called my bluff. He would rip my dick off if he found out I said he would go for a threesome, and I would like my dick to stay right where it is, so let's go. Time to punch some of that aggression out," he says, leading the way over to the sparring mat that has been claimed for them.

Liz slinks to the floor, watching Mikey step into the middle, dragging Matt with him. He may act like a dumb goofball but seeing him spar with someone other than Riley has her remembering why he is on the team.

Mikey expertly avoids every fist and kick thrown at him, while redirecting and teaching Matt exactly what he is doing wrong. Matt has had years of his own training, a good fighter by normal standards, but Mikey has him looking as new to this as she is.

Liz stops tracking the time, focusing instead on taking in every detail of how they move. She has never had the opportunity to study their technique like this. Normally, she is the one on the mat, trying to keep up. When she does get the chance to watch, she ends up lost in every hard line and muscle on Riley's body. She notes everything, trying to commit every movement to her memory.

"Bet you wish this was you, huh?" Matt calls out seconds before a fist slams into his abdomen, sending him dropping to the mat under his feet. She can't help but laugh, watching him finally get what he deserves.

"You're next, honey. I want to see what you know," he says smirking at her while he climbs back to his feet, dodging the next wave of attacks Mikey throws at him. The minutes tick by. Both men are covered in sweat, trying to catch their breath when they finally stop. A pair of gloves lands in her lap, followed by a mouthguard. Liz looks up to find Matt striding back into the middle of the sparring ring.

"I'm not training with you," she says, sliding the gear off of her lap and onto the floor.

"C'mon. I know you've been thinking about hitting me since the day we met. Worried you are going to like my hands on you a little too much?" he says playfully, bouncing back and forth. "I promise, I won't hurt you. Unlike your precious little Reaper, I don't get off on making women cry."

Anger bubbles in her chest.

Liz shoots to her feet, shoving her hands in the gloves. Once the mouthguard is in her mouth, she steps up. Training with Riley all these months has given her an edge she never expected to have. Maybe he was on to something, having her train with only the best of the best.

Matt swings, very obviously pulling his punches, treating her like some weak woman who can't handle a proper fight. He may be holding back, but she has no intention of doing the same.

She ducks, avoiding the next wave of hits, swinging her arm out just before he finishes his own. Her fist connects with his jaw, a satisfying *thud* echoing throughout the room. So focused on the fist swinging toward her face, she never saw the leg sweep coming. Liz goes careening into the mat, rolling out of the way just before Matt drops on top of her. Liz is up in an instant, kicking her own leg out, her shin connecting with the back of his head, sending him tumbling forward. She tiptoes around him, watching him climb back to his feet.

"Alright hold," Mikey exclaims.

Liz tumbles to the ground, the taste of blood filling her mouth before she can even register what happened. She heard hold and looked away for a second, that much she knew.

"Fuck!" Mikey shouts as she hits the mat, hard, unmoving as footsteps race to where she lies. Her ears ring and her head throbs, but she is conscious and that's all she needs. She prods her lip with her tongue and all she can taste is the coppery tang of blood. Her mouth guard is long gone, flying out of her mouth at the impact. Fighting past her mind screaming at her to stay down, she climbs to her feet. Her pure, unfiltered rage takes on a mind of its own.

"I am going to fucking kill you," she spits. Ripping the gloves off and throwing them, she ignores the symphony of voices surrounding her, all sounding panicked and lunges for him. She screams in frustration as too many hands grab her, pulling her back as she lunges for Matt.

It is too late.

She fights back like a captured animal, bending and twisting to get free, but there are too many of them. The moment she gets an arm or leg free, another pair of arms grips it again. Her vision is stained red, blood from somewhere on her face pooling into her eye. One minute she is fighting her way past three overgrown men, the next she is turned sideways, being swung onto one of their shoulders. She can't scramble out of Mikey's grip. He holds firm, fireman carrying her out the door and across the parking lot.

Each bounce as Mikey jogs with her pinned to him has drops of blood falling from her face. She watches them hit the cement below her, trying to focus on that instead of strangling her friend until he lets her go.

"Put me down," she seethes in his ear, resisting the urge to bite him so he drops her. "People are staring"

"Yeah, because you're covered in blood with wild eyes. They probably think you have rabies or some shit," he says, continuing his slow jog, each bouncy step making the throbbing in her head worse.

"I will be good, just put me down before my head fucking explodes," she begs.

He loosens his grip enough to hold out a pinky. She wraps her own around it with a sigh and is placed on her feet. When she sways, Mikey's arm comes around her, helping her stay upright.

"Ry is back," he states after catching her head turning back, anger flaring when she locks eyes with Matt, watching her be pulled away. She curses at him under her breath for saying the one thing that has her rethinking her need to sprint across the lot and finish what she started. "He is stuck with Ty and Alex, darlin. They might not show it, but they are just as protective as Riley and me. They will make sure he is taken care of."

She ignores him, forcing one foot in front of the other. She does her best to ignore the pain throbbing behind her eyes, not stopping until she is ripping the door to the housing unit open. Mikey trails close, letting her storm her way through the halls. Her anger fades the moment she charges into their living room. The fear and wrath painted on Riley's face is enough for the both of them.

He rushes to her side, gingerly gripping her face in his hands. She smiles, watching his eyes scan every inch of her, lingering on her lips. No words are spoken as he leads her into the kitchen, helping her settle into one of the chairs. She smiles through the pain, forgetting everything that happened while she watches the mountain of a man fumble with a first aid kit, trying not to wince when he starts to clean the blood from her face.

"Who?" he asks. She has never been afraid of Riley before, but in this moment, when she sees the murderous look behind his eyes, she feels what she never has, fear for the man in front of her. Not fear for herself, but for what he will do when he finds out who hurt her.

The haunting look turns soft as soon as his eyes settle on hers, gently wiping the blood from her brow with a damp cotton ball.

"Someone better tell me what the fuck happened," he orders.

"Matt gave her a two piece combo when she wasn't looking," Mikey says in one big rush. "The guys came in, I told them to hold, she looked up and he got her. Ty texted that the medic should be here anytime to stitch her eye up."

"Is he still breathing?" he asks.

Liz can see it in his eyes, the shift from Riley to Reaper. They darken, his soft gaze hardening, like all emotion was ripped away from him. It is truly terrifying.

She grips his hand in hers, refusing to let go. The last time she saw him this mad was the day he left to find her brother and, as much as she would love to give Matt that same treatment, Liz knows it is not so easy.

"Only because the three of us were there, and even that was a struggle. She was going to kill him," Mikey explains. His eyes find hers, softening when he finds her glancing up at him, even with her eye swelling.

Riley hands her a cool, wet rag, helping her press it against the side of her mouth.

"That's my girl," he coos. Liz and Mikey exchange a confused glance. Riley seems to be taking everything a little too well. They watch him disappear into the bedroom, returning a moment later, sliding a loaded clip into one of Liz's handguns. Liz stares at him with wide eyes, knowing that should not have turned her on.

"I'll be right back, princess," he says, placing a kiss on her forehead and sliding the gun into the waistband of his pants. She snatches his hand, stopping him from taking another step.

"Dude, you can't go shoot him," Mikey says, his voice raising slightly. "He fucked up, and we will handle it, but you can't fucking murder him."

"Why?" Riley shouts. "The fucker already told everyone I beat her. Because of him, they think I'm unstable and too dangerous to re-join the unit. I can let that shit slide, but this?" he gestures to Liz, watching her with a cloth pressed to her lip. "Look at her, Mikey. Everyone seems to forget how far I will go to make sure she is safe," he screams.

"I do know! I also know you will be court-martialed and they will throw your ass in jail. You want her to watch that? We both know what they will do to her with you gone," he shouts right back. The death glare on Liz's face has him grumbling to himself, walking away from the situation.

"He's right, sweetie. I need you here with me, especially if I need stitches. You know how I am with needles," she says, eyes pleading him to stay. There is no question that he is torn. "There is too much at stake. If you go, we will never find out what Scott is up to, we will never catch Dmitri, and I think this goes without saying, but I can't live without you. I won't."

A sharp knock on the door cuts through the silence. One glance at the terrified look on Liz's face, he knows he can't leave her, even if every fiber of his being screams at him to hurt Matt worse than he hurt her.

Mikey emerges from his room, seemingly done pouting, marching straight to the door to let the doctor in. Riley sits back down, pulling Liz from her seat and into his lap, rubbing idle circles on her back to keep her calm as the doctor sets up everything he will need to sew her swollen brow shut. Riley doesn't let her move, holding her steady while the medic gets to work.

CHAPTER 20

Liz prods her bruised, and still slightly swollen eye, in the bathroom mirror the next morning. The stitches holding the split in her brow together makes her nauseous as she thinks about the feel of her skin being tugged back together. Her entire left eye has shifted into a deep shade of purple. A bruise covers half her jaw, paired with a split lip.

While working on making herself as presentable as possible, she tries to listen in on the conversation in the other room. She can only catch small snippets of what happened in his meeting with the general, but when her name comes up, Liz does her best to act nonchalant walking into the room.

"Come to hear the plan? It's all on you today," Mikey says proudly.

"Why me?" she asks, puzzled.

"Tyler has some suspicions about whatever is on Scott's computer. Lucky for us, he should be heading off base any minute," Riley says, tossing her a small earpiece she quickly puts in her ear, stealing glances at the new mask he's wearing while she does, hating he has to go back to wearing it. Now that Scott has people watching them, Riley needs to be careful.

"Ty is across the hall, getting his shit set up. He is going to walk you through getting into the office and make sure the cameras stay off of you while you get this into his computer, it's your time to shine, baby." He sets a small flash drive on the table. She picks it up and puts it in her pocket for safekeeping, giving the men a puzzled look, hoping they will explain what she is meant to do with it.

"Don't ask us how his nerd shit works––" A knock cuts Mikey off mid-sentence. "That's probably him coming to explain," he says, pulling the door open, not revealing their friend, but the man everyone is ready to fire a round of bullets into. Liz's nose crinkles in disgust as he invites himself in holding a bouquet of rainbow roses.

"Why are you always around?" Liz snaps.

"I came to apologize." Matt holds the flowers out to Liz. "I swear I did not mean to hit you like that. My mind was ready to swing when he said stop. I fucked up, and you have every right to be pissed, but I was hoping you would let me take you out to lunch to make it up to you," he says, eyes darting from Mikey to Riley as they approach to stand behind her.

"You think lunch is going to make up for three stitches and a split lip?" Riley asks, donning a mask of cool indifference, even though Liz can sense the tension building. "She's busy."

"At least I didn't mean to hurt her, and I'm trying to make amends," Matt stupidly snaps.

Liz drops her chin to her chest, knowing the all-out brawl he is about to start. To everyone's surprise, Riley just laughs, not his normal, lighthearted laugh reserved for her, but one that makes every hair on the back of her neck stand up.

"Paula is waiting for you, princess. Don't want to keep her waiting," he says, stepping up next to her.

His voice in her ear sends chills across her neck and shoulders while Matt looks at them bewildered. "As for you," he says, eyes narrowing on the man in the doorway, still clinging to the gaudy flowers, "You can stay, get everything off your chest, maybe you'll even get it all out before I put a bullet between your eyes."

"No murder," Liz says whirling on him. Knowing she can't kiss him, despite desperately needing to. She steps around the group of raging testosterone and disappears down the hall, sending one quick text to Riley to make sure he keeps Matt distracted.

As soon as Liz is gone, Mikey excuses himself, knowing this is not his battle to fight. Riley will do what he wants whether he is there or not, and he is smart enough to not get in the middle of a pissing contest over a girl.

He ducks out of the room, darting across the hall to tell Tyler everything and make sure he starts helping her get to where she needs to go. The unexpected guest may have thrown a wrench into their plans, but they still need it to be done.

Riley stalks back to the table, slumping into one of the chairs, watching to see if Matt will follow suit, or turn and run. He doesn't bother trying to hide his shock when the man pulls out a seat on the opposite side.

"Now's your shot, kid. You have something you want to say to me, fuckin' say it." His tone is pure ice despite trying to stay the composed leader he's supposed to be.

"Why? So you can kill me? You know what will happen if you do it, right?" Matt snaps.

"Relax. If I was going to kill you, you would already be dead. I don't give a fuck about being thrown in jail. The only reason you are still breathing is because Liz is allowing it," Riley says, fighting the urge to wipe the smirk right off his face.

"I don't get you two. She clearly has feelings for you. You have a pet name for her. You would kill me for her. You make it seem like you have feelings, yet you put your hands on her because she questions your relationship. You make no sense," Matt admits.

"Well, good thing it's not your business," Riley snaps.

"You don't deserve her," Matt finally says.

"I know," Riley replies solemnly.

"She is so hopelessly devoted to you, no matter how many times you break her. I don't fucking understand it. I mess up, but at least I always try to make it right. I have done nothing but show her I can be what she needs, but she refuses to let go of whatever bullshit hope she holds onto for you. How is she so committed to a man who beats her just because he is nice sometimes?" he says, growing louder.

Riley almost feels for him. He knows how absolutely incredible she is, but he had no idea the man before him also held real feelings for her.

Riley goes to the cabinet, pulling a bottle of whiskey down and fills a glass, handing it to Matt.

"I told Liz I wouldn't kill you, but if you say that shit one more fuckin' time, I swear to whatever god you believe in, I will show you just how much the human body can take *without* dying," he says, all too casually.

"Why? Can't handle hearing it out loud? We all saw her when she came back—crying, wearing your handprint as a necklace. Your little buddies may ignore it, letting you do whatever you want, but I won't," Matt sneers.

"They ignore it because they know what happened over the arm of that couch." He looks over, picturing her bent over it again. Matt slams the glass on the table, hearing the confession, staring at

Riley with wide, panicked eyes. "She enjoyed every second, I promise."

"So, she was telling the truth." He leans back in his chair, shaking his head. "And what? You brought her over here to mark your territory?"

"No, I brought her over because you stressed me out, and I needed some relief," Riley says, attempting to sound indifferent. "I thought she told you we have a complicated relationship."

"I thought complicated meant she was in love with you, and you couldn't stand her. Not that you fuck her whenever the mood strikes."

"What can I say? She's hot, and I'm just a man," he says with a shrug.

"You are the reason she keeps turning me down, turning everyone down. Everytime you use her, you're giving her false hope," Matt yells, standing from his seat.

"What do you mean everyone?" Riley asks.

"There are plenty of men in other platoons that have been dying to talk to her, but they are too scared of you. Jesus christ, your own best friend wants to fuck her."

"What?" Riley asks, dumbfounded.

That was the last thing he expected to hear. Mikey has no problems making it known that he finds Liz unbelievably attractive, but when it comes to sexual feelings, he had assumed his friend wouldn't have any for her.

"He told her she had never looked hotter with the makeup running down her face before humping the air. She clearly felt the same way rubbing his damn stomach. The point is, you're keeping her from finding any real happiness." The words come out too fast to stop.

"Well, that's good to know, but believe it or not, I don't control what she does or doesn't do. I made my feelings clear, the rest is out of my hands. If you think you, or anyone else for that matter, can get her to agree to a date, she's all yours. I will back off," Riley says, knowing that was the last thing he expected to hear. "God, I can't believe I'm about to say this, but do you want to know how it happened? Why we have the relationship we do?" Riley groans, waiting to see his choice. Matt nods, slinking back into his chair.

Riley does exactly what Liz asked, he keeps him distracted, even if it means carefully picking and choosing what details to tell him, essentially handing him a playbook to her heart.

CHAPTER 21

Liz follows the voice in her ear across the eerily empty base. Tyler has timed everything perfectly to make sure she is able to make it to the office with minimal distractions. If anyone *does* speak to her, she is to tell them she is meeting Paula and keep going.

After only being stopped once, she reaches the building she is sick of seeing. As soon as she is in, Tyler starts turning the cameras just enough for her to walk by as close to the wall as she can without looking suspicious and out of place. She makes her way through the maze of corridors until Tyler finally points out the stairwell. Her heart thunders in her chest, taking the steps two at a time to make it to the top floor before the conference room empties.

The hall lined with photos and metals comes into view. Practically sprinting on silent feet, she stops just outside the door. Tyler gives her the all clear and she shoves the small lock-pick into the knob, doing everything he tells her to do until she feels the lock give.

"Alright, camera is scattered. There should be a USB port on the back of his monitor, just plug it in there and I can take care of the rest," he says through her earpiece.

Liz does as he says. With Tyler left to his work, she starts poking around in drawers. Mostly filled with junk and food wrappers, she carefully moves them around, trying to find anything of value. A glint of metal catches her eye as she pushes the very bottom drawer closed. There, tucked into the back, nearly the same color of the wood, is a lock.

"Hey, will this lock-pick work on anything?" she asks the void.

"Should. Why? You got something?" Tyler's voice cuts through the static.

"I think this drawer has a fake bottom," Liz says, gently knocking on it. It sounds hollow. Liz doesn't bother making sure it's fine to mess with before shoving the lock-pick into it. The pick jiggles around, finally springing the lock free. As if diffusing a bomb, Liz lifts the wooden plate, wrappers and all, disgusted by what she finds under it.

"How safe is my phone?" she whispers.

"Pretty safe, but not entirely. Depends on how fast you get it back to me to remove whatever you take."

Bile rises in her throat at what she sees: a pile of letters and photos lay scattered in the drawer, and on top, a grainy polaroid of Riley stripped to nothing but the tattered pants she found him in, Dmitri poses next to where Riley is struck up by a set of meat hooks like he was his prized fish.

She snaps a few photos with her phone, using it to move the polaroids to the side and get pictures of the letters underneath, hoping Tyler will be able to translate. Liz makes sure everything is put back in the exact positions before placing the piece of wood back in, attempting to relock it.

"Get my drive! You have incoming," he yells through the earpiece.

She rips the small device from the computer and throws herself into one of the chairs, screaming at her mind to settle before she gets herself killed. Her eyes close, listening to keys jingle just feet from where she sits. The handle turns effortlessly, and the general barges in, face bright red with anger the moment he spots her.

"What the hell are you doing breaking into my office?" Scott shouts, slamming the door behind him.

This was not supposed to happen. He should be miles away in town right now.

"I'm sorry," she says timidly, trying to think of an excuse.

"Tell him his secretary Sally let you in," Tyler whispers in her ear.

"I needed to speak with you. Sally said you should be back soon and let me wait in here," Liz adds, trying to appear less jittery than she is.

"Where is the rest of your team? Hiding in the shadows, waiting to attack me?" he barks, looking around the tiny space, eyeing her when he realizes she is alone.

"No, sir. They don't know I am here."

"And why *are* you here, Elizabeth?" he smiles, watching her squirm, opening her mouth to argue before snapping it shut loud enough for him to hear.

"I...I want to talk about Riley," she says. His too cautious eyes never leave hers as he slinks into his gaudy green leather chair.

"What about him?"

"You were wrong to not let him take his position back," Liz snaps, letting the smallest burst of anger out.

"Here I thought you were learning some respect," he scoffs.

"I am trying to be respectful. You don't like me, and I don't like you, those are facts, just like you making a poor choice based on lies is a fact."

"You think rather highly of yourself to think you are the reason he is not returning to lead the unit."

"Am I not? Was the decision not based on what Matt had told you?" Liz shoots back. "He told you Riley hits me, and you gave that as your reason to keep him from his position."

"You should be thanking me for working to get you away from him. I had no idea he was violent with you," he says, eyes softer this time, almost as if he can see the battered woman he believes her to be. "Though, I'm not surprised given his history."

"You and I both know he would never lay a hand on me."

"I trust Matthew, and for reasons I will never understand, he is fond of you. He came to me, worried for your safety when Reaper brought you into a room alone and attacked you," Scott says.

"Oh my god, he didn't attack me. He fucked me: bent me over the couch, grabbed me by the throat, and fucked me until my legs gave out. *That* is why I have marks, and that is the only reason I looked... disheveled," Liz blurts before her brain has the chance to think better of it. By the look on Scott's face, the general is torn between throwing her out of his office or himself out the window.

"Again, I'm sorry, but I can't have people thinking he is capable of such awful things. I wanted to tell Matt the truth, but if I did, he would think less of me, so I came to set the record straight with you," Liz says.

"Why on earth would you care if Matt thinks less of you?" he asks, watching every minuscule movement.

Liz adjusts in her seat, trying not to show how uncomfortable these talks make her.

"He's sweet, okay? I told him once Riley came back and we talked about our relationship, I would let him take me out. Well, we talked and it didn't go how I thought it would, so I have been thinking about everything he said. If Matt finds out that we... did that... he will never look at me the same again." The lies come easy, saying whatever believable thing the general will eat up while trying not to think about if she will have to follow through or not. "None of this matters, the only thing that matters is Riley did not do the things he was accused of, and it's wrong to keep him from being cleared," she quickly adds, an attempt to steer the conversation in any direction that will get her out of there.

"Let's say I believe you," he starts, pulling a small stack of papers out. They land on the desk with a small thud. "I let him return to lead the unit; can you guarantee Matt gets brought into the team, properly?"

"No," she says looking him square in the eye. "I will try, if and *only* if you clear Riley. But I cannot promise that the rest of the guys will listen. And I need to know why this is so important to you."

"Hmm," he says. Pursing his lips, he leans back in the chair, thinking over it. "I did not expect honesty out of you, Elizabeth. I suppose I can give you some in return. Matt is my nephew from a past marriage. He has always taken a shine to me, and I would like to give him his best chance at taking over for me some day, but Reaper has refused to teach him how a special operations unit runs."

"Again, no promises, but you have my word that I will try to convince them. Do we have a deal?" she asks, glancing at the papers he made a show of bringing out.

Hope blooms in her chest, watching him scribble his name across the bottom and hand it to her. She quietly thanks him, and leaves his office, forgetting if she is supposed to wait to be dismissed or not.

Rushing back the way she came, Liz quickly makes it outside, breaking into a fast jog the moment her shoes hit the pavement.

The paranoia hits hard. Dressed in everyday workout clothes, Liz can't help but feel like everyone she passes knows what she did.

She double checks her pocket, feeling the drive still firmly in place. An invisible weight lifts when she reaches the main door of their building. The forty-minute mission felt like a lifetime.

Not bothering to knock, Liz enters the room, going straight to the table, and tossing her phone and flash drive to Tyler.

"What's got you so spooked?" he says, eyeing her from behind his screens.

"The pictures on my phone almost made me vomit. Get them off, please," she whispers.

"I think Matt is gone," Mikey tells her from across the room. "You did amazing, darlin. Ty didn't think you could fake it like that. You should go tell Ry you got him his job back. We can deal with this and debrief later."

Liz stands, giving him a sad smile, mouthing thank you before dragging herself back to her room. She tries to put on a brave face to tell Riley the good news before she has to ruin it with everything else she found.

CHAPTER 22

Completely and utterly emotionally drained, the team sits around the table after having one of the hardest meetings they have ever had to endure. Tyler didn't want to wait until he went through the files after he saw what Liz found hidden in their general's desk, so he called an emergency meeting.

They spent the last few hours laying everything out, sitting in silence ever since. Liz wishes she could say something, anything to make it better, but she knows she has done enough damage agreeing to make sure Matt is included, making everything uncovered that much harder to face.

"Well, this sucks." Mikey is the first to speak since they showed Riley the photos. "What do we even do with this? As far as we know, those are ransom notes, ignored ransom notes, but it doesn't prove anything."

"I won't have proof of anything until I comb through the general's computer and get those photos translated. Either way, he was hiding that he knew exactly where Riley was, but with his connection to the joke of a man that runs the country, he will never face any consequences for it. He can justify it by saying it was to keep everyone else safe," Tyler says.

"I'm sorry, guys. I panicked when he came in. I never should have agreed to anything he asked," Liz says quietly. The hand that wraps around hers eases the guilt, but not nearly enough. She got Riley his position back, but it may have cost them everything. If they don't follow through and let Matt be as involved as he wants, Scott will, without a doubt, punish Riley for it. If they do let him in, they will never be able to figure out what Scott is really doing.

"Don't," Riley orders. "Don't do that to yourself. None of us knew what you would find, and that asshole was never supposed to show up. You did what you had to do and got the job done. I'm proud of you."

A sharp knock echoes through the silence, drawing their attention away from their defeat. Whoever it might be is not welcome, forcing Liz to grumble her way to the door.

She glances over her shoulder in time to catch Riley sliding his black neck gaiter over his face, covering the bottom half. Mikey tosses a handful of paper menus into the center of the huddle, clearly no one is taking any chances.

The door swings open, and to absolutely no one's surprise, she is left face to face with the last person she wants to see. Matt glances around her to the group of men watching them. His hazel eyes lock onto her, smiling wide enough to make his dimples pop.

"Can I please take you out to dinner?" he asks, more of a plea than a question.

Liz responds with a sigh, motioning for him to come into the apartment, beating back the urge to tell him to go to hell.

"We were just about to order something. Maybe next time," she says, flashing a fake smile.

"That's what you said last time. One date, and if you don't have a good time, I will never ask again," Matt pleads. A satisfied smile tugs at his lips when Liz looks at Riley, only to find him browsing a pizza menu, paying her no mind.

"I really can't. Ry had some things he needed my help with," she starts.

"I can manage," he says without looking up. "I think you should give him a shot."

The remaining men exchange glances, sensing the tension beginning to build. The three of them simultaneously stand, scrambling for the door before anyone can stop them, leaving with nothing but the promise to return with food.

"Okay. Fine. Where are you taking me?" she says through a sigh.

"Just a little Italian spot I know. Nice, but not too fancy."

She gives him a quick once over, thinking of what she can wear to match. "Give me a few minutes to get ready. I need to try and draw attention away from my fucked-up face," she says, glaring daggers at Riley. His lips shift under his mask, smiling mischievously, he winks, making her mad enough to walk away. If she didn't love the man so much, she would ring his neck.

The last thing she sees before ducking into her room is a chair kicked out in the way only Riley has mastered—a silent order for Matt to sit.

"How's it feel to finally get what you've been after?" Riley asks, trying to stop himself from looking at the door Liz is tucked behind, dolling herself up for another man.

"Incredible. Thank you, sir, for stepping back and convincing her to give me a chance," Matt says, following Riley's eyes to the door.

"Just know, if you hurt her, if you offend her, if you do

anything, and I mean *anything* that makes her even the slightest bit unhappy, we *will* kill you. Well, the other three will. I will take my good, sweet time, savoring every second of ruining you. I can break you in ways you can't even begin to imagine," he says coldly, smiling to himself under his mask. He watches Matt with the same intensity as any other enemy he has faced before.

Their heads snap up as Liz comes strutting out of the other room. The moment Riley lays eyes on her, regret hits him like a punch to the gut. She is stunning. A white and blue floral milkmaid dress hugs her waist while still hanging loosely around her legs, the bodice cinched just right. A set of white, chunky heels with thick straps wrap around her ankles and up her lower calf before tying neatly into a bow.

He catches Matt staring, both their eyes drifting to her exposed thigh where she is slightly bent at the waist, tightening the strap on the gun holster Riley had gifted her, his heart swelling at the sight. Her long, black hair is half pulled back into a clip, holding it away from her face and cascading over her shoulder before she stands back upright. The sway of her hips with each step has both men scrambling to their feet, rushing to her side.

"Fuck," Riley mumbles, barely loud enough for them to hear. Matt's head snaps to him, jaw clenched, fists balled at his side.

"Hey, beautiful," Matt says proudly. The only acknowledgement he gets is a tight smile, watching her step over to Riley instead of him.

"Are you sure you don't need me?" she asks, meeting his eyes, silently pleading with him to ask her to stay.

"God knows I do," his tone is a low, a sultry promise of what will be waiting for her when she returns. He leans in, just close enough so only she can hear, "But if you don't leave now, I will remind both of you exactly who you belong to."

"Okay," she says, trying to ignore the flash of heat growing between her legs. "I will see you later, I guess."

CHAPTER 23

The short car ride to the restaurant borders on painful, neither of them knowing what to say, so they choose to silently listen to the radio instead.

Liz can see the light at the end of the tunnel when Matt turns into the parking lot. At least inside there will be wine, enough to make the night tolerable.

He picks up her hand after opening her door, leading her inside. After giving his name to the portly man behind the podium, they only have to wait a few minutes before being led back to their table: small and round, tucked into a dark corner, and too far away from the others for her liking. She slides into her chair, ready to get this night over with, making uncomfortable small talk until their meals arrive.

"I have to ask, what did Reaper whisper to you before we left?" Matt asks, emptying his third glass of wine.

"That I'm better off with you," she says, sipping from her own glass, giving herself chills as she replays what he actually said in her mind.

"Damn. I did not expect that. He is so weird when it comes to you. I can't get a read on the guy. He fucks you, but won't date you, but threatens anyone who *does* want to date you. He encouraged you to move on but was staring at you like he wanted to take you right there in front of me," Matt begins, signaling for another refill. "I feel bad for you, being stuck around someone like that all the time."

"It's not that bad, especially when I have Mikey. But let's not talk about them tonight. Tell me about you," she says, batting her lashes.

He is the kind of guy who will boast about himself for hours, and she plans to take full advantage of that to get out of putting any real effort into the night. A few well placed *Oh wows* and *that's so interesting, tell me more* has him talking the entire meal. She waits until he switches from wine to whiskey to finally speak, hoping he is buzzed enough to loosen his lips.

"I owe you another apology, Matt. I have been so awful to you, and you don't deserve that. It has just been hard for me, seeing how close you are with Scott. That man has been nothing but horrible to me. Saying I work with Dmitri, calling me a whore, trying to send me back. I assumed that because you are close, you would be just like him," she says resting her crossed arms on the table, watching as his eyes drop right to her chest on full display. "The guys were the ones who saved me. They have been by my side, teaching me, and helping me heal since day one. It's a struggle to let anyone else in."

He looks at her with his brows knit, looking utterly lost.

"It sounds more like you have Stockholm Syndrome. You know what that is, right?" he asks, looking at her while she nods her head in agreement.

"It's pretty much when people hurt you, but you like it. Reaper has hit you, and they all keep you locked away, but they are nice sometimes, so now you love them. I think they convinced you to stay around to hold it over Scott's head. He tried to send you home, but they keep lying to you and saying he won't let you go," he rants, stumbling over words from all the alcohol coursing through his veins.

Liz waits until he spins around, flagging down the waiter to top him off, so she can pull her phone out to record the drunken confession.

"What do you mean?" she asks, trying her best to look hurt and confused, though with how drunk Matt seems to be, she could probably just demand he tell her everything.

"All your guard dogs. They are out to get him. Scott. They are keeping you hostage because he wants you to be safe." He leans in, dropping his voice slightly to what he must think is a whisper.

"They want to kill you. That's why I'm here. My job is to watch them and figure out what they are planning to do to Scott," he says, looking around. "Can you keep a secret?" he asks, beginning again before she has the chance to agree or not. "Scott is going to get rid of them. That Reaper guy was never supposed to come back, he was making sure of it, but now that you don't hate me, I can keep you safe. You can help me find out what they are doing, and we can stop it... together."

Unable to put up with any more of his booze-fueled nonsense, Liz picks up his hand, squeezing it slightly. "Thank you. You're a good friend, sweetie. But we should probably get back before they come looking for us," she says, trying to remember how to gentle parent.

He shoots to his feet, swaying slightly, tosses a handful of crumpled hundred-dollar bills onto the table, and walks out, bumping into three other tables in the process.

"Shit," she mumbles, chasing after him. "Hey, you took such great care of me, why don't you let me drive us back." Liz holds out her hand, looking at him with big doe eyes.

He smiles, digging into his pocket, leaning in for what seems like a kiss, when she sidesteps him and marches right to his car.

The walk through the housing building is, somehow, the longest of her life. Carefully dodging his wandering hand, Liz attempts to herd Matt back to his room. A few short steps and she will be able to wash her hands of this night.

With her mind focused on getting him to his apartment, she doesn't see the danger until it's too late. Her head cracks against the wooden door so hard she nearly goes unconscious. A hand grips her throat, squeezing until she is fighting for air while another one slips under her dress, caressing her bare leg. Every thought drains from her mind, nothing but sheer panic taking over the moment a warm, slimy tongue is forced into her mouth. Her split lip rips back open, dripping fresh blood down her chin. She tries to scream, to push him off, but she is tipsy, and he is drunk enough to not care about hurting her.

She reaches with one hand, fumbling with the straps on her leg, her other hand pinned helplessly above her head. Tears stream down her face when she hears the faint snap of a button release. Tearing the gun out, she shoves it under his chin, pressing it tight. Matt eases off, removing his hand, then his mouth, smiling like he just gave her everything she could ever want. The door behind her pulls open, sending her stumbling into an unfamiliar room.

She needs to get out. She can see the anger simmering in Matt's eyes, aimed at whoever opened the door. Using the distraction, she wretches her arm free of his other hand and takes off sprinting down the hall. Liz darts down the stairs while trying not to break an ankle, only slowing when she hits the landing of her floor. The only sound that follows is her heart pounding in her ears.

She presses her back to the wall, sliding down to sit on the dirty floor of the stairwell. Resting her head on her knees, she lets the tears flow freely, allowing herself a moment of weakness. All she can think about is what would have happened if his roommate didn't open the door when he did. And what is Riley going to think? He is going to be furious with her for getting herself into that situation. How can she go home, look him in the eye, and tell him she had another man's tongue in her mouth. Just the thought has her gagging.

Liz lets out a breath as she forces herself back onto her feet. She knows she will need to face him sooner or later, so crying about it won't change anything.

Liz walks with purpose back to their room, smoothing her dress as she does, trying to hold her head high no matter what happens next. The door handle trembles under her grip, nerves getting the better of her.

"Fuck," she whispers to herself in the empty hall. She lets out a breath, reaching for the door again. "You can do this. You *have* to do this, no matter how mad he gets."

She pushes the door open, stepping in before she loses the courage she grapples with, praying they are asleep and not waiting for her to return.

The moment her eyes land on Riley, she wishes she had never come back. It is going to be hard enough to talk to him without him looking the way he does now. He stands with his bare back to her, muscles and fresh pink scars glistening with sweat. A baseball cap is turned backward on his head, and his sweatpants are hanging dangerously low on his waist. Disgust and arousal is a crazy mix of emotions she never thought she would experience. And she hates herself for being aroused immediately after being assaulted.

"How was your date?" he asks, tone sharp enough to cut.

Warm tears slide down her cheeks, unable to form the words she needs to confess. She can't stand it, the anger and disappointment already lacing his voice. Not mentally equipped to handle talking, she heads right to their room.

"Liz?" he calls after her. His heart drops into his stomach when she doesn't answer. He runs after her, spotting the gun still in her hand. "Hey, what happened?" His hand wraps around her arm, stopping her from taking another step. He releases her the instant she turns back, looking up at him with pained eyes rimmed with tears and smeared make up.

He's softer then, reaching up to wipe the blood from her mouth with his thumb, holding her face in his hand for only a moment before letting her go. A storm of emotions rages inside his mind. Seeing the woman he loves hurt has him storming into their room, returning with his own gun.

"He did this to you?" he asks, trying to be gentle when he speaks to her despite what is going on in his own head when she nods.

"Please, don't," she begs when he storms to the door, his hand left hovering on the handle. The whimper in her voice, asking him to go against his nature, nearly breaks him. "It will ruin everything."

His hand drops to his side, forced to make an impossible choice. That choice is made for him when he looks into her eyes. Riley goes back, plucks the gun from her hand, and places it on the table alongside his, rushing back to her side. He holds his arms open for her, not sure if she is comfortable with being touched or not. He lets it be her choice, breathing a sigh of relief when she steps into him.

"Talk to me, love. I need to know what happened," he urges, stroking his hand down the length of her hair.

"He got drunk and told me everything," she says, sniffling.

"You know that's not what I mean."

"I don't want to talk about it right now, Ry. I haven't even had time to process what just happened," she says, hands trembling, wiping her tears from his chest.

"He *just* did—whatever he did to you?" he growls.

She nods again. "We got back a few minutes ago. Matt was really drunk, so I walked him to his room. I am so fucking stupid."

He is gone as soon as the words fall from her lips. The sharp smack of his hand slamming into the door echoes through the hall, sounding too much like the way her head sounded moments ago. She turns to find a groggy Tyler pulling his door open, glancing around with wild eyes when he sees the state Riley is in.

"Can you get access to the hall cameras?" Riley asks.

"Uh, yeah? Why? What's going on?" Tyler responds, rubbing the sleep from his eyes.

"Don't worry about it. Find when Liz and Matt make it back. Should only be a few minutes ago. Come get me when you do," he orders, turning back around and slamming the door shut.

He goes to her and drops to his knees at her feet. He loosens the ties behind her legs, letting the thick ribbons of her heels fall around her ankles before carefully slipping each foot free. He starts to drag his hand up her leg, stopping at the base of her thigh. "Did he—" Riley starts, unable to get the rest of the words out for fear of what she will say.

"No, thank fucking god," she says, peering down at him. "I would have blown his fucking brains out before it got that far." Her cheeks warm, flushing a bright shade of pink at seeing him kneel before her, every muscle on full display.

"Tell me if this is too much." His hands creep further, fumbling with the buckles on her holster until it clatters to the ground. "I would help you change, but I don't want to make things worse," he says, scooping the straps off the floor and walking them to where their guns rest on the table.

"I'm fine. Well—better now that I'm with you. I've dealt with worse. I'm just in shock," she mumbles, walking into their room.

He follows close behind, not wanting her out of his sight. Liz overloads her toothbrush with toothpaste, and violently scrubs every inch of her mouth, wincing when her lip starts bleeding again.

His stomach turns sour as he lowers himself on the bed, knowing at least a small part of what happened with the way she is brushing. He can't tear his gaze away, watching heartbroken as she rinses and spits mouthwash no less than four times.

"Ry!" Tyler yells, entering their apartment. "I got it."

That's all he needs to hear. He storms into the room, his anger reignited, ready to find out exactly what Matt did.

Liz follows, pulling her hair up into a messy bun, still in the dress that swishes with every step. She storms over to the table where they sit hunched over a computer, pushing it closed as she does.

"You need to hear what he told me before you watch that. I'm not kidding, Ry. If you go after him, everything will be ruined," she demands. "Should we wait for the guys?"

"Mikey's out with Lauren. I'm not pulling him from that," he states.

"Alex won't care if I tell him everything later," Tyler adds.

"Okay, well, buckle the fuck up," she says, pulling her phone out of her dress pocket. "There has been a lot of bullshit happening. Apparently, Scott has him convinced you guys are holding me hostage because he wants to save me. I'm your bargaining chip, I guess."

"What?" Riley chokes out.

"Yeah. He said you want to kill me, but General Grievous

wants me safe, so he is playing nice. Matt tried to convince me that you guys were the ones who refused to let me go in the beginning, and Scott has been fighting to free me from you this whole time," Liz explains.

"He does know that Scott has said everything to your face, right?" Tyler asks.

"I don't know, but he ended up hammered and—just listen," she says, loading the video on her phone.

She plays back every word he said about how the general was keeping them from finding Riley, and how he was sent to spy on them while their boss figures out a way to get rid of the team permanently.

"Now, I'm not saying Matt doesn't deserve to die. I think I would prefer it if he did. But doing anything to harm him will give Scott the excuse he is looking for to kill you," she finishes, standing from the table.

Riley watches her pace the room, waiting for her to say more. When she doesn't, he opens the computer and plays the footage. The men watch in stunned silence, anger twisting their faces while they are forced to watch what happened to her earlier that night. Clearly having seen enough, Tyler slams the laptop shut.

"How do you expect me to be around him after seeing that?" Riley quietly asks.

She simply responds with a shrug of her shoulders, walking to their bedroom. "The same way I have to after experiencing it."

CHAPTER 24

Each day that passes, Riley grows more protective of Liz, making each member of the team promise she will never be left unattended. He has given them all strict orders to pull her from whatever task or training is taking place and return her to their apartment if they spot Matt. The plan has worked so far.

Mikey switched up their workout routine, forcing her to the gym extra early to avoid any unwanted interactions, delivering her safely home right after. Tyler and Alex run interference, keeping Matt away from Liz with fake information about Dmitri and his operation. A task they happily took on after walking in on Mikey, Liz, and Riley wearing robes, fluffy headbands, and face masks while Liz introduced them to the wonders of trash reality tv.

Thanks to one man's deplorable actions, Liz is now back to being a prisoner. Unable to leave or see anyone other than her approved four people and, despite them trying to make it enjoyable, she misses the freedom she had.

Liz practically dances across the lot on the way to the gym, letting the warm sunshine blanket her face, the smell of freshly fallen rain soothing something deep in her soul.

She spent her morning snuggled up in bed with Riley, talking about all the things they have missed out on doing together. That prompted him to ask her to do some hand-to-hand training with him later. One of the things they have missed most.

Nearly halfway through their workout, Liz's phone chirps with a text. Her face lights up the moment she sees it is from Riley. He is on the way. She drops what she is doing, leaving Mikey to re-rack her weights while she rushes to the bathroom to freshen up. He may have already seen her at her worst, but things seem to always get a little—intense, when they workout together. Mikey separated them at home for that very reason.

Liz double checks herself in the long bathroom mirror one last time. Her eye is looking better. The stitches finally came out, and her lip is almost fully healed. She gives herself one more look before prancing out. Her excitement turns to dread when she steps through the door. Leaning against the wall, arms crossed like he has been perched there, waiting for her to emerge, is Matt. She frantically looks around, wondering how the hell he made it past Mikey.

"Hey, honey. I miss you," he says cooly, pushing off the wall, blocking her exit. "You haven't returned my messages. I was hoping we could go out again."

"Even if you didn't pull the shit you did, I wouldn't go out with you again. I told you, I am seeing someone. That night was a mistake, one I won't make a second time," she retorts.

He looks at her with his brows furrowed, a look of confusion on his face, one that quickly twists into anger.

"See, this is what's wrong with you. This is why no one will ever fucking love you, Liz. You are delusional. Batshit fucking crazy!" he shouts.

Liz flinches like his words physically slapped her.

"He has no interest in you! Everyone heard what he said that day. For fucks sake dude, he told me to try and fucking date you, practically begged me to get you the fuck away from him! I have been trying to help you, to keep you safe from the people who want to kill you and maybe give you the life you deserve. Yet here you are still, holding out hope he will have feelings for you someday!" he practically screams.

She looks around, frantic. She has no weapons. Fighting him will buy her time to try and slip away. But one of the stupidest things she could do is fight him while he is in a fit of rage and yelling to Mikey is no use. The second she walks away his headphones get turned all the way up.

"You don't know what you're talking about," Liz says with all the confidence she can muster, hoping if she refuses to play into his tantrum he will let her leave, though a feeling of unease grows with the volume of his voice.

"I know exactly what I am talking about. I could have kept you safe *and* made you happy if you would have let me. We could have built a relationship, one where you're not *only* good for a quick fuck while I hide behind a mask. How are you so fucking stupid that you think a man too ashamed of himself to even show his face could ever love you?" he screams, so lost in his anger he can't hear the figure approaching behind him. Liz's eyes light up, a smile tugging at her lips when she sees him reach and pull the mask off, tossing it aside.

"What the hell are you smiling at?" he demands.

"Her husband." A deep voice booms.

Matt jumps. He spins around to find himself toe to toe with Riley. He scrambles back, nearly bumping into Liz who is now watching him with amusement dancing in her eyes.

"Who the fuck are you?" Matt snaps, so lost in his anger he

forgets they are on a military base, filled with men and women who outrank him.

"I'm your fucking commander, and I will give you to the count of one to step away from my wife," he orders. The way his voice commands authority sends chills skating over her body.

Matt steps aside, allowing Liz to march right to Riley's side where he promptly wraps his arm around her and pulls her against his chest. He dips his head, placing a quick kiss on her lips before moving her safely behind him.

"You're commander Corson?" Matt sneers, sizing up the god of a man in front of him. "You think I'm stupid. He never goes anywhere without hiding his face."

"Right. Because I'm *too ashamed*?" he asks, voice dripping with sarcasm. "Thats what you said right?" He takes a step closer. "When you were screaming at Liz, berating her for not settling for you when she has me at home." He smiles at Matt when his eyes go wide. He may not have seen his face before, but there is no forgetting the edge in his voice.

Another step.

"What? Nothing to say? Only brave enough to scream at women you assault in dark hallways? Better get it all out because I am going to kill you this time."

"No murder!" Liz groans from behind him, looking around to find the gym nearly cleared of anyone who had been in there before.

"No promises, love," he calls back. His lip kicks up in amusement watching Matt's eyes dart between the two of them.

"Don't lose your nerve now," he says, stepping toward Matt once more, backing him up until he nearly touches the wall. "Not so fun, is it? To be cornered by someone bigger. Stronger. Someone who wants to hurt you. All *I* want is to see you dead, so imagine how scared Liz was when you tried to take more than just her life?"

"I didn't do any—" Matt stammers.

Riley's hand encases his throat, squeezing until Matt's hands fly up, grabbing at his arm.

"I saw the security footage," Riley shouts, slamming Matt into the wall. He grips tighter. Squeezing. Riley stares into his eyes, watching them turn from fear to absolute terror.

Matt weakly swings his arm out, the loss of oxygen getting to him already. Riley lifts his free arm, easily blocking his fist. Riley's first hit breaks something. Blood pours from Matt's nose, dripping onto the arm holding his throat.

"I watched you *touch* her." The second hit is harder. Drops of thick crimson spatter across his face.

"I watched you *hurt* her," he yells, swinging again.

"I watched you try to take something that doesn't belong to you," he shouts with one final swing.

Matt's head is sent flying to the side, blood spraying the wall beside them. The moment Riley loosens his grip, Matt crumples onto the floor, gasping for air.

Liz rushes back to Riley's side, letting him pull her into his side, listening to Matt's ragged breaths like it's a symphony. She has so many questions about what just happened.

"Clean yourself up," Riley says. "You should probably set that broken nose before your investigation starts." He steers Liz back down the hall, away from the scene he made.

"Stay here," he says, running to where Mikey absentmindedly lifts weights, either not knowing, or not caring about what just happened.

She can't take her eyes off of him. It has been so long since she has seen him in his element, thriving. It's an incredible sight. He jogs back to where she waits. Riley grabs her hand, pulling her out the door and across the parking lot to Mikey's truck. Liz scrambles in, scooting herself into the middle, needing to be close to Riley.

He climbs in next to her, starting the truck before gripping her leg with one hand and the steering wheel with the other. Butterflies erupt in her stomach as they peel out of the lot, heading somewhere off base. Liz snuggles closer, wrapping her arms around Riley's arm, careful to avoid any blood. She rests her head on his shoulder, ecstatic to have a small sense of normalcy back.

"Where are we going?" she asks, smiling up at him when he gives her leg a little squeeze.

"Home."

CHAPTER 25

The two of them are the happiest they have been in weeks when Riley pulls off onto the dark road leading home. Liz practically bounces in her seat when the hovel above their home comes into view. It has been so long since they have had any real quality time together. Even the days following Riley's rescue were spent having serious conversations with a constant flow of friends and doctors coming in and out.

His arms find their way around Liz when the elevator doors close behind them, keeping her held close until the very last second.

"We need a dog," Liz says as she is pulled into the living room, letting him steer her right to the couch, pulling her down with him as he flops onto it.

"If we make it out of this shit storm alive, I will take you to adopt as many dogs as you want," he says, burying his face in her neck.

She jumps back up, yanking on his still tender arm until he is standing, only feeling a little bad when she sees the slight wince.

That is what he gets for continuing to over do it. Despite being cleared and back to working out, Liz knows he still has some pain he tries to hide.

"You're covered in blood. Go shower," she says, inspecting the fluffy cushions for any sign of red, attempting to push him toward his room. She erupts in a fit of giggles as she is hoisted into the air. Riley slings her over his shoulder, acting as if she weighs nothing at all.

"Fine, but you're coming with me," he says, reaching up and smacking her butt, laughing at the squeal that escapes her. "I'm still too weak to be alone."

"Too weak my ass. I know you have been sneaking out before the sun comes up to go to the gym," she says as she rakes her nails over the defined muscles in his back. Riley tosses her onto the bed when they get into his room, leaving her sprawled out while he starts the shower, crawling in next to her while it warms.

"So," Liz says, rolling onto her side so she can face him. "Are we going to talk about what happened back there? That is going to be his excuse to hurt you. I can already see him saying you got mad that he took me out and attacked him"

"Nothing to talk about, love. There is footage of Matt attacking you. He can try to use it against me, but crying about it will do him no good. I would do the same to any man who tried to rape someone," he says, playing with her hair.

Liz watches him, mesmerized by the way he always does that when he talks about something serious. Remembering the shower is running, she pulls herself from the bed, holding both hands out to pull Riley up, too. If he says he needs help, help is what he will get.

She leads him into the bathroom, slowly pulling his clothes off before stripping out of her own, and joining him in his massive standing shower.

She has only been in his bathroom long enough to look in the mirror, she hadn't noticed how much detail he puts into everything. Black marble tiles with veins of white running through them cover the floor and make up the shower. Black walls are broken up by a floating, dark wood vanity, the color perfectly matching the gold accents scattered all over. A row of small, matching shelves sit on either side of the two illuminated mirrors above the sink, decorated with a few small plants and trinkets. The whole room is somehow both manly and elegant.

Liz turns back, finding his soap and a washcloth, loading it up. When it gets nice and bubbly, she steps over, slowly washing the blood from his arm.

A deep, guttural groan escapes him, sending heat flooding through her body. She washes every speck of red from him before ordering him to turn around. She squeezes more soap onto her hands, using it to make him slippery enough to massage his back, not stopping until the tension in his shoulders ease.

Riley turns, his hands encasing her waist. He pulls her against him, into the warmth of the water, letting it wash over both of them. Picking up a fresh cloth, he tries to return the favor, grumbling to himself when she refuses. He doesn't mind watching the show, seeing the woman he loves cover every inch of her body in suds. He is not sure what he likes more, seeing her covered in bubbles or watching them melt off her underneath the steaming water. When they finally leave the shower, Riley guides her right back into bed.

"Oh yeah? Jumping right into bed?" Liz teases, batting her lashes at him. She lets the towel fall to the floor before crawling under the covers. Her eyes drop to his waist, the bulge growing against his towel sending a wave of arousal through her. Riley drops it, getting in next to her. Liz scoots over, resting her head on his shoulder while one leg is slung over his waist.

"You have no idea how bad I want you, but I want *you* more," he says, idling, rubbing her arm. "When he had me, these are the moments I envisioned the most. Don't get me wrong, even being tortured didn't stop me from thinking about being buried deep inside you, but picturing you back in my arms is what kept me from breaking."

"I love you," she says as she peppers his chest with feather soft kisses. "So, I need to ask. Why did you take your mask off when Matt was yelling at me? What is going to happen now? You've been so careful about not being seen without it." Liz lets the questions pour out, concerned for what removing his mask means for him.

Riley rolls to his side, propping himself up on one arm. "Do you remember what I told you? The first time I brought you to our lake?" he asks. His rich, amber eyes scan hers, watching to see if she will put it together. Her brows pinch together and she purses her lips, getting a chuckle from Riley. "I'll remind you. You said that I would make a great boyfriend if you could ever get me out of the mask long enough to find someone," he starts.

"You said that if you end up with someone it will be someone who doesn't care. They will know why you wear it and respect that," she proudly states, beaming up at him.

"Exactly, but you're leaving out the most important part. I said that person might make me feel whole again, make me feel like I can finally be myself without hiding behind it," he explains.

"Right!" Liz exclaims. "If you find a person who makes you feel that way, you would think about whether you wanted to keep wearing it or not."

"I knew from the second you started being a brat in the interrogation room that you would change everything for me. Even when I was trying to get you home to James, I couldn't stop myself from falling for you, but I never thought you could ever feel the same way. When you gave me the smallest shred of hope that you could... I knew I would give it all up to give you the world," he tells her, watching the tears pool in her eyes.

"So that's it? You're giving it up because of me?" she asks, unable to hide her sadness.

"Not because of you, *for* you, well, us. I want to build a life with you, and we can't do that if I hide behind a mask. I made the choice when he had me. If I got out of there alive, I was done with all that. My past is nothing compared to our future," he says, reaching over and cupping her cheek in his hand, pulling her face to his "And don't worry, I'll still put it on and fuck your brains out anytime, you just have to ask nice."

He kisses her, slow and gentle, like he is trying to commit the feel of her lips against his to memory. His rough, calloused hands caress her leg, leaving goosebumps in their wake. He pulls it over his waist, forcing her to move closer until her body is pressed against his. Liz deepens the kiss, parting her lips for him. Their tongues dance around each other, soft and gentle. His hand squeezes tighter, like his restraint slips the more her mouth meets his.

She clenches her thighs, trying to ease some of the tension building between her legs. A soft, breathy moan escapes her lips when she brushes against the hard length of him. He stills, letting out a moan of his own against her mouth. He rolls them back over without ever breaking their kiss. Only when he is perched on top of Liz, settled between her legs, does he dare pull away.

"Is this okay?" he asks, scanning her face for any sign of discomfort, relieved to find nothing but love shining in her deep green eyes. It's not enough. After what happened only a few days ago, he needs to know he is not pushing her too far. Eyes still locked, she smiles at him, nodding her head. He drops onto his forearms, desperate to be as close to her as their bodies will allow.

"God, you're beautiful," he says, sliding an arm under her, keeping her head cradled in his hand. The breathy sound she lets out as he eases into her has every nerve in his body lighting up. Her hands fly around his back, digging her nails into his warm skin as he moves in and out of her, a slow, methodical pace, trying to savor every second.

Liz rolls her hips, a silent plea for more. Gentle and tender is amazing, but that has never been them, and they both know that. She can feel him fighting to hold himself together. A bite of sharp pain mixes with his pleasure when she rakes her nails down his back, finally snapping the last shred of control he had.

His hand clenches, holding tight onto a fistful of her hair. His pace quickens. Harder. Faster. He releases the grip he has on her hair, reaching down to pull one of her legs up, resting it on his waist. Liz screams in pleasure, the new angle letting him get impossibly deep, hitting everything just right.

She begs him to stop. It's too much. He ignores her cries, refusing to let up when he feels her start to tighten around him. She tries to move away, needing a small reprieve before he sends her flying over the edge. The only break she gets is the second he takes to adjust himself onto his knees, hovering over her.

"Don't even think about it," he growls. His hands dig into her waist as he pulls her back, slamming her onto his cock. She throws her head back, fingers gripping the sheets so hard her knuckles turn white. Every stroke sends her spiraling toward release. Her legs begin to shake. Riley reaches between them, his thumb circling her clit in teasing strokes, and she shatters around him.

"That's it, baby, come apart for me," he says through his heavy breathing. Her legs quake. Liz arches off the bed, seeing stars. He loses it the second she obeys. He doesn't let up, fucking her until he can't any longer. His orgasm crashes through him like a storm, stealing the breath from his lungs. He collapses on top of her, trapping her beneath him. Neither one has the strength to move, instead, staying in a sweaty heap, fighting to catch their breath.

It's Liz who reluctantly moves first, wiggling her slick body out from under Riley's. She props herself up against the headboard, pulling Riley to her so his head rests in her lap. Absent-mindedly, she runs her fingers through his hair, scratching his scalp, savoring every rumbling moan he lets out. He pulls himself away, settling next to her in the quiet. They will have to go back soon, but he knows what will be waiting when they do.

"I'm sorry, princess," he says, kissing the tip of her nose when she looks up at him. "I keep giving you moments like this just to drag you back into a fight."

Her soft hand slides into his, fingers lacing together. The weight of her head rests on his shoulder. "Stop apologizing. What is happening is out of your control. I need to have these moments with you between the crazy, or I will lose it," she assures him.

He can hear it in her voice, she means it. The constant fights don't bother her as much as the lack of normalcy. If that's what she needs, sneaking off to simply exist in each other's company, then he will make it his personal mission to give that to her. He just wishes he had more to offer.

"Well, how about this... I can hear your stomach rumbling, and I know none of the guys bothered to keep the kitchen stocked. So, I say we go back to base, order a pizza, and kick Mikey out so we can get some real alone time."

"That sounds amazing. I guess I should get dressed," she says, dropping his hand from hers.

Riley throws himself back onto her lap, pinning her in place. "Change of plans. We stay here, and you never put clothes on again," he mumbles into the blanket covering her legs, giggling as she gently rakes her nails across his shoulders carefully avoiding the angry looking scars.

"Too late. You already promised me pizza," she teases, prying herself from his grasp.

He watches her with an eerie focus as she darts across the room, naked as the day she was born. Only when her own door closes does he force himself to get dressed, meeting her in the living room when he is done. He isn't left waiting long when Liz comes strolling out. When his eyes land on her, he regrets ever suggesting they leave.

Her long, flowing hair is pulled back and twisted into a claw clip with his favorite strands refusing to cooperate and framing her face instead. A loose, light-blue crop top and matching shorts, with slits on each side that reach her waist, hugs her body, paired with low-top sneakers. He wraps his arms around her, sharing one last kiss before they go outside, leaving their home behind once more.

Liz connects her phone to Riley's truck the minute she gets in, excited to show him her favorite musical. She is singing along to the first few songs while he speeds along the winding roads when his phone rings, ruining his personal concert.

"Hey, Ty. What's up?" he answers.

Liz lowers the radio, not trying to be nosy, but also needing to hear what Tyler is yelling about on the other side of the phone.

"Calm down, man. What is happening?" Riley asks. The blood drains from his face. Liz goes flying into the dash as the truck comes to a screeching halt.

"You should wear a seatbelt," Riley says, ignoring the daggers she stares at him.

He turns back to the call, staying stopped in the middle of the road. "Okay. Send everything. I'll do what I can to get it secure. Tell them not to do anything stupid. I will figure something out," he says before hanging up.

"What the hell is going on, Ry?" Liz asks. Fear grips her like a vice.

Riley turns the truck around and drives them back, going as fast as he is able without terrifying her. "Scott knows why you were in his office. He is rounding everyone up. We can't go back."

CHAPTER 26

Riley and Liz are on high alert during the short dive back to their bunker, watching for any sign of Scott's soldiers. They speed along the winding road as fast as they are able without wrapping Riley's truck around a tree, only slowing once they pull onto the dirt trail leading home.

Every horrid thought of what is happening to their friends hangs in the air as they jump out of the truck, sprinting back inside. Liz watches, her anxiety growing by the second as Riley rushes to Tyler's room, loudly trying to find what he is looking for. When he finally finds it, he runs back to where Liz is waiting for him.

Now isn't the time for questions, instead, she stays quiet, sitting herself at the table, silently supporting him while he does what he needs to do. Minutes feel like hours while Riley messes with the computer in front of him. Eventually, the tension in his shoulders ease, the computer is shut, and the small hard drive attached to it is removed.

Liz slips her hand into his, outstretched to help her from her seat. The silence is heavy as they drag their feet to the couch. Pulling her into his lap, Riley finally starts explaining.

"We were right, and I am so fucking angry that we were. It's worse than any of us thought. Before I tell you anything, I need you to be honest and let me know if you want out. This is a lot, even for me, and I won't put more on you unless you want it."

"I'm with you, my love. Whatever is happening, I will stand with you through it all," she says, placing a tender kiss on his forehead.

"I only got glimpses when I was moving everything over, but Scott is up to something. I could be wrong, but I swear I saw something about getting rid of us. All of us." His voice is solemn when he says it, leaving out what they are both thinking.

Their team isn't being held for punishment, they are being held to die.

"We need to get them out," Liz shouts, jumping up from her perch on Riley's lap. "I told them he was trying to kill you. I saw him do it. He *will* kill them, Ry."

"We will. It's not going to be easy. I usually have a whole team behind me, but it's just us now, and no offense, princess, but you're not ready for making mission plans," he says, tracking every step of her panicked pacing, cracking a smile when she halts to glare at him.

"No shit. I have been doing this for like... eight-ish months. I have been training nearly fourteen hours a day everyday since the moment you asked me to join the team. I have been watching you guys plan, and I have been brought on multiple missions to rescue your ass. I know I'm not ready, but I'm also not useless," she snaps.

"I know. I didn't mean it like that."

"I think we can handle it, but if we need a team, why not just make one?" Liz asks, picking her pacing back up. "I was at the base for weeks. I know there are plenty of people who trust and respect all of you, and I'm sure at least a few of those people also don't trust Scott. Lauren can't stand him and adores Mikey, I bet she would help."

His eyes go wide. Riley climbs over the back of the couch, scrambling into her path. His hands grip her cheeks, squeezing them until her lips pucker. Her eyes search his, wondering what brought on his sudden burst of energy.

"Remind me to kick my own ass for underestimating you," he says, tilting her head up and kissing her deeply before running to his own room, leaving Liz dumbfounded.

Down the hall, more sounds of objects being shuffled around have Liz more confused than ever. It only takes a minute for him to come striding back out, phone in hand. One she hasn't seen before.

"Wanna tell me what's going on big guy?" she asks, ignoring her heart beating wildly in her chest. He is up to something, and she is not about to let him keep it from her.

"Sometimes I forget this is the whole point of having you trained exclusively by the spec ops team. You might not be there yet, but you see things we miss. I don't know why I didn't think of calling in some favors, but I am glad you did," Riley says, punching numbers into the screen, starting his own slow, methodical pacing around the kitchen, waiting for whoever is on the other end to pick up.

"Are you at the base yet?" he asks, skipping right over the pleasantries. "Good, I need you to come to my house first," he stops for a moment, opening and closing the cabinets before he adds, "And if it's not too much trouble, can you bring some groceries? You know how Mikey is," he gives a quick thank you before hanging up and starting all over again. This time, Liz knows it's Lauren. She listens patiently while he gives a recap of what is going on, asking her to figure out who will stand with them.

When the calls are over, Riley brings a blueprint of the base up on Tyler's computer. The table is scattered with pens and notebooks. Maps of the surrounding area as well as a U.S. map are placed throughout their mess.

Liz sits, watching intently while Riley scribbles notes into one of the books, going back and forth between maps. Unsure of what he is doing, she slides her own book over and begins writing down anything she thinks could be helpful.

Riley keeps a close eye on her, never saying anything or asking what she could possibly be working on, but just seeing her putting in the work next to him makes him proud.

The whirring of the elevator lowering has Liz jumping out of her seat, knowing the ones with access are all imprisoned. Seeing Riley not budge helps. He would be faster than her if he thought for a second someone had found them. Heart thumping out of her chest, the doors finally creak open, and a much too familiar woman steps out.

Riley leaves the table, greeting the woman with a hug, sending a wave of jealousy through Liz. She forces it back, reminding herself how absurd it is to be jealous over an innocent sign of friendship. Trying not to appear too nosy, Liz continues scribbling her notes into her book. She looks over every few seconds, trying to place where she has seen the woman before.

Dark brown hair falls just past her shoulders. She's dressed in a casual, comfortable outfit, no military insignia anywhere. What used to be white, well-worn tennis shoes are paired with plain jeans and a loose-fitting blue t-shirt.

Riley drops his arms, walking the woman over to the table where Liz still sits. When she sees them walking over, she stands to greet the woman, not wanting to be rude. Shock ripples through her when the woman strides right to Liz, pulling her into a tight embrace.

Liz looks at Riley with panic in her eyes.

"It's so nice to see you not chained to a table," she says, squeezing Liz a little tighter. That statement has her remembering exactly who this woman is. Paula, the one who defended her while she was helpless in the hospital bed, then again when the general screamed at her for the first time. Liz lifts her arms, returning the hug. They drop their arms and Paula takes a step back, looking Liz up and down.

"Groceries are in the car, so you may want to get them before the cold items spoil," Paula says in a motherly tone as she turns back to Riley.

His eyes dart between the two women, lingering on Liz, a silent question of if she will be okay without him for a few minutes.

She shoots him a smile, letting him know she will be fine. He backs toward the open elevator, his eyes glued to her until the last second when the doors finally close. Paula turns to Liz when he is out of earshot, laughing to herself under her breath.

"He is still so protective of you," she says, making her way to the table and looking over the various maps and charts Riley had been working on.

"I want to say he's gotten better, but I have had to stop him from committing murder more than once since we got him back," Liz responds with a quiet laugh. "I never got to thank you for treating me like a person when I first woke up, and for defending me."

"No need to thank me, dear. I just did what any decent person should have done. Not only did those men have orders they refused to follow, but they chose to treat you like a hardened criminal while knowing you were a victim." Her gaze softens when she speaks the last part, looking at Liz like she can still see the broken woman lying chained to that hospital bed.

Paula turns back to the papers on the table when the elevator sounds again. Riley emerges, both arms filled with plastic bags bulging with food, effortlessly carrying them into the kitchen. Liz rushes to his side, urging him to continue his battle plans while she puts the groceries away and makes them all some dinner.

The aroma of sizzling garlic and chicken fills the room while Paula and Riley sit around the table talking strategy. For the first time in months, their house is starting to feel like a home again, even if half their family is missing. Liz keeps cooking, trying to hear every word they say while she dumps pasta into a pot of boiling water. She pulls the chicken from the pan, setting it aside to rest while a glob of butter is melted with more garlic. Cream and a heaping pile of parmesan cheese are added to the mix, whisking it quickly so she can join the conversation across the room. As soon as the cheese melts into a creamy alfredo sauce, she dumps the noodles in and tops it with her chicken, loading it onto three plates.

"Thanks, baby," Riley says, rubbing the small of her back as she sets a steaming plate of food in front of him, much to Paula's surprise. Liz hands her a plate and runs back to the kitchen before anyone can see just how red her face has turned.

"Baby huh? Your overprotectiveness makes more sense now," she says, smiling at Riley.

"Spend ten minutes with her and try not to fall in love," Riley says, winking at Liz as she strides back over with her own food.

"I'm not surprised. I should have seen it coming the minute she told Scott off in that room," Paula chuckles. "You look happy," she adds, reaching over to squeeze his hand. "Now, let's figure this out so we can get the rest of the family back, shall we?"

"We need to get in. I can get them out, but I need access to the base. If Scott is rounding us up, he must be planning something," he says through a mouthful of food.

Liz continues to scribble into her notebook, oblivious to Riley watching her. His curiosity peaks.

"What have you been writing?" he asks. Reaching over, he tries to slip the book from her grasp only to have it yanked away.

"It's nothing you don't know already. You haven't been back for long, and I have been on base for a while now, so I know the schedule pretty well," Liz says timidly, laying her arms on the book to cover the information, embarrassed that's all she has.

"That's smart. Things change on bases, so having the current daily schedule will be a big help," Paula says.

"These are also the people who went to save you. Alex told them that we didn't have permission and they would most likely end up in trouble when we got back, but they went anyway. I figured if anyone would be willing to help, it would be them," she says, slowly sliding her book over to Riley.

He flips back and forth between the pages, studying every inch of the schedule she has written before scanning the list of names.

"Lauren, John, Neil, Liam. Can you try and talk to them when you go tomorrow?" Riley asks Paula. "I already know Lauren is on board, but I don't know the others well enough to get in contact with them."

"I'll take care of it," Paula states, bringing her empty plate to the sink. "I can't stay, but when you have a plan in place, let me know, and I will get the info to anyone willing to help. Liz, thank you for dinner, it was delicious," she says walking over to the elevator.

"No need to thank me, it was the least I could do," Liz says.

"Riley, I'll be in touch. Make sure you get those plans done. I'm afraid you don't have a lot of time," she says before stepping in and pushing the button to close the door.

Silence lingers in the air around them while Liz makes quick work of picking up their plates and dumping them into the sink.

Leaving Riley to think, she washes every dish, dries them, and puts them back in the cabinets. Anything to keep her mind off what could be happening to her friends. When the kitchen is spotless and Liz cannot find any more menial tasks to keep her busy, she goes back to Riley's side, looking over the mountain of maps and information. Thoughts continue to race as her eyes land on the tiny square labeled "Admin". She knows that is where the jail cells are, used for any soldier who steps out of line, or a team trying to simply get their leader back.

"What do we do now?" she asks, chin resting on the top of Riley's head while her arms wrap around his shoulders.

"We wait," he responds, reaching up to rub the arms holding him tight. "Paula and Lauren will gather any help they can find, while we work out what to do once they recruit those willing to help. I promised you some alone time, and I am not breaking that promise. So, until they assemble a team and it's time to go, I plan on taking full advantage of having the house to ourselves. Crisis or not, we need to make up for lost time."

"We can't just be all lovey dovey while our friends are being held prisoner, Ry," she says, pulling her arms from him.

"Why not?" he asks. The chair slides out, forcing Liz to step back. "I can make all the plans in the world, but we need bodies, and until I know how many I have to work with, no amount of planning will mean anything. I know exactly how we're getting them out. I know the best route to take, and what we will do when they are safe. All of that means nothing when an unknown number of people are added to the equation," he says. Riley picks up her hand, leading her to the couch behind him. He lands with a muffled thud, pulling Liz down next to him. "Now, if it's not too much to ask, I would like to have one fucking night where we can forget all the shit brewing out there and just be happy."

CHAPTER 27

The days that follow seem to fly by. Riley refuses to talk about strategy, or any planning for that matter, telling Liz she will find out when the time comes. They spend their time blissfully ignoring the storm brewing outside their home, instead pretending to lead a normal, domestic life. With each hour that passes, Liz can't help but wonder if this is how incredible the rest of their life could be if they were to leave everything behind.

The thoughts swirling in her head are cut short when one of Riley's many phones begins to ring. Craning her neck from her perch on the couch, Liz desperately tries to listen to what the person on the other end is saying. The call is short, ending after just a few minutes. Tossing the phone down, Riley spreads his piles of paperwork back out across the table.

"Okay, princess, that was Paula. We have a team. Come here, we need to go over the plan," he shouts from the other side of the room. Liz scrambles off the couch, rushing to his side where he now has a map of the base laid out.

"This is it? We're going to get the boys back?" she asks, practically bouncing with excitement.

"If we can pull this off, yeah. We don't have much time; we're getting them back tonight. Lauren is going to pick us up here." He points at a skinny dirt road on a worn-out map, "She will have uniforms waiting for us. I don't think you have been on base long enough for anyone to recognize you, and only a few people have seen my face, so we go in as soldiers."

"Okay, but won't everything be super secure? How are we going to make it to the admin building?" Liz asks, eyeing the map carefully. "Better yet, if we do make it, how are we getting *into* the building?"

"Like I said, we have a small team, so we will blend in with them. Paula and Lauren have a pair about the same size as us. They are going a few miles from base while we are driving in, so guards will get a tip that a man in a mask was seen in the woods. Scott will send everyone out, and that's when we get to where they are being held. There are plenty of people ready and willing to help us from the sidelines, so all we need to focus on is getting to that building," Riley explains, moving little figures around the map like they are playing out an action movie.

"What happens after? We can't come back here. It would only stay safe for so long. Eventually we would need to leave for food or supplies," Liz asks.

"We will have a van waiting for us about ten miles out. We get the guys, get them in uniform, and get the hell out. Paula is going to keep Scott distracted and focused on our decoys while we make the trek. Ty and Alex have a cabin in Michigan. We'll go there. If anything happens, we flee across the border into Canada. Now, go pack," Riley says. As if hopping the border while on the run from a corrupt army general is no big deal.

Seeming to have everything worked out, Liz does what she is

asked and slinks back into her room to change, packing a small bag of clothes. The moment the door closes behind her, and she is truly alone, the panic claws its way out. A million questions threaten to overwhelm her.

What if they get caught before they can get to their men?

What if something has already happened to them?

What will happen to anyone who helped them?

The last question sends a wave of nausea through her. Fighting to keep the food in her stomach, Liz takes a deep breath in through her nose, slowly exhaling through her mouth, as she continues to shove necessities into her bag. A soft knock echoes in the too quiet room.

"Ready to go?" Riley asks, arms enveloping Liz from behind, gently tugging her to rest against his body.

"No," she says with a sigh. "Am I a monster for wishing we could just stay here, together, and not have to deal with all this?"

"No, princess, you're not a monster. I wish this was something we could walk away from, but it's not. I promise, when this is over, I am taking leave, and we are going to start fresh—no more trying to build a relationship on a foundation of stolen moments in the chaos," he says, leaning down. His warm breath caresses her neck with each word, sending a shiver down her spine.

"Don't tease me with promises you may not be able to keep, Ry. If it's not this, it will be something else. There are enough shitty people in this world to keep you busy for a lifetime. This is your job, and mine now, too, I guess. I just need to get used to navigating everything," she says, her voice softer, laced with a deep sorrow that kills him to hear.

"I know. Things will calm down. I didn't know this is how everything would turn out," Riley says, squeezing her a little tighter, wishing he could tell her he feels the same. There is no point in bringing it up only to crush her more than she already is.

In his excitement at her joining the team, he had agreed to a five-year contract, for the both of them. His only thought in the moment was having her by his side for the next five years, selfishly not thinking about if she would even want that.

"I think I'm good to go," she says, missing his arms around her the second he pulls them away.

Walking to the elevator, hand in hand, Riley stops, wrapping his arms around her once more. They are running out of time. He spends the precious few minutes they have left doing what he loves the most, holding Liz in his arms, their lips locked in an endless kiss. This may very well be the last time they ever set foot back in their home again Riley makes sure the last memory there is a good one.

He reluctantly pulls away, leading her out the door and into the woods behind the cabin where they begin the long hike through the mountains. The silence between them stretches on forever. They march, listening to the sounds of birds chirping and twigs cracking under their feet. Liz peers at Riley, watching him trudge through the dense trees. She wants so badly to ask if he is as nervous as she is, after all, this is his first mission after being back.

His head is on a constant swivel, watching every shadow they come across as if someone is lurking behind it, waiting to ambush. The minutes tick by, each step bringing them closer to their mission.

"Will you just ask what you want to ask already?"

Liz jumps at the sound of his booming voice, so used to the quiet of the forest. "What are you talking about?" Her eyes stay fixed on the ground in an attempt to keep from tripping over roots and fallen branches.

"You get this cute look on your face when you're thinking about something, you've done it since the day you got out, and you keep watching me. You're not subtle, love," he says, stepping closer.

"God damn it," Liz mumbles under her breath, followed by a string of grumbled words even she can't make out. The restrained tantrum coaxes a light chuckle from Riley as he nudges her arm.

"What's wrong?" he asks, too playful for the situation they are in.

"Mikey said the same thing, now I'm going to be hyper aware of any dumb thinking face I apparently make," she says, quietly storming her way through the brush. "I was just wondering if you were doing okay, but I don't want to push it or make you uncomfortable. This is your first mission since being back, and I worry about you."

"What the fuck did I do to deserve you?" His hand finds hers, lacing their fingers together like they are on a romantic stroll through the trees, not hiking through a mountain on their way to break into a military base.

"I'm fine. This isn't my first time coming back from this shit. It sucks, and I'm anxious, but I have had what, six weeks to figure my shit out. My body is healed, and my mind is getting there. I still slip into a dark place, just like you do. It takes time, but if I thought for a second I was not well enough to do this, I wouldn't."

Liz gives him a small nod of acknowledgement. A silent understanding passes between them, no judgement, just two people fighting the same fight. The tension in Riley's shoulders ease ever so slightly. Hand in hand, they continue their journey, carefully picking their way around fallen trees and massive boulders, up hills and over streams flowing freely through the towering pines.

After hours of walking, Liz finally spots a break in the trees. This is it. Soon they will be storming the base, getting their friends back by any means necessary. They are so close, yet still so far. Somewhere in the distance, a car heads in their direction. Sprinting the last hundred yards to the road, they make it just as Lauren's little blue sedan pulls up next to the tree line. Riley throws the door open, guiding Liz into the front seat before he steps into the back.

"That bag has the uniforms. Get them on," she orders, peeling off onto the road, speeding through the twists and turns of the mountain. A perfectly pressed uniform lands in Liz's lap.

"When we get to base, I can't guarantee it's going to be one of ours at the gate, so I need you to keep that temper in check—" Lauren begins.

"I don't have a temper," Riley pouts.

"Not you, her," Lauren says looking over at Liz.

Her cheeks turn a deep shade of crimson as she wiggles her way into the cargo pants, fighting to change in the small seat of the car.

"Once we are in, two men from my platoon will be waiting with a duffle, and one is going to tell Scott they spotted you two headed this way. Paula sent one of hers to commandeer the security room. As soon as we arrive, he is going to do an update, blacking out the cameras for twenty minutes. You need to get them out and as far from here as you can before that time is up."

"Whats in the bag?" Liz asks, zipping her jacket up before sliding the hat onto her head.

"Three more uniforms and standard issue guns," she replies. "You should know how bad things have gotten in the last few days. Whatever you see in there, you need to promise you will let us handle it and get the hell out."

"What do you mean bad?" Liz's stomach turns to knots. A warm hand finds her arm, rubbing slowly up and down. She focuses on that feeling instead of the thoughts running rampant in her mind.

"Liz, you need to promise me you won't stop for anything. You can't save everyone, but if you get your team out, you have a better shot at ending things for good. I saw how you were when you tried to get Riley back. Promise me," Lauren says, her eyes darting between Liz and the road.

She can't form words, her tongue feels like ash in her mouth, so she simply looks over and gives a nod.

"He's locking people up, anyone who even thinks about questioning what is happening with your team," she says. Her voice is low and solemn. "Scott is running the base under some type of fucked up martial law, at least that's what he is calling it, but those of us smart enough to see through it know he is hiding something and trying to bury it. He is using his standing with that corrupt fucking president to do whatever he can to silence us." Barely more than a whisper, she says, "He has killed three people."

An eerie silence settles over the trio as Liz and Riley take in what she just said. Three people are dead. Three people lost their lives, and three families are now mourning a loved one because of them.

Devastated, Liz opens her mouth to speak before snapping it shut. Quiet tears roll down her cheeks. The guilt grips them tight, wondering if things would have ended differently if they had been there to stop it.

Riley knows the answer to that. Scott would have done it regardless, at least with them out, there is a chance of making things right. Liz, on the other hand, is racked with guilt, thinking they could have stopped it if they never left.

"They knew about your unit, said you guys would never turn into what you're fighting. They had threatened to go above his head to any of the general majors who would listen, and he had them fucking executed," she snaps, her voice cracking with each word. Lauren's knuckles turn white from her grip on the steering wheel.

"These are the coordinates to the bunker. Do not let anyone

you don't trust with your life get their hands on them," Riley says, tucking a small scrap of paper into the cupholder between the women.

Lauren picks it up, glancing at it for a few seconds before setting it back and digging something out of the center console. A thin trail of black smoke travels into the air as the paper goes up in flames, a lighter still in Lauren's hand.

"Anyone who can get out should go there. They will be safe, at least for a little while," Riley says.

"You should go too, Ren. If he finds out you helped us, he will kill you," Liz says, pleading, knowing it is falling on deaf ears. The two may not be close, but Liz knows her well enough to know she would rather die than leave any of her soldiers at the mercy of Scott.

Her stomach turns to knots when the car rounds the corner. The base looms in the distance, like a beacon of dread and despair. She reaches between the seats, finding Riley's hand already waiting for hers. Fingers interlaced, they sit in gut wrenching silence, their eyes never leaving their destination as it grows closer by the second.

CHAPTER 28

The energy shifts as they approach the gates leading to the base. Every face of the soldiers manning the entrance is sullen like they have spent the last few days subjected to the worst humanity has to offer.

The boy at the gate can't be older than his early twenties. Deep purple bags sit under his eyes with a haunting look behind them. He can barely make eye contact with Lauren as she flashes him her I.D card. He simply glances at it and waves her in. They made it over the first hurdle.

Lauren is already on the phone ordering whoever is on the other end to get started. The call is followed by one final call, the most important one. They sit, waiting until the alarms blare through the speakers. The base erupts into complete and utter chaos, allowing them to slip out, marching straight to the other side of the base.

The pair weave through the crowds of soldiers running frantically around the base. Two men join them, slipping a bag into Riley's waiting hand before peeling off and joining another group gathering in one of the lawns scattered throughout. Liz tries to listen as they breeze by, picking up bits and pieces of their superiors barking orders, but the only information she can gather is that they are searching for her and Riley. She already knew that, though hearing it out loud has her heart dropping into the pit of her stomach.

Time is running out. Their pace picks up, jogging across the pavement, trying to count the minutes in her head, not willing to risk looking at the watch adorning her wrist. The light jog quickly turns into a sprint when the platoons surrounding them begin running the opposite direction, leaving the base to hunt for them, unknowingly opening a clear path to their destination.

Hope blooms in Liz's chest as they approach the admin building. Getting through the crowds was the easy part. Now is where the real work begins.

Riley drops the duffle onto the ground, crouching to rifle through it. Liz bounces on the balls of her feet, trying to not look as anxious as she feels. He pops back up, card in hand, winking at Liz as he taps it against the small pad on the door, pulling it open the second the light flashes green.

Bag in hand, they stride into the building now swarmed with men and women of various ranks, all scrambling to figure out the general's orders. Riley walks with confidence—he knows exactly what he is there for and where to find it.

Liz follows his lead, walking a step behind, nearly bumping into him when he stops at the stairwell. With a quick look around to make sure they haven't been spotted, they disappear behind the door. Riley signals for Liz to stop. He listens for any signs of movement, and when they are clear, they sprint down the stairs.

The air grows thick, a musty, earthy scent replacing the crisp clean air. Each flight of stairs takes them deeper underground. The lights flicker overhead the lower they go. Liz fights to hide her unease. Instead, she watches her feet, making sure she doesn't send them both tumbling down the stairs.

Riley slows, once more listening for signs of life on the other side of the landing. The thick, metal door lets out a deep groan. Riley curses, hoping the noise hasn't alerted any guards to come running. He squeezes through the opening, sliding into the narrow hallway with Liz still close behind. They silently step down the hall. The only sounds are their muffled footsteps and the eerie water drips splashing onto the floor below.

"Something feels off. Where are all the guards?" Liz whispers. Her pace quickens to catch up to Riley.

"I don't know. Keep your head on a swivel. Scott could have gone overboard and sent everyone after Lauren's guys, either that or he knows we're here, and we're about to walk into an ambush," Riley whispers back, scanning the hall.

He stops when he turns the corner. One man sits on a worn-out metal folding chair in the center of the hall, doors lining the walls on either side. The man turns to them, a tight-lipped smile tugs at his face as relief washes over him. Every muscle in Liz's body goes tense, the feeling of something wrong never fully going away.

"You don't have long," he says. Standing, he tosses Riley a ring full of keys.

"I know. Get out of here. Lauren has a safe space for you," Riley says as he drops the bag, jogging over to the first cell door.

"I appreciate that, sir, but I can't leave. My family has a house on base. My wife and boys are there," he says, watching Riley fumble with the keys.

"If you stay here, he might find out you helped. He will kill you," Liz says.

"If I leave, he will kill them instead. I was assigned to guard the prisoners, so he will know I assisted you no matter what. I will happily die if it means my family stays safe," the man says, his mouth crooked in a sad smile.

"There has to be another way. You can get to them if you go now," Liz pleads. She pulls out the first uniform and runs it to the open door, tossing it in for whoever is on the other side. She looks back at the man, face lost in thought.

"Reaper, hit me." He says it is like a stroke of genius. "Maybe he will think you ambushed me," he continues, rushing to Riley's side.

"No, get your family and leave. I'm not hitting you," he says firmly, unlocking the next door.

"I can't. He has men stationed outside the houses. He has men everywhere. It may be the only way. General Murphy has gone crazy. If he thinks I tried, and was overpowered, he may spare us," he begs.

"Dude's name is Scott Murphy? No wonder he's a dick," Liz says, stifling a laugh. Riley shoots a stern look her way. "What? It's new information to me," she replies, grabbing the next uniform from the bag.

Liz watches Riley move on, tossing the next set of clothes into the cell while he tries to find the next key. His eyebrows are pinched, a faraway look in his eyes. She can see him fighting a second battle in his head. She knows what he is thinking. He blames himself for everything going on and can't bring himself to hurt anyone else.

Liz fights her own battle when Alex emerges from his cell, fully dressed in a standard uniform, gun up and ready to fight his way out. One quick nod and he is running to the cell next to his own, no doubt trying to make it to his partner. As much as she likes him, she needs to know Mikey is okay. Too much is happening. Liz tries to tune out the soldier begging Riley for help while the keys jingle in his trembling hand.

She pushes the nagging voice out of her head that says she's being too rash and marches right up to the man. Liz spins him around and drives her fist straight into his nose. Warm blood runs down his lips. He stumbles back against the wall, both he and Riley staring at her with wide eyes laced with fear. She looks at Riley, shrugging her shoulders.

"We don't have time for a moral debate, my love. You don't want to hurt him, and I don't give a fuck. You can yell at me later," she says, swinging again, and again, apologizing after each blow.

He leans back, blood spattered on the wall next to him, dripping onto the floor, mouthing his thanks to Liz. She pulls her arm back, hitting him with as much force as she can one last time before he crumples at her feet.

She pulls him into the now empty cell Alex was occupying, dropping him onto the floor, and pulling the door closed. If that doesn't convince them he was ambushed, nothing will.

Tears spring to her eyes when she turns back, finding Mikey standing just outside the cell, stuffing his arms into the uniform. She launches herself at him, jumping into his arms and wrapping her legs around his waist. He is quick to return the hug, wrapping his large arms around her and holding tight.

Their reunion is cut short. Footsteps echo down the hall, growing closer with each step. The men surrounding her lift their guns, aiming them down the dark hall, ready to open fire on whoever steps from the shadows.

CHAPTER 29

"I wouldn't do that if I were you," a chilling voice calls from the darkness.

Riley lifts a hand like its second nature, signaling his team to wait. Matt steps closer, emerging from the shadows, his gun trained on Riley. Liz steps in front of him, knowing he is the only person Matt will fire at. She goes tumbling back as Mikey yanks her by her pack, pulling her into the center of the four men. He and Riley shift to stand in front of her, protecting her from all sides.

"That's cute, pretending to keep her safe from me when you're the real danger," he taunts.

"We're the danger? None of us tried to rape her in a dark hallway. None of us hit her when she wasn't looking—"

"Well, actually…" Liz interrupts.

"You stabbed me," Riley barks, turning to face her, a playful smile tugs on his lips.

"I was scared!" she shouts back. Hands planted firmly on her hips she glares up at him, waiting for him to back down.

Riley lets out a breath, turning back to the man staring at them like they have nine heads. Struggling to take him seriously with two black eyes and a bandaged nose, he takes a step forward, ready to do what he should have done in the hallway.

"You can still come with me, honey. They are working for Dmitri. I can make sure you stay safe. Please, listen to me," Matt pleads.

Despite everything, she almost feels for him. The pain behind his eyes is genuine. Scott has brainwashed him into thinking her team truly is the enemy. But that doesn't matter. Every second they spend underground is time they don't have. She ducks between Mikey and Riley, dodging the hands grabbing at her, marching right toward Matt. With every step she takes, his smile grows wider.

"Matt, please just let this go," she says, wiping the smile off of his face. "You're not as stupid as you're acting. Think about it: Why the fuck would they go out, risking their lives for months at a time, if they are working with him? Why would I want anything to do with any of those men if they were working for the man who assaulted and tortured me?" she asks, watching his eyes go wide at her words. "You read my file, you know what Dmitri and his men did to me, right? To my family?"

"I redacted a lot, princess. If Scott didn't tell him, he may not actually know," Riley says. Even with his weapon aimed at Riley, Matt's eyes never leave hers. He gives his head a small shake.

"He held me for months, letting his people come in and beat the shit out of me. They pinned me down while he shoved his dick into my mouth!" she seethes, tears streaming down her face. "When I fought back, they started drugging me. They tortured me every fucking day until Riley found me and got me out," Liz says, sliding her gun onto her back. She unzips her coat and pulls her shirt up, exposing her stomach and the scars that cover it.

"They *saved* me," she says, looking back at her found family.

"But Scott—" Matt starts.

"Fuck Scott! He is the reason Riley was taken, tried to hand me back over to Dmitri, and has fucking pictures of Riley covered in blood in his desk like some fucked up shrine to his pain!" she yells, pulling her phone out of her pocket and showing him the photos.

"Why do you think all this is fuckin' happening? I'll tell you, it's because we found out what he is really doing," Liz shouts. She takes a deep breath, calming the fire burning inside her. "Look, we are running out of time. He will kill us, all of us, if we don't get out of here." Her eyes drop to the gun in his hand. It quivers slightly, almost like he wants to put it down.

"He isn't going to believe you," Riley says, walking to where Liz stands, keeping his weapon drawn, ever so slowly lifting it to look down the sight. Three other sets of footsteps shuffle closer until she has two men on either side of her, guns aimed and ready. "I'm sorry, love. I know you don't want anyone else to die, even if they deserve it, but we don't have time to try any longer. We need to leave."

She spins around, all four men staring down the sight of their guns, fingers on the trigger, waiting for Riley's signal. If they kill him, that's it. It won't matter what they find, they will always be painted as the evil that killed their fellow soldier. Behind her, Matt lets out a heavy sigh.

"Follow me," Matt says.

Liz turns. Matt disappears back down the path he came from. The team exchanges glances, unsure of what to do, but knowing there is only one thing they *can* do. They round the corner to find Matt waiting, looking utterly defeated, as if he is questioning his entire existence. "I can get you outside without being seen. After that, you're on your own."

"If you do anything to hurt them, I will put a bullet in you myself," Liz says, eerily calm. Not a threat. Not something to scare him. A promise that if any more harm comes to her men, she will push past every reservation she has and remove him from this world. His only acknowledgement is a single nod before striding away, Liz following a step behind.

"I never meant to hurt you," he says, nearly a whisper.

She speeds up, not slowing until she is walking next to him. The eyes she can feel staring into her soul are not helping the nerves running rampant. Liz shoves her hand behind her back, giving the team a small thumbs up, letting them know she feels safe. At least for now.

"He said you liked that. Men who are mean and take what they want. Scott's entire team told me you flirted with a pair of his men right after they got you out, all because they chained you to a bed. Said you called them *kinky*."

"I was terrified. I tried to fight them. I still have nightmares of them holding me down, trying to chain my ankles," she says.

"For what it's worth, I am sorry. Even if you *did* like it, I never should have acted the way I did. Kink or no, I have no excuse for not hearing consent come from your mouth. And I'm sorry it took your boyfriend beating my ass to see that," he says, eyes on the floor.

"Do you know why it was so easy to fall for him? He respects me. Riley never pushed. I mean, yes, he pissed me off beyond all belief, but everything was on my terms. He didn't do anything to me without finding out if it was okay first. He didn't even come into my room without asking, knowing I needed that control. And I could always see how much it killed him if he slipped up. He cares about making me feel safe and comfortable. He gave me space when I needed it and held me when I needed that, too. Riley respected every decision I made, even if it wasn't the one he wanted," Liz says, a small smile playing on her lips as she thinks about everything Riley has done for her and how grateful she is to have him by her side.

Silence stretches between them as they navigate the dark tunnels.

"You really trust them?" Matt finally asks, leading them down a narrow side hall she hadn't seen on the way into the cells the first time.

"With every fiber of my being, and I don't think you would be asking all these questions if you didn't have some doubts about general micropenis," Liz says, inciting a small laugh from Matt.

"I started thinking something was wrong when Aunt Paula showed up. Scott has been acting weird since your team got Reaper back. He said you guys traded something for Reaper's release, that's why everyone was locked up. Then, Paula shows up demanding they be let go?" he says, more to himself than the woman walking next to him through the dimly lit corridor.

"Wait," Liz says, stopping. Her brows pinched in confusion. "I thought Scott was your uncle? Is Paula his sister or something?" Liz asks, trying to piece the puzzle together in the little time they have before running for their lives through a field of men and women who want to capture them.

"Nah," he says, shaking his head. "Ex-wife."

His hand flies up, signaling everyone to stop while he creeps around the corner, checking for lingering soldiers before he waves them on. Liz wastes no time rushing back to his side, ready to pester him with questions.

"They were married?" she squeaks out.

"For over twenty years. She left him right around the time his little spec ops unit was formed." He points over his shoulder with his thumb, pointing it at Riley who still has his gun up and aimed, ready to fire. "She said he changed. That he wasn't the man she used to know." He takes a step closer to Liz, leaning toward her to keep explaining.

That's it, Riley has given Liz enough time doing... whatever it is she is doing. Every second she walks with him is a second too long. His pace quickens, catching up to them in a few easy strides. He pushes his body between the two of them, nudging Liz as far from Matt as he can. She shoots him that death stare he loves so much, unable to stop from winking at her in response, knowing it is going to drive her nuts. A smile tugs at his lips at the sight of her rolling her eyes. He would bet good money, if it weren't for the danger the rest of their team was still in, her gun would be aimed at him.

"The exit is just ahead," Matt says before being slammed into the wall. Riley holds him in place, pulling the handgun from its holster and pressing it to Matt's temple. The three other men surround him, waiting for orders. Everything happens so fast, Liz is left standing to the side, wild eyes scanning their surroundings.

"Riley, what the fuck?" Liz seethes, trying to stay as quiet as she can given the circumstances.

"We can't leave him alive. You and I know he is going to run straight to Scott. I won't let either of us be taken again, so if I have to become a disgraced soldier to keep you safe, so fucking be it," Riley says, his eyes finding Liz's.

She checks the watch on her wrist. Less than five minutes to get out. Even if she is not completely against it, killing him will alert everyone in the vicinity, making an escape nearly impossible.

"And then what? You're going to kill everyone else who comes after us? Because, if you kill him, that is exactly what will happen. We will never be safe. We will never have a shot at a real future," she pleads, checking her watch once more. Panic grows in her chest as the seconds tick by.

"Lizard's right, man. Half the base will hear the gun shot," Mikey says.

"Lizard?" she questions. "I'll deal with you later," she says with a fire raging in her eyes, sending a chill down Mikey's spine.

"They won't hear it if I beat him to death," Riley replies, smiling down at the fear swirling on Matt's face.

"That will take time we don't have. We need to go now if we want any chance of getting out of here, Ry." Liz steps toward him, wanting to reach out and take the gun from his hand, but can't risk setting him off. Who knows what demons he is fighting in his mind right now.

"Go. I will catch up. If I'm caught, at least you will be safe," he says, face softening when he peers over to where she stands.

"No. I just got you back. I won't leave you," she says, taking that final step toward him. "I trust him. I don't think he is lying about getting us out."

Riley searches her face for any tell that she is lying to keep him from doing what every instinct is screaming at him to do. He knows the longer he fights himself the more danger they are in, yet he can't stop. He watches her check the watch again. Her brows pinch, stress and fear etched into all her stunning features. They are almost out of time. If anything happens to Liz or the rest of his team it will be his fault.

"Please."

That one word hits him like a freight train. Not the word so much as the scared voice saying it. Realizing he was further gone than he thought, he drops the gun to his side, refusing to holster it. His grip on Matt loosens. A soft hand slides into his the moment it is free. The rest of the men let out a collective sigh, knowing that, like Liz, they would have stayed with their leader had things gone sideways.

Riley signals Matt to the back of the group. To everyone's

surprise, he listens, falling back to be flanked by the other three more than willing to wipe him from existence if anything goes awry. Riley is the first to make it to the door. It groans too loud for his liking as it's pushed open, just wide enough for him to peer out.

Less soldiers than he thought gather outside, none of which seem to be remotely interested in the building they are guarding, or the people sneaking out of it. Sticking to the shadows, they move quickly, tightening into formation in the hopes that keeps the attention off of them. The looming gate leading to the surrounding woods comes into view. So close to freedom Liz can almost taste it. There is a smaller gate, about thirty feet from the main entrance for small vehicles and personnel. A handful of Paula's top men are standing guard, waiting with a fresh bag of clothes for Tyler, Alex, and Mikey.

A wheezy voice crackles through the radio attached to Matt's vest. The team slows. The voice forces Riley to a halt. He leans into Mikey, whispering something inaudible to the rest of the team. One deep, steadying breath later, and he storms to where Matt stands.

"Follow Mikey. He knows where to go," Riley orders. His eyes scan over each member of his team before settling back on Matt, glaring right back at him. Mikey, Tyler, and Alex listen, running to their meeting spot. Matt's hand flies up to his head, activating the earpiece he wears.

"Not yet, sir. I heard they turned east. I am taking my men that way now," he says, letting his hand fall back to his side. "I told you I would get you out. You don't have to trust me, but you do need to let me leave. I will keep my word and bring my men east. I assume you're not headed that way. I don't know where you're going, and I don't want to know."

"Thank you," Liz says, stepping over to him, unsure of what

else to say, she simply gives him some advice. "Keep an eye on Scott, when you realize we're right, go talk to Paula. I'm sure there is more to the divorce than she wants to let on."

With nothing more than a nod, Matt turns and takes off running, shouting orders through his radio, telling soldiers to gather on the far side of the base, allowing them time to slip away.

By the time they make it to the gate, the rest of the men are changed into their usual black tactical gear. Crouched in a circle around two deep green duffle bags, the men carefully stuff backpacks full of weapons and gear. Liz and Riley break off, stripping out of their camouflage uniforms and back into their black clothing underneath. Liz loads the borrowed clothes into one of the bags while Riley fills the last two backpacks with whatever weapons remain. Slinging both bags over his shoulders, he stands, corralling everyone into the woods. The sun is setting, so they need to get as far into the woods as they can before it goes dark.

No more than ten feet into the treeline, a sharp chirp comes from the watch on Liz's wrist. They made it with seconds to spare. Liz snatches one bag from Riley's shoulder, digging out the earpiece before slinging it onto her back. From the looks of it, Mikey, Tyler, and Alex already have theirs in while Riley fumbles to find his in the bag, stuffing it into his ear after pulling it from his pocket.

The team spreads out, falling right back into mission mode. Far enough to not be ambushed together, but close enough to see the rest of the team weaving through the trees. Mikey and Riley both instinctively sandwich Liz in the middle, staying closer than they should.

"We have a sprinter van waiting for us eight miles out. It's going to be a rough hike with a lot of people looking for us. Keep your eyes up and your guns ready," Riley's strong voice says into her ear.

The confidence in the way he leads his team sends a wave of heat rushing through her body, settling between her legs. She curses at herself, now is not the time to be turned on.

"I have the map, but it's too risky to stop and check it. If you know the direction, I snagged the compass," Tyler tells him.

"Northwest. We'll follow you until the sun is nearly gone. We go the rest of the way together," Riley says.

They march on. Their escape is no different than any other mission. Although Liz struggles to slip into the mission headspace, she keeps quiet, focusing on picking her path through the underbrush, trying not to trip over the thick roots hidden beneath. That task becomes increasingly harder as the sun continues to set, taking away what little light she has. Every so often, Riley signals for them to stop, listening to their surroundings to make sure it is just the sounds of the forest and not Scott's men catching up to them.

"It's getting dark, huddle up. We should be clear to check the map," Riley orders, stopping to sit on a fallen tree. Liz is quick to join him. Her legs already ache from the miles they walked earlier in the day.

Tyler pulls the map from his bag, along with a flashlight in case it gets too dark before he is finished. He carefully goes over every detail with the team, explaining the safest route for them to take along with the fastest, suggesting one in the middle that will take them a bit longer, but should hide their position better. Alex pulls a handful of glow sticks from his bag, handing one to each member of the team.

"Crack it when it gets dark and keep it in your pocket. We don't know who could be out here with us." He looks right at Liz, and adds, "If it's in your pocket, it will hide the glow from anyone not in our formation, but we can still see it and know where you are."

She thanks him and slides it into her pocket, planning to wait until the rest of them activate theirs before she activates hers. After only a few short minutes, they get back to it. Eight miles will take them hours to walk on easy terrain, through the woods in the dark is only going to add time.

Sticking close, they follow Tyler as he leads them through the charted path. The forest is chilling at night. The birds are quiet, animals asleep. The only sounds are the twigs snapping and leaves crunching under their boots. They walk for hours before any of them feel safe enough to lower their weapons, slinging them across their chests when the moment allows. So focused on not falling flat on her face, she doesn't notice Riley getting closer, jumping when his hand brushes hers.

"The van isn't much further. Are you doing okay?" he asks, stroking his thumb idly across the back of her hand.

"Shouldn't you be asking them how they are doing?" she asks, struggling to make out his features in the darkness.

"Yes, he should," Mikey teases, taking a step closer as he pulls out his red glow stick, letting it illuminate his face.

"They are trained for this. I also don't love them the way I love you," he says, squeezing her hand despite the various boos now filling the silence.

"Van should be at the bottom of this hill. May have to walk around a bit to find where it's parked, but if I mapped it right, we should pop out within thirty feet of it. Give or take," Tyler announces, picking up his pace.

"I'm better after hearing that, but I don't think I'll be able to move my legs for days," Liz says, practically jogging, a death grip on Riley's hand to keep her from tumbling down the hill, taking everyone out with her.

If there is one thing Tyler excels at, it's land navigation. Even after being ambushed, thrown in jail, and forced to navigate in the dark with nothing but the light of a glow stick, he still was able to get them where they needed to go.

The van was even closer than she thought it would be, a true testament to his skill. Liz can't help the tears that spring to her eyes as that beautiful van comes into view. She blames it on the fact she is going on twenty-four hours with no food or sleep and hiked nearly twenty miles through dense forest that day.

Riley forces her into the middle bench seat with Mikey, claiming no one knows his face so he is the safest one to drive. Alex and Tyler take the back seat, snuggling up like teenagers, happy to be reunited after being locked away. Riley wastes no time pulling down the dirt road, heading right to their safehouse, leaving the evil overtaking the base behind.

CHAPTER 30

Pale moonlight filters in through the darkened windows, rousing Liz. Rubbing the sleep from her eyes, she scans the van. Alex has an arm thrown over Tyler's shoulder, his head resting peacefully on Alex's chest, both of them fast asleep. Mikey snores lightly next to her, their hands still interlocked. She pries her fingers out of his, gently placing his hand onto his lap, allowing her to sneak away.

Climbing into the passenger seat with Riley, Liz urges him to pull off the road so he can get some sleep. He has deep bags under his eyes, every line in his face hardened, filled with worry. His knuckles are white from the grip he holds on the steering wheel. Without looking over, his hand finds its way to her leg, holding tight while he drives.

"Are you doing alright?" Liz asks quietly, hoping she doesn't wake anyone. "If you tell me where we are going, I can drive so you can get some rest." Only then does he look over. His features soften, but only slightly.

"I'm okay. It's pretty normal to go days without sleep on

missions. This is nothing," he says a little too sharp, trying and failing to hide his stress. "And it will be a lot harder to find us if I am driving. There are no photos of me floating around and Scott's dumb ass wouldn't be able to pick me out of a line up, so, if he does use any facial recognition surveillance, it won't do him much good," Riley explains.

"Oh," she says, watching the dark trees whirl by each time they pass under a light. The time on the clock reads 2:17 a.m. while soft rock plays from the radio. If she wasn't panicking before, she is now.

Her breathing quickens. Unable to control her thoughts, her mind rushes back all those months ago. Like tonight, Riley was driving her through the woods, same music on the radio after the base had been attacked, and they were forced to flee. The hand on her leg starts slow, methodical movements, while another feels around until it finds her arm propped on the arm rest.

Liz peeks at Mikey, still fast asleep, now sprawled out across the bench seat with one arm reaching out for her. His hand sits against her skin, thumb lazily rubbing her arm. The deep scowl plastered on Riley's face has her gently setting Mikey's hand on the floor next to him.

"What's that look for?" she demands, crossing her arms to scowl right back.

"Nothing, love," Riley responds, trying to push the annoyance from his voice. Liz isn't buying it for one second.

"No. If you are going to make faces, you are going to tell me why you're making them," she demands.

"Calm down, killer. It's nothing important, just hard to see him grab for you, dead asleep, because your mind started to drift. And now, instead of checking on you, I have to explain that I'm jealous," Riley admits.

"Wow. I didn't realize you had a problem with our friendship," she says, bringing his hand up to her lips, placing a kiss into it.

"I don't, at least, I didn't before. Something changed between you two while I was gone. I'm not taking it well. I keep worrying one of you is going to pull me aside and tell me you slept together or some other bullshit."

Liz can barely stifle the giggle fighting to escape, only made worse when Riley's brows pinch together. He takes his hand back, squeezing the steering wheel like it owes him money.

"We did. A lot actually—"

"Do you want to give me a fucking heart attack? You can't start an explanation like that," he snaps.

"It's not what you think. I was so worried about you, it took everything to keep from falling apart. Mikey was there for me, even though he was struggling, too. He forced me to eat, shower, he kept me distracted with training as much as he could. And, when I would wake up screaming, he would come in, wrapped in a blanket, and lay with me, holding me on the really bad nights." Liz plucks his hand back from the steering wheel, saving it from Riley's deadly grip.

"All I'm trying to say is, he was there for me. That man didn't leave my side the whole time you were gone. He took the protector roll you bestowed upon him very seriously. Mikey is your best friend, Ry. You should know nothing like that would ever happen between us, even if he does think you would let him be our third," she teases.

"Excuse me?" he barks, so loud Liz spins in her seat to make sure everyone is still asleep. The last thing she wants is to wake them after being imprisoned for days, especially for something so stupid.

"Oh yeah, he said all I would need to do is tell you I'm into it, and you would make it happen," she says playfully.

"Is that... is it something you think about?" he asks, watching her reaction from the corner of his eye. His stomach drops as her lips are pulled up into a smile.

"Absolutely not. I have no interest in him, and he has none in me. We just happened to have a trauma bond over losing you, so our relationship is different now, but not in a bad way. Besides, that conversation ended with him saying you would cut his dick off for even joking about it," Liz informs him. The tension eases from his shoulders, but only slightly. She wonders if he will ever be able to fully relax.

"I'm sorry. I shouldn't have stressed you out with my stupid shit. Are you doing okay?" Riley asks.

"Yeah, this night just started to feel too much like when..." Liz takes a breath, struggling to get the words out, "when he attacked the base, that's all, just some anxiety." She pulls her feet under her, wrapping both arms around the one Riley has resting on her lap.

"I'm glad you have him. Mikey clearly cares enough to know when you're slipping. Next time I get jealous, do me a favor and tell me I'm a fucking idiot," Riley says. "Now, go back to sleep."

"Hey, Ry?"

"Yeah?"

"I love you," Liz says through a yawn while she lays her head onto Riley's bicep, thankful that all his time in the gym has made her a bigger pillow.

"I love you too, princess."

By the time Liz wakes again, the sun is high overhead. She cracks her eyes open to find Riley no longer beside her but laying across the back seat. His gentle snores bring a smile to her face.

Alex and Tyler take up the seat behind her, chatting quietly to themselves while Mikey drives. Finding herself constantly watching the mirror, trying to see if Riley wakes up, Liz forces herself to lean on the window, taking in the breathtaking views they pass by.

For hours, Liz stays silent, watching the mountains they leave behind turn into stunning, rolling hills. A mix of green and golden grass covers the ground as summer turns to autumn. Maybe someday, far in the future, Riley will want to retire. They can spend the rest of their days traveling, finding what good the world has to offer.

Eventually, the hills turn to farmland. They pass fields upon fields of corn, the land seeming to stretch on forever. The farms become more spaced out, replaced by buildings the closer they get to town.

Mikey pulls into a drive through, ordering enough food to feed an entire platoon rather than a team of five. Words pour from his mouth so fast she can barely make out what he is getting, not bothering to take personal orders. He pulls up to the window, handing the young kid working a small stack of bills. One after another, Mikey hands piping hot bags of food to Liz until her feet are swimming in a sea of brown paper bags. She happily munches on stolen fries while Mikey pulls back onto the road, driving them away from town. He pulls over at a small rest area, parking at the more secluded overlook.

The men scramble from the van, stretching and groaning like old men, after being cooped up for so long. Liz climbs over to Riley, gingerly running her fingers through his silky blonde hair, coaxing him awake. Regret hits as his eyes flutter open, peering up at her while the corner of his mouth tugs into a half smile. Maybe she should have let him sleep. He hadn't slept in far longer than her. Miles and miles of hiking through the mountains before jumping right into driving for nearly ten hours.

"Good morning," Liz says as she leans down to place a kiss on the scar crossing his forehead. "Mikey stopped for food, but I can save you some if you want to just rest."

Groaning, Riley sits up, shakes his head, and pulls Liz into his arms, enjoying the quiet moment alone. She leans into him, soaking up every second with him she can before they need to step outside and face the world. An angry grumble comes from Riley's stomach, sending Liz into a fit of laughter.

The view is breathtaking when they step out of the van. Liz has spent hours silently watching the world blur by, but that was nothing compared to stopping to see it. There is a mountain range off in the distance, dotted with deep, golden trees. The valley below is filled with delicate hills and a river cutting its way through. Long, tan grass sways in the breeze as they walk hand in hand to the battered wooden picnic table. Not bothering to wait, the three men are already tearing into the food like rabid animals. Liz is perfectly happy letting them gorge themselves, assuming they were refused food while locked up. Riley, on the other hand, is not. He runs toward them with impressive speed. Laughter bubbles out of Liz at the sight of them grabbing as many bags as they can in their arms, trying to keep them from being stolen.

It's that moment, seeing the joy on their faces and the camaraderie between friends, that has her wishing they could all simply disappear. The guilt wastes no time pushing that thought out of her mind. When she makes it to them, fully prepared to fight for her meal, Alex plucks the only preserved bag from the bench beside him and hands it to her.

"Thank you," she says, smiling sweetly. They all may be a bunch of feral creatures, but at least they are trained to take care of her.

"When did you two get so chummy?" Riley asks through a mouthful of food.

"Since your dumb ass got captured. And don't act like you wouldn't throw a fit if I wasn't nice to her," Alex shoots back, only half serious.

"Hey! I thought you liked me. We bonded." She pushes her bottom lip into a fake pout.

"You're growing on me," he grumbles.

"This seems like a safe enough spot," Riley begins, looking around at the vast expanse of emptiness. "How did all this happen?"

"I was working on breaking through an encrypted file. Scott must have had someone build a system around it to alert him if anyone tampers with it. I'm good at what I do, so I was already saving a copy before they reached us. I backed everything up to my own system and wiped the hard drive before his goons managed to get the door open and get Alex into cuffs," he explains.

"What did you find?" Liz asks.

"Not much. He is doing some shady shit, that's abundantly clear, but I wasn't able to comb through the files. I wanted to make sure I had them all copied first. I've only had the chance to go through what wasn't encrypted," Tyler tells them.

"So, right now we focus on getting to Michigan. Hope you don't mind us using your house. We don't exactly have a lot of options," Riley says apologetically. "Once we reach the house, Ty, Alex, you can go through everything we have on him. Mikey and I will figure out how the hell we can take Scott out of the equation and get back to stopping Dmitri."

"There's more, man. I assume Lauren told you, but he is telling anyone who will listen that he was right about Liz. Claims the reason we were getting locked up was because she has been working with Dmitri the whole time and charmed us into joining them. He branded us all AWOL," Mikey adds, unable to look at them.

The anger simmering around the table is palpable. Peace is no longer an option. The only way Riley will see this end is with a bullet between his general's eyes.

CHAPTER 31

The house is far more charming than Liz had expected it to be. For some reason she can't explain, she had assumed they owned a run-down shack outside of town. A place to run to if things ever got too bad.

The van stops outside a beautifully maintained two story modernized farmhouse. The house has pale yellow siding with blue shutters and a wrap around porch that has her swimming with jealousy. The moment she steps inside, it becomes abundantly clear that this is not just a safehouse to them. This is a home, a real home where they can live their lives in peace, even for only a few days between missions.

Liz hopes Tyler and Alex will be granted some time off when all is said and done.

Riley leads Liz to a large bedroom on the second floor, urging her into the shower while he commandeers Mikey's bathroom. Despite her protests, she listens, not wanting to admit it's for the best.

He meets her back in the room. They don't bother unpacking, not that they have enough to even justify trying. Instead, Riley dumps both bags onto the bed, organizing the gear by what they have. Frustrated, he throws everything back in, bringing his bag downstairs where he dumps it onto the restored wooden dining table. Still not satisfied, he asks Mikey to grab the rest of their gear and bring it to them, adding what little he has to the growing pile. Carefully, they begin to organize it: weapons go on one half, gear on the other.

"How the fuck are we going to figure out what Scott is up to and remove him from his position with a handful of guns, twelve boxes of ammo, five combat knives, and all this random shit?" he yells, the events of the last few days finally getting to him.

"Chill. You know they keep a stash here. I'm sure they have plenty for us to raid," Mikey reassures him, knowing good and well it won't help at this point.

"Do you guys come here a lot?" Liz asks while stacking bundles of paracord into a neat little pile for Riley to inventory.

"We try not to. It's not nearly as secure as the bunker, and the last thing any of us want is their home getting destroyed," Riley explains, helping her organize supplies.

They work in silence for what seems like an eternity. Once everything is sorted into groups, Riley and Liz start meticulously re-packing bags, making sure each one has the same supplies placed in order of necessity. Alex and Tyler arrive back, honking until Mikey gets up with a childish groan. Acting as if he is a teenager being forced into chores, he scoots out the door, returning with a brown paper bag in each arm. Liz places a kiss on Riley's cheek, leaving him to double check his work while she helps unpack the bags. Not knowing where anything goes, and not willing to mess up their organization, she opens every cabinet, leaving them open as she tries to put the new groceries with similar items.

"Alright, boys, what's everyone want for dinner? It's been a long couple days stuck in that god forsaken van, and you could use some real food," Liz asks when the rest of the team joins them.

Strong arms wrap around her waist, pulling her back. She can almost feel the smile on Riley's lips as he rests his head on top of hers.

"We are grown men, baby. You don't need to cook," he says, "I actually had other plans for us."

"What are we doing?" Liz asks, searching the faces of her team for clues.

"You and I us, not everyone us." He releases her and is gone before she gets the chance to ask what he means.

She looks to the men for any information. The ceiling suddenly becomes the most interesting thing in the world as they go out of their way to avoid looking at her, at least until Riley returns with a blanket tucked under his arm.

Mikey breaks first, unable to keep from smiling. Riley plucks a bag from the fridge that Mikey must have brought in. Handing her the blanket, he pulls her out the sliding back door onto a patio attached to one of the most amazing yards she has ever seen.

They really had carved out their own slice of paradise. Decorative bricks make up a large patio with a pergola overhead. Under it sits a built-in grill, complete with a wine fridge and pizza oven. Opposite the grill is a large outdoor dining table. The yard turns to loosely packed trees toward the back. Off to one side, closer to the house, is a fire pit with chairs carefully placed around it. The other side has a brick path leading to a warehouse-type building with three extra-wide garage doors on the front. Riley's hand slides into hers, interlocking their fingers.

"Where are you taking me?" she asks as they walk through the mostly golden grass.

"You'll see in a minute," he tells her, pulling her faster.

The further from the house they get, the more he becomes

himself instead of the hardened leader. His shoulders drop, relaxing with each step she takes away from their responsibilities. Liz releases his hand, instead opting to loop her arm through his, smooshing their bodies together as they walk. What she sees just past the tree line has tears rolling down her cheeks. It may not be their lake, but it's as close as they will likely ever get again. The small pond sits at the beginning of an open field, with carefully planted trees surrounding half of it, separating it from the back yard. In the center is a bubbling fountain, keeping the water from becoming stagnant. Two wooden Adirondack chairs sit near the waters edge, a rowboat left upside down next to them.

"This has to be one of the cutest ponds I have ever seen," Liz squeals.

"Alex had it put in when he realized he bought thirty-five acres of land with nowhere to fish," Riley explains, leading Liz to a flat patch of grass.

He lays out the blanket and helps her get settled before he sits with the food. He pulls out one of her favorites, handing her the caesar wrap she eagerly digs into. After having nothing but fast food and gas station snacks for three days, she is dying for something not swimming in grease.

"Thank you for this. I know it can't be easy for you to put everything aside," she says.

"It's not much, but I hope it's enough to keep you from losing it," he teases, lying back on the blanket. "I know I keep saying it, but when we make it out of this, I will make time for us to get away."

"As much as I want to believe you, we both know once your name is cleared, and Scott is in jail, things will shift back to hunting down Dmitri. There is no shortage of evil in this world, and you're the best at fighting it," she says lying next to him. "Are you going to go back to the big, bad, masked Reaper when you're done with Scott?" she asks, crawling onto his chest. His arms come up around her, pinning her to his body.

"Still thinking about those masks, huh?" he says playfully.

"I mean, as far as badass military personas go, you kind of hit the jackpot, tragic backstory aside. I wouldn't do a single mission without it if I had one. Actually, scratch that, I would make the whole team wear them. If all else fails, it would scare the fuck out of Dmitri's followers."

"You sure that's the reason? You don't just want me back in it because you think it's sexy?"

"Of course I do, but it's not the *only* reason. I just happen to like them. Besides, you said if I ask nice, you would put it on and fuck me in it. You already have," she says, kissing her way down his neck. Heat pools low in her belly as she feels him press against her.

"I have a few stashed here. Keep it up, and I will go put one on and chase your ass through the woods again." That, mixed with his hands caressing her body, draws a small moan from Liz.

"You think I'm going to let you leave when you're talking like that?" she says, sitting up to take her shirt off, leaving her bare breasts on display.

She nips at his neck. One second, she is on top of Riley, the next, she is flipped onto her back with him encasing her body.

Fiery need burns in his eyes. She reaches up, fumbling to rip his shirt over his head. Riley rocks back onto his heels, taking over for her. Liz lies back, drinking in every inch of hard muscle on his chiseled body. She follows the V created by his lower abs, guiding her eyes right to what she wants.

The sight of him, straining against his pants, has her threatening to turn feral. Before he can stop her, Liz climbs onto her knees, freeing his cock from its prison. She drops her shoulders, resting on one elbow while her other hand wraps around him, giving him the perfect view of her ass in the air and her head bobbing.

Liz wastes no time pulling him into her mouth, not stopping until he hits the back of her throat. The moan that comes from Riley only stirs her need to please him. Her hand works him while she sucks greedily, forcing him further down her throat with each movement. He reaches over her, forcing her pants down around her thighs. Arm stretched over her back, he slides his hand along the curve of her ass, settling between her thighs. Riley loses all control, feeling how wet she is for him. A rough hand grips her hair, forcing her in place while his hips start moving, relentlessly fucking her throat until she is coughing, tears streaming down her face. Liz tries to stop him as he backs off after only a few minutes.

"So greedy," he teases, pushing her onto her back. "It's my turn."

He rips her pants the rest of the way down, forcing her legs apart. He doesn't allow himself time to admire how stunning she looks, naked before him under the light of the setting sun. Riley has been thinking about this since the day he was on his knees before her, rubbing her leg to find a tracker.

He buries his face between her legs, licking and sucking like it's his last meal. Her breathy moans only push him more. He slips two fingers in, joining the rhythm of his tongue. Her hips buck against him. Fingers grip his hair and refuse to let go as he draws her closer and closer to the edge. Liz screams in pleasure, writhing against him as she comes.

"God, you taste so fucking good, baby. I've been dreaming of that since the day you took my mask off."

The confession sends a new wave of heat flooding her. There is something about him admitting he was having the same thoughts she was that day. She grips a handful of hair, tugging him up. A silent plea to give her what she needs. Riley is happy to oblige, seating himself between her legs. She is more than ready for him.

A deep groan escapes as he thrusts into her. He rolls his hips, pounding into her over and over. Everything about her is too perfect. Liz is too tight, too wet, he is not going to last much longer at this rate.

She starts to clench around him, winding tighter and tighter until the pleasure is almost painful. Riley reaches down, teasing her clit until she screams, back arching off the ground. He doesn't stop slamming into her, dragging her over the edge again and again. She cries out, begging him to come until he finally gives in, finishing deep inside her.

They lie together in a sticky, sweaty mess, fighting to catch their breath while the sun continues to set around them. Riley pulls Liz into his arms, staying like that until the light is nearly gone. Liz gets up with a sigh, searching for her missing clothing. For relatively stationary sex, her pants somehow made it fifteen feet behind them. The duo redresses quickly. Grabbing the rest of their things, they head back to the house before it gets too dark.

"I love you," he says. Riley wraps his arm around her shoulder, pulling her closer to him. "Thank you for getting me out of my head."

"I love you, too, but *I* should be thanking *you*. This was your idea, not mine," Liz says, leaning on him as they walk.

"Still, you make it so easy to forget the shit going on, and I appreciate that," he says, dropping a kiss into the top of her head.

CHAPTER 32

Liz wakes to an empty bed. She takes her time getting ready for the day, not at all excited to comb through more files from the general's computer.

After the first day they arrived, Riley had their supplies organized, catalogued, and repacked. Everyday since they have been forced to help Tyler and Alex with the technical side of things, spending hours reading emails and documents. Liz didn't mind at first, but the more she reads, the more she wants to drive back to the base and slit Scott's throat. They have more than enough evidence to open an investigation, but Tyler insists most of it will be considered subjective and likely get thrown out. They need hard, concrete evidence that he is doing something highly illegal if they want any chance of taking him down. As if getting a terrorist to murder your own unit isn't enough.

The only escape she gets from the computer screen is working out and cooking for the team. Despite it not being her home, Liz has all but banned everyone from the kitchen, insisting on preparing all meals and snacks. Since it is one of the only excuses she has to stop reading the evil Scott preaches, she has made it her personal mission to ensure the team is *very* well fed.

Listening to the clacking of keys and shuffling of papers around the other side of the large open kitchen, she gets to work on making another lavish breakfast.

Turning to start the scrambled eggs, her eyes lock on Riley returning from his run. Liz will never get over the sight of him. He's wearing nothing but shorts that sit sensually low on his hips, accentuating the deep V of his lower abdomen she loves so much. Every muscle of his torso glistens from a thin layer of sweat. Veins pop from his arms, driving her absolutely mad.

Eggs splatter onto the tiles under her feet, too lost in the sight of her love to feel them slip from her hand. He winks at her as he walks by and it takes every ounce of self control she has to refrain from kicking everyone out and taking him right there on the kitchen table. He knows exactly what he is doing to her, and she has never regretted her no sex in their friends' house rule. Riley rushes from the room, laughing the whole way, leaving her a flustered mess. Liz pulls herself together, cleaning the raw egg from the floor and starting fresh.

The house quickly becomes filled with the smell of sizzling bacon and fresh blueberry muffins. Crawling out from wherever he had been hiding, Mikey makes his way into the kitchen, trying to snack on anything he can. She playfully slaps his hand with the spatula as he reaches for a slice of bacon. Quicker than she is, Mikey snatches it from her hand before she can swat him again. He holds it high over her head, taunting while she reaches for it. The fight for it ends when Alex strides in the room, Tyler trailing behind. One look at their faces and her stomach drops. Alex's jaw is clenched tight, his eyes dark with worry. Mikey returns her utensil. His features harden as he turns from her goofy friend back into a hardened soldier with a mission. Liz quickly pulls the food from the griddle, attempting to listen in on the call as she does.

"We are all here, just waiting on Riley," Alex says to the mystery person on the other end.

Liz scraps her plans for an extravagant meal, opting instead for whatever is ready. With shaky hands, she loads four plates with food and begins setting them on the table in front of the men. Mikey comes back to help, taking the last two plates for her while she makes her own before joining them. Riley comes back a moment later with a shirt on, face still dewy with sweat. Alex puts the call on speaker and slides it into the center of the table.

"The gang's all here, Paula. How are things going where you are?" Alex asks. Riley drops a kiss into the top of Liz's head before sliding into his seat next to her and starts to eat. He tries to hide his stress, but she can see it in his eyes.

"Scott has gone completely off the rails. A third of the soldiers here are locked up while anyone who fights him on it is being dragged into the mountains and not coming back," Paula admits. Her tone is low.

Liz can feel her pain and anger in each word.

"Why the fuck is no one stepping in?" Mikey demands through a mouthful of food.

"And just what do you think I am doing here?" she snaps. "I am trying to do what I can. I don't exactly have my best people with me."

"Ignore him, Paula. What else is happening?" Riley asks in his powerful commander tone.

"Are you in the files yet?" she asks.

"Working on it, why?" Tyler finally speaks up.

"He has the green light for all of this. His friend, Mr. President, has granted him permission to hunt you down and stop those opposed by any means necessary."

Silence.

Every member of their rag tag team exchanges worried glances, but no one dares talk. There are no words for what they are feeling, for what's happening. She feels sick. The food turns to ash in her mouth. Liz reaches for Riley under the table, needing to ground herself, heart breaking for every person affected by her snooping. She takes a deep breath, shoving the guilt overtaking her deep into the recess of her mind. Liz refuses to let it consume her. Not yet.

"At this point, I am doing damage control. I can help you, or I can keep people safe here. You know what I have to do," she tells them.

"Don't worry about us, just keep doing what you can for the soldiers there. Is there anything else?" Riley asks.

"Tyler, did you get the coordinates I sent you?" Paula asks, ignoring Riley's question.

"Yeah, where do they lead?" Tyler questions.

"A safehouse. You may be compromised. He has Matt digging through safehouse files looking for where you might have gone. He came to me and asked what he should do. That's still my nephew, Riley. I can't watch him get killed. But, he is buying you time. He told Scott he thinks you went south, but he can't keep that up forever. You need to leave as soon as you can," she says, almost pleading.

"I understand. Make sure he stays safe. If helping is going to get him hurt, make him stop. Call if you get anything new," Riley says before abruptly ending the call.

Liz peers over at him, heart swelling with pride. He is still so protective, even of people who don't deserve it.

"You heard her. Gear up, time to go," Riley orders, standing from the table.

CHAPTER 33

It's not long before the team stands huddled around a table in a warehouse, less of a warehouse, and more of an oversized garage. Tyler has a map of the U.S. spread out before them. She watches intently as he marks the coordinates given to him by Paula. He defines multiple paths they could take to the safehouse nestled into a rural part of West Virginia. Her nerves grow as the men begin to bicker about which path is the safest to take. She tunes them out, eyeing the bright red lines following the winding roads from where they are to where they are going. At least, she tries to until she hears her name.

Liz looks up so fast it hurts.

"She's not fucking going with you," Riley snaps, stepping around her and closer to Alex.

She looks at Tyler and Mikey who are looking at each other uncomfortably. Realizing, maybe, she should not have tuned them out, she stays quiet, waiting to hear what they are arguing about.

"Don't pull this overprotective *she's mine* bullshit right now, Ry. It was your idea to split up," Alex barks.

"Since when does splitting up mean she is going with you over me?" he asks.

Liz closes her eyes, silently begging Alex not to be stupid enough to answer that question.

"Since she is safer with us," Alex snaps back.

Liz lets out a long exhale, knowing it can only get worse from here.

"My girlfriend is safer with you? I gave my fucking life to keep her safe," Riley states.

"And look where that got you! Got both of you!" Alex shouts back. "You were captured and she spent weeks having panic attacks, knowing exactly what the fuck was happening to you."

Riley recoils as if he had been hit. Liz drifts closer to him, wrapping her arms around his waist. Riley opens his arms for her, pulling her against his side.

"Everyone makes bad calls, Alex. That's not fair," Liz snaps, defending Riley. He may have made a mistake, but she won't sit by and listen to anyone use it against him. "What is the big deal with me going with Riley?"

"I already explained this to him," Alex says, glaring daggers at Riley. His grip tightens instinctively around her. "If you are together and get caught, they will use you against him."

"And if one of us is caught, they will use that to get to the other one," Riley snaps.

Liz looks to Mikey and Tyler for backup, not realizing they snuck away at some point as the argument grew heated.

"No one is going to tell me who I am driving with, for one," Liz starts, hoping to put an end to their petty squabble. "For two, it literally does not matter, and you both are being stupid. If I go with you and we get caught, they will use me to get to Riley," she explains to Alex. "If we are together and get caught, they will use me to get you to cooperate" Liz says looking up at Riley. "Bad people will do bad things, regardless of what precautions we take. I'm sorry, Alex, but if shit goes down, I need to be with him. I would rather be taken together than be used as Riley bait again."

"Suit yourself," he grumbles, walking away to join Tyler and Mikey who quietly raid the gun safe. Riley drops his arms, snapping a photo of the map laid before them.

"I'll be right back, I have something for you," Riley says.

She watches, confused as he rushes away. Liz turns to the map, running her finger along one of the bright red lines leading to their next hideout. The thought of them splitting up has her stomach in knots. While it makes sense logistically, the last thing she wants is to not be together. Every time they are forced apart, something bad happens.

She continues eyeing the lines, a deep sadness settling into her soul as she does, knowing this very well may be the last time she sees two of her friends. She turns to watch Mikey, Tyler, and Alex load up as many weapons as they can into bags, anxiety creeping in.

Packing more weapons is a waste of time. If Scott has men on their way to look for them, they should already be on the road. Footsteps approaching from behind eases her tension, only slightly, but enough to stop thinking about everything that could go wrong.

"Put this on," Riley says, shoving something hard into her hands.

A squeal escapes her lips. She bounces on her toes looking at the mask she's holding. A skull mask like his, modified for her, sits in her hands. Large, pointed ears top it while long sharp teeth jut out of the bottom. Small metal plates adorn the sides and top, matching it perfectly to Riley's favorite mask. The smile fades from her face. She pieces the color scheme together. With a look that could kill, Liz turns to Riley and asks, "What the hell is this?"

A wide smile spreads across his face. A smile that, for the first time in a long time, reaches his eyes. Liz almost drops it right there and throws herself into his arms, just happy to see him smile again, but she holds firm. She glances at the mask again, knowing if she looks at Riley any longer, she will break.

It's the perfect mix of beautiful and terrifying, if only he hadn't painted it to look like a honey badger. The colors are muted and far darker than the animal, but the pattern is there. And, based on the look plastered on his face, she knows she is right.

"I'm sorry, princess. I hate him just as much as you do, but I can see it," he says, wrapping his muscular arms around her.

"Of all the things you could have made it look like, you just had to go with the fucking badger?" she questions.

"Love... you *are* small and scary. You have been known to try to fight men four times your size just for looking at you wrong, and you fear nothing. Even you have to admit it suits you. But, if you hate it, I can make some changes," he starts, reaching out to grab the mask back.

"Don't you dare!" she shrieks, gripping the mask to her chest like it could disappear at any moment. "This is my new favorite thing."

Her grip loosens. Liz slides the cool, carbon-fiber mask over her head, settling it perfectly on her face. The immediate confidence has her ready to take on the world.

"How do I look?" she asks, playfully striking a pose. The way Riley's eyes glide over her body sends a wave of heat flooding her veins. The sensual way he licks his lips, watching her with an almost predatory intensity causes her breath to hitch.

"I get it now," he says, stepping into her. His hands instinctively grip her hips, pulling her closer. She peers up at him. Tilting her head back, Liz lifts herself onto her tip toes, praying she has enough skin exposed to kiss him.

"Will you two cool it?" a voice like thunder calls from across the garage, followed by footsteps that match.

Liz jolts away, ripping the mask from her face before turning her anger on Alex.

"What is your issue today? I thought we were friends, but you're still being a dick," she practically yells, ignoring her guilt for being so mean.

"We are, but I'm not going to pretend I'm not pissed. Neither of you will listen to reason and only care about being together," he snaps back. Alex glares at Riley who is moving to position himself between them.

"Yet you get to be with Tyler at all times? No one ever says a fucking word about you two being inseparable, but when we want to stick together, it's a problem," Liz barks, stepping around Riley.

His hands wrap around her once more. Riley may let her fight her own battles, but it will be a cold day in hell when he lets her give into the anger and actually swing at Alex.

"Scott doesn't care about catching us! He wants Riley!" Alex shouts back. The other two men finally find their way over, looking ready to jump in if it comes to blows.

"Okay, smart guy. What's his number one way to get Riley? Me. And if I'm with him, they won't need to keep hunting. You two will still be out there fighting to end things. If I'm with you, we get caught, then they will end up with all five of us and you fucking know it. You have the willpower to leave us behind and do what needs to be done, but he won't leave me, and you know damn well that I won't leave him," she says, leaning into the muscular arms snaking their way fully around her waist, morphing from holding her back to holding her close.

"You know she's right, Alex," Tyler finally says, speaking up for the first time since they started arguing over what route to take.

Liz softens, giving him the smallest amount of grace when

Tyler slips his hand into Alex's. None of what is happening is easy on any of them. She can only assume Alex is still grappling with the switch from their confident leader, back to his position under Riley's command.

"If you get caught, I won't bail your asses out. I'm not risking everything for your mistakes again," Alex seethes, turning on his heels, and storming away.

Riley's arms tense around her. Liz can feel how much that hurt him.

"He, uh, he has a lot going on right now," Tyler says, clearly trying to smooth things over.

"He's not the only one. Maybe getting space will do him some good, but he can't keep snapping like this. We're supposed to be a team, man. It's getting harder to trust that he will have our backs when he fights every decision Ry makes," Mikey explains.

Her heart sinks into her stomach. Tensions between the guys must be worse than she picked up on if Mikey is the voice of reason.

"Let's just get going. What route does he want us to take?" Liz asks Tyler, hopeful that following Alex's preferred route for them will ease the anger simmering within him before it erupts. She misses the tight pressure around her when Riley releases her from his grip.

They scan the map again, watching Tyler point to the lowest line drawn across it. Mikey gives him a curt nod before rolling the paper back up and handing it to Tyler.

Liz watches him go to Alex, seeming to argue quietly before getting into their blacked-out SUV and driving away. She hopes Tyler is right and things will go back to normal within the group once their names are cleared. Or, at least, what she knows as normal.

Maybe he had always been like this, butting heads with Riley's every order. Both men had admitted to having a complicated relationship. Even after Alex explained some of their past, she didn't expect to find jealousy at its root.

With a deep sigh, Liz goes to their own vehicle, helping load the bags into the trunk. Standing in a silent circle, the remaining three double check their weapons before climbing in. Insisting on driving, Riley gets in the front. Liz settles in next to him while Mikey clamors into the wide back seat, ready to take on the long road ahead.

CHAPTER 34

Three hours into the grueling, eleven-hour drive, and the tension still hasn't eased from Riley's body. Not wanting to make his mood worse, Liz resists the overwhelming urge to pry and get him to talk about his feelings. That much-needed conversation will come when their thirty-three-year-old child isn't groaning in the back seat, complaining about being bored. They have taken to ignoring him, but he is relentless.

The car goes quiet. The hairs on the back of Liz's neck stand at the feeling of being watched. She glances up, making eye contact with Mikey in the rearview mirror.

Liz pinches her lips together, trying to stifle the small laugh fighting to come out at the sight of Mikey raising his brows at her like the lead heartthrob in an old movie. Giving her head a little shake, she tries going back to watching the road ahead, but that only stirs him on.

The staring doesn't stop until Liz meets his gaze. Every time she does, she is met with another childish gesture. A wink. A kiss. Waving at her under his chin like the Little Rascals, Mikey does anything he can to hold her attention. Meanwhile, she can see

Riley fighting for his life to keep quiet and let them do whatever stupid thing they are doing. That is, until her phone buzzes in her pocket.

> Hey, good lookin. When are you going to get Ry to make me a mask?

> Um, what? Since when do you want one?

> Since always. Why does he get to be the only super cool, scary mask guy? Trauma? I can be traumatized too.

> You're insane... but I did kind of tell him a whole scary masked crew would be awesome.

"What the hell are you two texting about?" Riley's booming voice scares her so much her phone goes flying. Tossed away like it was the one yelling.

Mikey's laugh fills the car. Liz watches him lie on the seat, holding his stomach from laughing so hard. She has half a mind to go back there and throw *his* phone. Liz looks at Riley. Her eyebrows pinch together while her lips purse into a perfect pouting face. She crosses her arms and slinks back into the seat. Riley shoots her a wink, smiling wide as he looks at a still doubled over Mikey.

"So, you know I'm going to cut your dick off, right?" Riley asks in his all too calm tone. The laughing ceases. Mikey shoots up from his seat, perching himself between the two front seats, an elbow resting on each. Even Liz gets a chill down her spine from the ice in his tone.

"What? Why? Over a text? Why?" Mikey whines.

Liz can't hold back her laughter at the sight of Mikey's scared, frantic eyes searching Riley's face in the mirror.

Riley, desperately trying to hold back his smile and keep his composure, doesn't help the giggles bubbling from her.

"I only told her I want a cool mask, too," Mikey states. As if that could stop Riley now that he's started messing with his friend.

"It's not about that. I've been thinking about whether I wanted to warn you or just surprise you with my knife. You're like a brother to me, Mikey, so I'm telling you first." The words fall from his lips effortlessly. If Liz didn't know better, she would think he had put real thought into doing it.

"What the hell did I do?" Mikey pleads. His head swivels between Riley and Liz, both trying to hold in their laughter.

"You know exactly what you did. I should thank you for the idea though, very creative," Riley jokes. Liz watches him, she can see the gears turning in his head. Thinking so hard, she would not be the least bit surprised if smoke started billowing from his ears.

"Did you tell him?" Mikey asks, slumping back into his seat. His arms cross firmly over his chest, only reinforcing his image of a pouting child.

"Tell me what?" Turning to Liz, Riley asks, "Is there something you need to tell me?" She can't stop the giggle fit bursting from her chest watching Mikey's face run through his emotions. Confusion, fear, then back to confusion.

"Nope. This seems like a best friends thing," she says, calming herself and turning back to the window, leaving Mikey in the trenches.

"*We* are best friends!" he pleads with Liz. It's too late. There is no way she can look him in the eye and stay serious. She is shocked her outburst hasn't given it away yet. Liz quickly realizes he must be more stressed than she thought. That almost makes her let him in on it.

Almost.

"Okay, you're freaking me out, Ry. I can't tell if you're serious or not, man," Mikey says, his tone almost pleading. Every word is laced with genuine fear.

"It depends. Were you serious when you told my wife she has never been hotter after I fucked the life out of her? How about when you said I would let you have a threesome with us if it made her happy?" Riley asks, keeping his tone calm and level.

"Do you want me to be? You kind of sound like you want me to be serious. Is this happening? Are we doing it?" Mikey asks, practically bouncing in his seat.

Liz shakes her head, fingers pinching the bridge of her nose, regretting fighting so hard to go with her two idiots over the calm, quiet ride Tyler and Alex are no doubt enjoying.

"Okay. I *was* joking but now little Mikey is gone as soon as we get to the safehouse," Riley barks.

"I'm kidding!" Mikey responds. "She's hot, but I don't think about her in that way," he starts. "I'll admit, my mind went there briefly when I saw you two fucking by the pond—"

"What?" Liz shrieks, turning to face him so fast it gives her whiplash. The van veers into the opposite lane as Riley spins looks behind him. The tires squeal as he straightens the car out. Rage settles into every line of his face.

"Oh. Did you forget about their trail cameras?" Mikey asks, too innocently. "Alex kept getting notifications from one of them. Being the good soldier that I am, I checked to make sure we were safe. Turns out, it was just you getting railed."

"Mikey!" Liz shrieks. Her hands fly up to cover her face, embarrassed they had been caught in the act.

"What? I stopped watching *almost* right away," he says.

"Almost?" Riley asks, not wanting to know the answer. His knuckles turn white from the grip he holds on the steering wheel, no doubt debating on if killing his friend is worth it this time.

Liz reaches over and grabs one of his hands, interlocking their fingers. They stay silent for a long while. Liz watches the trees turn to towns and the town turn to fields as they make their way closer to their next safehouse.

"Can I have a mask now? I'm traumatized, too," Mikey asks sheepishly.

A smile tugs at Riley's lips. Liz watches the muscles in his cheeks flex and his jaw tighten with restraint. Since Riley has been back, they have had so little time where they can just goof off like friends. No one can forget the danger chasing them at every turn, but these small moments make them remember why they are fighting so hard.

A short burst of relief hits Liz when Mikey announces there is just over an hour until they reach the safehouse. Tensions have been high since Riley spotted a car following them not long after he and Mikey switched positions. They have been on edge ever since.

Every so often, Liz will glance out a mirror or try to spot the car from the back window. Each time, it's still there. The car has been careful not to get too close. Despite their best efforts to figure out if they are being paranoid or not, they have been unable to see who is inside.

After Riley announced they were being followed, Mikey had turned off their route, taking random streets, even getting on, then off, the highway. No matter what he did, the car stayed with them.

It has been impossible to focus on the world moving around them. Liz knows they are driving through mountains and farmland, but she can't pull herself from the dread building inside. She has checked her weapons seven separate times and checked Mikey's for him as many times as he would allow.

Crawling over the seats like an animal, Liz makes sure they have a small go-bag filled with anything they may need if their drive ends in a shootout. The warm hand on her back soothes, but it's not enough this time. Thoughts run rampant in her mind. Alex had warned them. It seemed so silly at the time. Now, they are faced with the very real threat of being captured.

"Breathe, princess. We're fifteen minutes out. If they were going to attack, they've had plenty of chances to. Ty and Alex should be behind us any second," Riley says.

His soft, comforting tone makes her want to believe him, but she can't shake the feeling that things are going to turn. She turns back from watching the car to nestle into Riley's waiting arms. His hand trails up and down her arm in long, soothing strokes. Her head rests on his chest, thinking if these are their last moments before a fight, at least they are together. There is only so much worrying she can do. The bags are packed. Their weapons are loaded and ready. If their stalker tries anything, at least they won't be going down without a fight.

"Look out the window," Riley whispers in her ear. She does as she's told, and there, behind the beat-up red car trailing them, is the blacked-out SUV that matches the one she is in.

She takes a steadying breath as her eyes drift closed. It's hard not to stare out the rear window, watching the rest of her team speeding up until Liz swears they are going to ram the car between them. Just when she is about to brace for the impact, they slow down, never falling too far behind. It takes a total of four minutes before the small car turns off onto one of the many side roads. They all let out a collective sigh of relief the second it's out of sight.

The rest of the drive is spent scanning the fields and trees, waiting for a vehicle that never comes. Liz has never been happier to pull onto a bumpy backroad. Every pothole Mikey hits rattles her bones. She grips the overhead handle, teeth clicking together at each impact.

The small house comes into view after a mile or two. Not nearly as nice as Alex and Tyler's home, but the safehouse has its own charm. At least, that is what she tells herself to cope with the new environment. It looks more like a run-down hunting lodge than a safehouse.

The small, two-story house looks like it has seen better days. Thick moss clings to the logs that make up the outside, one pillar on the covered porch is snapped, causing the roof to dip and most of the green shutters are on the ground.

Falling apart or not, Liz can't wait to get inside and get back to work. They may not have been followed this time, but the general will catch up to them sooner or later. She wants to be done before he ever gets the chance.

CHAPTER 35

A throbbing pain settles deep behind Liz's eyes, the whirring of old computers doing nothing but making her headache worse. The five of them have been hovering around the table, all staring at screens for hours with no luck, the same cycle repeating over and over again.

Tyler works his magic, pulling documents out of wherever they come from and sending them to one of them. Whoever is lucky enough to get said file proceeds to go through it, reading each and every word, scanning for any scrap of information they can use against their tyrant general. Everyone seems to be on edge. Liz wonders if, like her, they are thinking of the car that had followed them, or if there is something more they are not telling her.

Still, she pushes through, reading every boring email sent her way. Liz knows exactly why she is getting the mundane ones, and it makes her want to scream. She and Tyler have never been particularly close, not in the way she is with Riley and Mikey, or even Alex, more recently. But he has always been the quiet, rational one, directing Alex's anger away from her and making sure she stays safe in his own way. Close or not, he cares for her to some extent. That thought alone keeps her jaw clenched, holding her mouth firmly shut while she reads.

Her spine cracks as she stands, stretching her arms above her head to relieve some of the tension settling deep into her back and shoulders. She needs to move.

Compared to her, the guys have had a lifetime to prepare for this type of work. Riley had explained that this isn't their first time spending weeks collecting intel, and it won't be their last.

Liz steps out onto the porch, letting the crisp night air wash away the sounds emanating from inside. Four tired, hungry, men forced to huddle around screens and read for hours on end does not make for good company. She leans on the railing, letting her head rest against the chipping wood.

The night hums around her. Crickets and tree frogs form a steady rhythm while somewhere far in the distance coyotes let out bone-chilling yelps. She listens to the sounds, letting it ground her before forcing herself back indoors.

The hairs on the back of her neck prickle, shooting her head up. Liz reaches for the gun on her leg only to be met with air. Goosebumps crawl up her arms. Squinting, she tries to focus her eyes in the dark, scanning the near pitch-black tree line. She can feel it, that eerie, unexplainable way you know you are being watched.

Something is out there, watching, waiting. Not daring to turn her back on whatever, or whoever, is hiding in the woods, Liz backs her way inside. Her eyes don't stop scanning the dense trees until the door is shut and locked. Only then does she let her panic show

"Someone's out there," she announces to the men, fighting to keep her voice steady. Her guns are being strapped on without having to think about it thanks to muscle memory. Tyler pulls up the security system as Mikey sprints down the hall, legs kicking out from under him, nearly sending him tumbling across the floor.

"I'm not seeing anything. No motion has been detected. No vehicles are around. Nothing," Tyler informs them. His eyes never leave his screen, clicking through each and every camera, looking for signs of life.

"What exactly did you see?" Riley asks while strapping his own weapons to his body. Liz sucks a sharp breath in, thinking maybe she shouldn't have said anything. They are going to think she is crazy the second she explains what happened.

"Nothing, really," she starts, wanting to scream when she sees Alex's shoulders slump. It's obvious he has all but written her off.

"I know someone is out there. You know that feeling when you're being watched? Like you can feel their eyes on you even though you can't see them? I felt that outside. I was getting air, fine one minute, freaked out the next," she explains.

Her eyes snap to Mikey as he sprints back into the room, nearly tripping on the ripped carpet. Wearing all black and one of Riley's masks, he shoves her own mask into her hands before turning to Riley and doing the same. If anyone will believe her, it's him.

"There is no one out there, Liz. We are in one of the most remote safehouses at our disposal. They may suck, but we have cameras everywhere, and no one has seen or heard anything. I think you're still just paranoid about the car from earlier. No one will blame you if you need to get some rest," Alex says.

"Don't talk to me like I'm a fucking child, Alex," Liz seethes, stepping toward him. He may not be entirely wrong with the needing sleep comment, but she will never let him know that. "Someone is out there, watching us, whether you believe me or not." A strong arm comes around her waist. His hand grips her hip, stopping her from taking another step.

"Why are we not believing her?" Mikey's voice booms next to her head. Liz looks for Riley as soon as she realizes it's Mikey's arm around her waist. She finds him leaning against the wall, arms crossed watching her. Or rather, Mikey holding her. His jaw is clenched so tight it looks as if it might break. She shoots him her best "really?" face, smiling softly when she sees his face relax.

"Because there is no one out there," Alex shoots back, climbing back into his chair at the table, clearly ready to be done with the back and forth.

"So, you already checked?" Mikey asks, slipping his borrowed mask back off his face. She can feel the shift in him. His grip tightens ever so slightly. The playful tone he had earlier is nowhere to be found.

"We don't need to check. You know as well as I do that there is no one watching us. If there was, the cameras would pick it up," Tyler says with a shake of his head, still refusing to look up from his current task.

"Why exactly can't we just go check? It will take ten minutes. Am I the only one who remembers what happened last time we didn't listen to her?" he asks, pulling the front of her sweatshirt down just enough to expose the long scar across her neck. A permanent reminder that she notices things they don't.

If they had listened to her that day, she may have never gotten her throat slit, and Riley may have never been taken.

Liz looks at Riley from the corner of her eye. His face is softer now. His eyes linger on her neck before dropping to the arm still holding her around the waist. Unable to look away, she watches him slip his mask over his face, walking to her like he forgot they aren't alone.

"And you," Mikey says, turning to Riley the moment he attempts to pull Liz from his grasp. "I thought you would be the first one out the door."

"I would have been if I wasn't fighting past the urge to break your arm for wrapping it around her like that," he says, firmly tugging Liz out of his grasp. "If they don't want to go, they can stay here. The three of us can handle a perimeter check. And what the fuck is up with the masks?"

"I thought we would look cool, and I was right," Mikey says, shrugging his shoulders as if forcing the three of them to wear matching masks is a completely normal thing. "Maybe you should give *everyone* super cool gear and not just your favorite."

Responding with a giggle, Liz slips the mask over her head, ready to face whoever is waiting on the other side of the door. She doesn't make it far. Her cheeks flush at the sight of Riley. He looks just like he did when she was rescued, the only difference is he is no longer trying to hide his attraction to her. She looks away, heading to the door before she stares for much longer.

The trio slips out into the cool night air, cautiously eyeing the forest surrounding the house. Riley signals each of them to go in separate directions. Guns drawn, they start a slow sweep of the perimeter, looking for whatever is waiting for them.

Liz bumps into Mikey at the back of the house, both of them coming up empty handed. Liz wonders to herself if Alex was right. Maybe she is just over tired and imagining things. Tail tucked between her legs, she marches back to the front of the house, ready to go in and admit she was wrong as soon as they find Riley. When they reach the porch, Liz was expecting to see him waiting. Fear claws at her when he is nowhere to be seen.

"I'm sure he's just being extra thorough. You know how Ry is," he says, slipping his pinky into hers. The minutes tick by. Sitting under the moonlight, Liz listens to the bugs singing around her, trying to convince herself Riley is fine. A twig snaps in front of them, concealed by the thick trees. Liz instinctively raises her gun, aiming it in the direction of the noise, Mikey doing the same. Ready to put a hole in whatever emerges from the dark.

She stays prepared, listening to the crunching of leaves drawing closer and closer until an all too familiar face steps into the light. Nausea churns in her belly. Standing before them is Matt, hands held up in surrender, Riley right behind with a gun pressed to the back of Matt's head.

Like a bad car accident, she can't look away. She and Mikey rush off the porch, keeping Matt at gunpoint. Her eyes remain glued to Matt, watching for even the slightest twitch while Riley holsters his weapon and uses zip ties to force Matt's wrists together.

Mikey and Liz step aside, letting Riley lead their prisoner into the house while they follow behind, weapons still aimed. Alex's eyes go wide as he jumps up from his chair when Riley shoves Matt through the door.

"I told you, dickwad!" Liz shouts, unable to help herself after their spat. Pursing her lips as five sets of eyes all turn on her, she quickly adds, "Sorry, that was too much. You're not a dickwad, but I was right, and we need to go."

"No, you don't," Matt says, finally speaking.

Riley leads him to the table, roughly shoving him down into one of the chairs. The table shakes with the force. Riley rushes to Liz's side, wrapping one arm around her shoulder and pulling his gun back out with the other. "I tried to tell your fearsome leader, my aunt sent me."

"Why the hell would she send you?" Liz snaps. Paula knows their history with her nephew. There is no way she would send him of all people.

"I'm not alone," he starts, flinching at Mikey storming toward him. "Thats not a fucking threat. Jesus Christ, just let me explain."

"Why? So, you can stall? Buy your fucking master some time?" Alex argues.

"Isn't that exactly what you're doing?" Matt shoots back.

"You have thirty seconds to talk before I put a new hole in your face," Riley says in a tone that is all Reaper.

"I see you went back to hiding," Matt says, glaring over his shoulder at Riley.

"Twenty-six seconds," Tyler says.

"Scott was going to kill your friends. Aunt Paula got them out before he could," he explains.

"If that's true, why are you here and not them?" Liz asks, refusing to say the names of anyone she considered a friend in the likely case that this is all a ploy.

"Scott knows I sent him to the wrong house. He was going to kill me, so Lauren brought me with them. I assumed you would shoot first, ask questions later, so I volunteered to go in alone so they could stay safe. On the off chance you let me live long enough to explain, I have the coordinates where the rest of the crew is waiting. I am supposed to call if I manage to stay alive," he says, letting the words out in one big rush, no doubt taking Riley's threat to heart.

"Do you believe him, Liz?" Alex asks, looking at her like she is their built-in lie detector.

"I, um, I don't know. I want to say yes. He seems genuine. And he didn't fight. But he may know he has backup coming, so compliance is all a part of his plan," she says, growing increasingly uncomfortable that their safety is resting on her shoulders. "Exactly who is with you?"

"A few people who helped you get Reaper back. Lauren, Neil, John, and Liam. Lauren also forced Maya to run with us. They were the ones in immediate danger because they are all high ranking and friends with at least one of you. I sent Aunt Paula a picture of his hit list, and she had them ready to evacuate within an hour," Matt explains.

"Stay with him. If he so much as sneezes blow what few brain cells he has out of his fucking head," Riley orders before leaving the room, typing something into his phone as he does.

They stand watch, waiting for everything to turn. Their suspensions only grow the longer nothing happens. After a minute, Riley marches back into the room, combat knife in hand, heading right for the man with his arms tied together.

Matt scrambles to his feet. Deep red blood drips down his hand from the fresh cut on his wrist thanks to Riley's not so gentle zip tie removal. Covering his wrist, he eyes every one of them like they are going to pounce at any second. With an audible sigh, Liz walks out of the room.

She returns a minute later with a small first aid kit. No need for words, the look she gives Matt has him dropping back into his chair, looking anywhere but at her. Liz makes quick work of cleaning his cut, glaring at Riley when she sees how deep he managed to make it. He shrugs, not trying to hide the half smile tugging at his lips. Riley watches her work with a quiet intensity that sets her nerves on fire.

Two butterfly stitches and a gauze wrap later, her work is done. The rest of Matt's rag tag team picks the best time to come stumbling into the house. It's almost comical. Watching a group of five soldiers barrel through a single door, falling over each other, all shouting not to kill their man, Liz can't help but smile.

Seeing everyone gathered in the small living room, even while yelling and causing a ruckus, hope swells in her chest. They have backup. Six more people to watch their backs. Six fresh sets of eyes to comb through email after email.

In less than an hour, they have gone from fighting to stay afloat to having a fighting chance. That is all she could have asked for.

CHAPTER 36

The rest of the night is spent getting the newest members of the team settled, bickering about what they are going to do with Matt. After hours of lively discussions, Lauren pulled Mikey aside, angrily whispering something to him. He refuses to tell anyone what she said, but whatever it was has him convinced to let Matt walk free.

After agreeing to a full debriefing in the morning, the team breaks up and heads to their separate rooms for some much-needed rest. Morning is going to come fast, and when it does, they all need to be prepared for what's to come.

Finally alone, Liz watches Riley get undressed with the same intensity he had for her just hours earlier. She is practically drooling when his shirt is pulled over his head. Her eyes follow the lines of his toned body down to where his sweatpants hang deliciously low on his hips. He gives her a knowing look, stalking across the room to where she waits for him.

She may have had a rule about fucking in their friends' house, but she has no such rule about doing it in a government safehouse. She lets her hands trail up the hard ridges of his abdomen, admiring each defined muscle. His hands grip her waist backing her to the bed, ready to pounce when there is a thunderous knock on the door. His eyes darken, refusing to tear them away from the woman in his grip. He pushes her onto the squeaky bed, appreciating how much it makes her bounce as she lands. Liz scrambles back, making plenty of room for him to join her. The door handle jiggles as another loud knock echoes in the room. Riley throws his head back with a groan. He storms to the door, ripping it open with enough force to utterly terrify whoever is stupid enough to interrupt.

A loud laugh escapes Liz, filling the room as she takes in the sight before her. All six foot something of Mikey, wearing a silk pajama set covered in images of cookies and tiny glasses of milk. A pillow tightly clutched in one arm and a blanket in the other. They make eye contact as he peers over Riley's shoulder, a wide smile spreading on his face. He side-steps Riley who is glaring at him like he is plotting his demise. She clutches her side, stomach muscles on fire from laughing so hard.

"What the fuck do you think you're doing?" Riley snaps. He grabs Mikey by the shoulder, pulling him back before he can climb into the bed with Liz.

"Trying to go to bed, but someone..." he says, looking Riley up and down, "is stopping me." He tries and fails to shake off the hand holding him in place, instead just shimmying his shoulders like the saddest little dance.

"Why are you in our room? Shouldn't you be bunking with Lauren?" Riley asks, voice dripping in annoyance.

"She's bunking with Maya," Mikey says, holding up one finger. "Alex and Ty are obviously together. Neil and John are sharing a room," he continues, raising a finger with each occupied room. "You two have a room. That's all the beds. Liam's on the couch and Matt's on the floor, so I'm with you, roomie," he says, playfully ducking out of his grip and swinging his muscular arm around Riley's shoulders.

"There are two cars sitting outside. Pick one," Riley orders, trying to steer him back out the door. Before he can, Mikey looks at Liz. He pushes his lower lip out and furrows his brows, giving her his absolute best sad puppy dog face. It's not the first time he has had to use it, so he knows just how well it works on her.

"It's been so long since we have had a sleep over, darlin. You won't let him make me sleep in the cold car, all alone, will you?" he asks, quivering his lip for dramatic effect.

"Come on, Ry. He's our best friend. We had sleepovers all the time while you were captured, and I know you two have had to share a bed before, it's no big deal," Liz pleads with him, trying her best not to focus on how good he looks for fear of changing her mind. She almost caves and shoves Mikey out herself when Riley crosses his arms, making his biceps pop. He drops his head, looking defeated.

Mikey jumps into the bed like a child climbing into bed with his parents. Liz scoots herself into the middle, helping Mikey make his small section of bed. Riley shuts the light off and crawls in behind her, grumbling obscenities the entire time. He pulls her close to his chest, and she lets out a happy little moan.

"So, do you think T-Rexs are really dragons, but their wings didn't turn into fossils like the rest of their bones?" Mikey quietly asks.

The exasperated sigh Riley lets out has them both giggling.

"Oh, for sure. There is no way a big bad dinosaur would have those dumb little arms. They would be useless, unless they had wings attached," Liz whispers back.

"For fucks sake, will you two go to bed?" Riley begs.

"Okay, be honest, do you think giants were real?" Liz asks, ignoring Riley's pleas for sleep.

"One million percent, yes. Who else would be able to carry those big ass swords the science guys dug up?" Mikey answers, shaking the entire bed as he rolls onto his side to face Liz. She can barely see him, only a thin trickle of moonlight illuminates the small room.

"Thank god. I don't think we could be best friends if you didn't believe in giants," Liz teases.

"I don't trust anyone who doesn't," he says, matter of factly. "Aliens. Yes or no?"

"Fuck yes. The universe is too big. You're telling me there is an infinite amount of space, with infinite planets, but somehow, we're it for life? Absolutely not," she whispers a little too passionately.

"Is this necessary?" Riley asks

"Probably. Do you believe in aliens? That's something I should have asked before falling in love with you," she announces, wiggling herself against him, savoring the warmth of his bare body pressed against her.

"Princess, if you want him to stay in here, you might not want to do that," he groans into her neck, making her rethink her choices.

"So, is that a yes?" Mikey blurts out.

Riley tightens his grip on Liz. With his bicep over the base of her ribs and his forearm up the center of her chest, he rolls her over his body until he is firmly planted between the two.

"Yes. Now sleep, both of you," he demands in a tone that is too stern to argue with.

Mikey lets out a huff from the other side of Riley. Ignoring what he said earlier, Liz nuzzles herself closer into him, letting her legs get tangled up in his before closing her eyes and letting herself drift off.

CHAPTER 37

The following morning is just as hectic as the night before. They have gone from five people, all incredibly used to living and working with each other, to eleven. The new additions are trying to figure out their place while Riley is trying to figure out how to respectfully, but firmly, let them know he is in charge.

Once the chaos that is breakfast is over with, everyone gathers around the table. Before Tyler can continue going through the general's hard drive, they need to know everything the newcomers do and fill them in on what has really been happening.

"Alright, listen up. I am going to give out this information one time, after that, it's on you to figure out. General Murphy is attempting to get rid of Nemesis. As of right now, we don't know why. What we do know is he was heavily involved in my capture, and we have evidence of him communicating with Dmitri in an attempt to get rid of me," Riley begins.

A thick file lands in the center of the table with a *thunk*. Lauren snatches it first, her face turning solemn with what she sees inside. The rest of the newcomers pass it around while Riley continues.

"During a search of his office, Liz came across those photos, along with letters the two had been sending back and forth. Liz copied his hard drive and handed it over to Tyler who has been working to break into all his encrypted files. One file tipped him off causing him to brand us as AWOL. Whatever information we have, he doesn't want to get out, and he is now doing anything he can to end our investigation. You all know just how far he is willing to go. Right now, priority number one is combing through every word that man has saved and finding anything we can use to clear our names and bring his crimes to light. Any questions?" he asks, looking at each and every one of the faces watching him, determination shining in their eyes.

They collectively shake their heads, passing the file around.

"Good. Now, Paula has told us what she can, but being in such close quarters with Scott, there were only so many phone calls she could make. We are aware of his permissions from the president and their relationship. We had our suspicions about the two when Scott helped him restructure the entire military ranking system, putting himself on top. We are also painfully aware of all the death and destruction he has caused since we left. We are all here to put an end to it. So, who wants to tell me anything we don't already know?" Riley asks, settling into the chair next to Liz.

It's Laura who takes the lead, sliding her phone across the table before beginning.

"There isn't much. I will spare you the details of just how bad it is. Paula has been doing her best to keep him in check, but she's only one person. On our way out, we saw that man going into Scott's office. None of us know who he is, but he clearly isn't one of us," she explains.

"Fuck!" Riley shouts, startling everyone gathered around. His anger gets the better of him, and he throws the phone on the table, sending it bouncing to the other side. He leans forward, resting his face in his hands.

No one speaks, letting the silence settle into their bones. Curiosity gets the better of her, Liz reaches across the table only to be met with a hand tightly gripping her wrist, trying to stop her. She glares daggers at Riley, daring him to keep her from looking. He doesn't let up. Only when she reaches with her free hand does he let her go. The blood drains from her face when she looks at the man on the screen. Her hands shake as she sets the phone back down.

"What's the big deal with this guy?" Matt asks, clearly not picking up on the tension the man's photo has caused.

Liz catches both Mikey and Riley staring at him. Each looking as if they are picturing their own ways to end his life for asking such a blatantly stupid question. Liz swallows hard, working up the courage to finally say something.

"I don't know his significance for them," she says, nodding her head to the men sitting next to her. "But that's Ivan. As far as I could tell, he is nearly as bad as Dmitri. He is one of the men who beat me nearly every day I was held prisoner. And he was the one who held me down while Dmitri tried to rape me. I don't even want to think about what he did to Ry."

A wave of nausea rips through her. Before anyone can stop her, Liz is on her feet, rushing out the door into the fresh mountain air. Pushing past the guilt of what Riley is more than likely doing to Matt, she closes her eyes and takes a deep breath. Footsteps crunch on the gravel behind her. Knowing who it is, she walks away, heading right to the tree line where she can walk a long, slow loop around the house to clear her head. She will have to apologize to him later, but right now, she can't deal with another conversation where she is looked at as nothing more than what was done to her.

"We don't have to talk, princess, but I can't leave you out here alone," Riley says, as if he could read her mind.

She slows, allowing him to catch up. He keeps his word, walking a few steps behind Liz as she circles the perimeter. On their second lap, she extends her hand back to him, smiling when she hears his steps quicken to catch up, grabbing her hand like it's a lifeline tossed across a stormy sea. It might as well be with the storm brewing inside her.

"Why does it have to be him, Ry?" she whispers, just loud enough to shatter his heart. He tugs her to a stop, wrapping his arms around her like the most comforting blanket.

"I wish I had an answer for you, love," he says into her hair.

"I know what he did to me, and all I could picture while you were gone was him doing worse to you. It makes me sick to my stomach. And now he's back, and with general fucknugget, no doubt plotting to hunt you down," she says, bringing her own arms around his waist.

"Wait, that's why you're upset? Because you think he tortured me like he did you?" Riley asks, squeezing her tighter.

"Of course that's why I'm upset. He scares the fuck out of me, but I already know what to expect, and I can handle it. But you just got away from him a few weeks ago. The thought of him coming after you again terrifies me to my core," she says resting her head on his chest, listening to the steady *thump* of his heart.

"I'm torn between a panic attack and wanting to hunt him down, chain him up, force him to tell me every single thing he did to you... and inflict every wound he gave you back onto him," she says through gritted teeth. Her head shakes against his chest from the small chuckle he lets out.

She scrambles from his arms, storming away furious that he could laugh when she is opening up. Leaves crunch behind her.

Riley grabs her from behind, pulling her to a stop against his chest. "Don't be mad," he says, leaning close to her ear. His velvety voice that close has her melting back into him. "I don't deserve you. Everything he did to you, and you're out here worried about me."

"Of course, I'm worried about you. When he had me, I thought they would give me what I wanted and just kill me eventually. It made it easy to block out everything happening. But taking someone I love? That's not something I could ignore. Death turned into a worst-case scenario instead of something I begged for every day. And now, he's back, just like fucking Dmitri. What's next? Is my brother going to come back from the dead? Am I going to have to kill him again?" she sniffles, a silent tear rolling down her cheek.

"See, that right there is why I laugh. I have never met someone who can be so sensitive and violent at the same time," he says, placing a kiss to the top of her head. "Would it make you feel better to know I didn't see him much when they had me. Dmitri made a big show of being the one to torture me."

"No, that doesn't make me feel better!" she shrieks, twisting in his arms until she is looking up into his big amber eyes. "That just makes me want to kill Dmitri more than I already do."

"Have I told you how incredibly sexy you are when you're thinking about murder?" he asks. A small smile tugs at the corner of his lips. Liz rolls her eyes, still, she can't help but smile back at him.

"Let's go before Mikey gets worried," she says. Riley gives her a small squeeze before dropping his arms. They finish their lap around the tree line, listening to the crunch of fallen leaves under their boots. Liz ignores the dread building with every step they take toward the house.

Shouts grow louder as they step onto the rickety porch. Riley's arms find their way around Liz once more, pulling her in for one last second of peace before entering the eye of the storm. She squeezes her eyes closed, taking a deep breath, and tries to get in the right mindset for whatever is happening on the other side. Something warm and rough brushes along her cheek, bringing a smile to her face instantly.

His fingers curl around her chin, tipping her face up at him before placing one, tender kiss on her lips. The moment she feels him begin smiling against her lips the dread eases. He will be right next to her, so whatever is waiting for them inside, she can handle.

The scene they step into isn't as bad as Liz had suspected it would be. The team is piled around the small round table at the back of the room. Nine voices jumble together, all shouting over each other, attempting to agree on what their next move should be.

While they bicker, Liz and Riley slide in unnoticed. They hang back, listening to what everyone has to say, attempting to figure out what they missed. When nothing makes sense, Liz trails behind as Riley makes his way to the table, clearing his throat to get the team's attention.

"What did we miss?" he asks, looking at Mikey.

"Paula called. She saw Scott leaving in the middle of the night with Ivan and a few other guys. None of the higher ups believe her. I'll give you one guess who is getting blamed for abducting a general," Mikey quickly explains.

"Awesome," Riley mutters. "Anything else?"

"The five of us are all over the news. We are blamed for orchestrating the base being attacked last year and now kidnapping. As of today, we are all domestic terrorists. She has no clue where he is, but she suggests we get out of here today," Mikey adds solemnly.

Liz fights to stay standing. Things are always at their worst when Mikey isn't his joyful, goofy self. Right now, she sees none of that in him, only the soldier he truly is.

"I didn't want to say anything until we got their intel, but here…" Tyler says, tossing a thick manila folder onto the table. Riley snatches it up, thumbing through it.

"Ty, I could fucking kiss you right now," Riley says, passing the folder to Mikey. He strides up to the table, standing tall he continues, "I think it's safe to assume you two spent the night reading through everything. Tell us what you found." Riley orders. Liz watches him, beaming with pride. Whatever they found must be big to have him stepping back into full command mode. Tyler stands, clearing his throat, and outlines everything he found buried.

"First things first, General Scott Murphy is now our biggest enemy. I have backups of every word in that folder as well as backups of the backups. It will take a few days to encrypt them myself and get them sent to everyone who may be willing to hear us out. As for what is in that folder, he has been working with Dmitri for years. Some of their oldest communications go back to right after he took over Nemesis. All these years, he has been supplying weapons to K.E.I.M. Scott was also aware of Dmitri's plan involving Liz," Tyler explains.

"What plan?" Matt blurts out, watching Liz.

"Ivan met her brother in prison, to prove himself, offered her up as bait to get to Riley. Scott knew, that's why he ordered us not to look for her. He knew Riley would take the bait and ignore his orders. Riley was never supposed to make it out, let alone make it out with her in tow. Everything has been orchestrated," he says.

"They were working together when Fort Stryker was attacked, he informed Dmitri of our plans at the grove and when they changed, told him that, too. From what we could see, the president is also in on it, although he is letting Scott take the lead to keep his hands clean. His hard drive has years of classified, heavily encrypted emails detailing how they will help Dmitri overthrow the Russian government, allowing him to take over and create a union between our two countries to become what they call, a global powerhouse," Alex chimes in.

Liz didn't think it could get worse, but every word fills her feeling more and more hopeless. She's not alone. Everyone surrounding the table is watching Tyler and Alex, keeping themselves composed, but she can see it. Small things most wouldn't notice. The way Mikey and Riley clench their jaws at the mention of Scott or Dmitri. The way Alex keeps glancing at his partner, his finger twitching like he wants to reach out and take his hand. Even their newest members can't hide their disgust. Maya has tears rimming her eyes, tears she blinks back every so often, refusing to let them fall. Matt has begun pacing back and forth, brows knit in anger.

"In more than one letter, Scott bragged to Dmitri about blowing up the building, claiming if Liz didn't attack, he could have taken them both out that day. Everything will be put in a folder, and I will make enough copies for each of you. I suggest you read it thoroughly and learn everything we are up against," Tyler finishes, settling back into his seat.

"Thanks, Ty. Is there anything else? Any information that has not been said we should know? Now that we have physical evidence, we are in the home stretch. If you know anything that may be helpful, speak up," Riley orders. When no one does, he continues. "Now, anyone not a main member of Nemesis, go gear up and begin loading the cars," Riley orders. When the table clears, Liz slips into an empty chair next to Mikey. She wraps her pinky around his, refusing to let go.

"What's the next best safehouse?" Alex asks. He pulls out their map speckled with little red dots all over the country Liz never noticed before.

"It doesn't matter," Matt says cynically from behind them. He marches to the table, sliding in next to Tyler, unsurprisingly choosing the furthest seat from Liz.

"And why not?" Mikey responds.

"Because he is sending everyone who is afraid of him out looking for you. Every single safehouse is being searched. It's only a matter of time before we end up at the wrong place at the wrong time," he explains, locking eyes with Riley.

"So, what are you suggesting? We stay at the fucking four seasons?" Riley snarks back.

"No, sir. I shouldn't have said anything. I'm sure you were already worried about him finding us wherever we go," Matt responds timidly.

Liz almost feels bad for him. He may have done awful things, but he is showing remorse and trying to right his wrongs. That's more than most people would do.

"What if we had somewhere to go that isn't on his radar? Would he still be able to find us?" Liz asks quietly, looking only at Riley. She lets the rest of the team fade away before she loses her nerve. "I mean, he can find us no matter where we go, but it would be a whole hell of a lot harder."Riley says, eyeing her. "Why? Do you know a place?"

CHAPTER 38

None of the team knew what they were walking into when Liz told them she has a place where they could stay. Driving down a secluded back road that hasn't been maintained for years was the last thing Riley thought they would be doing.

The long dirt road has towering maple trees lining either side. Each one covered in leaves making up nearly every color of a sunset. He stays quiet, steering them down the road until it opens into a large clearing with a house sitting right in the middle. It looks like something plucked right out of a fairy tale. Long grasses surrounding the house blow about in the wind. To the right looks like what used to be a vegetable garden and the left has a small barn with an overgrown pasture. The whole patch of land resembles a serene postcard you could buy at any small-town store.

He parks in front of the house, taking it all in as he climbs out. It's bigger than it looks from the road. A patchwork of grey and white stones make up the face of the house with a towering arched doorway and a single arched window on either side, framed by wood so dark it is nearly black.

Deep green ivy snakes up the stonework, settling all over the rich grey slate roof. Riley hadn't thought about what kind of house he would give her when they finally got away, but seeing the house in front of him, it's easy to picture: Liz in the milkmaid dress he loves so much, tending to the garden while he carries the heavy baskets filled with fresh vegetables, their dogs bouncing happily alongside them, stealing bites right from the plants. At the end of a long day they can sit on the porch, watching the sunset. Peaceful. Serene. Everything she should have had.

Riley watches her get out, looking up at the house. It's clear something about this place holds a deep sadness, beautiful as it is. It's in the way she has carried herself since they got close. Less confident, trying to be as small as she can rather than commanding the room. The moment she shrank back into herself, he wanted to know what was causing it, but the pain swirling in her eyes made him stop. He refuses to make it worse by getting her to talk about it.

The guys notice it, too. It's been all of five minutes and each one has looked at him like he should have all the answers. God, he wishes that were true. At least then he would be able to pull her from whatever dark part of her mind she has retreated to.

"You okay, love?" Riley asks, walking over to where Liz is frozen, staring up at the house. She shakes her head, not in answer, but like she can physically shake off whatever thoughts are plaguing her, only adding to his worry. Remaining silent, they lock eyes. What he sees in her has his heart shattering into a million pieces. Liz makes her way to the door, digging around the bushes until she finds an old key. Forcing it into the lock, she twists hard, shoving the door open with a groan. Her head drops to the ground, rushing back to the SUV to grab as many bags as she can carry. Riley follows suit, sticking as close to her as he is able, refusing to let her out of his sight until he knows what she is thinking.

All his questions are answered when he steps into the house. Right inside the doorway is a staircase with a room to the side of it. The rest of the space is a large living room. He steps further in, dropping the bags on the floor. Past the living room is the dining area, and beside that is the kitchen. Everything is immaculately decorated. A mix of cottage core and modern. A large sectional sits in the living room, dividing it from the dining and kitchen areas, making each one feel open while maintaining their own space. There is a fireplace on the far wall and, hanging over the fireplace, is a large canvas threatening to send him over the edge. He can't look away from Liz in a white wedding gown, perfectly posed with who can only be her late husband. They are looking into each other's eyes while a little girl with eyes matching Liz's throws flowers above her head in front of them. Even as a painting, he can see the love and admiration on their faces. Drawn to it, he goes to the mantle, looking at each and every photo lined along the deep brown wood.

Wedding photos, a child's birthday, a man holding hands with a child walking toward a sunset. The most tragic array of love he has ever seen. He has half a mind to pack the car back up and get her as far from here as he can. The only thing stopping him is knowing she will fight to stay, insisting it's their best shot at safety.

Riley rushes from the room before he changes his mind, helping with the rest of the bags. He makes it back to the car in time to hear Liz telling Tyler about an old generator out back, asking to see if he can get it started. Her eyes flick to him for just a second, looking anywhere but Riley.

"Princess, why didn't you tell me?" he asks as soon as Tyler leaves.

"Don't," Liz orders, handing him the last two bags.

He follows her back inside, watching as her eyes drop the moment they make it through the door. Riley wonders if it's to keep from having to see her former life, the life she should be living, or to avoid all the looks of pity she is getting from the team.

"There should be plenty of room," Liz starts as she walks into a small closet built under the stairs, tossing out bags of fresh linens that had been vacuumed flat. "There is a room here," she says, pushing open the door at the bottom of the stairs, then climbing up.

The top floor is just a hallway with doors lining either side, most already open to reveal bedrooms and a bathroom. The walls between them are covered in family photos. She shows each pair that bunked together at the last house to their rooms, apologizing for not having something better, leaving them to get settled.

Footsteps come thundering through the house before Mikey appears behind him, huffing and puffing for breath. Ignoring him, Liz pushes open the last door to reveal the main bedroom and the king size bed sitting in the middle of it.

He wants to reach out to her, hold her, do anything to stop the cracking in her voice as she tells them that's where they will sleep.

Tears roll down her cheeks. Liz pushes past them, nearly tripping down the stairs and running outside. Riley stays a few steps behind, giving her as much space as he can allow himself while making sure she is safe. She slows after she makes it away from the house. He keeps watch, eyes never leaving her as she cuts through the long golden grass, billowing in the breeze. When she gets to the barn, he stops.

Five minutes. That is all the time he can stomach being away from her in this state. In five minutes, he will go talk to her, and if she truly needs more time, he will respect that.

It's the longest five minutes of his life, sitting outside, listening to her gut-wrenching sobs and shuddering breaths.

The smell of old hay hits him when he walks inside. Riley climbs the half rotten ladder to the second story, finding Liz sitting at the open hay door with her knees pulled to her chest. Slowly, he makes his way over and drops to her side, pulling her into his arms. The crying only gets worse, bringing him right back to that night she finally confided in them about her family.

Riley does the only thing he knows to do. His arms hold her tight. One hand gently rubs circles on her back while she lets everything out.

"I'm sorry," she sniffles into his chest, trying to snuggle closer.

"What could you possibly be apologizing for?" he asks, tightening his grip, struggling to understand.

"For crying over them... again. All I have done lately is become an emotional mess," she confesses.

"Don't ever apologize for having emotions. Especially now. If I knew this is where you were taking us, I never would have agreed. I would rather we all sleep in the car then see you hurt like this," he says, placing gentle kisses on the top of her head. Holding her in the silence, he watches the sun start to lower in front of them.

"Please talk to me," he says, those magic words always being her undoing. He can't stand knowing the only woman he has ever loved is hurting so much.

"He bought it for us," Liz starts, adjusting in Riley's arms so her back is against his chest, and her head can rest comfortably on his shoulder. "We always wanted a place away from everything. He found this cute house that was falling apart and surprised me with it. We worked nearly every day to build it into our forever home. It was so close, too. I started decorating and had new furniture delivered. There were a few more things we wanted to do before officially moving in. Then, they were gone."

His grip tightens, wrapping his hand around her wrist while her other hand idly traces one of his scars. Speechless. What is he supposed to say to her confession? What could he possibly say to make any of the situation better? Nothing. He knows there is nothing that can be done, and trying to make it better almost feels as if he would be minimizing her feelings and the weight of what she has endured.

"I thought I would be okay. It's been years since they died. I should have told you this is where we were going," she says, fighting back a fresh wave of tears.

"Love... please tell me this is not the first time you have come here since you lost them," he says, dreading the answer he knows she is about to give.

"We had nowhere else to go, Ry. Tyler may have gotten everything he was looking for, but you still need time to figure out what's next. You can't do that bouncing from one house to another, always looking over your shoulder, making sure Scott hasn't found us. I knew coming here would be safe and give you the time you need. And yeah, I never thought I would end up back here, and it fucking sucks, but I am a big girl and I will be fine as long as everyone is safe," she says with a sigh, finding a new scar to trace every now and again.

"I wish you told me. I never would have agreed to come here, not if I knew you had never gotten the chance to grieve this place, and the life your family should have had here," he says, eyes locked on the sun just starting to dip behind the mountains.

"You guys *are* my family," she says, following his eyes to the setting sun, trying to find the beauty in such a dark place.

"So, this is what you wanted huh? A calm, peaceful life, far away from the chaos outside? I really fucked up dragging you into my world," he says, settling further against a hard bale of hay, adjusting both of them so they can watch the sunset together.

"It is. Things were so hard for so long. I just wanted something simple with the most important people in my life. Somewhere safe, with everything we needed. It could still be that. Different, but someday, maybe we could make it something to be proud of again," she says, nuzzling into him.

"You would want to come back here? For good?" Riley asks, trying to hide the worry in his tone.

"For me? No, I will never live here again. There are too many memories. Too many ghosts haunting me here. But we both care about our team too much, and you know better than anyone that your own people can't be trusted. Maybe we can make it into an actual safehouse, kind of like the bunker. Someday, far in the future, when I can stomach being here." Liz raises his hand to her mouth, placing a tiny kiss on each scar.

"As soon as this is over, I'm taking you away from all of this, baby," Riley whispers in her ear. "I should have done it sooner. Fuck, I never should have asked you to sign those papers. I was so fucking selfish trying to buy myself more time with you. If I could go back and do it all again, I would have told you how I felt on that mountain top, and we could have a normal life right now. You wouldn't be on the run, you wouldn't be back here, forced to face your past before you're ready. You could be relatively happy," he confesses.

"Stop blaming yourself, Riley. I knew what I was getting myself into. Sure, I didn't know how bad it would be, but I knew I would not be going back to a normal life and that's okay. We have already talked about this. Do I still want that someday? Of course I do, now that I have you. But for now, and years to come this is our life, and that is okay. As long as I'm by your side I *am* happy, even if it doesn't seem that way right now," Liz says, wiggling her way out of his arms so she can turn to face him. "I told you, I may not like it, but I would never ask you to give up something you have worked your whole life building just so I can play wife again."

"Have you stopped to consider that I want that life, too? The one where we spend our days doing chores, playing with our dogs, cooking, then curling up on the couch to watch one of those trash TV shows you love so much. I want that just as much as you do. This is all new to me. I was so young when I was taken the first time. I never got the chance to experience falling in love and having a life outside of the military. I enlisted on my eighteenth birthday and worked my ass off to climb through the ranks. Figured I would get to a position where I could provide for a family, *then* think about settling down," he says with a sad sigh. "Obviously, shit happened, and that plan went out the fuckin' window. I stopped thinking I could ever have that. I knew no one could love me after I became Reaper. Then you went and stabbed me and changed everything," he says, watching her tears well up, rimming her emerald-green eyes, shimmering in the light of the setting sun.

He holds his arms open, silently pleading with Liz to snuggle back into him. He lets out a breath of relief when she does, holding her tight while the world fades into darkness around them.

CHAPTER 39

Liz is swept into a too tight hug, lifting her clean off the ground the moment she steps foot back into the house. She wraps her arms around Mikey's neck, hugging him back just as fiercely. She watches Riley try to pay them no mind, instead walking right to where the rest of the team is huddled around the fireplace. But she doesn't miss the way he glances back at her. The fireplace that now has every old photo of her past life turned around. Her grip tightens around Mikey's neck, grateful to have him in her life.

"Thank you," she whispers in his ear before letting him go.

"Next time, tell us what's going on, darlin. You had me worried when you started shutting down. Even Tyler was asking if you were okay when he went to tinker with the generator," he says, swinging his arm around her shoulders and guiding her to the group.

To her surprise, Matt moves from the couch onto the floor, making enough space for her to settle in between Mikey and Riley. Mikey grabs two MREs off the table, handing her one before he prepares his own. Liz sits back, silently listening to the chatter. Her heart swells at the sight. It may not be what it should have been, but to see family gathered in the space she thought would be lost forever gives her a tiny spark of hope.

"We are safe, for now. It will be harder to be found, but not impossible, so only use the devices Tyler has provided for you. We will be living off MREs and whatever food was packed when we left the last house. We now have everything needed to clear our names and keep the rest of yours from joining the treason list. Tyler has sent what he has to every single person who may be able to help us. We are no longer on the run, now we are on the hunt," Riley says with so much confidence it sends a chill down Liz's spine. She watches in admiration as he rallies the team, preparing them for the biggest fight of their life.

"We know Scott's motivations. We know what he is doing, and who he is doing it with. And, we know what will happen if we fail, so failure is not an option. If you have anything to say, any intel you have been keeping, any ideas or plans, now is the time to speak up," he says, eyes locked on Matt, nervously looking around the group following their leader's eyes to him.

"Why can't we just wait it out here?" Maya timidly asks. Her mousy voice is a shock to Liz, never having spoken to her before. She assumed anyone Lauren brought along would be just as powerful and confident as she is.

"Because that's not our job. Our job is to stop the bad guys, no matter where they are from. We cannot rely on others to solve our problems. There will never be a guarantee that our intel isn't intercepted, or that it will even matter if it *does* reach the right hands," Lauren carefully explains.

"I'm sorry. I just thought with all the proof, the people you sent it to would just kind of, handle it," Maya says, shrinking back into herself.

"No need to apologize. You are barely out of basic. You have never experienced anything like this before. Ask as many questions as you need, and we will try to explain the best we can," Riley says, his eyes softening when he looks at the girl.

Liz's heart does the same, melting at the man she loves being so gentle with the new recruit who shouldn't even be there.

"I say we go back to Montana, meet up with Paula... wait, what rank is she? Why can't she get this handled now that all the intel is in her hands?" Neil asks, looking around for answers.

"No one really knows. It's been kept under wraps my whole life. She doesn't have the same authority as most of the commanding officers, but she has clearance just as high, probably higher. The whole family used to joke that she was an internal spy sent in to investigate reports on higher ups. After all this shit, it doesn't feel like a joke anymore," Matt explains.

"Doesn't matter her rank. Who knows how many Scott supporters are crawling around that base right now. The second we step foot back there, we will face someone trying to detain us, or worse," Mikey says, digging into his food.

"We need to find him, that's the fastest way to end this. Wherever he ran off to, it's obviously with Dmitri. If we can find where he is clearly *not* being held hostage, that should be enough to prove we didn't kidnap the dumb ass. Then, once we know where he is, we find him and kill him. Easy peasy," Liz finally says, fumbling with the package of her food in an attempt to avoid smirks from half the team.

"As good as that sounds, love, finding him would be a mission in itself. We have no satellites, no tracking, no military equipment to use," Riley says.

"Great. Finally have what the information we need, and we still have no way of fixing everything that bastard caused," Alex snaps.

"Is there seriously no one in the entire military who wants to see him gone just as much as we do?" Liz asks.

She tries to fight off the bad thoughts creeping in. The voices fade to a muffled static while she falls into her own head. Every step forward and they are shoved ten steps back. They have been on the run for weeks at this point, fighting just to stay alive and out of prison. They haven't even begun the real fight, and just when she thought they could get ahead, life pulls them back.

A warm, rough hand wraps around hers, interlocking their pinky fingers. She takes a deep breath, then another, silently begging her heart rate to slow. Liz tips her head back, letting her eyes closed as she mentally fights with herself.

Yes, they are currently in a bad position, with seemingly no way out, but she has been in that position before. When she was, Riley came to save her, and since that day, he has always figured things out. He will do it again, even if it takes more time.

"Alright, kid, you're up. You've been kissing the general's ass for years, and he roped you in on this whole situation. You can't tell me he never told you who has it out for him," Riley says, turning to face Matt whose eyes dart around the circle of people like a wild animal being cornered.

"I don't know what to tell you. He was pretty convinced, or at least acted like he has no enemies. Besides you, I mean," Matt explains, twirling the spork from his MRE. "I could give you the names of a hundred people he didn't trust, but none felt the same about him,"

"There was really no one? You never overheard a phone call? Saw an email you weren't supposed to? He never freaked out about anyone? I haven't known him long and even I know that seems out of character for him," Liz says, trying to hide the annoyance on her face and make him feel comfortable to keep going.

"I mean, he hates Aunt Paula for obvious reasons, and the guy she started dating after they divorced, General Langford, or something like that, but again, that's for personal reasons," Matt tells the group. His cheeks flush a deep shade of pink and Liz can only feel bad for him having to talk about his family's personal problems with a group he barely knows. She knows better than anyone how raw that makes you.

"Look, guys, I'll admit, I fucked up following him blindly the way I did. I know that and if I had any real information to give you, you would have it already, but I don't," Matt says.

"Wait. Who did Paula date?" Riley asks, his eyes narrow on Matt. Liz looks between the two of them, hoping things don't take a turn.

"Langford, I think," he says

"Russell Langford?" Riley pushes

"Yes, sir," Matt says with a shaky voice. He drums his fingers against the dark oak coffee table , creating a steady rhythm. She watches him, making a mental note of all his nervous tics. Not the same ones he had when he was lying to them.

"Fuck, why didn't I think of that. Nice job, kid," Riley says. Liz joins the rest of the team in sharing confused glances, waiting for Riley to elaborate. No one dares talk. Not even Mikey has anything to say. They all wait, nibbling their now cold meals. "Again, anyone not in Nemesis, go get some rest. You will be briefed in the morning," he orders.

The new members continue to exchange glances. Lauren looks to Mikey for any type of answer. He simply shrugs his shoulders and blows her a kiss before she gets up and heads upstairs. Neil, John, and Liam follow close behind after cleaning up after themselves. Riley looks around at who's left. Tyler and Alex take up one half of the L-shaped couch, while he, Liz, and Mikey take up the other. Matt stays on his small patch of floor, making Riley do a double take.

"Why are you still here?" Riley asks.

"I'm technically still part of Nemesis... sir," he says.

Liz can't help but crack a smile at his boldness, especially after Riley was ready to take his life only a few short weeks prior. "Just let him stay, Ry," Liz tells him, sliding her delicate hand into his. He grips her tight, running this thumb back and forth across the back of her hand, savoring the silky feel of her skin against his.

"Fine, but one step out of line, and I'm dragging your ass out to the barn—"

"Why will I get punished?" Liz interrupts, looking up at Riley. He meets her gaze, looking at her like she is the only person in the room. Mikey fights to stifle his laugh next to her.

"I was talking to him, but we can put this meeting off, and I'll bring you out there right no—" Riley is cut off by a loud, uncomfortable cough from beside him.

"Can we continue, please? None of us want to see you two fuck," Alex says. "Don't fucking say it, Mikey," he barks.

Liz turns just in time to see Mikey slowly lowering his raised hand. She playfully slaps his chest.

"We're no worse than you two used to be," Riley shoots back. "But, and I am going to get my ass handed to me for this, I didn't consider Russell as an option. He was our Drill Sergeant when we were in basic. Our platoon was his last before he moved onto Company Commander. Alex and I got assigned to his unit. He's a mean old bastard, but he took me under his wing. I stayed with him as he moved up the ranks, up until everything went down. I've never met anyone more honest than him," Riley explains.

"So, you want to reach out to him?" Liz asks.

"No. He is running a base a few hours from here. First thing in the morning, we are leaving, and I need everyone to trust me. I'm going to get us caught."

CHAPTER 40

The days pass in a blur of shopping trips and coffee dates since they made it to town. Each morning the team gathers in Mikey's room to have breakfast and continue going over the plans and backup plans if something were to go wrong. To no one's surprise, he and Liz have received backlash every step of the way.

The newcomers had argued that leaving so soon after finally having somewhere safe to regroup and recover didn't make sense, even after explaining the reasoning multiple times. Then came the fight of staying in the hotel rooms. Even with the knowledge that Riley is their general's main target, not a single person was thrilled with the thought of him and Liz being the ones to reveal themselves. Even Matt had been against it, insisting that they are a team, and if the two of them can risk their lives for the plan, so can everyone else.

Despite the constant disagreements, Riley has made it abundantly clear that he is their leader, and they are to follow his orders. Not only is their safety his responsibility, but all of them being spotted adds too many unknowns to their mission. It's not possible to account for every way it could go down for every person. Liz and Riley are their best chance at being found, and the tip Mikey called in to the military base will assure they are not being picked up by ordinary police officers.

"Does anyone need anything or want anything while we are out today?" Liz asks the group, all lounging on the beds in Mikey's room. Every day she tries to do something to make their isolation easier, knowing more than anyone how hard it is.

"We're good, darlin," Mikey says, smiling while poking Lauren with his straw from breakfast.

No one else speaks up. She receives nothing more than a few head shakes and mumbled nos. Tyler and Alex already have their noses buried in their computers, still trying to get the intel they have out into the world. The soft clack of the keys dancing around the room. Liz fiddles with Mikey's paper straw wrapper, tearing it into tiny pieces while she waits for Riley.

"I'm sorry you guys are stuck here. I really wish it didn't have to be like this," she says, voice low and timid. Anxiety spikes, her heart starts beating out of her chest, overthinking about how that could come off as bragging about getting to leave. "I don't know why we haven't been picked up yet."

"It's the mask, babe. Reaper was always in a mask. There are no recent photos of him, and outside of a select group of people, no one knows what he looks like. I'm sure even with all the resources Scott has, it's been a struggle to get his photo out," Lauren explains, sliding off the bed and meeting her at the table. "And for the record, none of us are mad. We understand, but we also worry about what could happen to you two while you're out there with no backup. Stop overthinking so much, okay?"

"Thanks, Ren," Liz says with a soft smile.

Behind her, the door lets out two shrill beeps before the lock loudly disengages. The air around her stills as Riley strides in. Even wearing simple jeans and a hooded sweatshirt, he is breathtaking. Liz looks him up and down, drinking in every striking detail. She has half a mind to drag him back to their room and forget going out at all.

"Love, keep looking at me like that, and we won't make it to the elevator," Riley teases.

"No sex!" Alex barks. "They may be okay crammed in a room all day, but I'm not. Go get your ass caught."

Riley grabs Liz's hand, pulling her up from the chair. Not bothering with goodbyes, he leads her out the door and down the hall. After all this time, she still gets butterflies at the contact. Her excitement to spend another magical day with Riley quickly replaces the guilt she was feeling.

After a lazy lunch on the terrace of Liz's new favorite cafe, Riley leads her to the small local aquarium in the center of town. They wander past glowing tanks of jellyfish and deep ocean exhibits with sharks swimming laps through the shimmering blue water. Liz struggles to remember they are there for a reason, and something tells her Riley is forgetting, too. Every so often, they will remember to spot the cameras, looking right at them as they walk past. After a few more exhibits, Riley pulls Liz into the photo booth next to the gift shop, pulling her mouth to his as the camera flashes. Liz insists on stopping at the gift shop on the way out to get Mikey a souvenir. Just to be on the safe side, Riley leans into the ATM camera like an old man trying to figure out how it works, inciting a melodic giggle from Liz.

Leaving the aquarium, Liz spots an ice cream shop down the road, dragging Riley to it excitedly. Her excitement turns to dread when she sees the tan truck roll through the intersection a few streets down. Trying her best to stay calm, she places her order and grips Riley's hand while they wait. She doesn't bother telling him what she saw. If he didn't see it himself, she has no doubt he will pick up on her demeanor change and know something is up.

The once intoxicatingly sweet smell of the shop now has her stomach in knots. She sucks in a sharp breath, the rough hand gripping hers starts rubbing back and forth. Steadying herself, she focuses on the feel of his hand, letting it ground her.

"I think they found us," she says smiling as she links her arm through his, resting her head on his shoulder as they walk and eat. To anyone watching, they are nothing more than a happy couple living their best lives.

"You saw the truck too, huh?" Riley asks, pulling his arm from hers so he can wrap it around her shoulder. "We're almost back. I know how much you hate it but let me take the lead and stay behind me. I don't know what we will be walking into and you can be a hot head,"

"Rude," she sneers, "but fair."

The moment they set foot in the hotel, Liz feels that something is off. The sprawling lobby is empty, with only the hotel manager manning the front desk. His eyes narrow, locking on them, not even bothering to pretend to not stare. Their boots echo off the smooth tile floor, each one seeming to grow louder. Liz steps closer to Riley, tucking herself against his side. Her heart thumps in her ears as they make their way back up to the room.

"Remember princess, you do not leave my side. We might finally catch a break, or we may be walking into an ambush, but I can't keep you safe if you don't listen to me," he says, gripping her hand impossibly tight.

She gives him a curt nod, staying as close as she is able while they walk to the room. Not a single maid cart is left in the hall. No voices drift from behind the doors. The hotel feels abandoned, lifeless. Riley stops in front of their door. Gently, he takes her face in both his hands, tipping her head back to look up at him.

"No matter what happens, I love you," he says, looking into her eyes.

"I love you, too," she says, fighting back tears.

The way he's acting doesn't give her much hope for what is about to happen. He talks like this is the last time he will get to say those words to her. Liz lifts herself onto the tips of her toes, savoring the feel of Riley's lips against her own.

Riley pushes the door open, reaching for his gun while slowly stepping into the room. Liz peers into the dark, a sinking feeling in her gut. Someone is there. The room is too dark, even for late afternoon, like someone had blacked out the windows in anticipation of ambushing them.

They take another careful step inside while Liz holds the door open with the tips of her fingers, trying to keep as much light from the dim hall as possible. The light flicks on and her heart drops. Riley rushes back to her side, tucking Liz behind his back, safely away from the man sitting in their chair, or rather, as safe as he can make her in the situation.

Liz counts eight other gunmen, all with weapons aimed at them. She peers around Riley's side, watching the man look between them. She moves further behind him, shielding herself from his gaze.

"It's good to see you, Russ," Riley says, face to face with his old mentor again.

"Is this the woman you let turn you against your county? This mousy little thing who has to hide behind you? I expected better," he says, ignoring Riley completely. His voice is rich, warm like honey, and somehow comforting. That doesn't stop the anger bubbling out of Liz hearing someone blatantly insult her.

"Hey, fuck you buddy," she shouts. Riley wraps his arm around her waist, yanking her back as she storms toward the man in the chair. "Riley is risking everything to keep people safe. He didn't turn against his people, your little buddy, general fuck face, did."

"I stand corrected. She's a little spitfire," he says with a deep chuckle.

"Tell your men to stand down so we can talk," Riley orders.

"No matter the history I may have with you, I don't negotiate with terrorists," he remarks.

"With all due respect, sir, if you believe any of that bullshit, then you are a lost cause, and there is no point in attempting to talk," he starts, feeling Liz slowly reach for the other gun tucked into his waistband.

"These are my most trusted men, so say your piece," he says with a wave of his hand, signaling his men to lower their weapons.

"I don't have time to go over all the details. Tyler has sent you an encrypted message with all the intel we have. Long story short, Scott has been supplying the Russians with weapons in an attempt to bring on a new world order. He was behind Liz being taken, as well as my capture. When he was caught… well, I'm sure you have heard rumors of what's going on in Montana. He was recently spotted with Ivan, Dmitri's right-hand man. No one has seen him since," Riley quickly explains. The room is silent for a long moment, nothing but the sounds of electricity buzzing from the lights overhead.

Russell gets up, cracking the faintest smile. He walks to Riley and extends his hand. Riley takes it, allowing his mentor to pull him into a tight hug.

"I knew you wouldn't be stupid enough to kidnap a general," he says

"I also wouldn't be stupid enough to get caught. You trained me better than that," Riley says with a cool shrug.

"So, what is it you want from me Riley? Or is it Reaper, now?" Russ asks.

"It's Riley, sir, thanks to her," he says, pulling Liz into him. "We need help, any help you can give to find Scott. It's the only way to clear our names and put an end to his dealings with Dmitri."

"I saw what Tyler sent, and I will do what I can, but you, this little ball of fire," he says looking at Liz, "and the rest of your squad need to put your full trust in me and my men if this is going to work. You know better than anyone, I won't be questioned," he says, carefully eyeing the pair before him.

Liz squeezes Riley's hand in an attempt to ground herself. Something feels off, but if Riley trusts him, so can she. Riley nods in agreement.

"Cuff them," Russ orders, pressing a finger to an earpiece Liz missed before.

The men in front of her raise their guns, keeping them aimed while two men step forward. Her mind goes dark when she spots the glint of the metal cuffs.

CHAPTER 41

"Great plan, Ry. Really top notch. One of your best, really," Mikey drawls sarcastically, resting his head against the cold concrete wall of the prison cell they are sitting in.

Liz slides across the icy metal bench, pressing herself into Riley's side.

"Shut up, Mikey," he barks back. Riley closes his eyes and tips his head back, slumping against the opposite wall.

Liz watches everyone crammed into their small cell. A deep seed of distrust settles in her chest at the sight of so many furious faces. Riley asked for their trust and they willingly gave it. Now, they are all sitting in a jail cell on a military base after being ambushed. Their faces have been plastered all over the news as soon as a reporter got footage of them being walked out of the hotel in handcuffs. Luckily she was able to be led out without them.

"Well, someone needed to congratulate you on a job well done," Mikey remarks.

"I don't want to beat your ass, but I will if you keep this shit up, Mikey. Just shut the fuck up," Riley says, harsher than Liz has ever heard him speak to his friend before.

"Why should I? We blindly followed you into this plan and look where it got us?" he shouts, sitting up to look at their leader.

Liz's heart rate picks up, a soft buzzing filling her ears. There is a very real possibility they will come to blows in the tiny room. If they do, who knows who else will get involved.

"What did you think would happen if it was *you* who got caught outside? Do you really think we wouldn't be in the exact same situation if he gave in and let everyone run around?" Liz snaps.

"It's cute that you want to defend him, darlin, but speaking as your best friend, you need to stay out of it. He got us into this mess, and he needs to be held accountable. No one else wants to say it, so I will. He fucked up," Mikey tells her. That makes Riley sit up straighter, watching Mikey with a predatory intensity.

"Jesus, Mikey, give it a rest. Talking to her like that is only going to piss him off more. We all knew this was a possibility when we agreed to it. It was a gamble and we lost. Pointing fingers isn't going to change that," Alex says.

Mikey slumps back against the wall, looking anywhere but at Liz and Riley huddled together.

"Are you okay?" she whispers in his ear, getting as close as she can. Her hand rests on his leg, rubbing up and down, more to ground herself than anything.

"I'm fine. I want to kill him for snapping at you, but he's scared, and so is everyone else. If they want to hide their fear with anger aimed at me, I'll take it," he whispers back, leaning down so his lips practically brush her ear.

They sit in that room for hours. Liz tries to focus on anything she can. The different sounds of breathing from her team, the drips every fifteen minutes from the leaky toilet in their cell, counting the scars on Riley's hand over and over again, anything to keep her mind from drifting. When that stops working, she starts picking at any loose threads she can find on her clothes, meticulously pulling them off and creating a neat pile, followed by braiding tiny braids into her hair.

"Are you doing okay love?" Riley asks, noticing all the fidgeting.

"Oh, yeah. I'm doing awesome. Not thinking about being back in Dmirti's cell or that fuck ass interrogation room again at all," she says, trying to keep her voice steady. The last thing she wants is her team looking at her like she is weak, but she can't help the words that come tumbling out. She regrets it instantly.

Riley wraps his hand tightly around hers while Mikey watches them, looking as if he is torn between going to her and staying put. She lets out a breath of relief when she hears footsteps echo down the long hallway. It may not be a good sign, but at least the attention is off of her pathetic panicking.

The steps stop outside the door. The team perks up, bracing for whatever is about to happen. The old metal door glides open and three men step into the already crammed room. Each one carries an armful of handcuffs and chains. One look at what they are holding breaks the thin thread of restraint she has. Her eyes go wide, breathing rapid, she backs away from them as far as she can.

"General Langford has ordered you to be brought to his private briefing room. Everyone line up. Place your hands together in front of you. Once you are in cuffs, step to the door. You will be shackled together for transport," one man explains, looking at each of them.

Mikey slowly moves over to where she is pressed against the wall. Riley is already there, trying to calm her breathing. He doesn't interfere with whatever Riley is whispering to her, he simply reaches out and wraps his pinky finger around hers. She watches in horror as each one of her teammates does as they are told, getting cuffed and shackled together. Her body shakes when one of the men approaches.

"What's wrong with her?" the man asks, eyeing her up and down. She fights through her panic, trying to keep from a full breakdown. She focuses on the tag attached to his uniform: Callahan.

"Have you read our files?" Mikey asks, stepping up while Riley continues to try and calm Liz. "She was held for over six months by Dmitri Komarov. He kept her cuffed and chained to the floor," he explains, his voice remaining calm.

Callahan signals for him to raise his hands. Not wanting to make the situation any worse, he does, letting them put the cuffs on him before stepping to the side.

"You're not putting those on her," Riley seethes, never taking his eyes off Liz. "You can cuff me, but I am staying with her. Call Langford and tell him she has PTSD. It will only get worse if you try to force her."

Riley turns from Liz, just long enough to let them put cuffs on him before turning back to keep talking her through her panic. There are too many voices around, too much chaos for her to single in on one person. Her eyes drop to the cool metal pressed against her, going wide at the sight of the shiny handcuffs circling Riley's wrists. A second man joins them, but she can't bring herself to look.

"General Langford says you need to be cuffed." Her eyes snap to him the moment the words leave his mouth. "But you don't need to be shackled. He has given us permission to walk you separately and let you stay next to Reaper," he says, talking directly to her, giving her far more respect than the last group of men who brought her in.

Her mouth is too dry. She can't form words. She gives the

slightest nod and lifts her shaking hands. To her surprise, the man is gentle, opening the cuff completely before putting it on her, and letting it hang just tight enough to not slip out of.

She follows Mikey and Riley out into the hall, letting the soldier, Callahan, loosely grip her elbow to guide her. True to their word, she remains unshackled and next to Riley the short walk outside. Liz watches her feet as they go, breathing in the fresh air, ignoring the feeling of too many eyes watching. She listens to the leaves crunch under their boots, mixed with the chatter of soldiers making their way around the base. Before long, they are being led into a secure, windowless room.

"Hands out," Callahan orders as soon as the doors close behind them. One by one, the handcuffs and chains are removed, starting with Liz. She watches Riley's reaction, calming slightly when she sees nothing but respect in his eyes. The door swings open and General Langford strides in, walking past the line of prisoners and sitting himself at the head of the long oak table.

"Sit," he orders. He gets handed a thick tan folder that he begins thumbing through, carefully picking and choosing what papers to spread across the table.

Liz watches with curiosity. She had expected every other general to be short, balding, and portly like Scott. Now seeing him in the light, the man in front of her is the exact opposite. He is what she imagines Riley will look like when he is older. Just as tall as the rest of them, and nearly as muscular. It's clear he doesn't shy away from a fight. His hands are callused and dotted with scars. His hair is buzzed short, more salt than pepper, but it works on him.

He reminds her so much of someone, but she cannot put her finger on it. It hits her when he stands to walk around the table. She clamps her lips shut, trying not to smile at the realization.

Riley's brows pinch together looking at her. She can't speak, simply shakes her head hoping he forgets about it later.

"Alright, Riley. You trusted me, the least I can do is trust you. What is your plan?" he asks, stopping his slow circling once he reaches the head of the table once more.

"Simple, sir. We find him and bring him in. That's where you come in. We have the intel, and we should have the manpower. We just need the resources," Riley explains. "We know he is hiding out with Dmitri, no doubt waiting for us to be caught so he can magically be released. Once we know where he is, we just need to get there, find him, and capture him before he has the chance to resurface, claiming our team was holding him hostage," Riley says, watching his old mentor.

Sitting down, he picks the file back up, flipping through it while he casually leans back in his chair. "I have had my suspicions about General Murphy for years, and you now have everything you need to take him down. I can't be involved, but I can give you supplies. I have briefed the commanding officers on base with what they need to know. You won't get trouble from anyone. I also can't help you with satellites, but, if you happen to say... wander into command and convince someone to help you, well, then that is out of my hands. To anyone outside this base, you are all locked in my cells awaiting trial. You have one week to do what you need to do. After that, I will have to move you back into holding," he says with no room for discussion.

A weight lifts off her shoulders, and seeing how everyone else relaxes in their seats, they feel it, too. For the first time in weeks, it feels like they may actually stand a chance.

CHAPTER 42

Liz rubs at her wrists, feeling phantom handcuffs as she and the team follow Callahan across the sprawling base to the barracks. She was unsure of how much truth there was in General Langford's words, but seeing everyone puttering about their business, has her feeling optimistic.

Each person they pass pays them no mind. The team receives a few stunned glances that are quickly averted and the occasional slight nod. It is the first time in weeks she truly feels like they may be safe, at least until their week is up, that is. Safe or not, that doesn't stop her from eyeing each person, watching them as if they will attack at any second. Matching Riley's pace, she falls back to where Mikey is lazily walking behind them, picking her hand up as they go.

"Do you want to tell me what was so funny back there?" Riley asks, looking straight ahead as they continue walking.

"It was nothing. He just reminded me of a character from a show that was on when I was a kid. I shouldn't have laughed. I'm sorry," Liz says, resting her head against his shoulder as they walk.

Mikey's footsteps pick up somewhere behind her, clomping across the cement.

"Don't apologize, love. It was cute, but now I need to know who he reminds you of," Riley says.

"It's dumb. Just this cartoon about fairies. Their leader was a giant, buff guy in camo—" she begins only to be cut off by Mikey.

"Oh my god, yes! I know who you're talking about. That's exactly who he looks like," he says excitedly, inciting confused looks from the group ahead.

As they approach the building, Liz watches the team look around, no doubt looking for any potential ambush, just as she finds herself doing. Her grip around Riley's hand tightens when they step into the near empty building. They march, one corridor after another, until they reach a hallway that looks like something out of a horror movie. There is not a single sign of life anywhere. The fluorescent lights radiate a high-pitched buzzing, flickering softly above them.

"There were only a handful of rooms available. General Langford thought you may want to be somewhere more secluded. This is the best we can do. There are three rooms. You're not under our jurisdiction, so divide them up however you would like. You have one studio with bunks, and two, two bedrooms. One has a large bed, a bunk, and a single. The other has a large bed and bunks," he says signaling to each accompanying door. "Mess hall is across the lot from the door we came in. Armory is in the east wing of the base. We also have a small general store where you can get fresh clothes and toiletries," he says before turning on his heels and marching away, leaving the team standing in the hall to divide the rooms.

It doesn't take long to decide, although Riley is not too happy with the choices. They all agreed Lauren and Maya will get the single room. Alex and Tyler will take the room with the extra bed, opting to bunk with Neil, John, and Liam since they have helped the team before. Despite protests and Riley's failed attempt at pulling rank, they are forced to bunk with Mikey and Matt. She assures him they will be fine and reminds him that if Matt were to try anything like he has in the past, well, she has two of the best soldiers at her side.

The team splits, each group going into their respective rooms to get settled in before gathering in her room to make their final plan.

Tyler and Alex will spend every moment they can in the control room, hijacking equipment and recruiting anyone willing to help with satellites. Lauren and Maya are tasked with securing passage anywhere they may need to go, while Liam, John, and Neil get every weapon and piece of gear on Riley's list. Riley and Mikey begin mapping out plans for every environment they can think of. Matt is to stay with one of them at all times, while Liz is just to help with whatever is needed. They will take the night off to rest. First thing in the morning, the real work begins.

The days seem to pass in a blur. An endless cycle of meetings and disappointment. While most tasks are going smoothly, or even completed, they are still no closer to finding where their missing general is hiding. Alex has successfully taken over half of the command center, convincing the men and women working there to help their cause. The team works round the clock, checking base after base, looking for any sign of their old boss. It's been nearly four days of searching with little to no luck and morale is dropping fast.

Liz paces the living space, rattling off anything she remembers Dmitri talking about during her time with him. Nearly everything she overheard is long since outdated. Most of his compounds have been abandoned, missions scrapped, men killed. All come up as dead ends. Liz tries to ignore Riley pulling into himself, knowing he feels as if he is failing his team. There is nothing any of them can do to get him out of it. He runs on no more than three hours of sleep a night, spending every waking hour going over every mission file he can get his hands on.

"Why don't we just call it for tonight and start fresh in the morning," Alex suggests, closing his laptop.

"We only have three days to find him. You can go if you need to, but I can't stop until we have another lead," Riley snaps, not looking up from the mountains of papers in front of him.

"Ry, we have half the control room looking for him. We are there checking every location we know about and every location you two give us. There isn't much more we can be doing in the middle of the night," Alex protests.

Riley sighs, letting his shoulders slump.

"You're all free to go. I'll see you all back here at sunup to keep going," he says, digging back into his work.

Liz stops her pacing, saying goodbye to her friends as they file out the door. With the room nearly empty, she strides to where Riley sits. Wrapping her arms around his shoulders, she places a gentle kiss on the crown of his head.

"He's right, you know. Staying up all night, going over what you already know isn't going to find him," she coos in his ear. The folder drops from his hand with a soft *thud* onto the table. His hands grip her arms, holding her against him.

"I know he is, but stopping isn't going to end this either. No one at his base will be safe until it's over," he says. There is a deep sadness in his voice at the mention of all the men and women still suffering at Scott's hand. Too many families are missing loved ones because of Scott's hatred toward them, and she knows Riley blames himself for that too.

"Well, I'm with you. They can rest, and we can keep going," Liz says as she nestles her head into his neck. The moment he tenses under her grasp she knows what he is thinking. He wants to suffer alone, punishing himself while his team is fast asleep. She refuses to let that happen.

Liz releases him, finding Mikey and Matt watching their interaction. She gives them a small nod toward their door, silently asking them for privacy. With a small wave, Mikey shoves Matt into their room, pulling the door closed behind him.

"Okay. So, where you found me was blown up, where we found you is abandoned. The three compounds that were raided to find you are also empty," Liz begins, picking her pacing back up. The loud scrape of a chair sounds behind her. Riley forces her onto the couch, beginning his own slow lap around the room. "I know you don't want me to know all the details of what happened to you, and I respect that, but maybe talking about everything you overheard will help."

"It's not that I don't want you to know, it's that I don't want to upset you. I know you're still pissed at me for what happened, and picturing what I went through won't help," he says, stopping to look down at her, his eyes softening the moment they meet hers. "But, telling you what I remember can't hurt."

Soft light peeks in through the window. Hours have passed since Riley began telling Liz everything he had overheard. Jotting down each person or place, Liz cross references them with her own list. Nothing. Very few places match what she was able to remember, and even fewer people. Feeling hopeless, she picks up the list Tyler had left. Sounding out each word, she checks it against her own butchered spelling. Only one word doesn't quite seem to match up.

"Tell me about this one," Liz says, tapping her finger on the paper. "I spelled it how it sounds, sorry,"

"I don't know why I mentioned that, love. That was a fever dream."

"What do you mean?" she eyes him as he slides into the chair next to her, looking over her notes.

"It was when I was getting patched up. I was in and out, but I swear Scott was there, talking to Dmitri. He mentioned shipping something to that town. I just chalked it up to losing too much blood. It couldn't have been real," he explains.

"Ry, there were too many times when he would go missing. Scott was gone for about a week just a few days before we found you. After everything we have learned, do you really think that was just your mind playing tricks on you?" she asks, reaching over, taking his hand in hers.

He stays silent for a long moment. Liz watches his eyes dart from one paper to the next. Without hesitating, Riley stands, walking right out and pounding on the door next to theirs. Liz stays back, listening to the muffled voices outside. Offering a sad smile when he returns, she takes the hand reaching out, letting him lead her into their room. If they are lucky, they will get a few hours of sleep while Tyler looks into the only lead they have.

CHAPTER 43

They have gone over the plan so many times, Liz could run it in her sleep. Riley jumped into commander mode the second Tyler called him that morning. He didn't find Scott, but he did see shipping containers being brought into a remote base, a line of blacked-out SUVs following close behind. If she had to guess, she would say their missing general is in one of those cars.

Each member of the team was sent to confirm they will have everything they need when it is time to leave. Liz tags along, bouncing from person to person, helping in any way she can. The plane is secure. Neil and Liam had overseen the gear being loaded. Maya and Lauren made sure every weapon requested was brought to the cargo hold.

Gathered in Langford's private conference room, Riley goes over the plan again, drilling every detail into their heads. All the weeks of running, of fighting, has led them here. In a matter of days the tides could turn, their names cleared and the threat finally eliminated. Everyone needs to be in top form for what's to come. If they're not, it puts the whole team at risk.

Liz watches, filled with admiration as he tells them what to do should anything go wrong. Team or not, he gives them direct orders to get out. If they can quickly and safely help one of their teammates flee, great, if not, they are to get to safety. One person getting out alive is better than everyone dying.

Most of the team reluctantly agrees, although, no one looks like they will actually go through with leaving someone behind. Liz wouldn't doubt it one bit if that's the order every single one of them disobeys.

Riley leans over the sprawling map that takes up most of the table, going over their plan one last time. He makes each and every one of them recite the part they play in their mission. Only when they state the backup plan, and their agreement to flee should anything go wrong, does he move on to the next person. Confident in his team's abilities, he dismisses them, insisting they all get a good night's rest before leaving in the morning.

Liz says her goodbyes to each member as they walk out, flopping back into one of the plush office chairs when the last person is gone. There is something mischievous in the way Riley keeps peering at her while laying out his full report, hoping it will be enough to make General Langford change his mind.

"C'mon, princess, time for us to go too." Riley says, pulling her from the chair she's been curled up in. His arm tightly coils around her waist, pulling her against him. Liz leans into it, resting her head against his hard chest, trying not to shiver in the cold fall air.

She looks up, watching the stars as she is pulled through the empty base. Liz can't help but wonder if this is the last moment of peace she and Riley will have. In just a few hours she will be on a plane, flying halfway across the world, to a nearly impossible fight. Tonight very well may be their last night together.

Every thought rushes from her head when she steps into their room. Instead of Mikey and Matt arguing, she walks into candles dotted around the small space. Fresh Italian food wafts from the kitchenette, making her salivate. A large bouquet of deep red peonies sits in the center of the perfectly set table, drawing a small gasp from Liz when her eyes land on them.

"You planned all this?" she asks with a shaky voice, trying to fight back the tears threatening to break free. She lets him pull her to the table, sliding into the chair, in awe of the man before her. A large plate of her favorite pasta is placed in front of her before he speaks.

"I know I've said it a million times, but you deserve so much more than this. I don't know what is going to happen after tomorrow and I wanted to make sure we got one last night to forget all the problems outside of that door and just be a happy, semi-normal couple."

"It's perfect, Ry. Thank you," she says, smiling sweetly at him. "How did you manage to get peonies so late in the year? And how did you know they are my favorite?"

"I pulled some strings and had them shipped up from the south. Did you think I wouldn't know they are your favorite as soon as I saw that tattoo you got while I was gone?" he asks, raising an eyebrow.

"Honestly, I forgot all about that. I can't believe you figured it out from something so small."

"That's not small. I knew exactly why you got that tattoo, it's the same reason I got mine. That's why I never mentioned it."

The night speeds by, laughing and talking as if the next few days aren't going to take everything from them. Liz only wishes she had done more for him like he has for her. Every step of the way he has given her precious moments together, pulling her from the outside world and existing as nothing more than two people in love. She looks around the small room, realizing she will never be able to repay him for everything he has done for her. He gave her a home, a family, and a second chance at life. She will be damned if she lets some small man with an over inflated ego take that from her.

Dinner turns into slow dancing in the living room. Less dancing and more swaying back and forth, tightly wrapped in each other's arms, as if even an inch of space between them is too much.

Riley trails his fingers up her spine, leaving hidden goosebumps in their wake. Liz arches under his touch, pressing even further into him. A small groan escapes him. He leans down, bringing his forehead to hers. Her lips brush his in a single, delicate kiss.

Liz squeals as she is effortlessly hauled into the air, legs wrapping tightly around Riley's waist. His lips crash into hers. He kisses her with so much hunger and passion, Liz fears her legs will give out the moment he sets her back down. Lucky for her, he has no intention in doing that. She is carried into the bedroom, their kiss only breaking to pull his shirt over his head before removing her own. Her breath hitches when the warm skin of his chest meets hers.

Riley tosses her onto the bed, watching her with hungry eyes as she scrambles out of her remaining clothes. Drinking in every detail of her bare body, he walks toward where she waits, removing his belt with one hand.

She watches each fluid movement, practically drooling. The ache between her legs becomes almost painful. Her breathing picks up, and Riley lowers himself on top of her. His eyes dart to her lips, then lower, right to where their bodies meet. Liz's heart beats in her ears, every nerve in her body on fire. She brings her mouth to his, wiggling under the weight of his body in an attempt to get what she so desperately wants.

A hand works its way into her hair, gripping tightly against her scalp. The tinge of pain sends a fresh wave of heat coursing through her body. He wastes no time plunging himself into her, savoring the scream she lets out. His free arm snakes around her neck, lowering his entire body to rest against hers. He backs off, just to slam himself back into her. Nails rake down his back, enticing a sharp hiss. His deep groan rumbles through her whole chest.

Riley doesn't let up. Every muscle in her body starts to tighten, vision going blurry as she climbs closer and closer to release. He releases his grip, kissing her softly. His pace slows, as if he is savoring every moment like it could be their last. The switch from ravishing to tender sends Liz flying over the edge. She can no longer hold back the scream that had been building in her throat. Every muscle in her body tightens, sending Riley spiraling with her. Liz writhes underneath him, riding out the waves of ecstasy as they come together.

Riley rolls off Liz, pulling her into his arms as they fight to catch their breath, a thin layer of sweat coating their bodies. Listening to the rapid thump of his heart, Liz traces each hard line of his abdomen with her finger. He picks up her hand, interlocking their fingers with a deep sigh that sends Liz's thoughts racing.

"We need to talk, love."

"Okay," she squeaks, hoping he doesn't hear the underlying panic in her voice, but knowing he will.

He always does.

"Breathe," he orders. "Whatever thoughts are running through that pretty little head are wrong... Look, there is so much that can go wrong over the next few days. I gave an order to get out if the mission goes to shit. That goes for you too."

"No," she states, leaving no room for Riley to argue. "You can't ask me to leave you behind when you wouldn't do the same."

"That's different. I have spent my whole life doing this, you haven't. I need to know you will get out safely, whether I do or not," he says softly.

"If you go, I go. If you die, I die next to you. I told you, I already lost one love, I won't do it again," she says with a shaky tone.

"Together then. If anything goes wrong, we will meet at the rendezvous point. They have their orders, and I trust that they will manage. I offered up the bunker to anyone who can get there. But, if we don't come out on top, we will all be on the run again. Everyone knows to get somewhere safe and lay low for as long as they can, but we may not be able to do the same."

"Or we go back to my house. We fix it up and leave all this behind," she whispers.

"Could you really do that? Leave everyone behind knowing that Scott and Dmitri are hunting not only us, but the rest of the team? I can, but I think it will haunt you," Riley asks.

"You know I can't. And I don't think you really can either. I love them all too much to not finish this, no matter how long it takes. But a girl can dream, right? We could fix the house up, clean up the garden, maybe get a cow—"

"Oh, really? A cow? What happened to the dog?" Riley remarks, kissing the top of her head. She can hear the smile in his voice, sending her heart racing again.

"Don't worry, we will still have a dog. The three of us can tend to the garden and play with the cow, and every night we can have dinner like a normal family before we curl up on the couch to watch all the trash tv you secretly love," Liz lets out a happy little groan, picturing the future they could have. She pushes past the guilt of knowing that future comes from tragedy.

"I'm sold. If shit hits the fan, we find each other and go home. We can hide out for years and re-group. But speaking of our future," Riley says. He pulls his hand from hers, twisting to pluck something from his bag resting on the floor. When he returns, Liz wastes no time cementing herself to him once more. Suspicion grows as she peers down at his large hand gripping something she can't see. His hand trembles ever so slightly. Tears flood her eyes when a tiny green box appears. Riley pushes the top up with his thumb, revealing one of the most stunning rings she has ever laid eyes on. An oval cut diamond rests on a white gold band with two small marquise diamonds on either side, coming together to nearly form a heart, a small round diamond sitting at the bottom of them.

"I hope this is enough. You already had the big, grand declaration from the love of your life, and I didn't want to replace that. I just... I couldn't leave tomorrow knowing I might never get the chance to ask. So... will you finally make my life complete and do me the incredible honor of being my wife?"

She is stunned into silence. Liz knew he would ask someday if they made it out alive. Never in her wildest dreams did she think he would do it a second before Scott and Dmitri are found. She wants so badly to say yes, to say anything, but she is frozen, blinking back tears before they get the chance to fall.

"You don't have to say yes. Whether you want to get married or not, I am in this forever, Liz," he says, a sadness in his voice.

She opens her mouth to speak but no words come out. How is she supposed to tell him how much she loves him, and how much the gesture of keeping it simple means to her? Liz does the only thing she can, she lifts her hand slightly, holding it out to allow Riley to slide the ring on.

He lets out a breath and sits up, leaving Liz missing the warmth of his body. Following his lead, she wraps the blanket tightly around her chest, pushing herself up on shaky arms. Her hand can't stop quivering as she lifts it back up for him. The moment he plucks it from the box something catches her eye.

"What are those letters?" she asks, her voice cracking. Leaning it to get a better look at the engraving on the inside of the band, Riley twists it between his fingers, letting her see the J&M carved into the ring. The tears she fought so hard to hold back now flow freely down her face as he talks.

"I wanted to make sure they are always with you. You never have to choose between the life you lost and the one we're building,"

She doesn't let him put the ring on her before she throws herself into his arms, violent sobs wracking her body. He rubs her back, letting her get everything out that she needs to. "Should I take this as a yes?" Riley teases when her tears slow.

"Yes. Of course it's a yes. It has always been yes," she says as she reluctantly peels herself away from him.

Riley finds the ring hidden in the blanket and slides it onto her finger. Liz lets him pull her back down onto the bed. If this is their last night before the biggest mission of her life, she is determined to spend it tangled in her fiancé's arms.

CHAPTER 44

The bitter cold settles into every bone in Liz's body. The next few hours will test every member of their team. They have been hiking through deep snow for hours and still have miles to go.

Tyler managed to find an old abandoned air strip just south of where they believe Scott is hiding out. The team had agreed to jump ten miles out, opting to hike the rest of the way to avoid being spotted in the sky. Every so often, they switch off on carrying supplies in the hopes it saves some energy for the days to come.

Liz puts on a brave face. She had no idea the hike would be this brutal. Her fingers are frozen and the feeling in her toes is starting to go. The layers of thick, white camouflage gear succumbed to the elements after the first few miles. Still, they march, guns drawn with their heads on a constant swivel. Their mission is running on hopes and dreams. Following the only lead they had may not have been the best plan, but no one had a better one.

Finally, after hours, a small building with a tower stretching into the sky comes into view. Riley takes the heavy bag Liz has been carrying, allowing her to walk to the last stretch easier. She lets out a sigh of relief when she steps foot inside the building. Finally out of the frigid wind, she pulls her hood down and rips the white balaclava off her face. Liz takes a deep breath now that the air no longer burns her lungs.

It's not the type of airport she was expecting. It is an open room with old computers lining one side. A table and chairs sit on the other. Riley explained it was just a control center for small private flights, but she had still pictured a bustling airport, just with smaller planes.

The team gets to work, organizing their gear. A makeshift control center is built on the existing control desk that has seen better days. Bed rolls are laid out on the opposite side of the dusty room. Lauren and Maya work on building a small fire, just enough to keep them warm without smoking out the building. Everyone else works on their assigned tasks. Before long, the room looks like a functioning mission base.

"Hey, Ry!" Tyler shouts, walking over with a wire wrapped machine in his hands. "Did you sneak this into the gear?" Riley takes it from him, turning it over, inspecting the box from all angles.

"No. Russell said he's not able to help more than he has. I didn't sign for anything we didn't absolutely need," he says, looking around at the team now watching his conversation. "Liam, John, Neil. Get over here," he orders.

The team goes silent. Liz wonders if one of them betrayed the team and hid something that will get them caught. The muffled thumps of boots shuffling and the crackling of a fire is the only sound in the room. Everyone waits with held breath to see what Riley will do.

"Was this on the list of equipment I signed off on?" he barks, holding the box up to them. Liz can't help but feel bad as their heads drop to their toes.

"No, sir," Neil says, looking up at Riley. No longer is it two friends. Now, it's just the commander and a subordinate who didn't follow orders. "None of us packed that, sir. We followed your list to a T. Triple checked every item ourselves just to be sure."

"Alright, so no one knows how this got in our pack?" Riley asks the room. Every single member of the team shakes their head in denial. "Set it up, Ty."

"But, sir, that could tip off—"

"I said, set it up. That's an order."

They watch with held breath as Tyler expertly connects all the cords and wires. Alex walks to a supply closet hidden in a back corner, flicking what sounds like an electrical panel until the machines come whirring to life. Re-appearing moments later, he quickly announces to the team to keep the lights off. The solar panels on the roof are old, and in the winter, they are not storing as much as they will need to use. Power is reserved for equipment only. They all nod in agreement.

Liz isn't sure what they are waiting for. All she knows is with the way everyone stands like a deer in headlights, it's nothing good. A deep, crackling voice cuts through the silence, confirming her worst fears.

"I see you found my gift, Reaper," the voice says from the other end. A smile spreads across Riley's face while he picks up the small walkie talking connected to the box.

"I see you changed your mind, Langford," Riley retorts.

"Ehh, I want to see this end just as much as you do. I have had my men watching your satellites round the clock since you left. Both Scott and Dmitri are there. You were right," General Langford says through the old radio. "I have a team en route to topple Dmitri's empire. Once General Murphy gets word from your boy on the inside, I have no doubt he will scurry away."

"Sounds like a great plan, sir, except for the fact that as soon as

Scott knows your team is inbound, he will warn Dmitri's entire operation."

"Don't worry about that. Our man is going to get him out before he gets the chance to warn anyone. If given the choice between his life and theirs, he will choose his own," he announces.

He is not wrong. Scott will preserve himself over all others.

"How long do we have?" Riley calmly asks.

"Just stay alert and keep your end open. Someone will be in touch the moment he flees. We will make sure he ends up at that airstrip you're camped at."

The thick crackling from the radio stops. No one dares talk, instead choosing to sit in the calm before the storm. Even Riley takes a moment to compose himself before jumping back into his role as leader. He looks around, ready to bark orders, only to find everything done. Weapons are laid out and within reach. Their computer systems are all set, thanks to Tyler. The fire and beds are laid out neatly in an open square allowing each direction to have someone facing it. Seeing the worry in his face, and the overwhelming need he has to do something, Liz brings his extra pack to him.

"I found more gear I don't think you signed off on, Ry," she says sweetly, handing him the bag. Her heart swells as the smile returns to his face.

She found his little project weeks ago. Though he fought her on it at first, she convinced him this mission was the perfect time to reveal what he has been working on. Curious eyes watch the exchange.

"Mikey, sweetie, come here please. I know this is your fault," Liz announces, trying to hide her amusement at the flush of red on his cheeks.

As soon as he reaches them, Riley pulls a mask out of the bag and hands it to him. A carbon fiber half-skull with short, deep red horns poking out the top. Mikey looks like a kid in a candy store when he grabs it. His eyes go wide, a big smile on his face.

Riley pulls out his own mask, along with the one he made Liz, and sets them aside. The two of them then proceed to hand out plain masks to every member of the team. Each one is some variation of the two of theirs.

"I fuckin' knew I would convince you to do it," Mikey shouts, examining every detail of mask in his hands. "You have to admit, we are going to look so fucking cool."

"Sure, sweetie. As long as we don't die, we are going to be the coolest team of dishonored soldiers this select group of people has ever seen," she says, patting his arm.

"Yeah. I figured if we are all going to die, I might as well give you what you've been begging for," Riley adds.

"It will scare the fuck out of Scott when he sees us, though. He never said it, but he made it crystal clear, he is petrified of you," Matt tells Riley.

Liz gives him a small smile as she hands him his own mask. He looks from the mask in his hands to Liz, then back down in disbelief that he actually got one. He gives her a tight smile, gripping it like all the trust he has been fighting to earn is now placed in his hands.

"Listen up!" Mikey shouts, climbing onto a dusty, wooden chair that looks as if it will collapse any second. "Since I got us all super badass masks, I say we are no longer Special Operations Nemesis. That died with Scott's betrayal. We are now officially Reapers."

A small round of applause and cheers sounds all around them. Riley simply shakes his head and walks back to their pile of equipment.

"This is why your mask looks like a little devil. Because you're a brat, Michael," Liz says, looking up at him.

"Aww, don't full name me," he whines, hopping down from his chair.

"Then don't goof off right now. You know how on edge Ry is. He is genuinely worried about what is going to happen. You can celebrate and change whatever you want if we make it out of this. For now, can you just be Sergeant Michael Torres, super bad ass soldier and best right-hand man to your commander?" Liz pleads.

His face softens when he looks at the worry in her eyes. "You're right, darlin. This isn't the time or place, but you better believe when this is over, I am throwing the biggest party you have ever seen. We have a few things that need celebrating," he says with a pointed look at her left hand.

Her cheeks warm and she stuffs her hand into her pocket. He smiles, placing a kiss onto the top of her head before marching away to double check their weapons.

She lets out a shaky breath and goes to where the team is huddled around the fire, prepping their MREs. Dropping to sit on the floor with them, Liz starts mentally preparing for the longest night of her life.

CHAPTER 45

By the second morning Liz is positive she isn't the only one unable to sleep. The waiting and anticipation are slowly driving her insane. When the first rays of light filtered in through the tiny windows, everyone was on their feet. After a quick breakfast of rehydrated eggs, they got into their gear and spent the rest of the morning waiting for General Langford to reach back out.

She sits on the neat row of bed rolls with Maya and Lauren, laughing about how horrible she was during her jump training. Mikey has Matt and Liam outside, setting up a C4 charge just down the road.

The sharp static that comes from the small device forces everyone to a stop. Every set of eyes watches as Riley steadily walks over, waiting for General Langford to speak to him.

"Corson, you there?" his voice cuts through the thick crackles.

"Yes, sir."

"My men are twelve miles out. Ground forces are in position around the perimeter. The airstrike will be carried out within the hour. My lead satellite controller will update you from here on out."

"Thank you, sir," Riley says.

"We have eyes on Murphy. He was last spotted fleeing in a black SUV, unarmored. Three vehicles with ten men are with him, give or take. Murphy is in the middle. Taking the main road to your location. Approximately thirty minutes until he reaches you," the new voice calls.

Liz instantly feels nauseous. The rest of the team is on their feet, piling the last of their gear on. Mikey radios to Matt and Liam to get back to base.

"Thank you. I am putting one of mine on, relay any information you can to her, and she will get it to us," Riley tells him. He locks eyes with Maya, signaling her to go to him.

"You're sitting this one out. We need to know everything she says, the second he says it, understood?"

"Yes, sir," Maya practically whispers.

Liz watches the poor girl. She looks terrified, and it brings her right back to that first real mission she demanded to go on. The sound of a bullet tearing through flesh echoes through her ears. Pushing the thought out of her head, Liz throws herself into the rest of her gear and piles her weapons onto her body. When she is fully geared up, Liz takes over for Riley, teaching Maya how to relay messages so he can get ready.

Within minutes the team barrels out the door and drops into position. So full of fear and adrenaline, Liz is sweating under her layers. Slowly, she looks around, unable to spot any of the team in their positions, easing her anxiety slightly. If she knows where they are and still can't find them, chances are Dmitri's men won't find them either.

A soft, timid voice cuts through the silence. "Convoy is two miles from the explosives," Maya says into their earpieces.

"I have eyes on it. Everyone stay in position and wait for detonation," Mikey orders.

The world around them stills. The wind slows. The birds stop chirping. It's like the whole area is holding its breath, waiting to see what is going to happen. The only indicator of what's to come is the glint of sun reflecting off Alex's scope. While Mikey detonates his explosives, Alex will shoot through the window of the last car, stopping Scott's vehicle from escaping.

From there, the remainder of the team goes in on foot, wiping out the rest of the men transporting him. Unable to close her eyes, Liz focuses on breathing through the anxiety, trying to ignore her brain screaming everything that could go wrong.

The blast shakes her to her core. The ground rumbles beneath her as Mikey detonates his explosives, sending the first vehicle rolling onto its side. Pulling her mask down from her helmet, she climbs to her feet, gun aimed and ready. By the time she makes it the short distance to the explosion, most of the team is there, trying to shield themselves from incoming fire.

Gunshots on both sides ring out around them. Liz skirts around the building, finding Riley and Mikey ducking behind trees between shots. She stays hidden, firing her own weapon at the men tucked behind the cars. There is so much chaos hidden in the smoke, she has no way of knowing if their shots are landing. The only indicator is the sound of less and less shots being fired until they stop altogether. Riley signals to her, Mikey, and anyone else who may be concealed around them. They stop firing for only a moment.

"Push forward. The three of us will come in from this side. Matt, Neil, Lauren, go in from the back. John, Liam, Tyler, get to the other side. If they try to flee, stop them," Riley orders.

"Already here, no one has made it out, but the smoke is too

thick on this side. We can't fire into it without risking one of ours," Tyler responds.

With nothing more than a nod of his head, Riley leads the three of them out into the open. With nowhere to hide, they keep their guns up, watching every direction as they march into the smoke. Bodies litter the ground. The pristine white snow is stained with deep red blood and obsidian smoke sticking to it.

Stupidly, she checks each one, looking for both the masks on her team and faces of the men who once tortured her. So engrossed in the twisted faces under her feet, Liz didn't notice the man step from the smoke. The sharp crack of the gun yanks her back, looking up to find Riley slamming the man onto the ground. She aims her gun, ignoring the dull ache in her arm when she does.

Heart racing, she tries to aim at the man fighting with Riley. Her eyes dart to Mikey, but he is nowhere to be found. She can't hold the gun steady, every time she has a clear shot of the man, one of them throws a punch, moving them enough to put Riley at risk. Her breath quickens. All the training they have put her through, and this scenario has never come up. Riley's on top of the man, his fist slamming into the man's face relentlessly. When he finally stops fighting, Riley stands, firing a single shot into his chest.

His face is covered in blood as his head lolls to the side. Bile rises in her throat. There, on the side of his neck, is the strange devil tattoo, the one that seemed to mock her every time the man would beat her.

"Back is clear, last car is empty," a voice calls in her ear.

"First car is also clear," Mikey announces.

She stands straighter, lifting her aching arm again. The death and destruction can make her sick later. Now, she still has a mission.

Riley glances from her to her arm, then back to her. She

glances down, unable to see much past the thick coat. From what she can see, there is nothing out of the ordinary. She shakes her head at him and moves on. They trudge through the snow and smoke together, carefully watching each other's backs.

"Move up, everyone convene on the second vehicle. Stay focused, we don't know how many are left in there," Riley orders.

The words hit her like a truck. If she had stayed focused Riley would not have risked his life to keep her safe yet again. Boots crunch in the snow behind them. Liz would know those footsteps anywhere. Mikey pops up beside her, his eyes going wide behind his mask.

"Darlin, your arm—"

"Is fine. I'm a little sore. I think I was pressed against that rock a little too hard. Can we just get this over with?" she snaps, interrupting him. She lifts her weapon higher, hoping to push past the ache and make everyone stop looking at her like she can't handle her gun.

The three of them march on, meeting up with the rest of the team in front of Scott's car.

"I was right," Mikey announces. "We look fucking awesome. The smoke really helps."

Ignoring him, Riley carefully steps up to the car door. The team has it surrounded, guns up and ready to fire should anyone try anything. He tucks himself against the side, pulling a small handgun from his leg holster. Mikey steps up to the other side, completely in sync with Riley. He grips the handle. Riley gives him a small nod, and the door is ripped open.

Riley steps into the space, gun up, screaming at Scott to get on the floor. He reaches in, ripping the man free of the vehicle and tosses him onto the blood-soaked snow. Long gone is the man who would attempt to fight Reaper. Now, he is just a man with fear in his eyes, cowering in the snow while the people he once controlled stand ready to take his life. Riley grips his arm, pulling him to his feet where Mikey is waiting to zip tie his hands behind his back and lead him into their makeshift base.

The team surrounds him, walking him miles through the snow to where they can tie him up and figure out what to do now that they finally have him in their grasp.

CHAPTER 46

This is not what Liz pictured Scott's capture would look like. She had assumed the team would be cleared right away and they would be able to celebrate. But the reality is, his capture is just one small step in the fight, and they will never be able to fully undo all the harm he caused.

The room is somber. The team sits huddled around the fire, fighting off the demons of the day. Once Liz had peeled herself out of her heavy jacket, she finally felt the searing pain and warm liquid coating her arm. Riley insisted she let him take care of it. Instead of joining her team, she is forced to sit on the rickety table while her arm is crudely stitched and bandaged. She is lucky Riley was there, if he wasn't, the bullet would have gone right through her heart instead of grazing her arm.

To her surprise, Scott stays silent the entire ordeal. Liz wonders if he has something bigger planned, or if he truly knows it's over for him. She sucks in a sharp breath, hissing at the sting in her arm when Riley tightens the bandage just a touch too tight. Hopping off the table, she mumbles under her breath, "Ass."

"Don't lose focus next time and I won't need to sew you up, princess," he retorts.

Her eyes drop to her feet, ashamed that he is right. So much worse would have happened, all because she needed to see who lay beneath her boots. He grips her chin, forcing her to look at him. Tears well up when she meets his gaze. He doesn't speak. Doesn't get mad or scold, simply kisses her forehead, lingering for a moment before pulling her into a tight hug.

"Reaper," a voice calls out. Riley drops his arms. One more quick kiss, and he rushes to the radio on the opposite side of the room.

"Yes, sir," he responds, smoothly sliding into the free chair.

"Success?" General Langford asks.

"Yes, sir. We got him. What do you want us to do with him?" Riley asks, looking back at their old general.

"I will have an evac team at your location tomorrow morning, it is your choice if he comes home or not."

With that, the radio goes silent. Liz looks around the room, pain etched into every face. Giving Scott a wide berth, she makes her way over to where the team is resting, half eaten MREs going cold on the floor. No one has much of an appetite after the day they had. Nestling onto Mikey's shoulder, she stays quiet until Riley joins them.

"Okay. We went on the run as a team, planned as a team, and caught him as a team. So, we will decide what happens as a team," Riley announces, looking around the tight circle of his soldiers.

"You're making a huge mistake, Reaper. They think this is all your doing. I made sure of that. There is not a soul who will believe you," Scott spits from across the room, craning his neck to look at Riley.

"Trying to scare me while your life is resting in my hands is probably one of the stupidest things you could do," Riley says with a small laugh.

Scott lets out a huff of frustration, turning back to face the wall.

"I'm open to hear any and all thoughts on the matter. Why you think we should kill him, why you think he should live. Whatever you are thinking, now is the time to say it," Riley announces, looking around the circle.

"I think you know I'm team kill the mother fucker," Liz growls.

"Oh, surprise surprise. The mentally unstable, angry little gremlin wants to kill me," Scott seethes.

"I second that. He has done too much to too many for him to be allowed to live," Mikey says.

Neither Alex nor Tyler speak, they simply nod in agreement. Liz knew they would all side with Riley after having been on the front lines to the general's madness. If Riley truly is leaving it up to a vote, they will have to convince the new members.

"Shouldn't that be up to his superiors? Why does it have to be our decision? I have never agreed with the death penalty. I think he should have a trial for what he did," Maya says, looking at Lauren.

"Yes and no. You saw what he was doing. If we take him back, we risk his higher ups letting him free. And, with his ties to the president he may very well get pardoned, putting him right back in this position to keep on doing what he has been," she explains.

"If that happens, he will have a fresh list of targets. Everyone in this room will be in more danger than we have been. Not to mention every soldier on General Langford's base will be targeted," Alex explains.

"Is his life really worth more than all the lives he took in

Montana? How about the ones he took from supplying Dmitri with weapons for years?" Neil asks Maya. Her face drops as the words sink in.

"I can make this all go away. Every one of you can be cleared, go back to your lives. I can make things happen. I will get you out if that's what you want. An honorable discharge. You can move up in rank. Any promotion you want, it's yours," Scott pleads.

He is desperate now. Liz can hear it in his voice, the way he bargains for his freedom because he knows the vote is not in his favor. She watches him with morbid curiosity. Every so often, he will wiggle his wrists and ankles, as if gauging how hard it will be to break the ties.

"And what about you?" Riley asks Matt. "You look like you want to say something."

"I don't think it matters what I have to say," Matt says, fiddling with his spoon.

"Why? He tells you he can get you a promotion, and you're back to kissing his ass?" Riley snaps.

"No. But it's not easy to admit you think someone you looked up to your entire life deserves to die," Matt solemnly says.

Riley's face softens. "I'm sorry. I shouldn't have assumed. And you're right, that isn't an easy thing to admit."

"Thank you, sir," Matt says, still unable to meet his eyes.

Liz keeps watching Scott. From the corner of her eye, she can see him fiddling with the restraints. She moves closer to Riley to get a better view. His head swivels between the meeting and the door. She only gets small glimpses of his face, but it looks to her like he is seriously considering escape.

"Do what you're about to do, and I will take this knife," Liz starts, pulling a knife the size of her forearm from the holster on Riley's leg, "I will shove it under your knee, and shuck your kneecap like a fucking oyster. Let's see how far you make it then."

The air stills. Nervous eyes dart between Liz and their prisoner. A small chuckle escapes Riley next to her. He pushes himself off the floor with a groan, going to Scott and double checking each of the restraints. The loud rip of tape echoes in the room as he adds an extra layer of security.

"Okay. Before Liz turns this place into an oyster bar, let's vote," Mikey announces. "All in favor of ending this for good, raise your hand."

One by one, hands go into the air. In the end, even Maya's hand slowly raises.

Come morning, Scott will die.

Liz wakes to find Riley hunched over a small map. The rest of the team is either sleeping or beginning to pack up. She peels herself from the sleeping bag and tightly rolls it before checking in on Riley. She wraps her arms around his neck, resting her chin on his head. Wondering what he is thinking, Liz opens her mouth to ask three times. Each time she can't form the words and snaps her mouth closed.

"I can feel that, you know," he says, craning his neck to look up at her. "Are you up for a little walk?"

"A walk? In the freezing cold?" Liz asks, confused.

"I would go myself, but I knew you would never let me," he says, looking over at Scott. That's when it clicks, Riley is right, she needs to be there when it happens. Not just for Riley, but for her own closure. "I don't want them involved. This is hard enough on everyone without this weight on their shoulders."

"I'm glad you realized I wouldn't let you do this alone. Let me gear up and we can go," Liz says, placing a kiss on his temple before releasing him to go find Lauren. If she is going to hike through the snow again, she will need a jacket free of bullet holes.

No one tries to stop them as Riley slices through the tape holding Scott to the chair. Liz follows Riley as he leads them to the door. Holding up one finger, she rushes back to where Matt is sitting with his head hung.

"Hey. I can't imagine how much this sucks. No one will judge you if you want to say goodbye," she says, offering him a small smile.

"No," he says, barely meeting her gaze. "I said goodbye to the man I remember a long time ago. The man he is today, that's a monster who deserves exactly what Riley is going to give him," Matt says. Liz turns"Thank you, Liz. For checking on me, for giving me the chance to say goodbye if I needed it. I don't deserve that level of kindness, especially from you," he says. She turns back to face him, unsure of how to feel.

"You saw him for who he really is and changed the path you were on because of it. You fucked up and did some awful things for him, but when you saw his true colors, you risked everything to stop him. I may not be able to forgive you yet, but you do deserve kindness," Liz says, keeping her tone soft. "If you change your mind, Riley has an earpiece. And if you need to talk, we are all here,"

Matt gives her a small, forced smile. She doesn't push the matter. Liz rushes back to Riley's side, quietly filling him in on their conversation. Snatching a small chainsaw from the floor, Riley opens the door, shoving Scott out into the cold. Once outside, Riley takes the lead. Liz flanks them with her gun ready should Scott try to attack. The cold bites into her nose, making her eyes sting. The hike is short, just a few miles from the airstrip. Liz hadn't been told the plan before leaving, but seeing the frozen lake in the distance, she can imagine what Riley has planned.

The ice is solid under her feet. Liz stands guard while Riley cuts a hole in it. She had pressed him about the chainsaw he carried, and the pry bar strapped to his back. The only answer he gave was Tyler found it in the shed and made it run.

Her arm is on fire when he is finally done cutting the large square. Using the pry bar to push the block down, Riley tucks it neatly under the rest of the ice. Liz pokes the barrel of her gun into Scott's back, urging him to step toward the hole.

"This is how you're going to do it? Throw me to the bottom of a frozen lake? Drown me?" Scott stammers, spinning to look at them with wild eyes.

Riley finally lets his anger show, kicking the back of his knees to make him drop onto them.

"You're fucking monsters! Both of you," Scott screams.

"Shut the fuck up. Everything you have done to us, to all those fucking men and women who were under your command..." Riley yells, pacing behind Scott, looking as if it's a fight to keep himself in check.

"If I had my way, you would spend the rest of your life suffering. But we have a plane to catch, so you get off easy," Riley shouts, cocking the pistol in his hand as he walks away.

Knowing Scott can't go anywhere, Liz slings her rifle onto her back and goes to him. She may not be able to be there for him the same way he was when she killed her brother, but he won't be alone.

"Princess, close your eyes. You don't need to see this," Riley orders.

"Not this time, Ry. I hid from my brother, I won't hide from him, too," Liz says, holding her ground.

A soft click sounds from beside her. There, in the center of Scott's head, is a small green dot. The very same dot she last saw sitting between her brother's eyes. One hand drops from the gun, instead sliding into Liz's. He gives her a squeeze, and she sucks in a sharp breath, mentally preparing for what comes next. She has made a lot of comments about ending his life over the past year, but she never pictured actually doing it. The sight of death in such a brutal way still makes Liz queasy, she can only hope this time will be different. Riley stays perfectly still, like a towering statue of an executioner. The only movement comes from his lips, silently counting, just loud enough for Liz to hear.

One. Two. Three.

The deafening crack rings out, sending the birds in the trees fleeing. Scott falls face first into the snow. A thick pool of red already forming around him, staining the pristine snow.

Silent tears form a steady stream down Liz's face. She refuses to let go of Riley's hand, even when the sight of the golfball sized hole of mangled flesh threatens to make her sick. She fights past it, knowing this is what they fought so hard for. The fight may not be over, but they finally took a major threat out of it.

Snow crunches under her boots when she finally drops Riley's hand, walking to where Scott lies dead. She pushes him with her foot, sliding the weight of his body across the blood-soaked ice. Once he reaches the edge, she gives him one final kick, hard enough to send him splashing into the frigid water below.

Her eyes don't leave his body until he sinks so deep into the black water he disappears. In one smooth motion, Riley pries the ice block from where it rests under the water. Forcing it back into place, he seals Scott in his icy tomb.

CHAPTER 47

Walking off the plane is surreal. There is no more running and hiding while they fight to stay alive. No longer are they being hunted.

Liz steps onto the tarmac with a weight lifted off her shoulders, one that has been threatening to crush her for months. Her peace is short-lived. No more than four steps off the plane and the team is being herded across the base.

They file into the long conference room where General Langford is already waiting, perfectly organized files placed in front of each chair. Liz slides into the open seat next to Riley, waiting to tell him everything.

"Was your mission successful?" Langford asks, making eye contact with Riley.

"Yes, sir, it was," he responds.

"Good. If you will all open your folders." Langford pauses to give everyone a moment to do as he orders. "You will find everything we have gathered for you. I have had a team building a case since the day you arrived. That case is now in the hands of every general across the country. Paula has gotten relevant information, including satellite images of the disgraced General Murphy, hand delivering a shipment of U.S. missiles to Dmitri. Any and all information regarding each of you deserting and being brandished as domestic terrorists has been redacted. As of now, you are all free and re-instated to your positions," he explains.

A collective sigh of relief sounds from nearly everyone gathered around the table. Liz wants to be just as happy as the faces around her, but the nagging in the back of her head won't allow it.

She flips through the pages in front of her, skimming for the information she needs. Their names are clear. The world knows Scott was the mastermind behind every negative thing said about them. But nothing had been said about Dmitri.

"What about Dmitri? I don't see anything about him in here," she says, gesturing to the files.

"His operation is tied to more than just Scott. Details are classified as we work toward the bigger picture. Given that this has been the main focus of Nemesis, I can tell you the air strike was a success. I cannot say more than that at this time."

He doesn't need to. Any reservations Liz had going into their meeting are long gone. Her only struggle is holding her emotions in check while they finish. Warmth seeps into her thigh. She glances down to find Riley's hand gripping her leg, rubbing his thumb slowly back and forth. That one gesture says everything he can't.

It's finally over.

She can hardly focus on the rest of the meeting. Only when chairs scrape across the floor does she realize it has ended. Copying what the rest of the team is doing, she stands, plucking the folder off the table before walking to the door. Riley stays right behind her, sticking like glue as she moves through the crowd gathering in the doorway. A voice calls out, stopping them in their tracks.

"Corson. We need to talk," General Langford says before they can make it through the door.

Riley snatches Liz by the hand and pulls her back into the room. Russell looks between them as if he wants to say something, but the words never come. The two climb back into their seats, waiting for the room to finish clearing out before Riley reaches over and shoves the door closed.

"I looked into what you asked about, Riley," he begins, his tone softer than before. "You signed iron clad contracts. My hands are tied. I can, however, offer you Scott's position as general and leader of Nemesis."

"I appreciate the offer sir, but that isn't going to work for me. There has to be something I can do?" Riley says.

Liz watches him, confused.

"I know it's hard to hear, but—" Russell starts.

"But nothing. I made a promise and I intend to keep it," Riley snaps.

The moment the words leave Riley's mouth she pieces it together. He tried to get them out of their contracts, to give her the life he promised. All those times she snapped at him, told him not to make promises he couldn't keep starts running through her head. He had meant it, every word. Riley is willing to leave everything he has known for nearly twenty years behind. For her. She watches him with a mix of admiration and frustration, wanting to yell at him for being so stubborn.

"The base in Montana needs someone to help rebuild and pick off the rest of Dmitri's forces. And I need someone I can trust to help build and train a new unit of soldiers. Our oath was to our country and its people, and it's about time our president is reminded of that. There is more work to be done Riley, a lot more work. Without Scott holding you back, you can make a real difference in this fight," he explains.

"I said no. I will find another way to get us out of our contacts. I have to," Riley says in a rare moment of desperation.

"Like I said son, my hands are tied. The best I can do is give you the promotion. You are the best man for the job. If you would just take a few days, think about it—"

"He accepts," Liz says.

Riley's eyes go wide as he turns to her. "No, I don't," he argues.

"Yes, you do," she turns to him fully, interlocking their fingers before continuing. "Ry, this is your dream. This is everything you have spent your life working for. Even if you could have gotten us out of the contracts, you can't throw that away for me."

"I can and I will. You're everything I spent my life working for, I just didn't know it at the time," he says, tears rimming his rich amber eyes.

"And we will have that life. If you still feel the same when our contracts are up, we can walk away. But right now there are too many people who need you for me to let you give up."

"Did I mention you will need to sign a new contract with the promotion? You can make your service as short as one year. And, as a general, you can promote who you see fit, giving them a shorter contract as well," Russ presses. "It will also allow you to take a step back, organizing missions from your office instead of leading them, unless you choose to stay in the field. You can go home every night, have dinner with the missus, and pick back up the next day."

"See? You can get everything you want, just not exactly how you pictured it," she says.

"Liz, I made you a promise. I told you I would get us out of this. If I accept, that promise is broken," Riley says, turning to her.

"No, *I* am breaking that promise. You tried to keep it, and I stopped you," Liz argues.

"Look, why don't you take a few days and think it over," Russell offers again.

"No need," Riley says, peering at Liz while she smiles up at him, already knowing what he is going to say. "I accept."

EPILOGUE

The first year in their new roles flew by. Liz and Riley eloped just weeks after returning. Their days became filled with meetings, training, and executing plans to rebuild the base Scott had so eagerly destroyed. And their nights? Nights were filled with love and laughter. Each day ended with dinner as a family, the rest of the team joining them around the once empty table.

With Scott no longer hindering their missions, the new unit, lovingly named Reapers by Mikey, has more success under Riley than all the years under their old general. After the way he stepped up in Riley's absence, Riley eagerly appointed Alex the team's new commander.

Mikey took on the role of recruiter and trainer, officially adding Matt, Lauren, Liam, and Neil to the team and helping Maya transition to an admin role.

By the time the end of their contracts rolled around, Liz and Riley both knew they couldn't walk away. While Riley builds the ultimate dream team of soldiers for General Langford, Liz helps their personal dream team. Although Dmitri may not be a threat any longer, his followers are. Liz works tirelessly to set up new protocols involving hostages, drilling them into each and every soldier of their unit. Meanwhile, Riley lovingly builds a new building on base for the survivors. Now, every American prisoner, or captured soldier, has a place to return to where they receive the help they need with the dignity they deserve. Non-Americans have their own systems in place, ensuring they get the care they need in whatever place makes them the most comfortable.

Once a week, Liz and Riley board a plane, jetting off to whatever safehouse they are working on at the time. Riley uses the same technology and support he used in his bunker and the home he and Liz built for themselves.

They take on one at a time, allowing them to make each house perfect. The doors and windows are made with bullet proof glass and metal frames along with reinforced steel shutters that close with the push of a button. Riley outfits each house with the best security system he can get his hands on, making sure no one using it can be ambushed.

Remembering the shivering nights on the floor, or a mattress practically falling apart, each house is fully furnished. Knowing someone may need it with no notice, she also makes sure the pantry is fully stocked with non-perishables. Liz has insisted they hire someone to take all the food to a local food pantry before it expires, replacing it with fresh food every now and again.

Her old home was the first to be converted. What was once a ghost town is now a sanctuary for those who need it. Each time they work on a safehouse, Riley makes it a point to take Liz on a date. One night a week to put all work aside and enjoy the company of their spouse.

On their two year anniversary, Riley surprised Liz with the puppy she had been joking about for so long. They cooked dinner together, reminiscing about how far they had come since the day

Liz stabbed him. Neither made a move to bring up the retirement talk again. The three of them curled up on the couch that evening, finally able to breathe. They were still needed. The team still had work to do. But, for the first time since their meeting, Liz and Riley are exactly where they want to be. Side by side, savoring every moment of the life they fought so hard for.

ACKNOWLEDGMENTS

Thank you to every reader who fell in love with these characters, their chaos, and the world they live in. Writing them has meant more to me that I can put into words—ironic, I know.

To my ARC team: you are absolute superheroes. Thank you for reading early, leaving reviews, and supporting this book from day one.

And to Rob, thank you for cheering me on, for listening to me ramble about fictional people like they are real, and for supporting me during every single step of the way. Thank you for being my steady place, and for humoring me when the mask made an appearance for "research purposes." I love you.

I'm endlessly grateful you're here.

ABOUT THE AUTHOR

Ashley Davis is a new author living in a small town in Western Massachusetts with her husband, daughter, and two dogs. She has always had a deep passion for reading and writing. After being a stay at home mom for many years, she finally decided to take the leap and follow her life-long dream of becoming an author. When she is not writing you can find her building cosplays for her family and attending renaissance fairs.

You can find all her socials below.

SNEAK PEEK

Thank you for reading ***Her's to Defend.***

Before you go, I wanted to share a first look at an upcoming standalone project—one set in a completely different world, with new characters and a much darker romance.

This excerpt is an early draft and may change before publication, but I'm so excited to give you a glimpse of what's coming next.

PROLOGUE
DANIELLA

Fuck! I swear I sat down to write for ten minutes. How the hell did I manage to fall asleep? Stupid question. I know exactly how it happened. Running to and from the bathroom, vomiting all night– that's how. I snatch my laptop from where it landed on the floor, checking it for any sign of damage. Nathan is going to be mad enough when he finds out I called out of work. If I tell him I broke my computer writing after being too sick to go in? The thought alone has me nauseous all over again.

He always says sick days are for children, claiming a grown woman should have the willpower to tough it out. I learned to just suck it up after the last time. I dragged myself out with a fever, only to be sent home. He tossed my pillow onto the couch and didn't speak to me for two weeks. I told myself it was because he was stressed with work, so why am I so worried it's going to happen again?

God I hope today is different. It won't be, but a girl can dream. Too bad he is already in a mood since I kept him awake last night. This job is ruining him. Nathan used to be sweet and caring, at least most of the time. As soon as we got married, he dragged me across the country to this tiny town. Apparently, living in a town with a population of ten thousand works really well for his simple, rooted, family man image.

He told everyone I begged him to move away. Somewhere small, where everyone knows everyone else and our kids will be able to walk the street without fear. Somewhere I can get away from the hustle and bustle, letting me focus on my writing career.

What a joke.

He never supported my writing. Still, maybe if he sees how close I am to publishing my first novel, he will take me seriously. Proud is too much to ask for, but I'll be happy with silent indifference. On silent feet, I shuffle down the hall, carefully sliding my computer back into its place in Nathan's office. I need everything exactly the same as when he left. I pull out my phone, hoping he would have at least texted to check on me only to be met with disappointment when the screen is empty. It shouldn't come as a shock that the only thing on the screen is the time, but it hurts all the same. Shit. 3:24 p.m. He is going to be home in a few hours and I managed to get exactly... nothing done.

"These stairs are going to be the death of me," I mumble to myself, gripping the railing like letting go may very well kill me. Every creak of the wood under my feet sends a new wave of pain through my throbbing head. Dinner. A hot meal on the table when Nathan gets home. That is the only thing I need to focus on right now. Cleaning will have to come during dinner prep if I can even manage to stay on my feet that long. Hopefully a clean house and nice meal will soften him up a bit. I stuff my feet into my favorite pair of boots, throw my jacket on and sprint out the door.

It's a struggle to stay upright walking the three blocks to the store. Everyone I pass gives me a wide berth, eyeing me like I'm not a person but a walking petri dish. The chill of the air feels incredible on my warm face. That is, until the cold starts to bite at my already sore nose. Maybe I should have just called a cab instead of walking, sick, at the start of winter. It's too late now, I am already out, I just hope I can get what I need and make it home before Nathan does.

Relief hits when I turn the corner and spot the little sign outside the local grocery store. One good thing about being dragged to this quaint little town is the charming old main street. Shops line both sides of the road, with everything you could need all in one place.

Trying to keep my distance from all the healthy shoppers, I quickly pick out all the fresh herbs and vegetables I will need to make homemade chicken soup. He can be mad all he wants about soup, I need fluids and something I can keep down. A bag of noodles gets tossed into my basket and I dart for the front counter.

I'm already getting too hot. I need to get back out into the cool air before my fever spikes again and leaves me useless for the rest of the night. Today is my lucky day, not a single person is in line. I throw everything on the small counter, offering a tight smile to the small, older man scanning my items. He hands me my bag and I thank him profusely, rushing down the street to the butcher before I can head home.

The little bell on the door lets out a gentle ting when I step into the small butcher shop. Thank god I am so congested right now. If I wasn't, the smell of all the raw meat would absolutely send my stomach over the edge again. It's only been one stop and my luck has already run out.

I quickly step into line, trying to patiently wait my turn to order. Sweat is starting to coat my body from this god-forsaken jacket. Hopefully this line moves quickly so I can make it back into the cold. My heart drops into my stomach when the phone in my pocket vibrates. Did Nathan come home early? Did he find out somehow that I never went to work today? My traitorous hand shakes when I pull it out, relieved to see just a feel-better text from Amara. I shuffle forward with the rest of the line, grateful for the speedy men running the shop. Finally my turn, my phone gets stuffed back into my pocket as I make my way to the counter.

Stepping up to the glass, I point out the chicken breasts I want. While the man wraps it, I look around, accidentally locking eyes with the mountain of a man working in the back. My cheeks get hot, no doubt turning red for my utter embarrassment.

He has to be at least six-foot-four, with arms the size of tree trunks. He is covered in sprawling black and grey tattoos. I'm pretty sure the guy just tells the cows to die and they do. Stop looking at him dummy, you need to get your food. I peel my eyes away the second he smiles at me, going back to looking at the floor, pretending the wood grain under my feet is the most interesting thing in the world. The other man comes back, slipping a brown paper package into a bag for me. The small card reader beeps when I tap my phone against it and I can't get out of there fast enough.

The door lets out a painful groan when I make it back home. Maybe when Nathan is in a better mood I can ask him to fix it. And take a look at the stairs before I really do break my neck. The vintage clock in the entry reads 4:38. I don't have time to think about repairs right now. I strip my coat and shoes off, leaving them neatly by the door.

The chicken is searing in the heavy pot, while veggies and herbs are simmering away in bone broth, making the house smell incredible. I make quick work of scrubbing the counters and getting dishes put away, loading the dishwasher with everything I used to cook. I don't know if it's the steam from the bubbling soup, or the handful of flu meds I took, but I managed to get everything clean with plenty of time to spare. I'm in the middle of filling two bowls with the steaming hot food when the door groans open again.

PROLOGUE

"Hi sweetie," I yell as cheerfully as I can muster, grimacing at my own raspy voice. No response. Awesome. Rushing from the kitchen to greet him, I stop dead when I see the scowl on his face. There is no love, or worry, or any sort of kindness in his eyes. Just anger and disgust when he sees me. "Dinner is done, I was just plating it up. If you go wait at the table I'll bring it out."

He didn't even bother trying to hide how mad he is when I placed his bowl in front of him. His sigh is enough to tell me how disappointed he is in the meal. Why the hell didn't I just make one of his favorites? It's not like I didn't know he wouldn't be satisfied. I just had to go and give him something else to be angry about. His spoon scrapes against the bowl so loud I swear he is going to break it. I hurry back with my own food, gently setting it on the table. I push the noodles aimlessly around the bowl, taking only a few small sips of broth. Not much of an appetite anymore. Nathan watches me, barely taking more than a few bites of his own meal.

"How was work?" he asks, letting his spoon go clattering into the bowl, splashing liquid onto the table. I can feel his eyes on me as I reach over to wipe it up.

Nathan already knows the answer. He has to. Lying will only make him more angry. My eyes drop to my feet. Mustering up all the courage I can find, I quietly tell him. "I didn't go. I think I have the flu."

"I know. I got an alert from the camera in my office. You call out sick but you're well enough to sneak into my space and work on that meaningless little hobby of yours?" he shouts.

The table shakes from his hand slamming into it so hard. My heart pounds in my ears. I jump up, trying to clear the table, apologizing as much as he will allow. Something is different about today. Maybe he had a bad day at work and I just made it worse. I don't know, but the look in his eyes has me more on edge than normal.

"I'm sorry. I was up all night. I couldn't go to work like this—"

PROLOGUE

"Oh I know. You kept me up with you, forced me to be awake and miserable while you played sick!" Nathan's booming voice makes me stumble back. Seeing that only makes him worse. He shoves himself from the table, stalking over to where I am hopelessly trying to clean up.

"I'm sorry, sweetie. I really didn't mean to keep you up, that's why I ended up sleeping on the bathroom floor. I tried to rest all day, but that chapter I have been stuck on finally made sense–"

He slaps me so hard I go tumbling to the floor. The taste of blood fills my mouth. He hit me. That bastard fucking hit me. My fist is already clenched as I scramble back to my feet ready to hit back. I may have tolerated a lot, but not this. His eyes dart to my hand and his face twists into something dark, something I have never seen from him before.

Run.

Before he can grab me I turn on my heels and run through the kitchen, hoping I can make it to the door before he makes it to me. Nathan cuts through the dining room, beating me to it. I need to get out. I hate this stupid old house, the backdoor only leads to a dark alley that's been fenced off since the day we moved in.

Stairs. If I can make it up I can lock myself in the bathroom, call for help. No time to think, I sprint for the staircase, as fast as my legs will take me. My lungs burn with the effort. I duck under his arm, scrambling up. Almost to the top. Fingers dig into my ankle, yanking me down to my knees.

I have never seen him this angry. Gripping the rungs of the banister, I kick out with my other leg. A sick crack rings out under my foot. Nathan screams. Ignoring the sickening thuds, I scramble to get my footing and run, not stopping until I reach the bathroom.

The door slams closed. It feels like I fumble with the lock forever before it finally turns. I drop to the floor, letting the hot

PROLOGUE

tears burn my stinging cheek. With my back to the door, I fumble with my phone. My finger hovers over the numbers, but I can't bring myself to press the green call button. Minutes tick by. The house is quiet. Nathan has probably calmed down and realized what he did. I'm sure he is just giving me space, waiting for me to approach him before he apologizes. My gut twists and turns, screaming not to go out there.

Feeling like I am going to be sick, I slide myself across the cold tile floor, just enough to pull the door open. I crawl to the railing overlooking the entryway. When I look down, I run straight back to the bathroom to be sick. I empty the contents of my stomach before finally pressing the button. Tears stream down my face when the dispatcher on the other end answers.

"I think I just killed my husband."

www.ingramcontent.com/pod-product-compliance
Lightning Source LLC
LaVergne TN
LVHW091701070526
838199LV00050B/2233